Lynda G. Motterisbead

About the Author

HEATHER NEWTON's short stories have appeared in *Crucible*; *Encore* magazine; *Lonzie's Fried Chicken*; *O, Georgia!*; and *Wellspring*, among other publications. She lives with her family in Asheville, North Carolina, where she is an attorney and mediator. This is her first novel.

Under the Mercy Trees

Under the Mercy Trees

A Novel

HEATHER
NEWTON

HARPER

NEW YORK · LONDON · TORONTO · SYDNEY

HARPER

HarperCollins books may be purchased for educational, business, or sales promotional use. For information please write: Special Markets Department, HarperCollins Publishers, 10 East 53rd Street, New York, NY 10022.

FIRST EDITION

Designed by Fritz Metsch

Library of Congress Cataloging-in-Publication Data

Newton, Heather.
Under the mercy trees : a novel / Heather Newton.— 1st Harper pbk.
p. cm.
ISBN 978-0-06-200134-4
1. Older gay men—Fiction. 2. Brothers—Fiction. 3. Missing persons—Fiction. 4. Homecoming—Fiction. 5. Recollection (Psychology)—Fiction. 6. Families—Fiction. 7. Mountain life—North Carolina—Fiction. 8. North Carolina—Fiction. I. Title.

PS3614.E75U53 2011
813'.6—dc22

2010011500

11 12 13 14 15   OV/BVG   10 9 8 7 6 5 4 3 2 1

For my redheads, Michael and Madeleine

August
1955

That last night at Rendezvous Falls, the Ford Sunliner seemed to drive itself, the engine so powerful it felt as if some force were pulling them up the mountain. Martin drove one-handed, vibration from the steering column numbing his palm. Beside him in the passenger seat Liza clutched his other hand, her grip folding bone. The moon lit up fields on either side. The car entered woods and climbed north, its headlights sweeping the curvy road. Liza pressed a fist against her mouth and began to cry.

They rounded a bend and the waterfall loomed up, higher than a four-story building, its roaring water spitting white in the moonlight. Martin pulled over to the side of the road and went around to Liza's door to help her out. The air was cooler here than in town, and the water misting over them from the falls made Liza shiver despite her sweater. He almost told her to get back in the car, but she stepped past him and headed up the narrow path that led to the top of the falls. Martin reached in the glove compartment for a flashlight, then followed her. Rhododendron and holly branches slapped his body. Here and there bear scat dotted the path. Liza climbed on, her slender shoulders hunched, ponytail bobbing. Martin stumbled once or twice on tree roots before they came out onto the curving rock face just above the falls.

Liza stopped and breathed in the moist air, her shoulder blades rising and falling. Moon bled silver over the rock's smooth surface, illuminating ferns that claimed a toehold in tiny cracks and glistening streaks of wet where the falls had sprayed the gray-and-orange stone. She stepped farther out.

"Don't go too near the edge," Martin said. The thunder of the falls drowned out his voice. He took her arm. "Let's go back."

She pointed to a long crevice that ran from where they stood down to a shelf behind the curtain of solid water. The braver folk of Solace Fork used it to slide behind the falls. "Come with me," she said.

"No, Liza."

"Please." The moonlight seemed to stretch her skin taut over her cheekbones. Her face was fierce with all that she wanted from him, all that he couldn't give her. She took the flashlight from his hand, then sat in the crevice and eased down on her seat, disappearing behind the white water.

Martin stood alone in the mist of the falls, unable to follow.

The family of Leon Owenby, 65, has reported him missing from the home place, off Bryson City Road. Mr. Owenby's brother James Owenby saw him a week ago Tuesday when he went by to borrow a pair of tin snips, but nobody has seen him since. "It ain't like him to take off without telling somebody," said Hodge Goforth, Willoby County's director of Emergency Services and a family friend. "You couldn't run him out of the county."

—WILLOBY NEWS & RECORD,
October 14, 1986

I

Martin

Broken. His last scrap of dignity twisted off like a chicken wing. Martin Owenby climbed three flights to the Manhattan apartment he shared with Dennis on West Fifteenth Street, his heart fluttering idiotically in his chest. The battered leather strap of his suitcase threatened to give way as he bounced it up the steps. Nothing valuable left inside if it did spill. Air wheezed through his nose in an exotic bird call. Tiny bottles of Scotch from the plane rattled in his overcoat pocket.

On the landing, he stopped to get his breath, then unlocked the apartment door. Dennis was dozing on the sofa in his dressing gown, his antiques crowding around him. He waited up for entertainment, not out of concern. His corpulent body curled like a woman's. Martin and Dennis had been lovers once, until they both turned apologetically to younger men. Now they sniped at each other with the weapons of familiarity, like the worst of married couples.

Dennis blinked awake and saw Martin's slept-in clothes and the bruise smeared blue-yellow across his left cheek, smelled the scent of liquor spilled three days ago down his shirtfront. "He rolled you, did he?"

He. The blond midwestern god Martin took to St. Kitts ten days ago. "It was worth it," he said, wishing it were true.

Tickets charged above the limit on his sole unfrozen credit card. Past fifty, looks and wit were no longer legal tender, and sex was costly. In this era of AIDS Dennis seemed content to remain celibate. Martin was not.

Dennis sighed and heaved himself off the couch. "Your family's been calling. Your brother Leon has disappeared. It's been over a week since they noticed him missing."

"Missing?" Martin pushed his suitcase through the doorway of his closet-size bedroom. His head was less than clear, his tongue like cotton.

"I would have called you, if you'd left me a number," Dennis said.

"Maybe he decided to go somewhere." Martin didn't believe the words. His oldest brother, so like their father, not a spontaneous freckle on his body. Up at five every day, peed off the porch, lit his stove. Made black coffee and cornbread. Fed the leftovers to the dogs, God forbid he should buy dog food. Splashed water on his face and combed what was left of his hair. Rinsed his mouth out and spit. Did his chores. Walked his property. Smoked a slow cigar. Martin stayed in touch with his other siblings, putting in just enough effort to keep them from writing him off. The women still babied him, his sisters and sister-in-law, and he even considered his brother James a friend. But not Leon.

"James said they found his truck at the house. But his wallet was gone," Dennis said.

"Do they expect me to come home?" Martin knew the answer. He looked at his watch. It was too late to call his family. James would be asleep with his hearing aid out, and it would be Bertie, James's wife, who would be frightened awake. Martin could imagine her lying rigid in the bed, her prematurely white hair puffing around her head like a Q-tip, listening to the phone ring, expecting the worst.

"It's a family emergency. And your friend Liza is prepared to meet you at the airport." Dennis picked up a message from the telephone table and dangled it over Martin's head.

Dennis was jealous of Liza, or rather, the myth of Liza that Martin perpetuated. Her picture, dropped artfully from his billfold for years to reassure employers and others of his heterosexuality. His girlfriend. His long-lost love. His brother Leon snapped the photo at Martin's high school graduation, when Liza reached slender-necked to kiss Martin's cheek. It had grown as frayed and dated as the lies Martin told. He kept the photo hidden now, tucked behind his maxed-out credit cards, but it still made him feel handsome and romantic to have once had this girl love him so.

He snatched the message from Dennis and started to call the airline, then remembered he was out of cash and credit and put down the receiver. "Can you lend me some money?"

"Oh, for God's sake."

"I'll pay you back. I'm expecting a check for that computer manual I edited."

Dennis snorted. "I'll lend you the money but only for your family's sake. Put the plane ticket on my credit card, and I'll get you some cash tomorrow." He moved sideways between furniture to reach his wallet on an end table and handed Martin his Visa card.

Martin booked a flight for the day after next, giving himself time for the bruise on his face to heal, then dialed Liza's number. It was late, but her voice when she answered was clear, not graveled by sleep. At the sound of it he felt tears press against the back of his eyes and turned toward the wall so Dennis wouldn't see.

"Hey," he said.

"Hey, yourself." Her voice was young. She was still the auburn-haired beauty he had left in Willoby County more than thirty years ago. He gave her his flight number and arrival time.

"I'll be there."

He imagined her standing in the dim light of her kitchen. The last time he'd gone back to Solace Fork, a few years ago, she had cut her hair short, but her skin was as smooth and unlined as ever, her body trim. Martin wanted to reach through the phone line, have it take him back to when they were children. Liza was silent, and for a moment he thought he had lost the call. "Liza?"

"Yes?"

"Never mind."

"So I'll see you at the airport."

"Put the top down for me," he said, a reference to the baby blue convertible she drove when they were in high school, a lame joke to remind her who he was. They hung up.

"How sweet." Spit glistened in the corners of Dennis's mouth. "The two of you communicate without words."

Martin wanted to shut him up, but Dennis had just lent him money. Martin and Liza didn't need words because they invented in their minds the words they wished the other one would say. The image Liza had of him bore little resemblance to who he really was, but around her he was his best, most beautiful, and noble self. He was unbroken.

L i z a

At the Owenby home place, carrying a cooler full of sandwiches as her excuse, Liza Barnard hiked up to where bloodhounds puzzled cold dirt and dozens of men raked a slow, ragged line over the property, their backs to her. Hodge Goforth, Willoby County's director of Emergency Services, walked in the center. There was a pleasing softness about Hodge, inside and out. When he and Liza and Martin Owenby were children, Hodge may have coveted Martin's hard muscle and sharp wit, but somewhere along the line Hodge had accepted himself. In front of Hodge, brush and trees thickened as the mountain sloped upward.

The men reached the boundary of the quadrant they had marked off and turned back toward Liza. Hodge saw her and waved. She put her cooler with a pile of food and equipment near the edge of the woods. Hodge left the line and came over to join her. Too many years of his wife's good cooking hung around his middle, and he wheezed like an old dog.

"How's it coming?" she said.

He shook his head, keeping his voice low. "We searched a week for the man. Now we're looking for a body." Frost had covered fallen leaves the past few mornings.

"What do you think happened to him?" Liza said.

"No idea, but I don't have a good feeling about it." Hodge pointed to Sheriff Wally Metcalf, who was walking their way, talking to his chief deputy. "Wally didn't want to treat it as a crime, but I talked him into it. Old people wander off all the time, but this is different. Leon wasn't confused, and he'd never leave his front door hanging open like that." Over the ridge, Leon's house, just visible at the base of the mountain, looked ready to fall in.

"Did the sheriff find anything at the house?" Liza said.

"Nothing. He's told the family they can go back in."

The sheriff spotted Hodge and Liza and headed toward them, grinning. "You distracting Hodge, Miz Barnard? He's getting behind." After teaching English at the high school for nearly three decades, Liza was Miz Barnard to everyone.

"Sorry, Sheriff," she said.

"I needed a break. I'm not as young as I used to be," Hodge said.

"Uh-huh. But you're just as lazy," Wally said.

Liza envied the easy friendship between Wally and Hodge. Hodge's office was in the same building as the Sheriff's Department. The two men saw each other every day. With all their history and Martin Owenby shared between them, Liza and Hodge still weren't completely at ease when they were alone together.

"This would be easier if all the Owenby men got along," Hodge said. "We're having to keep them separated."

At the far end of the line, Martin's older brother James poked through underbrush without lifting his head. Closer by paced Steven Owenby, the son of Martin's sister Ivy. Ivy had mental problems and hadn't been able to take care of her children, but Steven had turned out well, considering. The muscles in his jaw and back twisted with impatience, and grizzled hair stood out from his head, but Liza knew he wasn't as wild and scary as he looked. Steven was Martin's favorite nephew. Martin wasn't as fond of his other nephew, James and Bertie's son, Bobby.

"You're the only person I know who gets along with all of them," Liza said.

"It's an odd spot to be in at times." Hodge called over to Steven, "Steven, come here a minute."

Steven walked over. "Hey, Miz Barnard." He took out a cigarette and lit it.

Hodge wiped sweat off his forehead. "You got any thoughts on this, Steven? You know this property about as well as anybody." Steven and his brother and sister had spent most of their young lives in foster homes, but in the summers Leon had Steven out to help him around the farm. Liza imagined a young Steven sleeping in the attic. The hundred-degree heat under the tin roof would have been stifling, but better than a bed in foster care.

Steven shook his head and exhaled smoke. "Leon wasn't afraid of the devil. He walked every inch of this property, in the light and the dark, at some point in his life." He pulled something out of his pocket. "Look what I found yesterday, back in a cove where you'd swear nobody had trod since the Cherokee."

They looked at what he held. It was the paper band off one of the cheap cigars Leon smoked, the words rubbed off by weather. Steven offered it to Wally Metcalf.

The sheriff shook his head. "He could be anywhere."

Steven carefully put the band back in his pocket.

Wally said, "Steven, your uncle James told me the last time he saw Leon, your mother had just been by and left his clean laundry. Then when James went back a week later, there was almost no laundry in his dirty-clothes pile and the dogs hadn't been fed. I wondered if you might have seen Leon during that week sometime."

"Naw." Steven shook his head. "It's been at least a month since I seen him."

Martin's brother James approached them, adjusting the hearing aid in his right ear so he could hear. He nodded to Liza, shy.

Wally pressed Steven. "You'd carry him around sometimes in that pickup truck of his, wouldn't you?"

Steven tossed down his cigarette and stubbed it out with his toe. "Everybody knows I'd drive him when he needed me to. What are you getting at?"

"Man wants to know if you drove Leon around any week before last," James said quietly.

Steven turned toward James, hatred on his face. "If I'd've drove him, I would've said. What are you saying, James? That I'd hurt the only one of you that ever showed my family a kindness?"

"I'm not saying any such thing."

Anger spurted out of Steven like water from a slit hose. "The rest of you treated my mama like dirt, like she embarrassed you. Well, you're the ones ought to be embarrassed. Walking into Solace Fork Baptist Church every Sunday of your lives like the saints of God or somebody, then letting us rot in foster care." He spat on the ground. "If I was going to hurt somebody, James, you better believe it'd be you, not Leon."

"Steven, come here a minute." Hodge took Steven's arm and led him off a few yards, close enough for Liza and the others to eavesdrop. "Nobody's accusing you of anything, son. Wally has to ask questions. James has a right to hear what you know. That chip you carry around on your shoulder is going to get you in trouble."

"That son of a bitch. That hearing aid makes him seem all harmless and innocent, but he ain't."

"When's the last time you saw Leon?" Hodge said.

"A few weeks, like I said." Steven turned around and raised his voice so they didn't have to strain to hear. "Leon didn't call me to drive him much anymore because he was getting James's boy, Bobby, to do it. Ask Bobby when he saw the man last."

"I'll do that, son," Wally said calmly.

Steven turned his back. "I'm out of here."

"Steven, we still need you to help look," Hodge said.

"Let James look for him his own damn self." Steven shrugged off Hodge's hand. "No old man could last in the cold this long, not even Leon. Any more looking would just be for a family that never did a thing for me. I'll see you, Hodge." He headed for the house, where the searchers' trucks were parked. Steven's hair was graying and his shoulders drawn up like an old man's, but to Liza's teacher eyes he was still a teenager with his feelings permanently hurt.

Wally called to Hodge. "He okay?"

"Yeah, he'll be all right." Hodge walked over to James and slapped him on the back. "Let's get to it."

"I'll head down and look by the sawmill," James said.

Hodge waited for the sheriff and James to walk far enough away, then said to Liza, "It hurts me to see family at each other's throats like that. The Bible says, 'first be reconciled to thy brother.' Seems like that ought to go for uncles and nephews, too."

"Have you told them that?" she said.

Hodge shook his head. "I've learned to be sparing with

Scripture around the Owenby men." He looked at her. "You've spoken to Martin?"

"I'm picking him up at the airport tomorrow."

"How'd he sound?"

"Hard to say."

"It'll be good to see him."

She nodded, not trusting her voice.

Hodge said good-bye and rejoined the search. The volunteers separated to cover the land that remained. Liza stood alone. She surveyed the expanse of land around them, exhausted fields and scraggly timber as far as she could see. A creek ran narrow through the Owenby property, past the house and down behind the old sawmill. She hoped, for the family's sake, that Leon wasn't lying out there somewhere. That he had gotten an urge to travel and climbed on a bus, off to see a lady friend no one knew he had. Around the property's edges, in the lace of bug-eaten leaves, the light was failing. She turned and went back to her truck.

With her headlights on she drove down the Owenbys' dirt road, then out onto paved state road. Her pickup truck hugged the same curves she and Martin had traveled in her Ford Sunliner convertible all through high school, before she knew Martin was gay, maybe before Martin himself knew he was gay. Deer eyes gleamed red in her headlights, and she clutched at time the way she grasped her steering wheel, her own selfishness appalling. Leon Owenby was missing, and Martin Owenby was coming home.

She was twelve. It was spring. Dandelion heads sloughed seeds like old men spitting teeth. Her father's mouth moved in a happy whistle, gusts of wind through the open windows snatching the sound. She trailed her hand out the window,

blocking air with her palm, then letting it go, searchi.
coded messages in the tire tracks that crisscrossed the n.
road. Morning sunlight rolled out like a carpet over low
mountains, and her father stopped in the yard of Solace Fork
School.

"You'll like it, Liza." He grinned at her, an almost-tug on
her hair melting her heart. Inside, the smells were oiled floor
and chalk.

She was new to this place, but her father was not. Summers spent here with cousins as a boy were his passkey, un-
locking lidded eyes. He had returned a doctor, a man "what
knew things." Liza stood as his daughter before the children
of Solace Fork School, her dress unpatched, in shoes that only
she had worn, the teacher's warm hand on her back. Her hair
curled, an alive, rich auburn, not baked to transparency by
the sun. Girls' hands twitched, wanting to touch it. Her well-
formed body had never hungered, and ten spines straightened
to match hers. Eyes widened at her that day and never closed.
Forty years later, waist thick, hair faded, and dues paid, her
life trailed out behind her like a tattered peacock's tail, yet the
folk of Solace Fork still treated her like an exotic stranger.

Only Martin really saw her. That morning he appraised
her, while Hodge Goforth blinked curious from the next
desk over. Martin's fingers tapered slender as beeswax candles.
Dark hair fell over his brow, covering one green eye. The other
winked at Liza, long-lashed and shameless, her father standing right there.

At recess, before the girls could draw near enough to claim
her, he was at her desk, Hodge shuffling behind. Martin might
as well have put his arm around her shoulders.

"Come with us. We've a place to show you." The mountain
had pressed his vowels flat, and "you" was "ye." She missed

that boy's voice, now that only perfect words dropped from Martin's mouth, all polished smooth like rocks from a tumbler.

She walked with him and Hodge down a rough deer path into the woods without a thought, something she would never let her two daughters do today. She heard the creek before she saw it, water burbling, heavy drops plopping from rhododendron leaves. The boys turned off the path. They ducked under limbs and came out into a clearing.

It was a sanctuary. Soft grass the greenest she had ever seen carpeted the aisles. Martin and Hodge had swept it clear of leaves. All around, mature hardwoods grew bent in the shapes of chairs, up, then sideways, then up again, a dozen giant church ladies sitting down. She could just see water through the trees, light brown where it flowed over rocks and almost black at the deep place where the creek branched.

Martin watched her, triumphant. Hodge looked worried, not ready to share this place.

She reached out to touch the closest tree. "How did they grow like this?"

Martin rested his hand next to hers, stroking the bark as if petting a horse. "A storm hit them in nineteen aught two, when they were too big to snap back and too little to come up by the roots. They grew sideways and then back up toward the sun."

Hodge cleared his throat and spoke for the first time. "It's the onliest hurricane to ever make it this far west. They say it sucked the water out of every creek between here and the coast and spat it out on Spivey's Bald."

Martin cupped his hands into a stirrup. "Want to climb up?"

She let him help her up onto the tree's broad bench, tucking in her dress. She could smell her own clean scent and Martin's, too, homemade rose soap that lingered in her nostrils. He hopped up beside her. From up there, the grove of trees was an eerie elephant graveyard, a field of bent bones.

"It's so odd," she said.

Martin's trousered leg touched hers. Sun filtered through the trees, dappling the grass and warming the top of her head. Down below, Hodge shifted from one foot to the other, opening and closing his hands.

A ladybug landed on Liza's knee. Martin reached over and gently brushed it off. "Maybe we'd grow crooked, too, if we got hit in the middle by a storm."

Liza drove to that place now, reaching her destination in the dark. She pulled a flashlight from under her seat and let the slam of the truck door puncture the cool silence. Solace Fork School stood abandoned, marked for demolition, the children bused to bigger buildings of aluminum and glass. The deer path was still there. She pushed through autumn-dried blackberry thorns to the clearing. The creek that forked wide here was the same creek that ran through the Owenby property. She could hear the water whispering.

Some trees had rotted and lain down tired in the undergrowth, but some still sat. She counted them in her flashlight beam, eight calm ladies murmuring a welcome. She touched the closest one, running her fingertips over dry bark. She wondered if the ladies minded the kinks in their trunks. Did they remember the trauma that bent them, or had they gotten on with things?

3

B e r t i e

Bertie Owenby stood at the mobile home's kitchen door, smoking a cigarette, waiting. Lately it was hard for her to leave the trailer. The sky outside strangled her, while the close walls of the mobile home were more comfortable than skin. Her husband, James, was just the opposite. He felt squeezed when he was inside. His shoulders were as broad as their hallway, and he made the floor shake when he wrestled the bathroom's accordion door back onto its runner.

Bertie would stay inside all the time if she could, but her sister-in-law, Eugenia, was insisting they clean Leon's house. She said she wanted it nice in case Leon wandered home, and she was worried that vandals or even the people helping search would break in and take Leon's valuables. There weren't any valuables. Eugenia was just embarrassed that other people might see how nasty Leon kept the place.

Bertie dreaded it. When Eugenia pulled up to the trailer in the new Mercury her husband, Zeb, had bought her for their anniversary last year, her bitty self barely peeking over the steering wheel, something in Bertie just put its head down and cried. Having to go out at all was bad enough. Worse was having to spend the whole day listening to Eugenia's critical comments about the size of Bertie's trailer, her and James missing a week of church, or some past mistake she'd said she was sorry for a million times. She put out her cigarette and picked up her cleaning things to meet Eugenia at the car so Eugenia wouldn't set a foot in her home. Even so, she caught Eugenia's superior glance across the road at the house where Bertie's parents lived.

"How your folks doing, Bertie? I heard your daddy was ailing."

Bertie got in the car. Eugenia knew full well that what ailed Bertie's daddy was the drink. "They're fine." She watched to make sure Eugenia didn't back over her azalea bushes getting out of the driveway.

A few raindrops plopped on the windshield. Eugenia turned on her wipers. "Your family is certainly blessed with longevity."

What Eugenia meant was, weren't Bertie's mama and daddy ever going to die off so Bertie and James could move into their house? Was it really the natural order of things for them to raise three children to adulthood in the single-wide they'd bought the week they married? The road opened empty in front of Eugenia's car. Bertie felt exposed. Her fingers itched for a cigarette.

Eugenia turned on her car radio to some preacher yelling. She pushed her silver wire-framed glasses higher on her nose. "You'll have to help me find Ivy's new place."

Ivy was James and Eugenia's sister. Ivy's son Steven had built the house for her more than a year ago, so it wasn't all that new, but neither Bertie nor Eugenia commented on the strangeness of not ever having been out to visit. "James said it's two down from Stamey's Feed and Seed, off Old Buncombe Highway," Bertie said.

"I called her, and of course her directions made no sense at all. We'll just have to look for her car."

At the Feed and Seed Eugenia slowed down, and they started looking. They found Ivy's beige Pontiac parked in the front yard of a cute little yellow wood-frame house. Eugenia pulled in, and they saw Ivy wave through the screen door.

"This house is precious." Eugenia sounded surprised. Bertie knew she was thinking Ivy didn't deserve such a nice place.

"I guess Steven's doing pretty well with his body shop. Whatever else anybody might say, he does take care of his mama," Bertie said.

"Humph."

Bertie didn't judge Ivy the way Ivy's own sister and brothers did, though she'd followed James's lead all these years and not had much to do with Ivy and her children. You could say Bertie didn't have room to finger-point at Ivy the way Eugenia did, or thought she did.

The rain was coming down a little harder now. Ivy lumbered out of the house, wearing a large dress too thin for the cool weather and a shapeless blue sweater that had seen too many washings. She smiled the wide dreamy smile she'd worn forever. She climbed in the backseat, causing the car to rock. There they sat, a generation of Owenby women by birth and marriage.

"What you been up to, Ivy? Still working at the Days Inn?" Eugenia said.

"No, it got too hard on account of my knees." Ivy raised her voice as if talking over somebody. "I do laundry for some old folks, like I did for Leon."

"When's the last time you were up there to Leon's?" Eugenia's arms dragged the steering wheel as she turned the car around to get out of Ivy's yard.

"I don't rightly know." Ivy wiped rain off her face. She was never one for dates and times. Days and months and years didn't seem to pass in a straight line for her the way they did for everybody else. Bertie caught herself feeling envious.

"Leon can't have had that much laundry to do. He always wore the same thing," Eugenia said

"Overalls and flannel shirts," Ivy said.

"We gave him a new shirt every Christmas. Zeb thought he'd come to church if he had something to wear, but he never did," Eugenia said. "We gave him underwear, too."

"He wore the underwear. Men's underwear can get right nasty," Ivy said.

That remark shut Eugenia up for the rest of the ride.

They drove up the gravel road to the Owenby home place, passing cars and trucks that the searchers had parked along the road. The home place was a hundred acres. James's daddy had built the house himself, starting with two rooms, then adding on as the family grew, until the house wandered all over its clearing. A buckled porch circled it, keeping it in check. Red clay stained its walls to waist-high. Behind the house tall poplars and other decent timber grew so thick you couldn't tell you were at the foot of a mountain, but most of the rest of the property was worthless except for raising ticks and snakes. Only Leon had stayed on there after their daddy died. None of the other children were interested in the place. Leon had eventually put in electricity but not indoor plumbing, and an outhouse peeked from behind the house. Next to the outhouse was the shed where Leon kept his tools. Beside the shed a fenced pen held Leon's three dogs. The dogs watched them drive up, barking a few times before going back to their own business.

Leon's old Chevy pickup truck sat under a tree in the yard, its dull green paint flaking. Eugenia pulled up beside it, and she and Ivy carried cleaning supplies into the house. Bertie lit a blessed cigarette on the porch to calm her nerves, looking out at the vehicles parked along the road. Her husband James's truck was the first in line. He'd been out since dawn. Bertie tried to spot him along the ridge, but the search had moved too far off to make out any people. She exhaled, frost from her breath mingling with cigarette smoke. Rain ran off the porch roof, drumming on dead leaves and making furrows in the mud below.

Bertie got married in front of this porch, by the steps where a butterfly bush used to be. They had the wedding at home because James's mama, Nell Owenby, was failing so bad by then she couldn't get out. James and his daddy carried Nell onto the porch, her arms and neck wasted thin but her belly swollen with fluid. Bertie's parents came, her daddy not drunk for once. James's people were there, except for Martin, who'd gone off to college, and Leon, who was supposed to be the best man but took a job at a mill down east all of a sudden right before the wedding. The service was short and plain. James had his hair cut like James Dean. He'd bought a new suit, light gray, and cleaned up his work shoes the best he could. It was a happy day, it must have been, but when Bertie thought of it now, what she remembered was the smell of urine mixed with earth that rose up from the ground beside the butterfly bush, from years of Owenby men peeing off the porch.

She pressed her cigarette out on the wet railing and went inside to help Eugenia and Ivy. In the short time since Leon had disappeared, the house had already grown cold and vacant smelling. She surveyed bachelor filth made worse by the sheriff's fingerprint powder. Leon's kitchen and living area, where he spent the most time, were the worst. Years of baked-on spills crusted the old-timey cookstove. The few pieces of furniture—a hard, stained couch, a couple of straight-back chairs, and a wooden chest—were covered with unopened junk mail, plastic bottles, dirty dishes, clothes. The only clean thing in the room was the television on its metal stand. It was a man's house, no sign of a woman's touch anywhere. Nothing soft to sit on. Nothing pretty to look at. When James's mama died, his daddy had cleared every sign of her out of the house.

A piece of yellow crime-scene tape fluttered in a draft that blew through a crack in the plank floor. Eugenia pulled the tape up and rolled it into a ball. "The dirt in here gives me the shivers." She put the tape wad into a black plastic garbage bag and went outside to get spring water for mopping from the gravity-fed pipe behind the house. Ivy started to scrub Leon's stove with a piece of steel wool. Bertie got out her duster to brush the fingerprint powder off things before they did the floor. She worked without talking, using the rhythm of the dusting to keep herself calm.

Through the room's low windows she could see Leon's truck in the yard, rain misting its windshield. It was queer how Leon just quit driving one day. A man who had always loved gadgets and anything mechanical and who had souped up his truck with a race car engine. It took the family a while to notice he wasn't driving anymore. If he needed to get to town he'd walk in, and there was always somebody who could carry him back home when he got ready. After a while James realized that Leon's truck hadn't moved an inch from where he'd parked it in his yard. He asked Leon if it was broke.

"No."

"Then why ain't you driving it?"

"I got out of the notion."

From then on if Leon wanted to go anywhere, he'd get somebody, usually Bertie's son, Bobby, to drive him in his own truck and give him a few dollars for his time. Leon liked riding in his own truck. Sitting in the driver's seat of that green monster, Bobby looked like a young Leon. Bobby and

Leon both favored James's daddy, Rory Owenby, though Leon's hair had been dark when he was young, while the hair that swirled in two long cowlicks down the sides of Bobby's neck was dirty blond. Bertie always itched to shave it.

Bobby acted like driving Leon around was the only work he needed. He quit his sometime job at the Tyson chicken plant and moved out of Bertie and James's trailer to go live with his girlfriend. In a way it was a relief to have him gone, since he came home drunk most weekends and never offered to pay any rent, but without Bobby around, the silences that settled between Bertie and James left her so on edge she wanted to rip her hair out by the roots. She and James rarely talked, not about anything real, and hadn't since Bertie left him that time, years ago. It was a mistake, and she came back after only four days, but James had treated her carefully ever since, like he was afraid she'd run off again.

Over by the stove, Ivy whispered, "hush, now," to nobody in particular as she scrubbed. It was typical of Eugenia to leave Bertie alone with Ivy and her craziness. Bertie walked down the short hall to where Leon slept, in the bedroom that had been his parents'. The overhead bulb was burned out, but dim light from the window streaked the wood floor. The bed in the corner was made, a faint smell of sweat rising from the covers. To Bertie's right a rusty mirror hung above the dresser where Leon kept his toiletries. His safety razor lay beside a bowl of old water. Leon's whiskers, gray and black, bled out of the razor onto the dresser top. Bertie picked up the razor. The handle was surprisingly warm in her hand. She pressed her finger against the blade.

"What are you doing?" Eugenia's accusing voice made Bertie jerk.

"Cleaning," she said.

Eugenia took Leon's razor out of Bertie's hand. "You don't need to mess with his things. I'll take care of them."

The bad feeling that had lain in Bertie's stomach all morning started to rise. "I wasn't messing. You said you wanted my help." Eugenia had no call to make her feel like a criminal. Bertie had belonged to this family for more than thirty years. She had as much right to touch Leon's things as anybody else, more maybe.

Eugenia set the razor back on the dresser. "I didn't mean it like that. I just need you to finish dusting in the other room. You missed some corners." She herded Bertie ahead of her back to the kitchen and living area.

Ivy had wiped down the stove with paper towels. The surface gleamed. Eugenia set to work mopping the floor. When Eugenia's back was turned, Ivy smiled at Bertie and walked over to put her big hand on Bertie's shoulder. "Don't worry," she said.

Bertie couldn't tell if Ivy meant, don't fret about the way Eugenia acts, or don't worry about Leon, or if Ivy was sharing a broader truth her simple mind had discovered. Whatever Ivy meant, somehow it made Bertie feel better. She started moving her duster, getting her rhythm back, and they got on with their chores.

4

Ivy

You'd think this house would have been full enough with the living, me and Eugenia and Bertie trying to stay out of each other's way while we dust and scrub. On top of them I also contend with the dead, crowding with bent necks under the eaves, warming their hands by the unlit stove, arguing, spilling out the door. And the yet-to-be born, baby spirits chortling, drifting by like the bits that float behind an eyeball. Kin mostly, I've gathered, both past and future, though few known to me in life. The weight of them all makes the house lean north with a sigh like an overloaded tinker. The mop water in Eugenia's bucket leans with it, threatening to spill out on the floor.

Is it a blessing or a curse, this seeing of mine? I've about decided it's neither, though it's made me look like a fool my whole life. Mama saying, "Ivy, what in the world," when I dipped and curved around the room as a girl, trying to avoid the ghosts on my way to set the table. I learned later to breathe deep and walk right through them. Pop's stares when I slipped and answered a question he hadn't heard asked. Me unable, still, to tell when a sight or sound is real to other people, not just to me. My brother James asked me once when we were young why it was that I felt bound to open my legs to every rounder between here and Lenoir. The answer is this: that sex is all smells and feeling, two things trustworthy and all of this world. Like the smells of my children, first Ivory soap and dirty diapers, then warm oil at the roots of their hair after a summer night of play, then the years the county had them when there were no smells, and I grieved that the three of them had never been real at all.

A baby spirit floats by, laughing, her hair red and curly. She passes through Eugenia's chest and Eugenia coughs. "I must be coming down with something."

"It's just dust," Bertie tells her. The yellow feathers on Bertie's duster flick and dart, flick and dart.

"Shoo," I say under my breath to the baby spirit, shaking a throw rug at her. "We're nobody here but old women."

"Speak for yourself, Ivy," Eugenia says. "Don't tell me you're groaning about a little housework."

As each of my children was conceived I saw its spirit leaping beyond the haunches of the father, grappling past other babies for a chance at life. Before I missed a month's bleeding I knew my sons and daughter from beginning to end. I saw Steven stocky and sweet, then a coarsened, bristled man. Trina, always a prankster in spite of want and battering. Shane, my oldest, twirling broken from a rafter in a last foster home. I catch sight of Shane sometimes now, always just behind the next doorway, ducking away from me when I try to follow.

I take stock of the room we're in. The old woman who was Pop's mother, Alma, swaddled in black to her wrists, ankles, and chin, spins by the stove, heedless of Eugenia mopping around her feet. Three of her teeth have died and turned a blue paler than a robin's egg, the only color about her. She is as hard in death as in life, the one spirit I don't dare pass through. Her mother, the carrot-haired Missouri whose adventures I've heard in family tales and seen for myself, appears her favorite age of twenty-one today and huffs with impatience, waiting for the rain to stop so she can leave the house. Two old fellows share a jar of moonshine across a checkerboard. I notice Bertie sniff the air, her nose sensitive enough to detect corn whiskey even from another world. Fair-skinned toddlers play around a mouse hole that Leon never boarded up.

Not every family member who passes on appears to me here. I don't know why some linger and some don't. But I wonder that Leon isn't here, as hard as he roosted here in life. I ask the old men, "You reckon he'll be coming soon?"

"Who?" asks Bertie.

"Who?" ask the old men.

"Leon," I say.

"I reckon not," one of the men says. "We ain't got room. They's too many of us as it is." He spits a big gob on Eugenia's clean floor, and I'm glad she can't see it.

"There's a spot for him there in front of the television, like always." I point.

The man looks at me queer, pondering what I mean by television.

Bertie and Eugenia swap looks.

"Ivy, honey," Eugenia says, "he might not be coming back." She whispers to Bertie, "Poor old addled thing."

"I know," I tell her. "I know it." But I clean with one eye out the window, watching for Leon to walk up through the cattails that grow along the creek, to come in and start up a pan of hard corn bread to throw in the yard for the ghost dogs that circle and whine out there in the wet.

5

Martin

Sober. The sun skirted cloud tops and pinned Martin to his window seat. He was brave for the stewardess, declined small bottles, heeded signs not to smoke. He prayed to his estranged higher power that the bruise on his face had healed enough that Liza wouldn't notice it.

The flight attendant came by, offering tiny bags of peanuts. The man seated next to Martin was asleep. "I'll give him his when he wakes up," Martin said, taking two bags. When the flight attendant was safely down the aisle, he pocketed both. He picked up the plastic cup that had held his ration of ginger ale and tipped an ice cube into his mouth. Smells settled in the cabin's circulated air, a mix of perfumes, peanuts, unbrushed teeth, the banana sandwich the woman across the aisle had produced from her carry-on bag. He looked out the window. The plane was flying west over North Carolina's flat Piedmont toward the mountains. Through holes in the clouds he could see the land below. Towns in this part of the state respected one another's space, spreading themselves out like strangers at a picnic ground, each centered on a miles-wide quilt of tobacco fields and curing barns.

*   *   *

In August 1954 he had taken a Trailways bus out of the mountains into the Piedmont, feeling the heat rise and wrap itself around his neck. Until that morning, when he'd climbed on the bus with his clothes and books packed into a mildewed duffel bag Leon had brought back from the war, Martin had never been out of Willoby County. He pressed his face to the grimy window. The bus zigzagged between stops, stitching a ragged line along patched and broken two-lane. An old woman in the seat behind him gave him a boiled egg, then moved forward to pester the driver. Diesel exhaust filled his nostrils, the smell of adventure.

The bus depot was in Whelan, the closest town to Solace Fork big enough to host a bus station. It was Liza who took him to the depot that day, one last ride in the Sunliner convertible that had elevated them to royalty as seniors at Solace Fork School. Liza's father, Dr. Vance, who bought her the car, also gave Martin the money to attend college at Chapel Hill. Martin's own father thought education was useless and had disappeared into the fields that morning without saying good-bye. His mother had felt too poorly to come with him to the station.

"Do you mind your family not seeing you off?" Wind rolled Liza's hair along her neck as she drove.

"No." His answer was honest. Greed for newness had banished fear, and he couldn't get out of Willoby County fast enough.

At the depot, Martin handed his duffel bag to the bus driver to throw into the underbelly of the bus, then turned and hugged Liza.

"You'll come over to Greensboro to see me at college, won't you?" she said when they separated. She blinked back tears.

Martin touched a finger to the corner of her eye. "Now, don't start that."

She tried to smile. "I know."

He kissed her good-bye. Her lips tasted of mint folded into tea and ice cream churned on a hot day, the slightest lacing of rock salt.

From the bus station in Chapel Hill, he walked north to Mrs. Bowen's boarding house, where Dr. Vance had lived as a student thirty years before. The doctor had written and secured him a room. The house, like the landlady herself, had not aged well. Gray paint peeled off the wide porch. Bricks had worked themselves free and fallen into weedy flowerbeds. Young men who would once have taken a place at Mrs. Bowen's table now lived more comfortably in university dorms. The only other residents were two old men, retired salesmen with no families, and Mrs. Bowen's own sister. In Martin's room, water stains mapped continents on the ceiling, but he didn't mind. To have his own room, after sweltering with snoring brothers in the triangular space under his father's tin roof, was a luxury.

On campus, he joined a swell of students moving toward the gym for registration. The young men were confident, dressed in new khakis and saddle oxfords. The girls wore clothing in textures he had never seen before, linen and cashmere. He resisted the urge to reach out and touch them. He took his place in a line of students picking up course cards. Two men ahead of him were returning from Korea on the GI Bill. Martin felt like a baby beside them. He tightened his jaw and stood up straighter.

Once registered, he wandered toward tables set up along the gym walls, where student groups advertised for recruits. A thin, plain girl with a name tag that said "Margaret" manned the table for the Carolina Playmakers, the university's drama group. She eyed him as he approached. "Actor, right?"

"Playwright." At eighteen, with life stretching before him

in all its promise, authorship of a few scenes acted out in the yard of a four-room schoolhouse was enough to make him think he was somebody.

"We do need writers. Especially writers who know how to use a hammer and paintbrush." Margaret pushed a sign-up sheet toward him and told him the date of the group's first meeting.

At dinner that evening, Mrs. Bowen gushed on about Dr. Vance. "The most intelligent young man I ever had stay here. And such good manners, too." Her eyes flitted to Martin's elbows, which were planted on the table. He moved them. The two old salesmen and Mrs. Bowen's sister ate without talking, their dentures clicking in unison.

Mrs. Bowen put more mashed potatoes on Martin's plate without his asking. "And his daughter. What's her name? Elizabeth?"

"Liza," he said.

"Beautiful girl."

"Yes, she is."

"I almost forgot." Mrs. Bowen got up from the table and rifled through a pile of mail on a sideboard. She handed him a package wrapped in brown paper. "Dr. Vance sent this for you."

The old people stopped chewing, watching Martin. He didn't want to open the gift in front of them, but it seemed he had no choice. He pulled off the paper. Inside was a dictionary, so new the thin pages stuck together. A note in Dr. Vance's handwriting said, "Something every playwright needs." Mrs. Bowen beamed. "Didn't I tell you the doctor was thoughtful?"

Martin excused himself and went upstairs to his room. He unpacked his few other books and placed them on a shelf above the room's scratched desk. A Bible from his mother, worn copies of Thomas Wolfe's *Look Homeward, Angel* and Faulkner's *Absalom, Absalom!* stolen from the county library and never missed, and a crisp new copy of Eugene O'Neill's collected works. His high school teacher, Mr. Samuels, had called the O'Neill collection a school prize for the play Martin wrote as his final English paper, but Martin knew Mr. Samuels had paid for it with his own money. Martin put Dr. Vance's dictionary with the other books and arranged and rearranged them, imagining how they would look to new friends coming to visit him, the conclusions they would draw about him from the titles. When he was satisfied with the display, he opened his billfold and took out the registrar's receipt for the $123 he had paid for his first semester's tuition and fees, and tucked it into the Bible, preserving it like a holy thing.

The Fasten Seat Belt sign above Martin's head dinged twice, and the plane lurched under his feet as the pilot began the approach to the Willoby County airport. Foliage and buildings gained definition as they descended. The plane turned and the mountains came into view, red and gold leaves vibrant on the trees near the base but already patchy at the higher elevations, where strands of gray cloud settled on low peaks. Martin's throat tightened with loss. Dr. Vance had thought him a man of honor and promise. Martin was glad the doctor had died before he could realize that Martin had failed him.

6

B e r t i e

The day after cleaning Leon's house with Eugenia and Ivy, Bertie sat at her kitchen table, smoking a cigarette, waiting for James to come home for supper. She had a meatloaf in the oven. The trailer was clean, every piece of bric-a-brac dusted, afghans lined up straight with the backs of the chairs and sofa. She had clipped all the articles about Leon out of the paper and set them aside to save for the family, and made her weekly calls to her grown daughters, who both lived near the coast. She was glad not to have to go anywhere.

She expected James to come home and eat, then head outside to escape the press of the trailer, finding excuses to stay out as long as he could, piddling with his tools and fixing small things that didn't need to be fixed. She and James used to sit in the living room after supper and watch *MacGyver* or *The Golden Girls* on television, but they couldn't watch together anymore because he had to turn the volume up so high. The lathes at the furniture plant had sanded down his hearing. Giant lathes that fashioned bedroom suites named after some French king, with carved mahogany pineapples on the bedposts. The company offered employees a discount, which was a joke. The bed alone was bigger than their living room and so heavy it would make the trailer floor separate from the walls.

She heard the wheels of James's truck kick gravel and the engine turn off. She waited for the sound of his door opening, his step on the little porch, the pause while he took off his boots, something he did for her to keep mud off her floors. When she didn't hear those things, she got up and went outside and saw James gripping his steering wheel, his seat belt still on.

He had brought home Leon's dogs.

Leon never named his dogs, just called them "dog" or "pup." When one died he got another. Every day since they'd discovered Leon gone, James had fed Leon's dogs at the home place, where he'd penned them up so they wouldn't bother the searchers. James treated it as temporary, as if Leon would be coming back to rouse the dogs out of the dirt and sit again with them on his porch, picking ticks off their necks. Now the dogs panted softly in the back of James's truck, just waiting for the next thing the way dogs do.

Bertie hurried around and opened the driver's-side door. James looked terrible. The muscles of his face looked like they were about to turn loose, about to let his eyes and nose and mouth slide right off like candle wax, on down his front. She undid his seat belt and took his arm to make him get out. "Leave the dogs in the truck," she said. "They'll be all right for a minute."

She walked him toward the trailer. Mud and rotten leaves caked his boots. At the porch, he tried to take the boots off, but his hands weren't working right.

"Stop. Just leave them on. Come on in the house," she said.

Usually James looked too big for their sofa, but he seemed

to have shrunk. "The sheriff's calling off the search." He wiped his hand over his mouth, then started to cry. When men cried the sound had to force its way up through muscle and thick bone. Men didn't learn how to cry the way women did. It scared them when it happened, the same as if they'd looked down and noticed they were gushing blood.

"Oh, God, he's gone." His voice was all out of control.

It was only the second time Bertie had seen her husband cry. The first time she had caused the hurt, and when she saw James break down over Leon she felt the guilt well up again, as if she'd caused the second pain as well. She sat down and pressed against him. Even with their bodies touching it felt like she couldn't get close enough to do him any good. "It's okay, baby." She scraped her fingernails through his hair, pushing it off his forehead, the way she would do a child with a fever. In the ridges of his corduroy coat she could smell his whole week, the smoke of barrels lit to warm searchers, metal from the sling blade he used to cut underbrush as he looked, the single paper-bagged beer she knew he had snuck on his way home, a thing she didn't begrudge him.

Outside, the wind came up. Dead leaves shook off yesterday's rain. James lifted a shoulder to wipe tears and snot off his face. "The sheriff wants to meet with all of us tonight over at Eugenia's, so he can tell everybody, announce it officially."

Bertie's mind started turning, trying to find an excuse not to go, but she knew she was stuck.

James stood up and moved away from her. "Let me see about them dogs."

From the kitchen window she watched him tie up the dogs, far enough from the house that they couldn't dig up her flower beds. Gray clouds tapered down into points, faking tornado shapes. James moved around the yard. She wondered which Leon James was grieving for. When they were all younger,

Leon was something, with that full head of black hair and smart grin always forming around some tall tale. But as he got older he talked less and less, until his mouth rusted shut like an old mason jar lid.

Of course, maybe Leon just didn't have anything to say to her.

7

Liza

Liza's husband, Raby, got home from work just as Liza was about to leave to pick Martin up at the airport. She waited for Raby to get out of his truck, watching him duck his head slightly as he climbed out. The jeans he wore for his job selling farm equipment showed off his athletic body.

"Where you headed?" he said.

"To pick up Martin Owenby. Leftovers are in the fridge."

He closed his truck door. "Martin Owenby. Your old flame." Laugh lines creased the corners of Raby's eyes. "Why doesn't one of his relatives pick him up? You can't swing a dead cat around here without hitting an Owenby."

"They're all meeting with Sheriff Metcalf. I volunteered to bring Martin."

"Does he know they've called off the search?" Raby said.

"No. I'll have to tell him."

Raby crossed his arms loosely over his chest. "Maybe I ought to come along to chaperone."

She knew he was teasing, mostly. "You're welcome to. I have nothing to hide."

Raby unfolded his arms. "I guess I trust you." He walked over, put his hands on her upper arms, and gave her a long deep kiss. "Just marking my territory," he said when he let her up for air. "Tell Martin I said hi."

Liza drove toward the airport, rehearsing what she would tell Martin about his brother. She visualized Leon Owenby in a ball cap with the local feed and seed's logo, large old-man ears with lobes that dripped down, his peculiar habit of wearing black dress shoes with overalls and polishing them on the backs of his pants legs when he thought no one was looking. She stopped herself before she could imagine further, Leon lying lifeless on that property somewhere, within shouting distance of the decrepit house or in the dark woods behind it, where even this time of year the undergrowth grew with sinister speed.

The first time Liza saw the Owenby farm she was thirteen. Martin had been to her house but never invited her to his. Liza's father kept a real home. When her mother died he refused to give in to depression or the male tendency to let things get dirty, mildewed, unaired. He hired a housekeeper, Mrs. Evans. Her baking and the oil she used to polish the dark wood in the doctor's study covered up the faint antiseptic smell that sometimes clung to his clothes. Martin loved their house. He stayed as long as he dared, talking to Liza in the lush backyard among her father's ferns and native orchids, or sitting with her father in the study's comfortable leather chairs, where light came in through French doors and a bay window. Her father's books and her own lined the shelves. Martin seemed bigger there.

There were no books at his own house, except his mother's Bible. Not even a piece of spare paper to draw on.

Liza's father got the call just after breakfast one morning

to come and deliver Ivy Owenby's baby, her first boy, Shane. School was out for the summer, and Liza convinced her father to let her come along. He shouldn't have allowed it, but he rarely said no to her. They drove up into the Owenbys' patchy yard. Chickens scattered. Martin's mother waved from the front door, then saw Liza.

"I hope you don't mind me bringing Liza," the doctor called, getting his bag out of the car. "I thought she could visit with Martin, or if he's busy, she can just read a book."

Mrs. Owenby walked to the end of the porch and looked around the corner of the house. Liza got the uneasy feeling that Mrs. Owenby thought Liza being there would get her in trouble. "Martin's out back, hauling rock. You can go talk to him, I reckon."

Liza's father followed Mrs. Owenby into the house, and Liza went to look for Martin. She found him on the far side of his mother's garden, in the middle of a large rectangle of plowed earth, tossing rocks into a wheelbarrow. He was shirtless, covered with red clay dust, sweat striping his wiry torso. Scratches on his arms beaded blood.

"What are you doing?" Liza called.

He turned around. She could tell he was happy to see her but also embarrassed, of the house, his bare chest, the dirt. "Mama wants a bigger garden space. Leon tilled it up, now I have to clear the rocks out, dump them over yonder." He pointed to a big pile of jumbled stone near the edge of the woods in back of the property.

She eyed the wheelbarrow. "It looks heavy."

"It is." He lifted his hair out of his eyes. "You having a good summer?"

"It's all right. Boring. You need to come over so I'll have something to do."

"Maybe Sunday afternoon I can come into town."

"Come for dinner. Mrs. Evans is cooking a roast."

As she spoke, Martin's brother Leon walked up from the direction of the lower field. He wore overalls over a dirty white shirt and was as sweaty as Martin.

"I need the wheelbarrow, Martin." He didn't bother to acknowledge her.

"You can't have it. Pop told me to get these rocks cleared."

"I'm taking it." Leon grabbed the wheelbarrow by the handles and dumped all of Martin's rocks out onto the ground.

"What are you doing!"

"I said I needed it." Leon started to push the wheelbarrow away. Martin grabbed the front. As they tussled, Martin's father came around the corner of the house. "Quit that!" Martin and Leon both stopped where they were.

Mr. Owenby was tall, like Leon. His farmer's hands were permanently dirt stained. Martin appealed to him. "He just dumped my whole load."

"I need the barrow to take that seed down. You told me do it today," Leon said.

"Take it," Mr. Owenby said. Leon took the wheelbarrow and left the way he had come.

"How am I supposed to clear the rock?" Martin was so frustrated he was close to tears.

"Carry 'em by hand." Mr. Owenby looked at Liza, then back at Martin. "And get back to work. You ain't the one having the baby."

Martin's face reddened with humiliation.

"I'll just go in the house," Liza said, not wanting to cause him any more grief.

"Best you did." Mr. Owenby headed toward the lower field.

Martin wouldn't look at Liza. She walked back to the front

of the house and went inside. Through the closed bedroom door she could hear Ivy moaning and her father and Mrs. Owenby murmuring. She found a tub of unshelled peas Mrs. Owenby had left on the kitchen table and took them outside to the porch to make herself useful. The porch boards were bowed and cracked, all moisture sucked out of the wood. The only thing to sit on was a high-backed chair with a frayed cane seat. The Owenbys didn't even have a rocking chair. She sat down in the chair and snapped the peas, popping one or two in her mouth as she worked. Sweat trickled down her face. The chair's hard slats dug into her back. She heard Martin throw a rock on the pile behind the house. She imagined him working like Sisyphus in her Greek mythology book, pushing a boulder uphill only to watch it roll down again. When her father finally came out of the house, displaying Ivy's newborn baby in a blanket and announcing, "Now, isn't he a fine big fellah?" Liza was never happier to see him.

Liza turned in to the airport. How a boy like Martin grew at all in the rocky earth of the Owenby farm amazed her. She blamed his parents for giving him no soil in which to take root. His mother tried, but she didn't have the time, or didn't know what to give him in the moments she found. When he left here the wind so easily ripped him up and blew him away.

She parked and went inside to baggage claim. A voice behind her said, "Liza." The fluorescent glare of the airport lobby yellowed Martin's face. He was too thin, but still good-looking, with almost no gray in the hair that fell rakishly over his eyes. When she hugged him, wanting substance, his body seemed to collapse backward into air, leaving her embrace unsatisfied. He felt boneless, like a baby's foot. He had always been like that, his physical self as hard to grasp as his mind and heart. There had been times when she had gone back and read letters from Martin that she had saved, remembering them as being long and full of heavy meaning, only to find a few scrawled sentences, his letters mere notes. She had filled in the rest.

He held her at arm's length. She could feel the strength in his hands. "You are absolutely beautiful." His voice, tobacco roughened, made it true.

"So are you," she said, laughing. Lines of sadness crossed the laugh wrinkles around his eyes, but the green eyes themselves belonged to the mischievous boy who had led her into the woods on her first day at Solace Fork School.

"It's so good to have you home," she said, then wished she hadn't when she remembered what had brought him.

"Is there any news?"

"The sheriff has called off the search for now. He's taking a personal interest in Leon's case, out of friendship to Hodge. He's meeting with your family tonight at Eugenia's. I'm supposed to take you straight there." She watched Martin's face but couldn't tell what he was feeling. "I'm sorry about your brother, sweetie."

He nodded. "Thank you."

They claimed his suitcase and walked to her truck. Martin hefted his bag into the back, and they climbed in. It had been a long time since they had sat so close.

"How's my family handling it?" he said.

"Not so well."

"Tell me."

Liza pulled away from the terminal and out onto Aviation Drive. "From what I gather, Steven suspects Bobby, and James suspects Steven. There are probably other theories I haven't heard yet."

She saw a familiar look on Martin's face. He would bolt if he could, but her truck was already in motion. They passed gray factories with half-empty parking lots and hit country highway. Corn browned in the fields on either side. In her rearview mirror, a last sliver of hazy sun dropped behind hills.

Martin tried the radio, then gave up when he remembered how the mountains blocked airwaves. "I should feel more than I do. I barely knew him." He rolled down his window and stuck out an elbow. "When I visited, we ran out of words after three minutes. You can't have a conversation with a person who has no answer when you ask him what's new."

"His life got small," she said, thinking that Leon's life was best kept small. When his life was bigger he harmed people.

"I guess all of our lives have gotten small." In the fading light, Martin's profile showed his years. The shadow of a bruise outlined the ridge of his cheekbone, and tiny veins broke along the side of his nose. Liza suspected that even as he navigated the broad avenues of cosmopolitan New York, his life was bounded on all sides by alcohol, guilt, self-hatred. She took his hand and squeezed it before letting go and turning her truck toward town.

They passed the turnoff for Solace Fork School, where she and Martin had gone to school through the twelfth grade. "Did Hodge tell you they're planning to tear the school down?"

"No."

"Next month. They're going to replace it with a book depository."

"Didn't any of our famous alumni raise a stink?"

"You're our only famous alumnus."

"That's sad."

"It's really falling apart, from being empty for so long. We'll go out there tomorrow if you want to."

"Don't you have to work?"

"I have so much accrued time off I could play hooky for a semester and they couldn't say anything."

They drove the rest of the way to Eugenia's house, catching up on safe topics. Liza wanted them to find the familiar groove of old friendship, to fall into the banter, the finishing of each other's sentences, but the ride was too short. She told herself to be patient.

At Eugenia's, the curb was lined with cars. Liza stopped her truck in the street and let it idle. "I'll see you tomorrow."

"Don't you want to come in with me?" Martin's voice half-teased, half-pleaded.

"I'm not family. It'll be all right." She waited while he lifted his suitcase out of the truck bed.

Martin's family didn't know he was gay. As he trudged across Eugenia's yard he seemed to remake himself, squaring his shoulders, losing the give in his limbs.

On Eugenia's porch, he turned around and waved. Liza waited until she saw him open the door and go in, to make sure he didn't flee.

8

I v y

My daughter, Trina, drives us to Eugenia's house in the low-slung black Corvette that is her pride and obsession. My son Steven squeezes in the back, and I sink into the front seat, afraid I won't be able to get myself back out. Trina keeps her car clean. She washes and vacuums it twice a week and won't let anybody eat or drink in it. I understand her care, this girl who for so long didn't own a nice thing to tend to. At twenty-eight she looks like she did as a youngster, with dark brown hair she cut into wings in front of the bathroom mirror, corduroy Levi's and a plaid shirt hanging out at the tail. Her pug nose leads her fierce and hopeful into life. She has always kept her head above water, a dunked dog bobbing, intent on surviving. She does Steven's books at the body shop. She and Steven neither one can keep a boyfriend or girlfriend, because they are more loyal to each other and to me than they are to any mate.

At Eugenia's, Trina helps me out of her car, and Steven climbs out behind. Hodge Goforth stands on the porch, here to support the family and explain things to us. "Y'all come in."

We go inside, and Trina whispers in my ear, "This house smells like old lady."

I swat her arm. "Hush."

Eugenia has furnished her living room with the laminate furniture they make at the furniture plant where her husband, Zeb, worked before he retired. Flat olive green carpet with a wave pattern covers the floor. Her shelves are full of pictures of her only daughter and her grandchildren, who don't come visit much but who send her pictures to put up on her fridge. Eugenia doesn't put pictures on her fridge, of course. There is nothing on her fridge but a magnet shaped like praying hands. Nothing out of place in her house. She has not made coffee for us or the sheriff, and there aren't even enough seats for all of us to sit down. She doesn't want us to stay long. I expect she is suffering particularly to have me here. Eugenia has not spoken to me any more than necessary since I was seventeen and got pregnant with my first boy, Shane. I embarrass her, hard as I try not to. The ghosts must feel unwelcome here, too. I only see one, a baby spirit tumbling around the room, looking for somebody to pester.

Steven finds me a place on a love seat at the far end of the room, facing the door. He and Trina stand up behind me. I can feel Steven protecting me, the way he's done ever since his big brother, Shane, died. I lean my head back and look up at him. Steven's hair is wiry, the gray ones poking out above the brown. His arms are strong, and there is auto body paint under his fingernails. He is scowling at my brother and sister. He feels their slights more than I do. I want to reach up and smooth out the groove between his eyebrows. He sees me looking up at him upside down and smiles.

James and Bertie's boy, Bobby, has come. My Steven can't abide Bobby. I hope they can both behave themselves tonight. Bobby slouches against a wall. His baseball cap is on backward and lifts up every time he leans his head back. James and Bertie sit in metal folding chairs. Bertie's arms are crossed against her chest. When Bertie wishes to be somewhere else, she can't take it off her face. Eugenia and her husband, Zeb, claim the couch, leaving room for Hodge at the end. The sheriff chooses to stand. We are all of us here but Martin, who is supposed to get in this evening but hasn't appeared yet. Martin is the baby. The family has never counted on him in weighty matters, any more than they've counted on me. Sheriff Metcalf goes ahead and starts without him.

"I thank y'all for coming. There's so many of you, I wanted to say things just once so I didn't have to repeat." The sheriff looks around at us, making eye contact with those of us that will let him. "Y'all may have already heard, we're discontinuing the search for the time being." His jaw kind of clenches, like he's expecting an outcry from us, but he hasn't said anything we don't already know. We stay quiet. He looks relieved. "Now, that doesn't mean we're giving up. It just means we've covered everywhere we can think of to look. If we get any new information, we can start the search again. I'm going to summarize what we know, then y'all can ask questions."

We all nod. The baby spirit, hair curling reddish gold all over her head, settles on Bobby and pulls on his ball cap. Bobby doesn't notice.

"The first Monday of the month, Leon cashed his Social Security check at the bank, so we believe he had some cash on him. His wallet wasn't in the house. Maybe he had it with him, though James says he didn't generally carry it when he worked around the property."

"That's right," James says. I picture Leon's wallet, shiny with wear, a ring worn in the leather from a condom he's had in there ever since I can remember.

The sheriff goes on. "That same day, Alvin Richards saw him at the Piggly Wiggly. The next day, Tuesday, James saw him when he went over to borrow a tool. That's the last sighting we know of. When James went by again a week later,

Leon wasn't there and the front door was hanging open. The dogs were hungry. That's when y'all called us."

The sheriff's focus on timing makes me nervous. Time confuses me. I worry about saying the wrong thing, getting it wrong. As the sheriff starts to ask his questions, I keep my mouth shut.

"Do y'all know anybody who had a reason not to like Leon?" The sheriff doesn't look at me, but an answer forms in my head all the same.

Did I have a reason not to like Leon? Yes I did.

I had just turned thirteen. It was April and the air was warm, but the water in the creek that flowed down from Spivey's Bald was so cold it hurt my toes when I dangled them in. Pop had put a pipe where a spring ran out of the rock and into the creek, so we could get water without dirt or leaves in it. I kept a jelly jar down there so I could get me a drink when I wanted. The water out of that pipe tasted sweet and clear. I felt it clean me as it went down. This was my special spot. I sat on bright green, star-shaped moss. This was the only place on the property where such moss grew. Its springy softness was worth the damp that eventually seeped through the seat of my dress. I was building stick houses, using two Y-shaped sticks to start a tiny lean-to, then cutting out a piece of moss as sod to fit the roof. Underneath, in the rectangle hole I'd left, roly-poly bugs panicked in the light, rolling into balls. I was flicking them like marbles when I heard young men's voices hiking up toward me, on the other side of the creek.

First I saw their heads, bobbing as they walked. Leon and two of his friends. Leon was tall, like Pop. New spring sun had pinked his face and neck. Dale Mabrey, as tall as Leon but heavier, carried a big stick he'd picked up and whacked at saplings as he walked. Skinny Nathan Coffey followed behind like he always did, not saying much. They were already in their twenties. All three had been in the service during the war. They rarely gave children like me the time of day. They came out on the rocks across from me.

"Look here." Dale Mabrey grinned at me across ten feet of shallow water. "That your sister, Owenby?"

"One of them." Leon looked bored.

"Which one are you?" Dale Mabrey asked me.

"Ivy," I said.

"What kind of name is that?"

"I don't know."

"Ivy, Poison Ivy, Creeping Ivy." Dale looked around at Leon and Nathan, grinning, showing off for them. He splashed across to my side of the creek and poked at my dress with his stick. "What you doing, Ivy?" He lifted up the edge of my skirt with the stick.

I moved away, smoothing it down. "Nothing."

Nathan Coffey stood nervous on the opposite bank. "Come on, Dale. Let's get going."

Dale waded back across the creek. He took out a pack of cigarettes and shook one out for himself, tucking it in his overall pocket. "I think I'll stay here." He held out the whole rest of the pack to Leon. Leon looked over at me and then took it. There I was, sold for half a pack of Salems.

"Come on, Nathan," Leon said. He walked away. Nathan looked at me across the water and hesitated for half a minute, then he followed Leon. Their sound faded into the laurel, and Dale Mabrey came back across the creek.

He sat down next to me, squashing one of the little houses I had worked on so hard. I didn't say anything, for fear he'd call me a baby. He grinned at me. Pimples covered his face and neck. He fiddled with the fly on his overalls, and his thing popped out and waved around. I had seen male things before, when I took baths with my brothers when we were younger, but this was big and red and ugly looking. When he grabbed my hand and wrapped my fingers around it, it was warm and sticky, and it smelled bad.

"Don't." I tried to pull away, but he was strong.

"Up and down, Ivy," he said, his hand over mine. Our two hands rode up and down, faster and faster. Dale's jaw slacked and his breath came quick. His eyes closed. "Faster," he said, though it was him making our hands move. I felt his thing get wet, and then white stuff squirted out, all over my hand, some on my dress. I got my hand away then. He went up and down a few more times on his own until his thing wilted over. He opened his eyes.

I backed away and bent down to wash the white stuff off my hand in the creek. Dale jumped up and grabbed my wrist. "Don't waste it, Ivy." He slung me back down on the bank, pulled up my dress, yanked down my drawers. With one finger he collected the white stuff from the end of his thing and off my hand. Then before I knew what he was doing he jammed the finger up me. Jammed and jammed. It burned and I cried out. I tried to get away, but his left hand dug into my collarbone.

He finally stopped and let me go, wiping his finger on his overall legs. "I'll see you around, Creeping Ivy." He left me there on the bank.

I lay down with my cheek against moss and stared at the creek, focusing on orange rocks polished round by the burbling water. Waxy laurel leaves floated upside down like little boats. Long-legged water bugs skimmed the surface.

My great-grandmother Missouri appeared on the bank as a seven-year-old child. A tight braid tried to tame her red hair. She carried a homemade rag doll that she took no care with. She flung it around, dashing its head on the rocks.

"I want a drink," she demanded.

I stared at her, dazed.

She stamped her foot. "Get me a drink!"

I got up off the bank and brushed leaves and sticks from my clothes. I found my jelly jar, walked slowly over to the pipe to fill it and brought it back to her. She grabbed it and took a loud drink, handing the glass back to me with a sigh. I drank what was left, my hands and lips shaking, while Missouri kicked pebbles into the creek. No amount of water could wash away what had happened.

After that day, I moved my spot. I left my jelly jar at the pipe but found a new place up the hill, hidden by bushes and long grass, where I could see down but nobody could see me unless I wanted them to.

Did I have a reason not to like Leon? Yes I did. Do I begrudge him selling me out for a half pack of smokes? I do not. I can't hold onto resentments any more than I can hold on to a long thought. Both slip off my mind like a silky ribbon loosing itself from a girl's hair and falling to the dirt on her way home from school. And at least Leon didn't judge, as mean and thoughtless as he was. He was the same to me and my kids always, unlike the back-turning of the others. And lately he had helped me out with something.

No, I didn't keep a grudge.

Sheriff Metcalf is finishing up. I'll get Trina to tell me later what I missed. Eugenia asks Hodge to lead us in a prayer. I am not the only one who doesn't bow her head. We are all watching each other.

Eugenia's front door bangs open. We hear a loud wiping of shoes and smell cologne. Martin leans in the living room doorway, looking older than last time. The grin on his lips is half-desperate. The baby is home.

9

Martin

His family. The faces that turned toward Martin were all like his parents' in some way—his mother's ears sticking out from his sister Eugenia's head, his father's nose on the faces of his sister Ivy and nephew Bobby, a certain turndown of the mouth that afflicted them all. If Martin walked down Main Street in Whelan today, passersby might recognize his own unoriginal face and stop him to ask if he was Rory and Nell Owenby's boy. He lifted his hand in a wave. "Hello."

"Martin!" Eugenia got up from the couch and ran to him. Her head barely came up to his collarbone, but her wiry arms were strong enough to hurt when she hugged him. The others merged toward him, hugs from the women and handshakes from the men.

Hodge grabbed his shoulders, grinning. "Good to see you, buddy."

The sheriff, polite, waited for the greetings to subside and for people to take their seats again, then Hodge introduced him. Martin shook the sheriff's hand. Wally Metcalf had a pleasant, intelligent face. Martin liked it all the more because it bore no family resemblance.

"We were about to wrap it up here. I've got to get to another meeting across town," the sheriff said.

"Hodge can fill me in." Martin wasn't sorry to have missed the meeting. How was one supposed to act at such events? What face did one put on as law enforcement gave the briefing?

"I'll be in touch, folks," Sheriff Metcalf said. He showed himself out.

Eugenia planted herself in the living room doorway so no one else could leave. "Y'all heard what he said, now. If you hear of anything, you're to tell him. And us, too." Then her face crumpled and she started to cry. "This is all so terrible." Martin was nearest to her, so he put his arm around her. Her husband, Zeb, a tall lurch of a man whom Martin had heard say maybe a dozen words in forty years, got up from the couch and came over to pat her on the shoulder. With a big sniff Eugenia composed herself and moved away from Martin, clearing the exit.

Hodge spoke up. "Eugenia's right. If you think of anything at all, tell the sheriff. You never know when something small will turn out to be important."

Martin's nephew Bobby leaned against the wall, one dirty boot resting on Eugenia's clean paint. "There's people in this room that do know something and they ain't telling."

Steven bristled. Ivy reached a calming hand back and touched his wrist.

"Now, Bobby, you don't need to be saying that. I'm sure if anyone here knows anything, they'll tell it," Hodge said.

"Not if they're the one did it," Bobby grumbled.

James, looking uncomfortable, spoke to his son. "That's enough, Bobby."

Bertie sat in her chair, her pointer finger drawing the same circle over and over again on her thigh, beading the pink polyester of her pants.

"No, let's hear what he has to say." Steven walked around

to the front of the room and stood between Bobby and the
door, his arms crossed. "I'm inclined to agree that somebody
here ain't telling the truth."

Bobby spoke without looking at Steven. "You didn't like
it that Leon was favoring me now. You knew he was going
to let me and Cherise put a trailer up there on his property,
behind the house."

"You a damn liar, Bobby. Leon wouldn't've let you do that
in a million years, and he was getting tired of you asking."

"He was going to let us."

"All right." Hodge held up a hand. "Nobody's going to put
a trailer up there now, anyway. Not until we know something
for sure about Leon."

"But Leon said we could!" Bobby's boot scraped down the
wall. Eugenia flinched.

"Son, this is not the time." James's quiet voice was firm.

"Shit. You stupid—" Bobby stomped toward the door. As
he passed Steven, he stumbled over Steven's foot and almost
fell. Martin couldn't tell whether Steven had helped Bobby
trip or not.

Bobby recovered and got up close to Steven. "You're asking
for it, man!"

Steven didn't budge. "Get out of my face, you sorry bastard."

Bertie crossed her arms and legs and closed her eyes. Martin
could almost hear her counting to calm herself.

Hodge moved between Steven and Bobby, using his two
arms as a wedge. "Y'all cut it out."

"There's stuff missing from Leon's place, and I think you
took it," Bobby said.

"I don't have nothing but what Leon gave me."

James took Bobby by the arm and led him out of the
house. Bobby protested all the way out into the yard. Steven

headed for the door, but Hodge stopped him. "Let him get on the road first, son."

Eugenia heaved a sigh and looked at Martin. "Are you going to stay with us?"

Bertie spoke up. "I have a bed all ready for you, Martin."

Martin was trapped, bound to hurt someone's feelings. "I'll go in alphabetical order, starting with Bertie. Then I'll be back over here tomorrow night to stay with you, Eugenia."

"Must be nice to be fought over," Hodge said. Eugenia didn't smile.

Trina and Ivy joined Steven near the door. "Martin, come by the house while you're here," Steven said.

"I will," Martin said. Steven always had good dope. A night partying with him and Trina was a tradition Martin made time for on his rare trips back to Solace Fork.

Once Ivy and her children had left, Hodge turned to Martin. "I hate that it took this to get you back home."

Martin didn't remember a time without Hodge, whose family had lived a half mile away from the Owenby farm, easy walking distance, even barefoot. Hodge was a little pudgier, his hairline slightly more receded than when Martin had last visited, but his good nature hadn't changed. No matter how many years passed, Hodge welcomed Martin as if Martin were still the shining star he'd been as a boy and Hodge was his trusty sidekick. Hodge's loyalty was more than Martin felt he deserved.

"We're doing all we can about Leon. Wally Metcalf knows his stuff. We'll find him," Hodge said.

Martin nodded. "Thanks for being our liaison."

"Happy to do it. Now listen. I know you've got to make the rounds to see all your family, but after that me and Claudie want to get you out to our place. There's something I want to run by you." Hodge looked over at Eugenia, who was making

Bertie stand up so she could put away the folding chair Bertie was sitting on.

"I'll give you a call," Martin said.

Martin told Eugenia good-bye and walked outside with Bertie. James was standing in the yard, alone. The three of them got into James's pickup truck, with Bertie in the middle. Martin could tell Bertie needed a cigarette. He did, too. Nobody spoke. James was usually an easy talker, but he seemed distracted. Martin felt guilty that Leon's disappearance hadn't affected him the way it had James, but James and Leon were closer in age. And Leon hadn't bullied James.

James and Bertie's trailer hadn't changed in thirty years. Bertie kept it immaculate. Eugenia disdained the trailer, but it was nicer than the house they had grown up in. It had indoor plumbing and heat. Martin took James's cue and removed his shoes on the porch. Inside, it was sweltering. Bertie liked it warm. Martin took off his coat and rolled up the sleeves of his dark purple dress shirt. He could feel sweat stains starting to form under his arms. James stripped down to his undershirt.

"You want something to drink?" Bertie said.

He wished he could ask for a Scotch, but Bertie didn't allow liquor in her house. "Just water, please."

Bertie filled a glass from the tap and handed it to him. The water tasted the way he remembered, delicious, the no-taste of cold rocks.

They walked into the tiny living room. Martin and Bertie sat on the couch. James sank into his recliner. Martin set his water glass on Bertie's polished coffee table.

"What's the name of that firm you work for again?" James said.

"Glenkinchie, Talisker and Craggenmore," Martin improvised.

James had worked for the same furniture company for decades. He didn't understand or respect self-employment even when it was done well, and Martin didn't do it well. Martin appreciated James. James had treated him decently as a kid. When James and Bertie were courting they took Martin places, once to the state fair in Raleigh. Got him gloriously sick on cotton candy. Bertie was easier then, just a sweet, uncomplicated girl. Now she sat on the sofa, her white hair pulled back with a bow-shaped barrette that was too young for her, so tense that if he reached over and touched her with his finger she would jump.

She reached for a pack of cigarettes and a lighter on an end table next to the couch, shook a cigarette out for herself and handed Martin one without his asking. "You can sleep in Bobby's room."

"Where will Bobby sleep?"

"He stays at his girlfriend's house."

"Ah. What's her name again?"

James leaned back in his chair, raising the footrest. "Cherise. Cherise LaFaye."

"Good lord."

"She made it up. She cuts hair. She must think it makes her sound fancy for her customers," Bertie said.

"Ah. Her *nom de cosmetologie.*"

Bertie didn't smile. "People ought to use the name they're given. That goes against my grain of salt."

"What's her story?" Martin lit up with his own lighter, not waiting for Bertie to get through with hers. He imagined them both relaxing a bit there on the couch as the nicotine hit.

Bertie inhaled. "She's not much good." She exhaled and looked over at James.

"She'd sooner climb a tree and lie than stay on the ground and tell the truth," James said.

Bertie passed Martin a plastic ashtray. "She's going to get Bobby in trouble."

Bobby had never needed help getting into trouble. Martin could tell by Bertie's face that she knew it.

"What was that about Bobby putting a trailer up at the home place?" Martin said.

"He got this idea in his head of selling that big pile of rock back behind Leon's house, and him and Cherise putting a trailer back in there," James said.

Martin remembered the heap of stone, between their mother's garden and what used to be their father's corn field. It was huge, made up of all the rocks his family had ever turned up plowing. The pile had been there so long that grass had grown up through it and the snakes considered it theirs. "Who'd buy rock around here? Doesn't everybody have plenty of their own?"

"You'd be surprised. New people moving in want it for walls and such. There's a man parks a truck full down at the Piggly Wiggly parking lot, gets eighty dollars a ton for it," James said.

"Selling the rock isn't the problem. Talking Leon into it is," Bertie said. "Bobby told us Leon was still thinking on it, but I don't know."

Martin couldn't see Leon going along with Bobby's plan. It would have required Leon to make a change. Getting Leon to do anything different would be harder than moving that pile of grassed-over stone. Martin wondered how pissed Bobby had been when Leon said no. He looked over at Bertie. Her index finger was scratching a circle on the fabric of her pants again. He wondered if she even knew she did it and thought of the pills he could get her, cheap, to smooth out the bumps in her road.

Bertie set her cigarette in the ashtray and got up. She picked up a long manila folder from the top of the television and brought it over, opening it on the coffee table to reveal a collection of newspaper clippings in various shades of yellow. The clipping on top was about Leon, with a picture of the home place, more dilapidated and overgrown than when Martin had last seen it.

"I've saved all the ones since Leon went missing," Bertie said.

James made a small sound in his throat and stood up. "I'm going to turn in." He walked down the hall toward the back bedroom.

The corners of Bertie's eyes pinched with worry. "All he's done since Leon went missing is search and sleep."

Martin didn't know what to say. He lifted the top clipping and read the sheriff's plea to anyone who might have seen Leon, then moved the articles about Leon aside, curious to see the rest of Bertie's collection.

"You can look at all of them if you want. I don't know why I save them. I guess because no one else in the family cares to."

She had created an archive of Owenby memorabilia, including every mention of their family that had ever appeared in print. Martin's fingers stopped at his father's obituary, with a muddy snapshot someone had taken shortly before he died. He looked ancient. In contrast, his mother was young in her photograph, barely a girl. Dots of ink fragmented her young face.

"She was a pretty woman in her day," Bertie said, watching him.

"She looked nothing like this," Martin said. It seemed dishonest to have put this picture in the paper when she died.

"I don't know that anyone ever took a later one. Your mama wasn't one to call attention to herself."

Martin thought of the one time his mother got a break from her work of tending the men. She and Martin caught the mumps together. His father had never had the mumps and feared what it would do to his manhood. He let Martin's mother sequester herself with Martin in their bedroom, and he slept on the porch. She may have been miserable trapped in bed with an eight-year-old, but to Martin it was heaven to have her to himself for long quiet days at a time while his father and brothers were in the fields.

Bertie gently moved the clipping of his mother aside. "Here's one about you."

The piece she pulled out was about one of Martin's plays. The town librarian had organized some locals to come to Chapel Hill to see it his senior year of college. His mother was dead by then and his father had refused, but Eugenia and Zeb came. Bertie and James didn't. Bertie had left James that year, briefly, and she and James weren't facing anyone yet. Martin never knew the details, just Eugenia's righteous condemnation of Bertie for running off with some man to the Peabody Hotel in Memphis. It was months before Eugenia would even speak to Bertie again. Martin wondered if Bertie was thinking about that now as she showed him the clipping.

He flipped to the next piece in the stack. The picture, from ten years earlier, was of North Carolina's favorite son, Deke Armstrong, shaking hands with a grinning Andy Griffith. The caption celebrated a coup by the North Carolina film commission. A movie Martin had never heard of would be shot entirely in North Carolina.

Deke Armstrong. A man who had dumped Martin with such bruising finality that Martin, usually shameless with acquaintances who had money, had never bothered him for a loan.

"I saved it because you knew him at college," Bertie said. "Do you ever hear from him?"

"We haven't kept in touch."

She straightened the papers in her folder into right angles, then got up. "I guess I'll go to bed." She stopped in the doorway and studied his face. "It's good to have you here, Martin. You know, you don't have to change houses tomorrow. It'd be easier if you just stayed here."

"Sorry, Bertie. I'm more scared of Eugenia than I am of you."

Bertie left and Martin looked out the window. He had forgotten how dark the country was at night. No streetlights for miles, not even car headlights from this side of the trailer. And the sounds. No ocean sound of city traffic. Insistent scrapings of insect legs, dogs howling, and every shuffle, every flush, every step of the other two human beings in the trailer. The walls might as well have been made of cardboard. If Bertie and James had conversed in whispers in their bedroom down the hall he would have been able to discern every word. But they didn't talk.

He turned back to Bertie's folder to see if there were any more articles about himself. There was a brief mention when he graduated from college but nothing else. Deke Armstrong had gone on to a respectable career in Hollywood, making sure that he returned to North Carolina often enough to preserve his place as the big fish in a little pond. Martin's fleeting career as a playwright hadn't made the news in Willoby County. He picked up the picture of Deke again. Grainy newsprint softened Deke's sharp cheekbones and jaw, but the haughtiness Martin remembered was still there.

At the end of Martin's first week as a freshman at Chapel Hill, brain-tired from five days of classes, he took a seat in the second row of the Playmakers Theatre for the drama group's organizational meeting. Twenty other students sat around him. At a table in front of the theater's stage, a pretty blonde and a thin, pale-faced boy watched the clock for the time to start. Also at the table, reading while he smoked a cigarette, was a dark young man who looked older than everybody else. As Martin watched, the man's cigarette burned down, a bridge of ashes arching over his book, until Martin was sure it would fall and singe the pages. At the last moment, the man took it out of his mouth and flicked it into an ashtray to his right. His dark eyes evaluated the gathering audience. Martin looked away before the man's gaze reached him. The blonde called the meeting to order.

The girl named Margaret who had signed Martin up slipped into the seat beside him. "Hiya, playwright," she said.

As the blonde went over preliminaries, Martin asked Margaret, "Who's that fellow in black?"

"Deke Armstrong," she whispered.

He tried the name out in his mouth.

"He saw action in Korea," Margaret said. "He's brilliant onstage. He played John White in *The Lost Colony* this summer."

The thin boy took the floor. "We're holding auditions for *Tartuffe* in three weeks. I have scripts for anyone interested. If you want to work on costumes or scenery, see Bess after the meeting." He pointed to the blonde. "The other thing we're putting on this semester is a series of student-written one-act plays. Submit them to Deke before September fifteenth if you want your work considered. No suicides or people waking up at the end of the play to discover it was all a dream, please."

Martin blushed. The play he'd written for Mr. Samuels, *Fortunate One*, featured a suicide. He started to rewrite it in his head.

"And now, to get us all in the dramatic mood, Deke Armstrong has agreed to do a reading for us from Shakespeare's *King Lear.*"

With so many people fawning over him, Deke could have been pretentious. Martin watched him, ready to snort and poke Margaret in the ribs as a homely substitute for Liza if Deke seemed too impressed with himself. But Deke gave an easy smile and rose. "Let's see if I can do the Bard justice."

" 'Blow, winds, and crack your cheeks! rage! blow!' "

Except for his own play and occasional movies in Whelan, Martin had never seen a dramatic performance. Deke's smooth voice reading old words, the way his jaw muscles flexed as he read, riveted Martin. At the end of the passage, when Deke spoke the last lines and closed the book, Martin couldn't move.

That night he dreamed that the Playmakers were hazing him in a fraternity initiation. He ran naked with his pledge brothers through a canopy of hands and feet that kicked and punched. He slipped on cold grass and looked up to see Deke. Deke's hands on his shoulders lifted him up, then slammed him back down hard on the ground. Deke's hands didn't rest on him any longer than any other brother's hands, but the shock that went through Martin at Deke's touch was like nothing he had felt before. He woke up alone in his bedroom at Mrs. Bowen's, embarrassed at his physical response.

He reworked *Fortunate One* and left it in Deke's mailbox in the Playmakers office. In October the temperature dropped into the thirties. Martin excused his thin coat by telling people he was warm natured. On a miserably cold day, as he walked through a wind tunnel between class buildings, he heard someone call his name.

"Owenby! Hold up." Deke finished a conversation with another student and walked over to Martin. Martin hadn't thought Deke knew his name. "Your play," Deke said.

Deke had the play in his hand. Martin could see the flimsy watermarked paper he had used, the lower case *e*'s from Mrs. Bowen's typewriter all filled in with ink. Deke had read his play.

"You have potential." Deke walked beside him, less than two feet away. Martin could smell him, a cold smell like air before it snows. "The cause and effect bit, sin and retribution, is juvenile. When you've lived a little you'll learn that sinners go free and the innocent suffer all the time." Deke's smile twisted bitter for an instant. "Anyway." He handed the play to Martin. "See my edits, and if you can live with them, we'll put on your play."

"Great," Martin said, ever the brilliant man of words.

He wished he could write to his high school teacher, Mr. Samuels, to tell him about the play, but Mr. Samuels had moved away right after graduation, and no one knew where he had gone. Instead Martin wrote to his mother and told her that the Carolina Playmakers were putting on his play. She wrote back, in her even, sweet penmanship, telling him how proud she was and sending him ten dollars to buy a new shirt for the performance. She must have saved the money out of the stingy bits Martin's father gave her for the household. Martin washed his old shirt and pressed it with Mrs. Bowen's iron. At a second-hand store he ran his fingers over used coats, imagining what it would be like to be really warm in one instead of just pretending. He chose a dark brown calf-length wool coat from the 1920s that had the flair of a costume so he could claim he bought it used on purpose. He wore it out of the store, hoping to air out its camphor smell. With his hands in his pockets, he was warm for the first time that fall.

The upperclassmen who would direct the student plays invited him to a working meeting at the Carolina Coffee Shop, near campus. He could tell his star had climbed. When he entered the smoky coffeehouse, group members looked at him with interest. Deke waved him over to the booth where they were sitting.

"Nice coat," he said.

"It costed a whole ten dollars," Martin said, as if ten dollars wasn't a lot of money.

"Cost," Deke said, correcting his grammar. "It *cost* ten dollars." Before Martin could feel embarrassed, Deke moved over and made room for him. When others arrived after that, Martin had to move closer still, until his leg pressed against Deke's and Deke's arm jostled him when he tapped his cigarette in the ashtray. Deke didn't try to move away. Martin relaxed. This was how he had always imagined college, sitting around with intelligent people, exchanging ideas. Thanks to Mr. Samuels's recommended readings list, he sounded as though he knew more about philosophy and literature than he actually did. He nursed a cup of coffee, his stomach growling.

Deke sparred with the thin boy who had run the Playmakers meeting. Their argument over whether writers had to live dangerously in order to have anything worthwhile to say progressed to a discussion of the parallels between Homer's *Odyssey* and Hemingway's *For Whom the Bell Tolls*. Martin listened, remembering the spring he turned twelve, when his father found him under a tree, buried in a boy's version of the *Odyssey*. His father made him put the book down and gave him a bag of peas to plant. Martin pressed peas into exactly three holes before the characters in the book started to call to him like sirens. He dug one big hole, poured the rest of the peas into it, covered them up and went back to his book. When his father asked him if he had planted the peas, he said yes. In the spring, when the peas came up in a tangle and died, his father beat him with a belt so badly he had to miss school for two days. Lying in bed, trying to find a position that would ease his bruises, Martin ran pictures through his head of Odysseus's adventures and told himself it was worth it.

"Great literature requires suffering," the thin boy insisted.

They wondered why Martin laughed.

A waitress brought two baskets to the table, each holding a burger and fries. Deke took them and passed one to Martin. "I've got this," he said quietly. No one at the table noticed the charity. Martin ate ravenously. The next time Deke tapped a cigarette from the pack he'd set in front of him on the table, Martin reached for one and lit up, waving away the disappointed face of his Baptist mother, who thought smoking was a sin. To his left Deke's body seemed to radiate heat.

Liza couldn't come to the performance of *Fortunate One* because of exams, but caught a ride from Greensboro to see a rehearsal. Martin took her to the theater. They slipped into seats and listened to Deke give directions to the two actors playing the hero and heroine. Martin had wanted Deke to play the male lead, a young man remarkably like Martin himself, but Deke preferred to direct. Stoney, the fellow he'd picked for the part, was unimpressive, but homely Margaret, who had won the role of Martin's female lead, was talented enough that they soon forgot she wasn't pretty and worth falling hopelessly in love with.

"This is great!" Liza whispered. She nestled against him. "I've missed you."

Martin slouched happily in his seat, proud to have Liza there. Up onstage, Deke's hands cut the air, moving the actors around as if he had them on strings. His voice echoed through the theater, sometimes calm, sometimes biting. Martin tried to catch his eye, but Deke didn't look his way.

During a lull when the actors were walking through scene 2 for the fourth time, Liza whispered, "Daddy asked me to tell you that your mother doesn't look well. He'd like to examine her, but she keeps putting him off. He thought you might at least be able to talk your father into letting her get some rest."

Martin had no hope of his father excusing his mother from working. "I'll write to her. Maybe I can convince her to go visit her sister."

At the front of the theater, Deke called it a day. "Dress rehearsal next Wednesday." Martin led Liza down the aisle to introduce her. Deke shook Liza's hand, looking bored. Martin saw Liza observing Deke, trying to figure him out, but Martin was too giddy at being around Deke and having his play produced to be concerned about Liza's keen eye.

Snow began falling early the day of the performance. Martin watched, anxious, as it accumulated on his bedroom windowsill, afraid the play would be canceled, but when he got to the theater an hour before showtime, the Playmakers were in place. Deke was as cool as ever.

"You can watch from backstage if you want," he offered.

"No." Martin wanted to sit anonymously in the middle of the theater to gauge the audience's reaction.

The theater filled with students who shed coats and hats

and jiggled the seats in front of them with booted feet. *Fortunate One* was the second play to be performed. Martin suffered through the first piece, not hearing a word. After a brief, torturous intermission, the lights dimmed again, and Margaret and Stoney took the stage. Martin stopped breathing. He listened in terror for yawns or muttered remarks from the audience, but heard only a respectful hush and a few inevitable coughs. He relaxed and concentrated on the action onstage.

Even dress rehearsal hadn't prepared him for the real performance. Sitting in the dark, he stopped reciting lines along with the characters and eventually forgot he had written the play. When it was over, too soon, he saw that several girls around him were wiping their eyes. He was sure that the applause for *Fortunate One* was louder than the applause for the first play. When Margaret and Stoney came out to take a bow, Deke came with them and motioned for Martin to stand where he was. "The playwright," Deke told the audience. Martin basked in the admiration of the people around him, pocketing their congratulations to savor later.

Backstage, the Playmakers spiked orange juice with vodka and smoked in a crowd until a faculty adviser told them they were going to set the theater on fire.

Deke's hand brushed Martin's elbow. "Let's get some air."

They left the theater. Campus walkways were deserted. Their feet squeaked on pressed snow. A few flakes still danced in the moonlight.

"It's cold as hell," Martin said happily, blowing on his hands.

Deke pulled a flask from his coat pocket and offered it to him. "This'll warm you up."

Martin took a swallow, the unfamiliar taste of Scotch burning his throat and then, as promised, warming him through. He took another swig and handed the flask back to Deke.

Their fingers touched briefly. Deke seemed unperturbed by the cold. Compared to Korea, Martin supposed, tonight was balmy.

At the intersection of Franklin Street and Airport Road, the world came to life. Two squads of fraternity boys hurled snowballs at each other while their girlfriends squealed on the sidelines. Martin felt like dancing. Instead he rehashed the performance. Deke listened, tolerant.

"Margaret really clinched that final scene."

"Mmm-hmm," Deke agreed.

"I should send flowers to her and Stoney to thank them for not screwing up my work."

"Hey, what about your director?" Deke cuffed him on the back of the head and tugged at his hair. The touch made Martin burn all over. He unbuttoned his coat to let cold air blow in.

The moon and streetlights skimmed white and yellow light across the snow. Martin couldn't help himself. He took off running, testing how far he could slide in the snow without losing his balance. He skidded in front of a car in chains moving slowly up the hill. The driver swore at him. He ran farther, gaining speed in icy tire tracks in the middle of Franklin Street. He heard another car crawl up behind him. He skated in front of it, swerving back and forth, ignoring its honking horn until someone yelled, "Stop! Police!" He slumped to his knees in the snow and turned around. A police car. He climbed to his feet and dusted himself off. Deke walked up behind the patrolman, calmly smoking a cigarette.

"What's your problem, son? You want to get yourself arrested?" The policeman was livid.

Martin metamorphosed into the picture of prep school politeness. "No, sir. I apologize, sir."

"Is he with you?" the cop asked Deke.

Deke, unflustered, tossed his cigarette in the snow. "I'm afraid so."

"Well, make sure your friend stays out of the street or I'll arrest him. We've got enough going on tonight. We don't need this aggravation."

Deke took Martin's arm. "I'll see that he gets home."

"I apologize again, sir." Martin bobbed his head in a little bow that stopped just short of insolence. When the police car had driven out of sight, he tore away from Deke and sprinted down the sidewalk, howling at the top of his lungs. In front of the Carolina Theatre he skidded into a snowbank and lay still, gathering his breath, playing dead, wanting attention.

Deke reached him and nudged him with his foot. "Up."

Martin kept his eyes shut, his face serene.

Deke sighed. "You asshole." He bent and grabbed Martin's forearm, his strength surprising, and hauled Martin to his feet. Martin tried to run again, for fun, but Deke's grasp was too tight. Deke spun him around. Their faces were inches apart. Breath steamed between them. Deke grabbed Martin's numb ears and pulled him close, giving him a rough shake. *"Shape up!"* Their cheeks touched. Stubble on Deke's face scraped Martin's skin, intimate as a kiss. Martin's breath caught and he leaned in, wanting to feel the scrape again, wanting to press his body against Deke's, for everyone else on Franklin Street to disappear and leave them alone in the snow.

"We're going to my place," Deke said in his ear. He shoved Martin away from him.

Martin would have followed him anywhere.

10

Ivy

The day after the meeting with the sheriff, early, I drive up to the home place. It is just light. Frost covers spiderwebs on the ground, turning them into little silver tents. The searchers have all gone and won't be back. I walk around to the side of the house to Mama's garden. I call it hers though she's been dead these many years because her plants still thrive around its edges. Irises and day lilies that will come up in spring in colors you can't get anymore, a country rose that puts out a smell far bigger than its tight, thorny flowers, a quince bush whose knobby apples look like people's faces. Maybe her plants do best when they're ignored, like Mama herself. I've come up to harvest Leon's vegetables. No sense in wasting them. The garden is a mess. Squash and pumpkins have jumped their rows. Greens have gone to seed and potatoes to black. One stalk of corn still holds its head above the weeds. I'll gather what's left and spend my day cutting the bad spots into my sink.

This garden is where I sat with Shane when I was eighteen and he was nine months old, the first time the state came to take him. Sat with him on that rock over there, enjoying the delicious, melted-crayon smell of his little old dirty head. I sang his favorite song in a whisper, the riddle song. When he yawned and stretched, I yawned and stretched. The sun was warm on our hair and the rock cool beneath.

Old Alma hobbles out the side door of the house and steps off the porch to join me. Without a word she bends to pick squash, dropping them in one of the baskets I've brought, not as a favor but because work is her habit. I keep quiet, grateful for the help. I try to make my two hands work as smooth as hers, one over the other, hardly rustling the leaves that grow around the squash as she twists and plucks.

I hid my pregnancy for the longest time. Eugenia was the one who found me out. She wasn't living at home then; she got married as soon as she could to get out of the house, but she liked to come back and remind me that she was a grown-up and I was still a child. Mama had measured me for a new dress and took her time sewing it. By the time she had me try it on to fit, it didn't. Eugenia was at the house that day. She took a long look at my belly. "Mama, she's pregnant!" Mama chased me around the room, whipping me with the end of her measuring tape. When she calmed down she decided I could stay.

I stand up now to ease knees that hurt already. Missouri comes outside, the young woman in bloom she prefers to be. She stays on the porch. Our labor doesn't tempt her. "Law, daughter," she says to Alma. "Save the work for the living. We did our bit."

Squash falls from air to ground, and Alma is on the porch now, too, churning butter in a rusty churn. She turns the wheel harder and harder as cream stiffens against the dasher. "You never did your bit." Her old face is sour under her white cap. Her three blue teeth glisten when she sneers.

I leave them to bicker. I finish the squash and turn up earth to hunt potatoes.

The social worker came out one time before they took him.

I know who called Social Services on me, a girl at the glove factory who didn't like me because my production was higher than hers. I kept to myself at work, didn't socialize. You couldn't really talk to anybody anyhow with the machines so loud. I worked alone at my station, sewing thumbs on gloves as they came off the line, so many per hour. Once in a while I had company, ghost men missing their work, a bored Missouri with nothing better to do, Alma looking for Missouri so she could nag. Sometimes Alma chased Missouri around the plant floor or up among the metal beams of the factory's high ceiling. I tried to ignore them, but Missouri in particular won't be ignored. If I tried, she would stick her hand in my machine and mess it up, or smear grease on the gloves, so sometimes I had to talk to her a little bit, just out the side of my mouth. And at least two times I know that girl, Wanda Harper, saw me talking to the air. She didn't say anything, until I had Shane. Then she, I'm sure it was her, called Social Services to report the crazy woman had a baby.

First the social worker made a home visit, driving up into the yard on a Saturday afternoon. I wasn't smart enough to be wary. She convinced me they came to check on everybody's babies. Mama was out in the fields when the lady came, or maybe she would have stepped in and made me keep my mouth shut. The social worker seemed so nice. She asked about Shane, what I fed him and whether Mama minded caring for him while I was at work. I told her what a good baby he was. Then she steered the talk around to my hearing voices. I was so young and dumb, the way she asked it, she made it seem like it was nothing queer to hear voices nobody else could hear, or see people nobody else could see. I was so happy to find another human being who understood what that was like. I told her about the ghosts I talked to. She went away that day and wrote up a report with the word "schizophrenic" in it. The next time she came back, she had the law with her.

Now I know better. Now when somebody hears me talking, I just tell them I'm bad to say things to myself, and they leave me alone.

Up on the porch, the door behind Alma and Missouri cracks open a wedge. My son Shane lurks behind it. I recognize the red and blue of the nylon windbreaker he wore the night they cut him down.

"I could have cared for you," I say across the garden rows, loud enough for him to hear. "I tried."

He shuts the door.

Martin was still a boy at home when they came for Shane. I'd have thought that even if Mama didn't love me enough, she would love Martin enough not to let that happen in front of him. He was fourteen then and loved the baby. He danced Shane around the room until Shane fairly shrieked with glee. He made up stories for Shane, and Shane seemed to listen.

They came in a sheriff's patrol car, the deputy and the same social worker. I was so comfortable there in the garden with Shane on my lap that I didn't get up. Pop talked to them first, then Mama went over. Then they all walked around to where I was. The social worker pointed to me, and the deputy handed me some papers.

"What's this?" I said.

"Emergency custody order." He may as well have spoke Greek, though I did later learn the language of Social Services. "We're going to have to take your child, ma'am. You'll have a hearing at the courthouse next week to see if you can get him back."

Some moments in life can still make you feel sick when you turn your mind to them, even years later.

I looked to Mama and Pop. Pop was a fierce man, but

the social worker and the deputy, so official, had cowed him. "Go along with them there, Ivy," he said. Mama didn't say anything.

"You can't have him." I stated the fact. I slid off the rock and backed toward the house with Shane. The papers fluttered away into the vegetable beds. Martin had stepped out on the side porch behind me. He let me in the door, and I ran for Mama and Pop's room, the only one that locked.

I could hear the deputy trying to reason with Martin to let him past. Martin kept saying, "No, sir." I believe he spread himself out and grabbed both sides of the doorframe. The deputy didn't want to touch a boy to pry his fingers off the jamb. I locked the bedroom door and held Shane close. Oh, he was so warm in my arms. Even his pee smelled good. I tucked the ends of his blanket up under him.

"Miss Owenby, don't make this hard. I don't want that baby getting hurt," the deputy called.

"You're not taking my baby!" My shriek woke Shane up, but he didn't cry, yet. I heard the deputy struggle with Martin. Then the social worker was outside the bedroom door, she must have come in the front. "Ivy, you need to cooperate or it'll go worse for you." How could it go worse?

The deputy got by Martin and started kicking the door. Shane began to cry at the noise. The lock on the door was just a piece of wood. The kicking splintered it, and the deputy fell into the room. Martin was still after him, grabbing the man's muscled arms, jumping on his back. "Leave her alone!"

The deputy got free of Martin and grabbed Shane out of my arms. The blanket Shane was wrapped in unrolled, and the man nearly dropped him. Shane and I both screamed. I tried to take him back, but the deputy held him high over his head and made for the door. He handed Shane off to the social worker, and she ran to the patrol car while the deputy blocked me and Martin. Mama and Pop stood as shadows and let it all happen.

When the social worker was in the car, the deputy abandoned us and ran for the car himself. He got in and locked the door before I could get there. I banged on his window and ran after them on our dirt road, choking on dust, until they disappeared from sight. Then I sat down in the road and howled. Martin was the only one to come and touch my shoulder.

I find I am crying now, over Leon's vegetables. I have nothing to wipe my face with. Missouri, ever one to spot weakness, calls over from the porch, "Don't blubber like that, girl. So you weren't fit to mother. It's past."

The two pieces of wood that top Alma's churn bounce violently. "What do you know of mothering? You were no mother to us, barn cat, rising up to leave when your kittens drew close to nurse." Her words age Missouri, dull her bright hair, draw her mouth up tight. Ghost children twirl around her on the porch, grabbing her skirts, harassing, asking for this and that. She puts her hands to her ears and screams them away, flings them off into the yard with a great shrug of her shoulders. "Go!" The children disappear, leaving Missouri as young as before but frazzled. She advances on Alma, small fists knotted, unpeeling one finger to slice across the air in front of her daughter's face. "Do not!"

Alma knocks the top off the churn, grabs a handful of fresh butter and throws it in Missouri's face. She wipes the rest across Missouri's dress front, ruining fabric.

"Oh!" Missouri rears back to slap.

I yell, "Stop!"

They stop.

"Be ashamed." I wipe my nose on my sleeve.

They aren't done. Alma spits at Missouri, "Three children, with three different fathers, nary a one named." Alma forgets that I myself repeated this bit of family history.

Missouri calms. She licks new butter off her fingers. "My name was as good as theirs. Ain't no man worth letting move into your house. Why keep just one when you can have which-ever one pleases you on a given day?" She gives herself a shake, and her frock is clean of butter. "Choosing one surely never did you any good."

I turn back to the vegetables.

After the law came with the social worker and took Shane screaming out of my arms, I heard his cry in everything. Running water, radios, tires on gravel, a dog's bark miles away. I nearly lost my job at the glove factory because I kept stopping my sewing machine to listen.

They did finally let him come home, three months later, to Mama, not to me. He had to learn all over again who I was. Mama could have ignored Social Services' instructions. Instead she took them to heart. She wouldn't leave me alone with Shane. She watched everything I did with him. When the social worker came to check, Mama talked about me like I wasn't there, like she was Shane's mother. I sometimes think Shane must have remembered that time. I want to explain, but he won't come near enough to me now to listen. I didn't really get him back until Mama got sick and wasn't strong enough to keep him from me anymore.

The side porch door moves a little on its hinges. I wonder if it's Shane or just the wind. In case it's him I start to sing, of cherries without stones and chickens without bones. Alma and Missouri cross insults on the porch. My baskets fill, my harvest the browns and yellows of a passing fall.

11

Liza

Liza stood with Martin in the yard of Solace Fork School. Heavy yellow demolition equipment circled the school. The building's roof sagged in the middle, the chimney separating from its base. Most of the windows were broken. The front door was propped open with a brick.

"It looks smaller than I remembered," Martin said. "Shabbier."

"It's been vacant nearly fifteen years," Liza said. In their day, grades one through twelve somehow fit into this school's four rooms. Now three elementary schools and a middle school fed Willoby High, the concrete monstrosity where Liza taught. The high school had twelve hundred students. Its windows didn't open even when the air-conditioning broke down. Between classes the noise in the halls was almost unbearable, metal lockers slamming, students screaming profanity, the class bell going off. She missed the quiet of Solace Fork School, the smell of oiled floors, the miracle of the boards not bursting into flame under the stove in the winter, bird sounds through the open windows in warm weather.

Martin stepped up on the low porch and went inside. She followed him into the dim hallway that separated the classrooms. The old smells were gone, replaced by sour mildew and the musk of small animals that lived and died inside the walls. Martin went to the end of the hall and into the classroom that was theirs as seniors. Mr. Samuels's classroom. Liza stepped in after him.

The floor was discolored under years of polyurethane and scarred where desks had been bolted down. The stove was long gone, someone having finally realized the risk of conflagration. One broken desk sat in a corner, waiting to be cleared away with other trash, or not worth salvaging before demolition. Its hinged top leaned separately against a wall, covered with decades of carved initials and scratches of pen that had gone through paper. Liza sat down at the desk. Wads of chewed gum pressed into the corners of its lidless case. Her knees bumped the underside. "How did we ever fit?" she said. Martin was staring out a window at the woods behind the school and didn't answer.

The fall Mr. Samuels came to teach the upper grades, the students reported to class with a sense of expectation. Liza liked school anyway, and a new teacher represented possibilities. Mr. Samuels was writing on the chalkboard as the students filed in. She, Martin, Hodge, and the Gaddy twins, Nancy and Betty, were seniors that year and shared the classroom with a dozen ninth- through eleventh-graders. They all sat in their seats, staring at the new teacher's back. He wasn't tall, maybe five nine, his body solid and compact. The sleeves of his spotless white shirt were rolled up. His forearms were muscular and tan, the hair bleached light by the sun. His trousers weren't new but were pressed. As he wrote on the board Liza was not above joining the other girls in admiring his physique.

He turned around and smiled. The ear pieces of his gold wire-framed glasses left red marks on both sides of his head. "Good morning. My name is Robert Samuels." His accent was neutral, not southern. He sounded like the people on the radio news.

He was new and they could have tested his boundaries, but they didn't. None of the seniors were troublemakers, except Martin when provoked, and the younger students took their lead from the seniors. Or it may simply have been that Mr. Samuels exuded authority.

He took the roll, staring at each student as he or she answered to memorize the name. Then he put his roll book down. "Today, class, we're going on a hike."

The students exchanged looks. Some didn't have shoes, or if they did, the soles had worn through or separated from the shoes like flapping mouths. Mr. Samuels examined their feet. "A walk, then, not a hike. A half mile at the most. Bring a pencil and a piece of paper." He picked up a canvas rucksack from beside his desk.

They lined up and followed him outside. It was the best kind of August day, not too humid, the sky a pure blue, the air so clear you felt you could see every little thing. Mr. Samuels led them down the deer path in the direction of the secret clearing. Liza worried that he had discovered it, but he took them left through the woods. They came out on a dirt road and walked along it until they reached a meadow surrounded by tall pines, former farmland. A tumbled chimney rose from blackberry thorns, the only memory of some family's homestead. Mr. Samuels led them over grass to a small spring. He knelt down, cupped his hands, and drank. "Have some water," he invited. "Be careful not to stir up the mud."

"It might pizon us, Mr. Samuels," a ninth-grade boy said.

"I had some Saturday and I'm still here," Mr. Samuels said.

Liza and Martin went to the stream and drank. The water was perfect, worth the risk of contamination.

After everyone drank, Mr. Samuels led them farther into the meadow. "Stop here." They looked around, wondering what he had brought them to see.

"Pair up," he said. Martin moved closer to Liza, leaving Hodge to look around for a partner. Mr. Samuels pulled a pocketknife and a skein of brown yarn out of his canvas satchel and began cutting lengths about three feet long, handing one to each pair. "Make a circle with your yarn. Then sit down and observe. Write down everything you see inside your circle, every type of flora and fauna, every mineral. Don't disturb anything. The couple with the most impressive list at the end of a half hour will win a prize."

Younger students began running around, looking for the most diverse patch. Liza looked at Martin. "Do you have a preference?"

"Somewhere soft to sit."

They walked over to the meadow's edge and draped their yarn in an oblong around an anthill.

"Can we count every ant?" Martin said.

"Start observing," she said.

They peered at their little patch of ground and grass. Liza served as secretary. "Ant. Spiderweb. Wild onion. Grass."

"Dirt," said Martin. "Stinkweed. More grass."

Mr. Samuels walked around the meadow, checking on each pair's scientific methodology. When his back was turned, Martin plopped down, rear end first, inside their circle. "Observe me, Liza."

"You're squashing my flora and fauna," she said. He scrambled out before Mr. Samuels turned around.

The world inside the circle seemed to grow bigger as they examined it, and louder, teeming. Blades of grass bent as insects crawled up them on their way to nowhere. Indignant ant scouts came out of the red hill and shook their little fists. A small clumsy beetle bumped up against the yarn enclosure and ran in a panicked circle until he reached the break and escaped.

"Stupid fellow," Martin said.

Liza listed the rocks poking out of the dirt, some brown, some crystal white. Clover, the edges nibbled by rabbits.

Mr. Samuels came over with his field guide and read their list over Liza's shoulder. He fingered the tall weed flowering white in the middle of their circle. "Now, what are you calling this?"

"Stinkweed," Martin said.

"Ah. *Daucus carota*. Wild carrot. Poetically known as Queen Anne's lace. True stinkweed is something else altogether."

"It does stink, though. If you smell it for too long it'll give you a headache," Martin said.

"Thank you for the warning. And what is this? We don't have these in Ohio, where I'm from." Mr. Samuels squatted and hooked two fingers under the pinkish purple blooms of a small fuzzy-leafed plant, as if he were lifting its chin.

"We call it shepherd's whistle." Liza pulled off one of the tiny, tube-shaped flowers, bit the end off and squeezed a drop of nectar onto her tongue. "Try it."

Mr. Samuels copied her. "Very nice. The leaves look like something in the mint family." He opened his field guide and began flipping pages. "Here we go. Henbit. A weed introduced from Europe. Latin name *Lamium amplexicaule*." He showed them the picture. "But I like shepherd's whistle better. Thank you for teaching me the local name."

Hodge called over, "How many things y'all got?"

"It's quality, not quantity, that counts," Mr. Samuels called back.

"I'm waiting for a rabbit to come out of this hole," Hodge said. The younger boy who was his partner got up and went searching for more interesting things to drop into their circle.

"That's cheating," Martin said.

"You can't import objects," Mr. Samuels said. "Just write down what's already there."

Over to their left, Liza heard Betty, the slow Gaddy sister, observe, "Bird doo."

Mr. Samuels was still crouched over Liza and Martin's circle. He poked at a piece of quartz embedded in the earth inside the circle, then pried it out of the ground.

"I thought we weren't supposed to disturb anything," Martin said.

Mr. Samuels held the rock out on the flat of his hand. He had the callus of a writer on the inside of his middle finger, but his palm was hard. He was a man who worked as well as studied. "Look."

They looked. The rock was an Indian arrowhead.

Martin raised his eyebrows, asking permission to pick it up. Mr. Samuels nodded. He held perfectly still, as if inviting a wild bird to feed from his hand. From where Liza sat she could see the vein in Mr. Samuel's neck pulsing faster than it should have. Martin took the arrowhead and held it up, testing its sharpness. Sunlight shone through the thin edges. "That's a nice one." He handed it back to the teacher.

"Do you find many of them around here?" Mr. Samuels said.

"Depends on the place. One of my daddy's fields turns one or two up every time we till."

Hodge gave up waiting for his rabbit and came over to look. "We find some every summer in the creek."

"What do you do with them?" Mr. Samuels said.

"Skip 'em in the water. They make good skipping rocks."

"Next time you find one, bring it to me instead of skipping it." Mr. Samuels pocketed the arrowhead.

"Does that mean we win the prize?" Martin said.

Mr. Samuels let the class vote. Liza and Martin lost to a team who put their yarn around a half-eaten frog. The winners got horehound candy to suck.

On the walk back, a boy grabbed the Gaddy twins' list and began making fun of Betty Gaddy's bird doo. "Stop it," Mr. Samuels said sharply. "Miss Gaddy did exactly as I asked. Her observation of avian feces was entirely appropriate." He reached in his pocket and handed her a piece of candy. Betty Gaddy had never heard praise from a teacher before. Her face turned a mottled red. She walked back to school sucking her candy, not looking left or right, her shoulders straighter than usual.

Liza and Martin fell back. "What do you think of him?" Liza said.

Up ahead, Mr. Samuels walked beside Betty Gaddy, talking to the students around him, pointing out plants along the side of the road. Afternoon sun turned his hair a dark gold. Martin studied him.

"Well?" she said.

He looked over at her, as if he'd forgotten she was there, then grinned. "Good," he pronounced.

Now in the dusty classroom, Martin traced a finger over faint images that had been erased from the chalk board. He caught Liza looking at him. "What are you thinking about?"

She laughed. "Betty Gaddy."

"Good old Betty." Martin slacked his jaw in a perfect imitation of Betty.

"Don't be cruel." Mr. Samuels never made fun. Liza appreciated that now, the temptation to single out one student to torment. She had seen her colleagues do it, choose one irritating, unpopular student to pick on, reaping the reward of having the other students laugh with you. Eye-roll about him or her in the teachers' lounge. All the others will love you, only one will hate you. In memory of Mr. Samuels she was careful not to do that.

She eased out of the desk and stood up.

Martin reached up to the top of the chalkboard, where a map was rolled up like a window shade. "I bet that's the map they had when we were here."

"Probably."

He grabbed the bottom of the map and pulled it down with a rip of vinyl, then screamed when something flew out of it. Liza jumped back. A small brown bat hurled itself at the water-stained ceiling, then at the chalkboard, then at Martin. Martin ducked and covered his head. "Jesus!" The bat slammed into a cracked window and dropped to the floor, stunned.

"Don't touch it! It might have rabies." Liza made sure she stayed back several feet.

"Thank you, teacher. I was going to pick it up and give it CPR." Martin grabbed a decayed cardboard box from a corner and put it over the bat. "I thought their sonar was supposed to keep them from running into things."

"We must have panicked him. There the poor thing was, curled up between Ceylon and Basutoland, minding its own business. Look at all the bat droppings under the map. He must have lived here a while."

The bat came to and started thumping against the sides of the box. Martin looked at her. "What do we do now?"

She started laughing. She couldn't help it. "You should have seen your face when that thing flew out."

Martin started laughing, too. "Scared the shit out of me."

The bat hit the side of the box hard enough to shake it. Liza and Martin both jumped, then got even more tickled at themselves. Martin had to lean against the windowsill. It had been a long time since Liza had heard him belly laugh.

"Oh, Lord." He got his breath and wiped his eyes. "I can't leave him under the box. He'll get bulldozed."

She went and picked up the desk lid that leaned against the wall. "If we slide this under the box, you can carry him outside."

"*I* can carry him outside?"

"It's a man's job," she said sweetly.

They maneuvered the wooden desk lid under the box without letting the bat escape, and Martin lifted it up. He carried it toward the door, like a waiter carrying a tray.

She followed him out onto the little porch. "I'll just stay here while you take him into the woods."

"You're a big help."

He carried the box out into the schoolyard, to the worn place at the edge of the woods where the deer path began. His body was as trim as when they were teenagers, arms wiry, back strong. Liza wished he still were that boy and would turn around and call out an invitation for her to walk with him to their clearing of twisted trees.

After school the day Mr. Samuels assigned them the yarn circles, Liza went swimming with Martin and Hodge in the creek near the clearing. It was the perfect place to swim. The creek was less than fifteen feet across, but where it forked it was four to five feet deep, deep enough to play in, with a gentle current that pulled at their legs as the water debated whether to flow left or right. The water was freezing. Long grass softened the bank. The warped hardwoods screened them from anyone walking through. Younger trees, wild cherry and mulberry, bent over the water, some trailing their fingers in it. In warm weather, Liza and the boys went there whenever they could sneak away. Having no mother meant Liza got to do what she pleased. The first time she swam there, her body was straight and long legged. By the beginning of their senior year, a woman's curves showed under her modest bathing suit, and Martin and Hodge had hair on their chests.

When they got there that afternoon, she and Martin went right into the water, heads under, to take the sting out of the cold. Hodge stepped in up to his ankles, then stopped, with his arms crossed over his chest. His belly, painfully white, stuck out over the band of his cutoff dungarees.

"Come on in, Hodge. It's not going to get any warmer." She blew water out of her nose and turned over on her back to float.

"Didn't seem this cold last time." Hodge ventured out a little farther but stopped before the drop-off, the water now up to his shins.

"Get in or I'll pull you in," Martin said.

Hodge worked up his nerve and finally eased in up to his shoulders but kept his hair dry.

"Get your head wet, Hodge," Martin said.

"Naw, I gotta leave soon. I told the preacher I'd help him set up for the revival this evening. I don't need wet hair."

"Another revival?" Liza and her father went to the Episcopal church in Whelan. Things Baptist fascinated her. "Didn't you just have a revival?"

"Yeah, Hodge, how many times you gonna get saved?" Martin said.

Hodge was too good-natured to take offense. "Oh, Lord, save me from these heathens."

They paddled around until Hodge said he had to go. He got out, shook himself like a dog, and went behind a tree to change into dry overalls. He emerged and walked to the edge of the water to wring out his cutoffs. "Come by the house later if your daddy will let you," he said to Martin. Hodge rarely got to spend time with Martin without Liza.

"Yeah." Martin didn't sound hopeful. Once he got home his father would put him to work.

"Bye, Liza," Hodge said.

"Enjoy your revival." She lifted her toes out of the water in front of her.

Hodge turned and walked down the path that led back to the school. "Pray for our souls," Martin called after him, and swam over to Liza. "Are you getting too cold?"

"No."

He dove down to the creek bottom. She leaned back against tree roots that stuck out into the water, letting her legs float on the water's surface in front of her, her eyes half-closed. Martin surfaced, holding a handful of the rich gray clay that lay beneath the sand on the creek bottom. He dribbled some of it onto her bare thigh. It beaded where it landed, like mercury from a broken thermometer. She gave him a look and closed her eyes.

"Mr. Samuels seems all right." Martin let more clay squeeze from his fist to her leg.

She opened her eyes and lowered her legs into the water to wash the mud off. "He's bound to be better than Miss Yates." Miss Yates, the woman who had taught them since the eighth grade, had left to marry a lawyer in Asheville. "I feel like I hardly learned anything last year, she spent so much time scolding the younger kids. We need somebody who can get us ready for college."

"College," Martin said. "Not sure I'll be able to go."

"Of course you'll go, silly." She lifted her feet out of the water and put them on his chest and pushed him over backward. He came up sputtering. She stood up from her nest in the tree roots, giggling.

"I'll get you for that." He dove under and grabbed her by the ankles, tipping her over. He came up and she started to run away, in slow motion, squealing when he grabbed her around the waist. The water lubricated their bodies, so that every touch was slick, his forearm along her rib cage, his hand on her hip, her shoulder against his chest. They made excuses for more, pushing each other, wrestling.

"Hey," she said. "Let me get on your back. I think I can reach those grapes." She pointed to a wild muscadine vine that hung five feet above the water, clinging like a parasite to a tree branch.

"Get on."

She climbed on his back and wrapped her chilled legs around his torso. "Not high enough." She hooked her right leg over his shoulder, then her left, so that she rode on his neck. She could feel her pubic bone against the back of his head as she stretched to reach the grapes. His hands rested on her thighs. He looked up at her. She moved so that he could see the curve of her breasts under her conservative bathing suit, the white underside of her arm. She tugged off part of the vine. The grapes weren't quite ripe, their taut skin black with a sheen of green. She looked down at Martin, her left hand resting on the top of his head. "Take us over to the bank." He waded over, holding her lower legs to steady her. Her body glided against his as she slid off his back.

"You weigh a ton." He lay back on the grass, pretending to be exhausted. His chest was muscular, a man's chest.

"Your reward." She held a grape over his face and lowered it to his mouth. He wrapped his lips around it, popping the skin with his teeth to suck out the fruit, swallowing the seeds. She dabbed his lower lip with her little finger. "Grape juice." She leaned over him. "I don't think I got it all." Her wet hair fell in a slow curl in front of her shoulders. She leaned in closer, until her hair touched his chest. She kissed him, licking the grape juice off his lower lip. His lips were full and soft. She could feel her pulse all over her body.

Something nudged her through Martin's cutoff dungarees. She looked down at the rise in his cutoffs and laughed, resting her hand lightly on his crotch. "Now, what is it I'm supposed to do with this? I know there's something." She slid her fingers under the waistband of his cutoffs and pulled them down, then wrapped her hand around his penis and left it there, still. Sophistication abandoned her. She didn't know what to do next. Neither did Martin.

Still holding him, she leaned in to kiss him again. Their bodies were cold from the water, but their breath was warm. He moved his hips almost imperceptibly, his tongue pushing hers. She dragged her kiss from his mouth to his chin, to his chest, along the hair that grew down to his navel. The yearning she felt terrified her. She opened her mouth and pressed his warmth against her lips and tongue, the roof of her mouth. Martin's breath caught. He raked his fingers through her hair, pushing her head down roughly with both hands. She moved to the rhythm he chose, clumsy at first but then losing herself in Martin's low moaning, the scrape of her teeth against skin, the pulse of hot liquid when he cried out into the air, frightening birds out of the trees.

He held her head down, still moving. "Don't leave."

She wouldn't leave. He let go of her head, and she lifted her face. He pulled her up so that she lay along his chest. He kissed her, a thousand tastes mingling in their mouths. Her whole body felt swollen. She rubbed against him, thinking she would die if he didn't touch her, but his arms rested passively alongside hers. She took his hand and pushed it into the warmth between her legs, pressing it hard against the thick fabric of her bathing suit until pleasure surged over her. She let go of his hand and relaxed on top of him. Their two hearts pounded at each other, unsynchronized.

Her bathing suit strap had slipped. Martin wrapped his hand around her breast and entwined his legs with hers. She nestled her head against his chest. She could feel the storm-bent trees close by, nonjudgmental, beneficent. Water whispered through the grass along the bank. Far away the Owenbys' sawmill droned in the summer air.

She and Martin were children then. She thought that day was a beginning, that they would do it again and do more. Instead, after that, they rarely did more than kiss. The not-doing was delicious in its way. When she was near him her skin felt electric, the high-voltage current that encircled them giving out an almost audible hum. But Martin always had a reason not to go where she so badly wanted to: the imagined steps of someone who would discover them, Hodge's constant presence, a pretended concern for her honor. It was years before she understood why.

Across the schoolyard, Martin put the cardboard box down and pushed it over with his foot, then ran toward her. The bat flitted into the bushes. Martin was winded when he reached her. "My good deed for the day," he panted.

She pointed to the head of the deer path. "Let's go down to the clearing."

He looked toward the break in the rhododendron. "No. Not today." He turned to face her. "I've got to meet Eugenia and Zeb at Bojangles'. Besides, I just released a rabid bat into those woods." He started across the yard in the direction of her truck.

"Good point," she said to his back, but her feelings were hurt. She wanted him to remember what she remembered. She wanted it to matter to him.

12

Martin

Martin got Liza to drop him off in the parking lot of the Whelan Bojangles' restaurant. It was only eleven forty-five, but Eugenia's burgundy Mercury Grand Marquis was already there. His relatives ate early. He went around to Liza's side and lifted his suitcase out of the back of her truck.

Liza rolled her window down. "How long do you think you'll be in town?"

"Not sure. I'd like to get some news on Leon. At least a few more days." If he could stand it.

"Come to dinner at our house day after tomorrow. I'm sure Raby would like to see you."

Martin was a little afraid of Liza's husband. Raby always greeted him with a grin and a crushing handshake that told Martin Raby could kick his ass if he wanted to. "That'll probably work. I'll call you."

She squinted up at him. "It really is good to have you home."

"You and Hodge make it bearable, Liza."

After she drove away, Martin put his suitcase and coat on the backseat of Eugenia's unlocked car and went into Bojangles'. The heavy smell of chicken grease hung in the air. Eugenia and Zeb sat side by side in a booth near the entrance, eating chicken and biscuits. Eugenia waved him over. "Martin, make sure you ask for the senior citizens' discount. You get ten percent off and a free small drink."

Martin was horrified. "I'm not a senior citizen."

"They give it to anybody over fifty."

He went up to the counter to order. He didn't ask for the discount, and blessedly the big girl working the register didn't offer. "The number two combo, with green beans, mashed potatoes, and a large iced tea," he said.

"That'll be two forty-nine."

He handed her three singles. Money went further here than in Manhattan. He lowered his voice so Eugenia couldn't hear. "Can you tell me where the nearest liquor store is?"

The cashier pointed. "About four blocks that way, on Main Street. It'll be on your right, next to a antiques store."

"Walking distance?"

"Everything's walking distance around here," she said.

He moved down the counter to pick up his food and carried it to the table, trying to figure out how to get to the liquor store and smuggle a bottle into Eugenia's house before evening lock-down. He wasn't going to go another night without a drink.

His brother-in-law, Zeb, had always moved in slow motion. He chewed his biscuit as if it were a cud, periodically raising a heavy finger to swipe crumbs off his face. His mind worked in slow motion, too. If he contributed to a conversation at all, his remarks were likely to pertain to something someone had said ten minutes earlier. Zeb and Eugenia together were like a hippopotamus and one of those tiny, quick birds that live on hippos' backs. Somehow their symbiosis had worked all these years.

Eugenia saw Martin's large drink. "Martin, you didn't ask for the discount."

"I was thirsty."

"It must be nice to have money to throw away. When you're on a fixed income like us, you'll take any discount you can get." She sighed. "I just can't stop thinking about Leon, wondering what happened. He went through enough in life. It's not right."

"What do you mean, 'he went through enough'?" Martin bit into his chicken.

"The war, of course. You were too young to remember, Martin, but he had a hard time."

Martin remembered a letter saying Leon was injured but not bad enough for the army to send him home. "How did he get hurt?"

"A piece of shrapnel. It about sheared his breast off." Eugenia traced a curve under her own small breast to demonstrate. "Opened him up like a can of tuna. Left a flap of skin and muscle an inch thick." She shuddered. "When he told it, you could see how bad it had scared him."

"I never heard him tell that story," Martin said.

Zeb cleared his throat. "I don't reckon he told it to us but the one time."

"A scare like that would turn some men to Jesus, but it seems like it scared Leon away from religion even more." Eugenia's eyes watered, and her sharp little nose turned pink. "I do worry about his salvation, Martin."

"After he got back he never would work without a shirt on, because of the scar," Zeb said. He finished his biscuit and washed it down with the last swallow of his small Coke. "Social Security just gave us a increase. Six dollars more a month." His straw hit the bottom of his empty cup, and he slurped air until Eugenia glared at him. He put the cup down, looking as if he wished he'd used his extra Social Security money to buy a bigger drink.

A woman about Eugenia's age approached their table and

patted Eugenia's shoulder. "Eugenia, I'm just so sorry about Leon." Eugenia looked up. "Oh, Peggy, thank you." Her eyes filled with tears. "We're just doing the best we can."

"I know it's hard."

"Peggy, do you remember my brother Martin? Martin, this is Peggy Sasser, used to be Peggy Gaylord."

Martin stood up to shake hands.

"Why, Martin, you were just a little thing last time I saw you," Peggy said.

Martin had no memory of her at all. He sat back down.

"Honey, you just let me know if I can do anything for you," Peggy said.

"Just keep us on your prayer list," Eugenia said.

When Peggy had moved toward the exit Eugenia said, "She was so slender as a girl, do you remember, Martin? And now look how much she's put on."

"I don't remember her," he said.

"They lived just over in the next cove."

He shrugged.

"Well, they were Methodists," she said, as if that explained why he wouldn't remember. She wiped her fingers on a napkin and stacked her trash in a neat pile on her tray. "Zeb and I have a church supper tonight. You're welcome to come, Martin, or I could pick you up a frozen dinner."

"Don't worry about me. I'll figure something out. Maybe I'll give Steven and Trina a call."

Eugenia raised a thin eyebrow. "I know you're close to them, but Steven scares me to death. That temper. I can't help but wonder if he might have done something to Leon."

"Now, Eugenia," Zeb spoke up.

"I'm serious," she said. "You know, the sheriff found Leon's gun still in the house. But nobody ever found Leon's knuckle knife. You know the one I mean?"

Martin nodded. Leon had brought the homemade knife back from the war. The blade was seven sharp inches, with brass knuckles welded to the handle for gripping. "He probably had it with him when he disappeared," he said.

"It was awful big to carry around. I just have a terrible feeling about it. Like somebody, Steven maybe, got mad at Leon and used the knife on him."

Zeb coughed, blowing biscuit crumbs across the table.

Martin added his trash to Eugenia's. "I'm sure Steven had nothing to do with it. He and Leon got along well."

"Well, Bobby, then. You heard what Steven said at the meeting the other night, about Bobby being mad that Leon wouldn't let him put a trailer up there."

"Bobby can be a pain in the ass, but I don't think he'd hurt a family member," Martin said.

"If he is family. Bobby was born nine months to the day from the time Bertie left James. To the day, Martin," Eugenia said.

Martin looked around for the garbage can. "That's just silly. Bobby looks more like an Owenby than I do. Like Pop, with hair."

"I'm just saying."

They got up to leave. Martin dumped their trash, and they stepped outside. It had warmed up to a crisp Indian summer day, the temperature in the sixties. "I'm going to walk around town for a while. You can take my things on to the house. Let me just get my coat." He opened Eugenia's rear car door.

"You won't need your coat. Let us take it back to the house with your suitcase," she said.

"It might cool off later." Martin needed the coat to hide the booze he was about to purchase. He grabbed it out of the backseat and bent to give Eugenia a quick kiss on the cheek.

"You sure you want to walk back?" she said.

"I'm sure. See you in a couple of hours."

Zeb went around to the passenger side and held the door open while Eugenia climbed in. "Y'ought not to talk about family like that," he muttered to her.

Martin waited for them to pull out of the Bojangles' parking lot, then headed up the street toward the liquor store, thinking about Leon's war story.

Plenty of young men from Willoby County fought in that war. On Veterans Day when Martin was a senior in high school, Mr. Samuels offered extra credit to anyone who went to Whelan for the local celebration. A parade honored veterans of the two world wars and any from the Spanish-American War who might still be hobbling around. Liza and Nancy Gaddy were marshals. They stood up in the back of Liza's convertible, waving white-gloved hands at the crowd while Dr. Vance drove. The silk sash that draped from Liza's shoulder to her waist made her look like Miss America. After the parade was over, the mayor of Whelan called for men who had served to step up in front of the crowd. Mr. Samuels walked forward. So did Leon. At least twenty men, of various ages, went up. From where Martin stood, no more than six feet away from Mr. Samuels and Leon, he could hear them speak. Mr. Samuels offered Leon his hand. "You're Martin's brother. I'm Robert Samuels."

Leon took the offered hand. "What was your division, sir?"

"Eighth Armored. You?"

"First Infantry."

Martin wanted to hear more, but they had said all they planned to. Both turned to face the crowd. Mr. Samuels stood at ease, low autumn sun flecking his hair. As the mayor finished his remarks, Mr. Samuels's eyes locked with Martin's, the way they sometimes did in class. Martin met Mr. Samuels's gaze, feeling a kind of power over the teacher, until Leon caught their exchange and scowled.

After the Veterans Day speeches, Mr. Samuels gave Martin a ride home, telling Martin that he reminded him of a young Thomas Wolfe. The teacher's nervous hand reached out to him, then drew back, then reached out again to rest on Martin's leg, where Martin let it stay. They parked on a side road, and Martin allowed Mr. Samuels to put a hand down his pants and stroke him there, then touched Mr. Samuels the same way, feeling pleased and terrified when the teacher climaxed, losing all dignity.

Martin hoped Mr. Samuels hadn't left because of what they did together. He hoped he had simply decided to go in search of a place big enough to have crevices and folds, hiding places for men like that. Men like Martin. Willoby County, for all its mountainous topography, was as flat as Kansas when it came to places of privacy.

Martin spotted the brick facade of the liquor store, squeezed between an antiques store on one side and the Junior League Bargain Box on the other. He quickened his pace. When he pushed through the door a bell announced his entry, and the clerk called a greeting from the back. All those nice, full bottles. He felt himself relax. He arranged his coat on his arm, figuring out how best to cover his Scotch bottle on the walk back to Eugenia's.

13

Bertie

Why did one thing send her spinning? Bertie felt a small minute of peace when she first woke up in the morning, then one thing, like an unexpected bill or a saleslady not treating her friendly, and she was sour the rest of the day. Up and down, up and down. Some days she couldn't even figure out what was eating at her. She'd run a list through her head and not be able to point to a thing. It was just a bad feeling, like her body was full of chemicals and she had to suffer until they got flushed out.

She stood in the doorway to Bobby's room. Today the thing bothering her was Martin leaving after only one night to go stay at Eugenia's. Bertie's home was as nice as Eugenia's. Bobby's room wasn't big or fancy, but it was clean. The bed was firm. She had put away Bobby's stuff so there was space for Martin's things. She knew Martin had left because he was afraid to say no to Eugenia, who had bossed him around since he was small, but Bertie still felt like she'd done something wrong. Like maybe he'd seen a roach, which was impossible as clean as she kept things. Or like he'd found a pubic hair on the bathroom soap, which Bertie would never let happen either.

She stripped Martin's dirty sheets off the bed. As she was

putting them in the wash, Bobby and his girlfriend, Cherise, drove up and came barging into the house.

"Ma, I need my WKIX T-shirt, so I can get in free to see Nantucket at the mall. Where's it at?" Bobby said.

"The clothes you left here are all folded in the bureau drawers in your bedroom. I wish you'd take them with you."

He headed down the hall.

"Don't be loud. Your daddy's sleeping. And don't strew everything all over," she said. He didn't pay any attention.

Cherise sat down at the kitchen table. For someone in the cosmetology business she sure let herself go on her days off. Her hair was pulled back tight with a fabric ponytail holder, and it didn't looked like she'd washed it that morning. Her red-orange fingernail polish was chipped, and she needed to bleach the hair above her upper lip. She didn't even try to make small talk, just ignored Bertie.

Bertie crossed her arms. She could hear Bobby pulling out drawers in the bedroom.

"Found it!" he called, not bothering to be quiet. He came back in the kitchen, wearing a T-shirt with the radio station logo. It had fit him in high school but was way too small now. When he lifted his arms his belly button showed, along with the trail of hair leading up to it.

"Bobby, that shirt doesn't fit," Bertie said.

"That's okay. I'm getting in free."

"What about me?" Cherise said. "Don't you have another shirt?"

"No. You'll have to pay."

"Bullshit," she said.

A horn honked outside. Bertie looked out the window. Hodge Goforth's truck idled in the driveway. Bertie left Bobby and Cherise arguing and went outside to see what he wanted.

Hodge rolled his window down. "I can't stay, Bertie. I'm just dropping these off." He handed her a stack of photocopied flyers, black and white, with a blurry picture of Leon under the big word "MISSING." Leon was turned sideways, like he'd been trying to get away when the camera flashed.

"Where'd you get the picture?" She hadn't known anybody had a photo of Leon recent enough to identify him with.

"Eugenia had it. I've already put these up all around Whelan. If James can do Solace Fork today, we should have it covered. Here." He handed her a staple gun and a roll of duct tape. "I'll get the staple gun back from you next time I see you."

"I'll make Bobby help," she said.

"I'm sorry I have to run. I'll talk at you later." Hodge backed out of the driveway.

She went back inside. Bobby was looking in the refrigerator for something to eat. Cherise was working on a package of turkey she'd pulled out, peeling one piece off at a time and sucking it into her mouth. The girl did not need to be eating like that. She already looked heavier than the last time Bertie had seen her. Bertie put the posters down on the table and took the package of meat away from Cherise. "That's for James's lunches," she said.

Bobby handed Cherise what was left of a baked chicken. The girl sat down at the table, digging her fingers into it, stripping off the meat even down to the red-streaked pieces that lay right next to the bone. Bertie had been saving that chicken to make chicken and dumplings, but she wasn't going to eat it or serve it to James after seeing Cherise paw all over it.

"Hodge brought these posters by. I'm going to give you half and James half to put up this morning around Solace Fork," she said.

"I ain't doing that today. I got a show to go to," Bobby said.

"What time is the show?"

"Two o'clock."

"You have plenty of time."

"Why don't you do it?" he said.

"I'm going across the road to do chores for my mama today. Here." Bertie's pocketbook was on the counter. She dug out a ten-dollar bill and offered it to him. "Put up the posters, and you can use this to pay for Cherise getting into the show."

Cherise snatched the money out of Bertie's hand and put it in her jeans pocket.

"Fine, we'll do it," Bobby said. He picked up Hodge's staple gun and squeezed the handle. It went off with a bang and a staple flew across the kitchen, dinking the refrigerator and then hitting the floor.

"Stop fooling around, Bobby," Cherise said.

"You're going to put somebody's eye out," Bertie said.

Bobby took half the stack of posters. "Come on, Cherise. We've got to get these done before the show starts."

Cherise stood up, licking chicken grease off her fingers, and headed out the door without washing her hands or saying good-bye. Bobby followed her.

"I'm sending James out later to make sure you put them up," Bertie called after him.

"I said I'd do it, Ma. Get off my back!" The door slammed behind him.

Bertie picked up the chicken Cherise had mangled and tipped it into the garbage can.

James wandered into the kitchen, his hair messed up from sleep. His shoulders were slumpy all the time these days. "What did Bobby want?" he said.

"A shirt he'd left here." She showed James the posters on

the table. "Hodge brought these by for you to put up. Bobby already took half."

James nudged the posters with a finger but didn't really seem to be looking at them. It was like his spirit had left him. He was going to have to go back to work the next week, and Bertie wasn't sure how he'd do.

She tried to offer him some hope. "If we get the posters up today, maybe somebody will call."

He sat down at the table and picked up Hodge's duct tape, peeling up the edge with a bitten fingernail.

"I'm going to head over to my folks'. Mama will be wondering where I am," she said.

James turned his hearing aid off and took it out, rubbing his ear, shutting her out.

She went and got her coat and walked across the road. Her mama had got so she couldn't bend to clean, and her eyes were too weak to see the dirt. And it wasn't like Bertie's daddy was going to help out. She made her parents lunch and cleaned up the clutter so they wouldn't trip over anything. At four o'clock she walked home to watch her soap operas.

James got home as *Guiding Light* was ending and the local news was coming on. He sat down on the couch next to her. She handed him the remote control. "I'll go get supper started." He didn't answer.

In the kitchen, the chicken carcass she'd thrown away that morning was making the trash smell. Bertie tied the garbage bag to take it out. Outside, it was getting dark. A short wind blew dried leaves along the ground around her feet. The cold had shut the bugs up. James's truck door wasn't all the way closed, and his interior light was on. She went to close the door so his battery wouldn't drain and noticed papers sticking out from under the passenger seat. A whole pile of papers, with Leon's face over and over again. She reached in and pulled them out to look. James had been gone all day and hadn't put up a single poster. She pushed the stack back under his seat and shut the truck door. Inside the trailer James turned up the volume on the TV. A commercial blared, loud enough to hear through closed windows and doors. She stood there with the garbage bag in her hand, feeling scared. Being the depressed one was her job. They couldn't afford for her and James both to be like that.

14

Martin

After Eugenia and Zeb left for their church supper, Martin walked to his nephew Steven's body shop, where Steven had an apartment over the shop. Martin was glad it was close to Eugenia's house. He could drink all he wanted and walk back to Eugenia's without worrying about driving.

At the body shop, the day's last customers were claiming their cars. Martin's niece Trina, Steven's younger sister, waved to him from behind the register in the small business office. Martin could hear Steven inside the garage, yelling to his help over the shrilling of some piece of machinery. Paint fumes wafted out of bay doors. Martin leaned in the office doorway. There was no place to sit.

Trina handed her last customer his key and the man left. She took a twenty-dollar bill out of her register drawer and locked it. "Chinese food okay with you, Martin?"

"Fine."

"We'll just eat upstairs at Steven's place. Come tell me what you want." She untaped a dirty menu from the wall behind her and handed it to him. He chose cashew chicken, and she picked up the phone. "Hey, Fong. It's Trina, over at the body shop. Bring me a number thirty-four, a number forty-five, a number twelve, and three wonton soups. All right, hon." She hung up. "I'm his best customer. There ain't anywhere else good to eat around here."

Steven came in through the door to the garage, wiping his hands on a rag and whistling. He was a generation younger than Martin, but his wiry hair had more gray in it. Martin's hair was still almost completely brown, and he hadn't inherited his father's tendency toward baldness. From the back, he still looked like a young man, though from the front the sag of his cheeks and the broken vessels around his nose gave him away.

"I ordered you a mu shu pork," Trina told Steven.

"Good. The guys will close up."

"Your shop seems busy," Martin said.

"We got plenty to do. One of the big insurance companies picked us to do all their work," Steven said.

"Steven beat out eight other body shops to get that contract," Trina said, proud of her brother.

Martin was proud of Steven, too. Mr. Samuels and Dr. Vance had helped launch Martin on his way, and he had gotten nowhere. No one had helped Steven.

"It's a lot of paperwork, but it's worth it," Steven said. "Martin, you ought to stay with me next time you come to town. My couch is as good as anybody else's."

"I actually got a real bed at Bertie's. Bobby wasn't home."

Steven balled up the rag he was holding and lobbed it into a metal trash can in the corner. "Bobby. Don't get me started. I despise that boy."

"And that bitch he goes with, too," Trina chimed in. "Cherise, or whatever she calls herself now. In high school she was just plain Cheryl."

"We're going to have it out one of these days. He's all but said I murdered Leon. If he keeps it up, I will murder somebody—him. Mama and Trina want me to promise not to hurt him. Shit. He better stay out of my way, or they'll be visiting me on Sundays at Central Prison," Steven said.

They waited downstairs until a small Chinese man with a brown paper bag hurried across the street, dodging traffic.

"There's Fong." Trina picked up her twenty-dollar bill and went out to pay him. When she came back in, the smell of Chinese food filled the office.

"Come on upstairs," Steven said.

They went around to the back of the shop and climbed the long wooden stairs to Steven's apartment. The apartment hadn't changed much since Martin's last visit three or four years ago. It was clean, by male standards. Steven worked so much, he wasn't there enough to mess it up. The entry door opened into the kitchen, and the first thing Steven did was check the fridge. Martin looked over his shoulder. Beer and baking soda. He approved.

Steven dug around among bottles that rolled around in the crisper. "Rolling Rock okay?"

"Sure."

"Y'all probably drink fancy beer up there in New York." He set three bottles on the counter and popped the lids off with a church key.

"Whatever's cheap." Martin took a beer, wishing for the bottle of Scotch he had hidden under the guest bed at Eugenia's that afternoon. Beer filled him up before it got him drunk.

Trina claimed her bottle of beer and leaned against the counter. "I might come up and see you some time, Martin. I've never been to New York."

"Or anywhere else. Myrtle Beach don't count," Steven said.

Trina pretended to kick Steven. "Big brother here won't give me the time off. But seriously, I'd like to come up and

maybe see a show, or come at Christmas to see the ice skat-
ing."

"At Rockefeller Center," Martin said.

"That's it. They have packages out of Winston-Salem, with
cheap airfare and all."

"I would love for you to come." Martin meant it. Trina
would eat up New York. And she was the first of his relatives to suggest coming to visit him in all the years since he'd
moved to the city.

Trina got paper plates out of a cabinet. They took Fong's
takeout into Steven's living room and spread it out on the
coffee table. The food was bland and heavy on the cornstarch.
Fong had taken all the spice out to appease the local clientele.
After they ate all they wanted, Steven disappeared into his
bedroom and came back with a pipe and a bag of pot. They
passed it around until Martin was so relaxed he felt like his
body had merged with Steven's couch. Between hits, Steven
and Trina entertained him with stories about their customers
and employees. Then the talk turned to their brother, Shane.
The talk always turned to Shane.

"Remember how he used to like to fish?" Trina handed
Martin the pipe and went over to Steven's entertainment
center. She picked up one of several framed photographs—
Shane, at about age fourteen. His hair was long. He wore bell-
bottom jeans and a checkered shirt. His teenage mustache was
a smudge of dirt on his upper lip. He was holding a trout and
a cardboard sign with its weight written in Magic Marker, six
pounds two ounces.

"Leon's the one used to take Shane fishing. He'd take me,
too, once in a while. He was real patient with us," Steven
said.

It was hard for Martin to imagine Leon patient or kind.

But one couldn't speak ill of the missing. He took a hit off the pipe and passed it to Steven.

"Shane was so proud of that trout," Steven said. "He wanted to stuff it. Got mad at Leon because Leon said fish were for frying, not for stuffing. It did taste good, though."

"Shane could get mad." Trina put the photograph back among the others, carefully straightening it. It was the closest Martin had ever heard her come to admitting that Shane had a fault. She and Steven wouldn't let anyone talk badly about their brother. If he had rages, if he assaulted his foster brothers or his teachers, it was because they deserved it. Shane was troubled. He never had a chance.

Steven lifted the pipe to his lips. "He tried, man. One time we all got to go to Mama's for Christmas. She had a place out Springfield Road for a little while. It was small, but she could fit us in for a few days. An ice storm came up. Mama's car completely iced over. She sent Shane outside with the scraper to scrape the ice off her car windows. The ice was so thick and hard it wouldn't scrape easy, so Shane goes and gets a hammer out the shed and starts shattering the ice. He totally forgot he was shattering the glass along with it. Mama didn't even get mad. She just sat down and cried because she didn't have the money to replace the glass. Shane was so upset. He wouldn't come home for another visit for months after that—too embarrassed. Mama tried and tried to tell him it was all right. She borrowed money for the front window and put plastic over all the rest, but Shane couldn't stand to look at that car. It reminded him of what he'd done."

"He was always sensitive," Trina said. "Me and Steven got the thick skin. Shane didn't have any skin at all."

Martin felt guilty that all his memories of Shane were from when Shane was small, before Martin left home. His mother teaching him the proper way to hold Shane, love for the baby softening her weathered face as she demonstrated. "Like this, Martin, in the crook of your arm." Shane's tiny fists flailing. Martin taught Shane the alphabet when Shane was two. Shane would say a few letters, slurp a breath, say a few more. Ivy and his mother were so proud. "He's going to be a smart one, like you, Martin," his mother said, handing Shane a biscuit with butter and fig preserves. Shane beamed and climbed up on Martin's lap, his breath sticky on Martin's cheek.

Martin had to think hard to remember seeing Shane at all during the boy's teenage years. Shane must have been at the funeral when Martin's father died, but Martin couldn't remember. Rory Owenby had died about a year before Shane committed suicide. Martin went home for his father's funeral only because he didn't want Eugenia and James and Bertie to think ill of him.

Trina and Steven didn't seem to notice that he had no memories of Shane to contribute. They gave Martin more credit than he deserved for being an ally. Martin never did anything more for them when they were kids than the aunts and uncles who were here. He just had the excuse of living far away.

Steven reached for the bag of pot. "Mama tell you about the monument?"

Martin watched as Steven expertly repacked the pipe. "Monument? No."

"She's ordered a real nice one for Shane's grave, finally. Me and Trina would have helped her buy one a long time ago if she'd let us, but she didn't want our help."

"It'll have his name on it and part of a poem I wrote," Trina said.

"Poem?"

She looked shy. "We're going to run it in the paper this

year, on the anniversary of the day he died." She looked around.
"Where's it at, Steven?"

"On top of the TV."

She went and got it and handed it to Martin.

> *It has been twenty years*
> *Since you went away*
> *We loved you so much*
> *But you could not stay*
> *We remember your laugh*
> *And your big appetite*
> *You were our star*
> *You were our light*
> *Not a day goes by*
> *That we don't think of you*
> *We will always remember*
> *We will always be true.*
> *Love forever, Mama, Steven, and Trina*

It was painfully bad and painful for other reasons.

"Do you like it?" Trina said.

Martin was the family poet. His opinion mattered. "It's lovely." He handed the poem back to her.

"We're going to install the headstone that day, too. You should come, Martin," Trina said.

Martin breathed in the haze they had created with Steven's pipe and suddenly didn't want to be there anymore. "I doubt I'll be able to make it down." He stood up and waited for the room to stop reeling. "I'd better go. I don't want to get back to Eugenia's too late."

"I'll drive you," Steven said.

As impaired as Martin was, he knew Steven was in no condition to drive. "No, I'll walk. It'll help me sober up."

"Suit yourself." Steven shook his hand, and Trina gave him a hug. It was seven o'clock. Trina turned on the porch light. He made his way down the steps, both hands on the rail. Traffic had quieted. Streetlights marked the way for the few cars that passed. He pulled his coat around him, wishing it were warmer. As he walked, he thought about Leon taking Shane and Steven fishing. He just couldn't see it. Leon was mean. He was mean when he left for the war in 1942 and even meaner when he got back.

Not long after Leon got out of the service, when Martin and Hodge Goforth were eight or nine, Leon caught them down behind the sawmill, showing each other their penises. They weren't doing anything other little boys didn't do. Hodge didn't grow up to be a queer because of it. But Leon went nuts. He didn't hit Hodge, but Martin remembered his friend's face as Hodge cowered against the wall of the sawmill, his pants still down around his knees. Hodge expected Leon to kill him.

Leon did hit Martin, cuffing him so hard on the side of the head that he fell down. "Go on home," Leon told Hodge. Hodge took off running, crying, pulling his pants up as he ran.

Leon turned on Martin again. "You mama's boy, candy ass, sissy." He kicked him with every word. Martin crab-walked backward in the dirt, trying to dodge the blows. It seemed to Martin now that Leon must have suspected he was gay, even that early, and was determined to beat it out of him. He nearly did. He kicked Martin in the crotch. The pain was blinding. Martin curled up in a ball with his fingers over his groin to protect it. Leon kicked him again. "I hope your pecker swells up like a watermelon. Then maybe you'll be ashamed to show it around." He left Martin lying there and went back up the hill toward the house.

When Martin recovered enough to walk he went home, crying. His mother was in her garden and wanted to know what was wrong. "Leon beat me." He showed her his bruised fingers only. She wiped his tears away with callused thumbs. "Don't mind him," she said. "The war was hard, and now he's back he don't know where he fits in. Just stay out of his way." Martin did stay out of Leon's way, nursing his swollen balls until they went back to normal size and he could stop walking bowlegged. God, Leon was mean.

When they were ten, Hodge apologized for leaving Martin that day. As if Hodge's soft little body could have shielded Martin from Leon's blows and his staying could have made a difference. Hodge apologized the day he and Martin and the Gaddy twins were baptized. At Solace Fork Baptist Church, when you turned ten years old, you got baptized by total immersion, whether you wanted to or not. Martin never knew any child who said no. It was simply what you did. The preacher, Brother Pike, met with the four of them beforehand. He was a tall, gangly man with dark yellow hair and a droopy mustache, who worked as a plumber during the week. His sermons were full of plumbing analogies, of sin blocking people's drains, the need to flush out the waste in their lives and be purified. They met with him the Sunday before the baptism to rehearse the one-line profession of faith they would mutter before they went under, JesusChristismyLordandSavior. Brother Pike explained how he would have one hand under their backs, while the other held a cloth over their mouths and noses so they wouldn't swallow water and embarrass themselves and the Lord by coughing. The slow Gaddy twin, Betty, had adenoid trouble and breathed through her mouth. Martin wondered if she would smother when the preacher put the cloth over her nose and mouth.

The baptism didn't mean anything to Martin, except that it made his mother happy. Hodge, though, took it very seriously. He talked about his personal walk with Jesus until Martin began to feel jealous that Hodge had found a new best friend. The creek ran behind the church, a good twenty feet wide, close enough that the sanctuary flooded every few years. The day of the baptism, the four candidates waited in the doorway of the church, watching the rest of the congregation assemble on the bank. The preacher's wife was in charge of them, to make sure they had clean underwear on under their white cotton robes and another dry pair to change into afterward. They couldn't hear what Brother Pike said from where they were, but when he raised an arm and motioned to his wife, she told them to come on and led them toward the bank and their waiting families. Crabgrass cut the bottoms of Martin's bare feet. The Gaddy girls were in front, then Hodge, then Martin. Brother Pike beckoned for Nancy Gaddy to come forward.

While the preacher was prodding Nancy to state her profession of faith out loud, Hodge whispered, "Martin?" His face was even more earnest than usual. "I ask your forgiveness," he said.

"Huh?" Martin said.

"I ask your forgiveness," Hodge hissed as Nancy Gaddy rose dripping from the creek and Betty Gaddy started forward.

"What for? I'm not God, you know." Martin watched the preacher put Betty Gaddy under and counted one-one-thousand, two-one-thousand, wondering how long he would be able to hold his breath.

"That time, when Leon came down to the sawmill and started hitting on you," Hodge said.

Martin remembered. He'd had other beatings from his brother, but that one stood out.

"I'm sorry for running away. I'm sorry for leaving you like that."

Martin wasn't sure what to say.

The preacher beckoned to Hodge. Hodge grabbed Martin's arm. "Do you forgive me?"

"Sure. Sure I do," Martin said, because it seemed important to his friend.

Hodge breathed a sigh and walked down to the water. As the preacher immersed him, Martin's mother leaned forward from the front row of people on the bank and caught Martin's eye, smiling at him. He smiled back. Hodge rose dripping from the creek, his thin hair plastered to his head, and Brother Pike called, "Martin Owenby."

Martin walked down to the bank. The sand was wet and cold under his toes. The preacher put a bony hand on his back, just as he'd said he would. Martin told the crowd that Jesus was his Lord and Savior. Brother Pike tipped him back. He could feel the cloth on his nose. Above him, a mockingbird left a branch and flew into white sky. He went under the water and came up, catching his breath, his robe heavy around him.

"Martin Owenby, you are a child of God, and He takes great delight in you," the preacher declared.

From the bank, Martin heard his mother's clear, plain contralto begin a melody, and others join in, weaving harmony.

> *From every stormy wind that blows,*
> *From every swelling tide of woes,*

There is a calm, a sure retreat;
'Tis found beneath the mercy seat.

There is a scene where spirits blend,
Where friend holds fellowship with friend;
Tho' sundered far, by faith they meet
Around one common mercy seat.

Brother Pike helped Martin wade back up the bank, and Mrs. Pike shoved him up the hill to get changed. Martin and Hodge never talked again about the day Leon caught them.

At ten, Martin had no sins to wash away, and the baptismal cleansing didn't last for him like it did for Hodge. In particularly drunk moments since then, he had wished he could do it again. He could use a wash now, a good soak or scrub, to remove all the sins he'd accumulated. But God only lets you go under one time.

He turned onto Main Street. The few trees that lined the street had dug their toes into the dirt, pushing up squares of sidewalk. Martin tripped and stumbled, noticing as he caught himself how much less nimble he was than just a few years ago. Time was taking the spring out of his step. He sat down on a bench in front of the liquor store he had visited that day, now closed. In the window of the antiques store next door objects vied for space, iridescent dishes of carnival glass, old *Life* magazines, delicate silver picture frames holding photos of people long forgotten. He lit a cigarette and waited for the cold October air to dull his buzz.

A sheriff's patrol car pulled up to the curb. Shit. Martin exhaled smoke all around him, waving his cigarette back and forth like the pope swinging incense on Christmas eve, to cover up any marijuana smell that hadn't yet aired out of his clothing.

The patrol car's passenger-side window rolled down. Hodge leaned out on his elbow. "Want a ride?" The sheriff was at the wheel.

Martin couldn't refuse. He exhaled one more time and crushed his cigarette out on the sidewalk. He got into the backseat of the patrol car, realizing only after he closed the door that there was a cage between him and the front seat.

"Make you nervous?" Hodge grinned back at him.

It did make him nervous. He stared out the window to his right to keep from feeling claustrophobic.

"We were just over in Punkintown, talking to a witness who told one of my deputies she'd seen your brother," the sheriff said.

"Really?" Martin leaned forward.

"Yep." Wally's strong, square-nailed hands rested at two and ten o'clock on the steering wheel. The hair on the back of his neck was cut in a perfect straight line. "Old lady called and said she saw Leon at the bus station yesterday, getting on a bus to Charlotte. Me and Hodge go out there to her house, turns out she hadn't seen a thing. She heard it from somebody who heard it from somebody." He shook his head. "Happens all the time. Witnesses are useless. I'll take good, hard physical evidence over an eyewitness any day. The deputy who sent me out on this goose chase is going on crosswalk duty tomorrow."

"What'd you do tonight?" Hodge asked Martin.

"Ate Chinese with Steven and Trina."

"Fong's Fine Foods. Gives me indigestion," Wally said. His police radio blurted something unintelligible. He ignored it.

"Did they tell you about Ivy buying that nice headstone for

Shane?" Hodge always knew the Owenby family news before Martin did.

"Yes."

"Who's Shane?" Wally said.

"Ivy's oldest son. He killed himself, maybe ten or twelve years ago," Hodge said.

"Twenty years ago." Martin felt carsick. He tried his window, but it was locked. He leaned his head against the cool glass. An oncoming car's headlights swept over them, imprinting him with the cross-hatched pattern of the patrol car's cage bars.

"Has it really been that long?" Hodge said.

"Before my time," Wally said.

Wally pulled into the well-lit parking lot of the Municipal Building, next to Hodge's pickup truck. Hodge freed Martin from the back of the patrol car, and Wally drove off. They got in Hodge's truck and drove toward Eugenia's, where Martin would be able to retrieve his bottle from under the bed and finally get a decent drink.

"I've been wanting to float an idea by you," Hodge said.

"What's that?"

"The dean over at the community college told me last week there's an opening in the English department. They need somebody to teach literature. I mentioned to him that you'd be in town and that I'd tell you about it. He was real excited. He was a student of Liza's in high school. She makes all her students read your plays."

"Oh, God."

"Don't be embarrassed. The Lord gave you a talent. You should be proud of it."

Martin wondered if Hodge had ever read his plays. Hodge loved him enough that he'd probably tried. "Hodge, I can't teach at the community college. I live in New York."

"But you don't have to go back just yet. You could stay in the apartment we built for my mother-in-law in the basement. She was only in it six months before she died, and now it's filling up with junk. We'd charge you two hundred dollars a month rent, you could come and go as you pleased."

Martin looked over at him. "You've got it all planned out."

"This situation with Leon is hard on your family. They need you. Every day that passes without us finding him, I think about your mama, how much her family meant to her. She would have wanted you children to look out for each other. Think about it."

Martin knew it would make his family happy if he stayed, not because he could do anything, but for the comfort of having one more person to stand with while they waited for word.

Hodge's headlights swept over cornfields. A night fog was descending. A possum scuttled off the side of the road.

He had once assumed he would stay in this place. Despite his experimentation with Mr. Samuels and the games he played with Hodge as a child, he assumed he would grow up and marry Liza. Deke Armstrong changed that. If Deke hadn't, some other man would have.

The night of Martin's play, Deke's muscled chest pressed against Martin's back, slick with sweat. Warm hands defined Martin's body. Deke opened him up, split him in two, and the old Martin dissipated into air, leaving a new Martin breathing hard into cool sheets.

When Deke fell asleep, Martin slipped out of the house, wanting time alone to think. He was aghast and exhilarated at what he had just done, guilty and triumphant when he imagined what his father and brothers would think if they knew. His muscles were sore, as if he'd been in a race and won. The night was silent, except for the occasional sound of tire chains chinking or the metallic scrape of a snow shovel on concrete. He hoofed across backyards, snow spilling over the tops of his shoes. He lost the feeling in his toes, but the rest of him had never felt so sharp and alive. As he approached Mrs. Bowen's boardinghouse, the glare of the bare yellow bulb that lit her porch hurt his eyes. Mrs. Bowen opened the door and peered out. He began to formulate the excuse he would give her for coming in so late, but when he reached the porch she called out to him, her voice kind.

"Martin, come in here."

He climbed the steps. Mrs. Bowen's gray hair hung long down her back. Her face, instead of being angry, was full of pity. "It's your mama, son." She pulled him into the stale warmth of her foyer. "Dr. Vance called and said she passed."

His mother had died while he was luxuriating in applause and pleasure. He felt his whole body go numb, like a slept-on limb. In front of him Mrs. Bowen's mouth opened and shut. He couldn't process her words.

He stumbled upstairs and stuffed his good suit, tooth-brush, and a change of underwear into his duffel bag. Out in the hall he could hear Mrs. Bowen whispering to her sister. His ears cleared, and he understood the word "cancer." Mrs. Bowen tapped on his door and handed him an envelope. He opened it. Eight five-dollar bills. Mrs. Bowen had tears in her eyes. "You pay me back when you're able," she said.

No one met him at the Whelan bus station. A man he knew by sight offered him a ride to Solace Fork. The man had known his mother. "Nell Owenby was a fine woman," he said, leaving unsaid the trials and harshness of her mar-ried life, perhaps because such hardship was unremarkable for a woman. Martin thanked him and stared out the window.

Deer had chewed bark off the trees that lined the road, trying to avoid winter starvation. A young deer, tossed off the road by a car, rotted in a ditch.

The snow that had hit Chapel Hill hadn't swept this far west. From the crossroad at Solace Fork he walked the rest of the way to his father's house, feeling under the thin soles of his shoes every familiar bump and rut. When he was younger he had walked home from school this way, reading as he walked, and never tripped or slid, even when Leon rode by in the truck and veered toward him, laughing when Martin jumped. He rounded a final curve, and the house came into view. The porch was bowed, propped up by cinder blocks. Sweeping the yard had been his mother's job. In her sickness, chicken leavings had piled up in forlorn drifts.

As he approached the house he smelled smoke. His father came out of the front door without seeing him, carrying a knot of sheets, and went around to the side of the house. Martin followed him.

"Pop," he said as his father tossed what he'd been carrying into a fire he'd lit on the ground.

His father looked up. "Martin. You got here all right."

"Yes, sir."

The wind changed, and Martin moved away from the ashes from the fire. "What are you burning?"

His father didn't answer. Martin moved closer. He saw in the fire charred leather and paper, wood and sepia, his mother's framed photograph of her parents, her Bible, softened with wear, her clothing, the sheets she must have lain on in her final sickness. His father was burning all of her intimate things, all the things Martin might have tucked away to remember her.

"What are you doing!" Martin reached into the fire for the Bible.

His father knocked it out of his hands with the stick, crack-ing two of his fingers. "Don't touch it! It's got the sickness on it!" Flames lit the Bible's pages, eating words, erasing the penciled comments his mother had written in the margins in her years of close Bible study, gnawing at the leather cover.

Martin felt sick. His mother had lived with this man for decades, borne his children, borne her tumor, and she hadn't been dead a full day before he started burning her things in fear of catching her cancer.

"You ignorant bastard!" he screamed. His father ignored him, stoking the fire higher. Leon emerged onto the porch. He looked at them, curious. James walked up from the henhouse to check on the commotion.

Martin pleaded with his brothers. "He's burning Mama's things." They blinked in response, as if they couldn't see why he was upset.

Martin headed back down the mountain. The smoke of his father's fire wouldn't leave his lungs. "You ignorant bastard," he rasped, striking the air with his duffel bag. Around him the mountain was still, even cowbells keeping a respectful silence.

At the general store the owner, Perry Riddle, put his hand on Martin's shoulder. "Sorry about your mama." Martin could only nod. It hurt to breathe. He asked to use the phone, shield-ing himself from Perry's curious eyes as he asked the operator to dial Deke's number in Chapel Hill. The phone rang and rang. He imagined the sound echoing into emptiness in the room where he and Deke had lain, what seemed like a long time ago. The silence was indifferent.

After twenty rings, when Perry coughed politely, he hung up. He told Perry good-bye and went outside. Behind the store where no one could see, he leaned against weathered boards and doubled over, with a cry that came out as a whisper. He sat on the ground and sobbed. Wetness seeped through his trousers, freezing him through.

"Martin?" Perry Riddle rounded the corner of the store.

"I'm all right." Martin dragged his coat sleeve across his eyes and stood up. Somewhere a mourning dove's call pushed at the cold. He accepted Perry's pat on the back and walked out to the road.

"Martin?" Hodge was beside him in the driver's seat, waiting for an answer.

"No," Martin croaked. "No, I can't stay here." Then to hide his revulsion at the idea, to spare Hodge's feelings, he made things up, commitments and deadlines waiting for him in New York, friends who had actually noticed he was gone.

"I understand," Hodge said, sounding disappointed. "It was just a thought."

They had reached Eugenia's dark house. Hodge waited, engine idling, until Martin let himself in, then pulled away. The house was still. As quietly as he could Martin went to the living room, turned on a low lamp and found his plane ticket in his wallet. Hodge's proposal had chilled him. He called the airline and scheduled his departure for the first flight out in the morning.

A prayer vigil will be held at Solace Fork Baptist Church on December 14th at six o'clock in the evening, to mark the two-month anniversary of the disappearance of Leon Owenby, age 65. Mrs. Eugenia Nash, sister of the missing man and an organizer of the vigil, tells the public to bring their own candles, as the church needs to save its candles for the Christmas eve service.

—WILLOBY NEWS & RECORD,
December 10, 1986

15

L i z a

"Please join me in the singing of 'Amazing Grace.' I want y'all to sing loud at the part that says, 'I once was lost but now am found.' Here we go, now." Charlie Davis, the part-time reverend of Solace Fork Baptist Church, lifted a hand to direct the hymn.

Liza stood shoulder to shoulder with Hodge on the church's winter brown front lawn, with forty-some other citizens who had come to pray for Leon Owenby. Their collective breath puffed white in the cold night air. She and Hodge were positioned next to a crèche of large plastic manger characters, which someone had plugged into a multi-outlet adapter and then connected to three consecutive extension cords that ran from the yard into the church. Underwriters Laboratories would not have approved, but Liza appreciated the heat she was getting from the light bulb that burned within Mary. The scent of melting plastic was a comfort.

"Amazing Grace, how sweet the sound . . ."

Martin's sister Eugenia, standing on the church steps with Reverend Davis, got the crowd started with a vibrato that was surprisingly powerful for someone so little. At the other end of their uneven row, Bertie's lips barely moved. She'd come alone, saying that James was under the weather.

"That saved a wretch like me . . ."

Liza mouthed the words, fingering the unlit white candle she'd brought, with its homemade paper collar. Beside her, Hodge sang out enthusiastically, sometimes hitting the right note, sometimes not.

"I once was lost but now am found . . ."

If Martin were here, he'd be making faces at the reverend's literal use of this particular hymn. Liza kept her eyes straight ahead, afraid she might burst into inappropriate laughter if she met anyone's eyes.

"Was blind, but now I see."

The singers finished up, all at different times, and Reverend Davis put his arm down. "Let us now light our candles for our missing brother. Please remember to hold your candles upright so the wax won't burn your hand, and, ladies, don't catch your hair on fire."

Reverend Davis tilted his candle to light Eugenia's. She turned and lit her husband Zeb's. He walked down the far end of the crowd, lighting the candle of the first person on each row. Dots of light staggered slowly down the line in Liza's direction.

She and Hodge waited for the flame to reach them, stamping their feet for warmth. "I wish Martin was here," Hodge said.

"His choice." Liza was still miffed at Martin for skipping town without saying good-bye.

"I think I drove him off," Hodge said.

"How?"

"I tried to get him to stay here and take that teaching job Jay Daniels has open at the community college."

She laughed out loud, then put her hand over her mouth when people stared. "Martin Owenby teaching freshman English. Good lord, Hodge. No wonder he hightailed it. That would scare anybody."

Hodge sighed. "I know. It was just wishful thinking on my part. I shouldn't have counted on it."

"I don't think Martin wants to be counted on," she said.

"Have you heard from him?"

"No."

"I haven't either."

The woman next to Hodge lit his candle, and he lit Liza's. Around them the tiny flames gestured wildly at each other.

"Pray with me silently," Reverend Davis said. They dutifully bowed their heads and closed their eyes. A cold, slow wind moved behind them. Liza cupped her hand around her candle to keep it from going out. She could feel Hodge beside her praying hard, hard enough for both of them.

It was always wise to bar the door if you wanted Martin Owenby to stay.

The January of their senior year of high school, Mr. Samuels made Martin, Hodge, and Liza stay after school to complete their college applications. He sat at his desk, correcting ninth-grade essays.

"Why do we have to do this today, Mr. Samuels? Mine ain't due for another month," Hodge said.

Mr. Samuels didn't look up. "No time like the present, Hodge. And if you're still saying 'ain't' when you graduate from here, I will have failed as a teacher."

"Sorry, sir."

Martin nudged Liza. "I'm putting your address down. The mailman knows where your house is."

"Good idea," she said. His parents wouldn't see the response before he did.

Mr. Samuels finished red-inking one essay and reached for another, peering over his glasses to check their progress. "Hand your applications to me when you're done. I'll mail them."

"I'll mail mine," said Martin.

"No, I'll mail it. I don't want anyone changing his or her mind at the last minute." Mr. Samuels went back to grading papers.

Three months later, in April, Martin's letter came from Chapel Hill. An all-day rain bruised the sky the day it came. Liza ran from her car to the porch when she got home from school, shook water from her umbrella and saw it, stuffed in the brass letter box by her front door. The thin cream-colored envelope poked out from between a power bill and one of her father's medical journals. She plucked it out. The sight of the admissions office address embossed in gold made her heart pump faster than it had when her own acceptance letter had arrived from Woman's College in Greensboro two weeks before.

She took the mail inside, where her father sat reading in the leather chair in his study. Rain dimmed the usually bright room, giving the feel of evening rather than midafternoon. A floor lamp behind her father's chair molded weird shadows out of the furniture. She fluttered the envelope in his face. "Martin's letter from UNC."

He grabbed it and stood up. Before she knew what he

was doing he ripped the shade off the floor lamp and held the envelope to the bare bulb, using his thumbs to press the envelope against the letter inside.

She was horrified. "Daddy!"

He squinted as he read. " 'We are pleased to inform you.' " He lowered the envelope. "He got in."

"I can't believe you just read somebody else's mail."

The light bulb's glare deepened the crinkles around his eyes and glinted off his grinning teeth. "I've got to call Samuels, get him over here to help me talk Martin into going. We need to plan this right."

"That's silly, Daddy. Martin wants to go to college."

"The boy's got nobody at home to even imagine it with him. He doesn't think he's going. We've got to make it so there's no way he can't go." He reached for the telephone and got Mr. Samuels at home. "Samuels? He got in. The letter came today. Yep, I'm proud of the boy. I think you're right. It'd be best if he didn't have to work his freshman year, while he's getting adjusted. I'll lend him enough so he won't have to. Lend, give, call it what you want. When should we tell him?"

Liza listened in amazement. Her father and Mr. Samuels had obviously been conspiring about this for some time. Her father seemed to have forgotten she was in the room.

They concocted a plan, with Liza as the lure. The next day, Friday, at school, she invited Martin to come to her house Sunday afternoon, on the pretext of working on their graduation recitations. Sunday was the only day Martin's father didn't make him work.

The occasion felt momentous. She dressed with care, choosing a straight black skirt that fit her twenty-three-inch waist and a light gray cashmere sweater with a scoop neck that showed off her mother's pearls.

Mr. Samuels arrived a half hour early. He winked at her before disappearing with her father into the study. "Don't give us away, now."

"I won't." She went to her room and brushed her hair to a sheen, tucking it behind her left ear. When she heard Martin's steps on the front porch, she met him at the door.

He eyed her. "You look like you're about to pop. What gives?"

"Never mind. Come in. Daddy wants to see you."

He squinted, suspicious, but followed her down the hall. She knocked on the door of the study. Her father opened it. Mr. Samuels stood behind him, looking proud enough to cry.

Martin nodded to both men. "Hello, sir. Sirs."

"Come in, son." Her father moved aside to let them in. He had set out his good sherry. Afternoon sunlight shone ruby-colored through a cut-glass decanter. He and Mr. Samuels already had their glasses. He poured two more for her and Martin. Martin took his, raising it to his nose for a discreet sniff.

"A toast," her father said. "To college-bound seniors."

Martin lowered his glass.

The letter from Chapel Hill lay on her father's desk. Her father picked it up and handed it to Martin. "I believe you got in, son."

In an instant she saw that her father and Mr. Samuels had been right to worry. Martin froze. His eyes shifted right, as if seeking an escape. Mr. Samuels moved to the study door and shut it. "Open the letter, Martin."

Martin had no choice. He set his glass down and slid a thumb under the envelope flap, peeling it open, closing his eyes for a moment before he unfolded the letter. In the silence as he read Liza could hear blood whooshing through her veins. Martin looked up and cleared his throat. "I got in."

She put her sherry glass down and gave him a hug. He stood as if paralyzed, but her father and Mr. Samuels moved into action.

"You're going, son." Her father put a hand on Martin's shoulder and led him to the closest chair, then sat with Mr. Samuels across from Martin, leaning forward. Liza took a seat behind her father's desk, out of the way. "Don't worry about cost. I'm lending you the money." Her father held up his hand as Martin started to protest. "It's a good investment. I'm sure I'll be happy with the return." He glanced at Liza, and she blushed a little, imagining herself married to Martin.

"Don't think for a minute that you aren't smart enough for college," Mr. Samuels said. "You'll hold your own. I'm not concerned about that a bit."

Martin set the acceptance letter down on the arm of his chair, as if he didn't want to touch it. He pressed the heel of his hand against his forehead. "I can't believe I got in."

"Well, you did," said Mr. Samuels.

Martin put his arm down. He tried to laugh. "What's Pop going to say?"

"You've got to decide, son. It's your decision, not your daddy's," Liza's father said.

Something changed on Martin's face, as if he realized he had a choice, that he could go even if his parents said no. He breathed out a long, slow breath. "I don't know how to tell them."

Mr. Samuels leaned forward and patted him on the knee. "The doctor and I will go with you."

"And me," Liza said, indignant.

"Tomorrow, then, when he gets in from working." Mr.

Samuels picked up his sherry and stood up. He waited for them to join him, glasses held high, then toasted Martin. "To a fine future."

They drank. Martin coughed, his eyes watering. Her father and Mr. Samuels moved close, pounding him between the shoulder blades. Each blow shook him, making him seem frail.

In the schoolyard the next day, Hodge recited Scripture to shore them up. " 'The Lord is on my side; I will not fear: what can man do unto me?' Psalm 118."

"My daddy can do plenty," Martin muttered.

Younger children streamed past them, walking down the road in pairs, siblings tormenting each other. Martin was pale. Liza squeezed his pinky finger, borrowing a favorite assurance from her father. "In twenty-four hours it will all be over."

He looked ready to vomit.

She pointed to her car, parked in the side yard of the school, where its pure white top and shiny chrome put Mr. Samuels's duller ride to shame. "Let's go. We'll tell your mother we're working on some project for school."

They got in her car, Hodge in the backseat and Martin next to her in front. The pearl-colored interior hadn't lost its new leather smell yet. Her charm bracelet hung from the rearview mirror. She backed skillfully out of the schoolyard and headed for the Owenby farm. Martin rolled his window down and stuck his elbow out. She slowed down to buy him more time.

Since her first visit to Martin's house, she had done her best to ingratiate herself with his mother. With the car, she could show up any time she wanted, and she did. If she hadn't been the doctor's daughter, Martin's parents would never have tolerated it. When the Sunliner pulled into the yard, Mrs. Owenby was in her garden at the side of the house. She straightened up from weeding. Amid the growing vegetables, with her arms akimbo and a man's straw hat on to protect against the sun, she looked like a scarecrow.

"We're going inside, Mama. Schoolwork," Martin called.

"All right."

They went into the house. Bread dough rose in a bowl on top of a pie safe. A pot of pole beans slow-cooked on the stove, a chunk of fatback flavoring the beans and the air in the room. Hodge's stomach growled. They opened their books on the kitchen table, to make it look as if they were studying. The Owenbys didn't have electricity. The only light came from windows along the porch, but they knew if they went outside into the sunlight Martin's mother would put them to work.

"We might as well do some real studying," Hodge said.

"I never thought I'd hear you say that," Martin said.

"I must be feverish."

They did homework at the long plank table until they heard a car in the yard. Liza and Martin jumped up and looked out. Her father and Mr. Samuels got out of the doctor's car. Mrs. Owenby went over to speak to them. When the men gave her Martin's news her shoulders rose in delight and then fell, her arms sweeping right, toward the fields where Mr. Owenby was finishing his day. Beside Liza, Martin's breath came faster. The adults walked toward the house, and she and Martin rushed back to their seats.

The house shook when her father and Mr. Samuels stepped on the porch and opened the door. Mrs. Owenby came in behind them. She put a hand on Martin's shoulder. "I'm so proud." She went over to a cabinet and pulled out a pitcher of water and stacked metal cups.

"Nell, don't let us put you out," Liza's father said.

"You're not putting me out." She set the cups down on the uneven table and they fell over, clanging like bells. Martin grabbed them and set them upright. Mrs. Owenby poured water for Liza's father and Mr. Samuels and raised her eyebrows at the young people to see if they wanted any. They shook their heads.

To make room for Liza's father and Mr. Samuels on the far side of the table, Hodge moved so that he and Liza flanked Martin on the opposite bench. Mr. Samuels and Liza's father slid into their bench, their knees jostling the table. Mrs. Owenby took a chair facing the door, as if she didn't feel entitled to more space. Her hands played in her lap. "Rory will be along directly."

"We're not in a hurry," Liza's father said.

"I hope we're not imposing," Mr. Samuels said.

"I appreciate you coming. I just don't know what Rory is going to say."

Liza's father sipped his water. "That rose of Sharon in your garden is the finest I've seen, Nell."

"My grandmother brought it with her from Virginia, it's that old."

"I'd love a clipping someday when you have time."

"Get you one on the way out."

A silence ensued that even the doctor's good manners couldn't break. Liza, Martin, and Hodge all stared down at their books.

Footsteps pounded on the porch. Mrs. Owenby jumped. The door banged open. Mr. Owenby held onto the doorjamb with one hand and used the threshold to wipe mud off his boots. He was a balding version of Leon, but whereas Leon's face sometimes gave up a smile, Liza had never seen Mr. Owenby smile. He worked, he went to church, he worked some more. He had no time for foolishness. He looked up and saw Liza's father and Mr. Samuels. "Somebody sick?"

Under the table Liza grabbed Martin's cold hand.

Her father was up, headed toward Mr. Owenby with his arm outstretched, shaking Mr. Owenby's hand before the man could think to refuse.

Mrs. Owenby stood up behind her chair.

Mr. Owenby looked at the crowd of people in his kitchen. "What's all this?"

"Rory, Martin has something to tell you." Liza's father nodded to Martin.

Martin's face flushed pink. He kept his eyes down. "I got into college, Pop."

"College?" Mr. Owenby repeated the word as if Martin had spoken French.

"The University of North Carolina at Chapel Hill," Mr. Samuels said.

Liza's father spoke up. "Rory, I want you to understand what this boy has achieved. Not every student can get into the university. He has a fine mind. There's no end to what he might accomplish if he goes."

While Liza's father talked, Mr. Owenby shook his head, shaking off the words. "He ain't going to no college."

Mr. Samuels struggled to get his legs out from under the table so he could stand up. "Sir, if cost is the issue—"

"I don't care if it's free. He's already had more schooling than a man needs."

"Rory, I know you never had need of an education yourself—you're a self-made man," said Liza's father. "But times are changing. Young people today need an education to compete."

"I believe the doctor's right, Rory."

Liza was so unused to Mrs. Owenby speaking in Mr. Owenby's presence that at first she didn't recognize her voice.

Mrs. Owenby's hand fluttered from her throat down the front of her dress. "Martin's smart. He can make something of himself."

"You saying I ain't made something of myself?"

Mrs. Owenby shrank back, holding the back of a chair in front of her, as if its slats could protect her. Eyes down, she said so softly they could hardly hear, "I believe he ought to go."

As quietly as she said it, the fact that she spoke at all made her words resound. Then, as if she had used up everything she had to speak up that once, she receded, brown and gray, almost invisible against the floor boards and furnishings of the unlit room.

"He ain't going. And I'll thank y'all to leave now."

Liza heard Martin let out a breath he'd been holding. He looked at his father. "I am going. I am going, Pop."

Mr. Owenby stared at him. Martin didn't flinch. Hodge moved closer to Martin, shifting the bench. Wood screeched on wood, deciding something. Mr. Owenby's hands dropped to his sides. "You'll get no help from me. You're no 'count, boy." He turned and stomped toward the door, dirt clods from his work boots leaving a Hansel and Gretel trail behind him.

"I'll work the summer for you," Martin called after him, but Mr. Owenby didn't turn around.

Mrs. Owenby sat down at the kitchen table, blinking, trying not to cry. Martin reached across the table and put his hand over hers. "It's all right, Mama."

"Nell, you've got a special boy there. You've done the right thing," Liza's father said.

"Y'all best be going," Mrs. Owenby said. Hodge scrambled to obey.

Before standing up, Liza whispered in Martin's ear, "Meet me at the bottom of your road at ten." He nodded.

She and Hodge followed her father and Mr. Samuels outside. The yard was completely quiet and still. Not even a chicken clucked.

"Do you think he'll be safe?" Mr. Samuels asked in a low voice. Liza's father just shook his head.

That night Liza pulled the Sunliner over to the shoulder at the bottom of the road that led to the Owenby farm and turned off the engine, leaving the headlights on. She opened the car door and stretched her legs out. The Owenbys were all in bed. No one else would come up this road.

What humans called silence was really layered sound. The rustle of leaves in light wind, a bark from a dog up the hill, insect scrapings that overlapped like the mixed-up radio signals her car antennae pulled from air coming up Bostic Mountain. The smells, too, were layered—first fetid undergrowth, then, with a lift of the wind, the open smell of new mowing in a field to her left, a hint of crab apple blossom.

She sat watching moths play in the dusty beams of her headlights until Martin came into view, moving slowly down the hill. She turned the lights off, making the car invisible, and walked toward him on the dirt road.

She couldn't see well in the dark. When she kissed him his lips were swollen and she tasted blood.

He yelped and held his hands up to keep her away. "I'm sorry. I'm sorry. It hurts. Please don't touch me." He reached out a finger and trailed it down her arm. "It wasn't too bad. I'll be all right tomorrow. That's the last beating I'm taking from him."

She stood two inches from him. The heat from their skin formed a magnetic repulsion, allowing them to get only so close. He was a voice in the dark.

16

Martin

Martin woke up hungover, mouth dry. Another gray winter morning in the city. Behind the shade of his tiny bedroom window pigeons elbowed the glass. He threw a pillow, and their stupid cooing stopped. He checked his alarm clock. Ten-thirty. Dennis would be at work at his antiques shop. The apartment was quiet, except for a rush of water when the tenant above flushed the toilet. He swung his legs off the bed and sat up, checking his image in the mirror over his dresser. It wasn't pretty. His eyes were puffy, whiskers grew in patches, he suffered from bed head. He stood up, turning away so he wouldn't have to look at himself, and made his way to the kitchen, feeling every stiff muscle.

The light on the answering machine blinked—seven new messages. He hit the play button. One collection agent after another, wanting to know why he hadn't paid his credit card bills. He deleted them, knowing there would be more before the end of the day. Yesterday he had finished the only freelance job to come in since his trip to North Carolina two months ago, an updated edition of a manual he'd edited before, the changes so slight he'd actually finished it on schedule without having to make excuses. He had nothing else lined up, and the dry spell was starting to worry him. His plan for the day, his only plan, was to deliver the edits to his client in person in the hope of rounding up more work.

He opened the refrigerator. Dennis had taped a big note to the top shelf. "Buy your own food!" He ignored it and poured himself a glass of Dennis's orange juice, the only thing he could stomach. He washed the glass and put it away to hide his crime, then took a shower to get the smell of Scotch off and got dressed to pay a call on his client.

He caught the subway at Fourteenth Street. Ever since his return from North Carolina, he'd felt as if his train face had atrophied. He was marked. Odd people singled him out for conversation. An old man whose speech he couldn't understand tried to say something to him and handed him a card proclaiming Saturday the true Sabbath. A nicely made-up woman with her hair tied back in a classic bun told him that aliens were speaking to her through her wisdom teeth. He was glad when the train reached Fifty-third Street and he could escape.

The Christmas tree was up at Rockefeller Center, and the tourists were in for the season. The software company he did most of his work for had two floors in a modern glass office building on Forty-ninth Street with an option to expand to a third. They were growing and had kept Martin fed the past few years, translating their user manuals into plain English. His contact, Arnie Lloyd, was on the eighth floor. Martin got off the elevator. The receptionist and another woman were using a ladder to hang evergreen garlands around the reception area. Someone had laid out a long table of holiday food and bowls of green and red punch. The receptionist waved a sprig of mistletoe at him from up on the ladder. "Hi, Martin. Can I interest you?"

"Sorry, I'm afraid of heights."

"Oh, well. Go on back. Arnie's expecting you."

He walked down the hall. The offices on either side had glass windows, so anyone could peer in and see the occupant working. Or not working. He wondered what they did when they needed to put a head down for a nap or pick a nose. Were they really reading official reports, or had they tucked a *Mad* magazine inside? He reached Arnie's office. Arnie sat at his neat desk, engrossed in reading a document. A real document, not a *Mad* magazine. Martin tapped on the glass, and Arnie waved him in with a smile.

"Season's greetings, Martin!" Arnie was tall and slender. He looked like an old book jacket photo of J. D. Salinger but without the angst. His cropped hair and dark suit were more 1950s ad man than 1980s anything. He performed a valuable service for his company, as a liaison between the public and the hackers that came up with new products for the expanding personal computer market.

He got up and Martin shook his hand. "Arnold. Got all your holiday shopping done?"

"Gift certificates, my boy. Gift certificates are the way to go. Have a seat." Arnie motioned to one of the sleek black leather chairs that faced him.

Martin handed him the floppy disk with his edits and sat down. "Let me know if there's anything else you need on that."

Arnie put the floppy in his inbox. "I'm sure it's fine."

Martin marveled again at the absolute cleanliness of the office, the lack of a single fingerprint on the glass top of the desk, and yet Arnie didn't wince when, without thinking, Martin picked up a glass paperweight and examined it. Martin put it back down.

"Your roommate told me about your brother. Terrible, terrible thing," Arnie said.

Martin made an appropriate grunt, not wanting to talk about Leon. "I have some free time, Arnie, if you have any other projects for me. I'm not planning to go anywhere over the holidays."

Arnie got a pained look on his face. "Actually, I need to talk to you about that. The company is making a change. We're getting so big, the higher-ups have decided to take editing in-house. No more freelancers, unless we really get buried. I might have something for you once in a while, but I wouldn't want you to count on it."

It was a blow. Martin came back as best he could. "Have you hired your in-house people yet?"

"Two gals fresh out of school, anxious to get to the city, willing to work for nothing. You wouldn't want to work for what we're paying them."

Martin couldn't be mad at Arnie. He wasn't really interested in working for anybody nine to five. The hours would interfere too much with his hangover recovery schedule. He had a feeling Arnie knew this.

"I'm really sorry, Martin. It wasn't my choice. I'll make sure we get you paid for this last job before Christmas."

"Don't feel bad." Martin stood up and shook Arnie's hand. "Do keep me in mind if anything comes up."

"I will, you'd better believe it. And anytime you need a reference, have them call me. I mean it." He came around to Martin's side of the desk and clapped him on the back. "Hey, our holiday party starts in fifteen minutes. Why don't you stay?"

The offer of free refreshment was tempting, but Martin couldn't see introducing himself to strangers as the technical editor the company just canned. "Thanks, but I have a few more clients I need to see today."

Arnie wished him luck, and Martin saw himself out. On the street, he stopped and breathed cold air. Arnie's firm wasn't just his biggest client. It was his only client. If he had been a more ambitious person, he wouldn't have allowed himself to become so dependent. He didn't have the energy or initiative to round up new work. No one hired this time of year anyway. They were all too busy clearing the decks for their Christmas vacations.

People passed him on the sidewalk, noses red and dripping from the cold, shopping bags full of Christmas gifts. A bag lady stopped a few feet away, singing to herself. A dirty pink Barbie suitcase held her worldly goods. Her skull showed through the parchment-thin skin of her face, no fat left to humanize her deep eye sockets and sharp cheekbones. She rocked as she sang.

Martin's mother had grown thin like that toward the end, but he had been too self-absorbed to notice.

The week before he left for college, as he repacked his duffel bag for the tenth time in the attic room he shared with James and Leon, he could hear his mother downstairs with Eugenia and Ivy, trying to reason with Shane.

"Those biscuits are for supper," she said.

"But I *want* one," Shane wailed.

"Honestly, Mama, if one of us had acted like that, you would have tanned our hides," Eugenia said.

"He's just little," Martin's mother said.

Martin closed his bag and went downstairs. Shane was sitting on the floor, kicking his legs. He started to scream.

"Stop that," Eugenia said, without going near him. Eugenia was married but had been coming over to help their mother around the house.

Ivy moved from the corner where she was peeling potatoes and bent over Shane, murmuring softly. He rolled away from her but stopped squalling. "Let me take him outside," Ivy said.

"You know I can't do that." Martin's mother reached down for Shane's arm and tried to pull him up, then gasped and grabbed her side. She let go of Shane and leaned on the back of a chair, her eyes closed. Pain carved lines at the corners of her mouth.

"Are you all right, Mama?" Eugenia said.

"I'm fine." His mother spoke without opening her eyes. "Martin, can you play with him for a while?"

"I'm supposed to meet Liza and Hodge. It's my last chance to see them before I leave." His voice sounded almost as whiny as Shane's.

"Eugenia?" Mama said.

"Oh, all right." Eugenia stomped over to Shane and hoisted him up. "But I hope when I have children I don't have to depend on other people to take care of them." She dragged Shane by one arm toward the door, his bare feet sliding along the splintery floor. Shane began to screech again, reaching out his free arm to Ivy. She started toward him, but their mother stopped her. "Potatoes, Ivy."

Afternoon sunlight beckoned Martin. He followed Eugenia and Shane outside and then half-ran down the road, not stopping until he had rounded the bend at the bottom and was safe from anyone else asking him to do anything.

The bag lady finished her song, and gave Martin a hopeful smile. Her teeth were terrible. "Spare any change?"

He patted his empty pockets. "Wish I could."

She shrugged and rolled her suitcase down the street.

He put his hands in his coat pockets and began walking, lowering his head against the wind. There was nothing for it but to go home and have a drink.

17

Ivy

I stand in my nice big laundry room, pretreating old Mrs. Larson's favorite polyester blouse. Grandmother Alma sits and spins in the corner of the kitchen near the open laundry room door. Her black dress gathers lint.

When Steven built the house for me, he made it all one level so I didn't have to carry laundry up or down stairs, and he put in a commercial-size washer and dryer. I like doing laundry for old folks. It helps them out and gives me some extra walking-around money. Old people don't have too many clothes. Most of them don't do enough to get sweaty or dirty, so they can wear things more than once. Except that Mrs. Larson does tend to drop food on herself and can't see it, so I have to pretreat. I pull old lady nylon underpants out of the dryer and peel them apart, listening to the static. I like the smell an electric dryer leaves, the softness of the clothes when they first come out. If I'd had a dryer when my babies were little, I'd have warmed a towel for them after every bath, winter and summer.

The laundry money, all cash, helps stretch my disability check. Hodge found a lawyer to help me get my disability a few years ago. My bad knees weren't enough by themselves, so the lawyer used what he called my mental health history.

Being called crazy had never got me anything but grief before. I figured if it would get me something from the government after the government had taken so much away from me, I'd do it.

My disability hearing was in front of a judge but not in a regular courtroom. They stuck us in a room that looked like the court people used it mostly for storage. Lots of files and empty boxes, and a long conference table squeezed in the middle, wired with a microphone to record what we said. I told it to the judge flat, all about the ghosts I saw. The judge was polite while I told him about my regulars, Alma and Missouri. I didn't mention Shane. Then I told him about the one ghost I saw in the room with us, a tall, bent-over fellow with old-fashioned glasses, who was very busy with the files in the room. I described him down to the rough brown wool of his trousers and the smell of tonic on his neat-parted hair. I told how he stood behind the judge like a page-turner behind a church organist, putting papers down on the table for the judge to look at. He took his job seriously, even though the judge couldn't see him or his papers. When I told that part the judge got real still and thoughtful. Anyway, he decided I was crazy enough not to be able to do gainful work and gave me my benefits. It's not a lot because I never earned much, doing factory work and cleaning motels, but between the disability check and laundry money, and Steven paying my mortgage, I get by. They send my disability checks to Steven, but he knows I'm not crazy and hands them right over to me.

Alma has been quiet all morning without Missouri here to rile her. Then, as I pull the next wet load out of the washer, she speaks out of nowhere, "They say your Steven did it."

"Did what?" I drop the clothes in a basket.

"Leon."

I stop what I'm doing, hurt. "Who says it?"

"I hear the whisperings."

"He never did." I untangle Mrs. Larson's worn-out brassiere from around my washing machine agitator and pull it out. Alma's fingers twirl thread. I wonder how much thread she has spun since she passed on and what she does with all of it. "You're as bad as Missouri, weaving trouble," I say.

"I tell you for your own good," Alma says, righteous. "Your sister, Eugenia, has been running her mouth, talking about that knuckle knife being missing."

When she says it I see the knife in my mind. It was made for slashing, but I've seen Leon use it for everything from pounding tomato stakes to picking his teeth.

"Your Steven has the knife."

I drop Mrs. Larson's bra into the basket and stand there with my arms hanging down.

"Don't stare at me like a stupid cow." Alma picks a piece of lint from between her blue teeth. "I just done you a favor."

Missouri appears with a flounce in the doorway between the kitchen and living room, a young woman as usual. She shakes her red hair like a show pony. Alma's look tells me not to mention the knife in front of Missouri. Missouri wears a store-bought dress of pink cotton, paid for with money from a source she will not name. Her small hands love the creases in the skirt. She holds the skirt out in front of her. "Press this for me."

Alma makes a disapproving noise.

"I can't." I untie my apron. "I'm just on my way to see Steven."

Missouri stamps her foot.

I know the trouble she can cause. "All right." I get my hand-held steamer down off the shelf above the washer and plug it in. Missouri loves the steamer. If they had had such things in her time, she would have owned one. When the steamer is ready I run it down her skirt, all around.

"Ow! Don't char me, girl," she says.

"Sorry." I squat down to get the wrinkles near the bottom. My knees crack. Missouri doesn't care that I might not be able to get back up.

"Why you going to Steven's?"

"Just to visit." Steam pours out in a stream. I concentrate on her hemline.

"There's a gathering over there."

I look up at her.

Her face is wicked. "The sheriff's over there, talking to him."

Alma's spinning wheel stops. I stand up, knees aching, and pull the steamer cord out of the wall. I get my apron off and pick up my pocketbook and car keys off the counter. I walk out of my house without locking it.

"Hey!" Missouri calls after me. "What about my dress?"

18

Liza

Liza drove her truck toward Steven Owenby's body shop, with wind whistling annoyingly through a space at the bottom of her driver's-side door. Her older daughter, Sandra, had had an accident at the mall the day before, and now the truck door wouldn't close properly. Liza pulled one of her gloves off with her teeth and stuffed it against the crack to try to stop the noise. It didn't work.

"Mom, I'm *so* sorry," Sandra had said. "There was this low wall in the mall parking lot, and I didn't see it. The truck door scraped right over it, and then I had to pull it loose." She was close to tears.

"These things happen." Liza ran her hand along the bottom of the driver's-side door to feel the damage. With a teenage daughter driving it was a wonder her truck didn't have more dents and scrapes.

Her husband, Raby, squatted down to get a better look, then stood up and closed and opened the door a couple of times. "I'm afraid if I try to bend it back out I'll make it worse."

"I can take it to Steven Owenby's body shop tomorrow before work. Somebody there can give me a ride to school. I don't have a first-period class," Liza said.

"Am I in trouble?" Sandra said.

"It's coming out of your Christmas money," Raby said.

"Dad!"

He poked her in the ribs. "I'm just kidding. Can't you crazy women take a joke?"

At Steven's body shop, Liza eased her truck between cars that were parked in the small front parking lot, ready to be worked on. Someone had sprayed the windows of the little office with artificial snow, spelling out "Merry Christmas!" She went in. Martin's niece Trina was on the phone, ordering a part. She waved. Liza worked her key off her key ring. The office smelled of acetone, motor oil, other vital fluids.

Trina hung up the phone. "Hey, Miz Barnard. What can we do for you today?"

Liza handed her the truck key. "My daughter bent the bottom of the door. It doesn't close securely."

"Steven!" Trina called.

Steven came out of the garage. "What's up, Miz Barnard?"

"Her truck door's bent," Trina said.

"Let's take a look."

He went outside with Liza and examined the door. "We can probably get it done for you today. It might not even need any paint."

"That would be great."

As they stood there, a sheriff's cruiser pulled in right next to Liza's truck. Wally Metcalf was driving, with Hodge as his passenger. They got out of the car and walked over. Hodge looked uncomfortable.

Wally nodded. "Steven, Miz Barnard."

"How's it going, Sheriff?" Steven peered behind the sheriff at the patrol car. "Got a problem with your vehicle?"

"No, the car's fine. I need to ask you some questions, son."

Steven wiped his hands on his coveralls. "Go ahead."

Trina came out of the office and stood with Steven.

"It's about a knife Leon had. With brass knuckles for a handle. About this long." Wally held up his hands to illustrate. "You know what I'm talking about?"

"Yes, sir."

"A customer saw you with it at the shop this week. He recognized it as being Leon's and mentioned it to me."

"What customer was that?"

"I'm not going to tell you."

"Well, I wasn't trying to hide the knife. Leon gave it to me. I can use it if I want."

The noise from the garage behind them had stopped. Steven's two employees leaned in the open bay doors, listening.

"When did he give it to you?" Wally said.

"A few weeks before he went missing."

"Did anybody ever see you with it before he went missing?"

"I did," Trina said quickly. "Several times."

Liza didn't believe Trina, but she approved of the lie. She knew Steven was telling the truth. He wouldn't harm Leon.

"I understand that knife meant a lot to him. Why'd he give it to you?"

Steven crossed his arms. "I didn't ask him why. I got the feeling he was just ready to pass it on."

A beige Pontiac pulled into the last open spot in the parking lot, and Ivy Owenby got out. Her normally placid face was anxious, and she hadn't taken the time to put on a coat. She went right to Steven and Trina, her breath wheezing.

"They're asking Steven about Leon's knuckle knife, Mama.

You know, the one Leon gave him back in the summer?"
Trina said pointedly.

"Don't do that, Trina," Wally said.

Ivy recovered her breath. "Sheriff, Leon was giving stuff away right there at the end before he went missing. He gave me twelve hundred dollars, after never giving me a thing in my life."

"It's true, Wally," Hodge said. "I told you he was thinking of giving his truck to James's boy, Bobby. He hadn't decided on it yet, but at least he was thinking about it. Leon didn't spend a big part of his life thinking about giving people things."

Wally sighed. "Where's the knife, now, Steven?"

"Hanging in there above my work bench. I'll get it for you."

"I'll get it." Wally pulled a plastic evidence bag out of his pocket and went into the garage.

Hodge stepped closer. "Steven, did Leon say anything when he gave you the knife?"

Steven glanced toward the garage then back. "It was weird, Hodge. You know Leon wasn't a talker. I never heard him tell one tale about the war, but when he gave me that knife something opened him up like a spigot. The man was crying, talking about how the skin on his chest peeled up. Said he saw his heart beating in his chest, but the doctors told him it didn't go that deep and he imagined it. Embarrassed the hell out of me. I don't know what to do with a crying man."

Wally came out of the garage, carrying the knife in the plastic bag. The knife was cruel looking, the brass knuckles tarnished and scratched with use. "I've got to take it to have tests run. Don't leave town without telling me, Steven."

Steven had had enough. He opened his mouth to give the

sheriff what for, but Hodge put a hand on his arm. "You weren't planning to go anywhere anyway. Don't get upset."

"Shit," Steven said to Wally. "Why don't you do some real police work and find out what happened to Leon instead of harassing me?"

"We're doing our best," Wally said. "Hodge, you ready to go?"

Hodge gave Steven's arm a squeeze. "I'll check in with y'all later." He and Wally got back in their car. Wally backed out carefully so he wouldn't scrape Ivy's car. Nobody moved to help guide him.

When the patrol car had driven off, Steven turned to Liza. "Come on, Miz Barnard. I'll carry you over to the high school."

Liza followed him to the curb where his tow truck was parked and climbed up into the cab. Steven fumbled in his pocket for his keys. When he pulled them out his hands were shaking. He started the engine and moved slowly into the street. Liza looked back. Ivy still stood with Trina in the body shop's parking lot, hugging herself to keep warm.

Liza wondered how Ivy had known to come.

19

Bertie

Bertie could never get warm this time of year, when the days were so short. The sun was fickle, by midafternoon snatching back any warmth it had allowed, the trailer's shadow darkening dead grass in the yard. A few snowflakes floated in the dry air, disappearing before they hit the ground. The sight of them made her feel even colder. She knew it was just her. She had the heat set on seventy-eight while she worked with James on the Christmas decorations, and James was peeled down to his undershirt and still sweating as he twisted branches into the artificial tree.

Making much of decorating for Christmas was something she and James had agreed on early in their marriage. They had to learn how from television and magazine pictures because their own families hadn't paid any attention to it. Bertie never was completely sure she'd got it right, but the kids didn't know the difference. Bobby and the girls always had a nice Christmas, at least one big present they really wanted even if it took until March to pay it off.

Usually James was as into the decorating as she was, but this year she'd felt shy about asking him to help. He was quiet as he put the tree together, staring at nothing while his hands inserted the branches. Bertie opened a cardboard box, lifting out familiar ornaments, wanting to hold up each one to ask James if he remembered. At the bottom of the box were broken bits of ornaments her children had made when they were little—Popsicle sticks with glue hardened at the ends, cotton balls from a long-lost Santa's beard, green and red construction paper, faded and curled. Bertie couldn't bear to throw the pieces away, especially the things Bobby had made, when he was still little and sweet and she held out all the hope in the world for him.

A car drove up outside, and Leon's dogs started barking. Through the window Bertie saw Eugenia getting out of her Mercury, using all of her strength to shut the heavy car door behind her.

"Who is it?" James asked.

"Your sister." Eugenia didn't just drop in to see them for no reason, and Bertie was suddenly afraid. Hodge had called them about finding Leon's knuckle knife at Steven's shop. The sheriff was supposed to have it tested. She glanced over at James, wanting to shield him from any bad news Eugenia might bring. She went to open the door before Eugenia could knock.

"I've about had it with this weather," Eugenia said. Snowflakes rested on the faux fur of her coat collar before melting in the heat of the kitchen. Bertie let her in, relieved. Eugenia wouldn't waste time complaining about the cold if she had something bad to report about Leon.

James came into the kitchen. "What's going on?"

Eugenia's glasses had fogged up. She took them off and wiped them with a glove, then put them on again. "You heard about the knife?"

"Yes. Anything new today?"

"Not about that, but look." Eugenia pulled an envelope out

of her pocket. "You know I had Leon's mail forwarded to us. He hasn't gotten much, just one Social Security check before I called and told them to stop, but then today this came." She handed the envelope to James. Bertie stood beside him so she could see. The return address was some medical place in Lenoir, the Imaging Center. James pulled out the paper inside.

"It's a bill," Eugenia said. "For diagnostic services."

Bertie looked at the bill, for $648, from a date back in August. Leon had never cottoned much to doctors. He could have gone to the VA for free, if he'd wanted to drive to Asheville, but he seemed to believe, like a lot of older folks did, more in dancing by the light of the moon than going to a doctor.

"What's 'diagnostic services'?" James asked.

"I called to ask, and they wouldn't tell me anything. The girl said I had to have an authorization signed by Leon. I told her I couldn't very well get him to sign anything, seeing as he was missing. Then she said I'd have to get the sheriff to subpoena the records." Eugenia unbuttoned her coat. "I called the sheriff and gave him the account number. He's going to get those records and also see if Leon went to the emergency room for anything around that time. Sometimes it's the emergency room that refers people to this Imaging Center."

"Why wouldn't he tell us if he was sick?" James's face looked tortured.

Bertie pointed to the bill. "What do they do at that place, anyway?"

"The sheriff said X-rays, MRIs, CT scans." Eugenia rattled off the list like she knew what she was talking about. Bertie had heard of X-rays. She wasn't sure what those other things were and didn't think James knew either.

"I told the girl at the Imaging Center she better not expect us to pay this bill if she wouldn't tell me what it was for," Eugenia said.

"I don't think we'd be responsible for paying it," Bertie said. Leave it to Eugenia to worry more about that than about what the medical records might show.

"Y'all excuse me." James put the medical bill down on the table and went outside. Bertie could see him through the kitchen window, just standing there in the yard looking up at the sky, his ears turning red with cold. His nice thick coat hung on the back of a kitchen chair, not doing him any good at all.

Eugenia put the bill back in her pocket. "I bet you're relieved they caught Steven with that knife."

"I don't follow you," Bertie said.

"It takes the suspicion off Bobby."

Bertie crossed her arms. "Who says suspicion was on Bobby in the first place?"

"Now, come on, Bertie."

Eugenia had a lot of nerve. "If James was standing here you wouldn't be talking ugly about his son like that," Bertie said.

"About his son?" Eugenia looked at Bertie over the top of her glasses. Her little nostrils flared, like she smelled something bad. "If you say so." She opened the door and stepped outside before Bertie could answer, stopping in the yard to speak to James.

Bertie pushed the door closed, harder than she had to. Nobody held it against her the way Eugenia did, not even James, who had the right. She wished she could grab Eugenia by her scrawny throat and explain it to her, make her listen.

There was one good part of Bertie's life, when her youth bloomed, her skin was buttermilk smooth, and the curves of her rump and breasts and calves drew wanting looks from every man in the county. Her hair curled soft in the 1940s perm Willoby County girls still wore a decade later. She dressed herself up in ribbons and nylons bought at a discount at the five-and-dime where she worked in Lenoir, her money all her own. She shared a room with two other working girls. They rubbed each other's feet at night, complaining about their bosses but as happy as could be to be free of parents and answerable to nobody but themselves, a precious selfishness. They spoke aloud daydreams of moving on to Winston or Raleigh, of meeting handsome, wealthy men, of brick homes in Cameron Park and maids to stroll their children.

Bertie thought the blooming was forever, a hard-won reward she'd earned for living through a childhood of deprivation and her father's violence. Nobody told her it would pass in a blink like the blush of a morning glory.

She chose James because he was handsome and good, didn't drink too much, and because if she squinted her mind's eye, she could fit James into the daydreams she clutched at the way a child does her blanket.

Her looks weren't the type that survives past girlhood, that require fine bones to hold skin in place. Jowls sagged and eyes sank in, the deepness of the lines at the corners surprising her anew every morning. It happened so fast. One day, one minute, even, she was getting the up-and-down from the boys at Riddle's general store. The next, nobody was looking at her anymore. She had to give up the daydreams she'd carried into her marriage because she couldn't play the parts any longer. She was too heavy-hipped and old for her fantasy heroes to love. Birthing two big-headed babies had made it so she wet herself when she laughed or picked up something heavy. When she should have been enjoying her husband and daughters, instead she watched her life burn like a wad of newspaper thrown on a fire, one last grand flame passing into gray ash, with her hollering after it, "Wait! Wait!"

She did it to bring herself back.

All it took was one appreciating look from a man she hadn't paid any attention to before, a rascal who didn't care what anybody thought. Riding along with him, with her elbow out the window of his truck, Bertie felt how beautifully her hair blew back. Everything she said seemed clever, sexy. Afterward, the he-say-her-say was that she'd run off to the Peabody Hotel in Memphis, the one with the duck fountain in the lobby. Bertie let the rumor stand. Really they'd stayed at a motor court outside of Asheville. It wasn't fancy, but somebody else cleaned up after them, and when she stretched out on her side on top of the sheets she found again the lovely curve her pelvic bone made, a smooth ridge that disappeared into extra pounds when she lay any other way.

For three nights and three nights only, she had it all again. Then the fourth morning she woke up and saw an ordinary man. Bad breath. Snoring. Coarse black hair growing ugly all over him. He was as embarrassed as she was. Later that day, he took her to the bus station and gave her twenty dollars for the ticket home.

James came and got her at the station. He cried himself into hiccups and she just held his head. She saw that time had folded the corners of his eyes as well, but a man doesn't disappear when sun creases his face or his hair grays or thins. As deep as his hurt went, it couldn't touch what she herself had lost.

James's mouth shook the whole drive home. They reached the trailer at dusk. Her peonies had blossomed while she was gone, and lines of ants followed their sweet smell, swarming the beds. Her parents' screen door opened, and Bertie's older girl, Dacey, came running across the road to hug her. Her younger, Sue, toddled along behind, already not quite sure who Bertie was. Bertie tried to feel joy, but all she felt was despair. It would have been better if James had written her off then, instead of taking it upon himself to make things right for her. She had stolen his life as she'd wasted hers, never feeling anything good inside, and worse, not able to pretend for him. James never said another word about it, even when she told him she was pregnant and he had to know the baby wasn't his. He had always claimed Bobby as his own, no matter what kind of mess Bobby got into.

Bertie looked out the kitchen window, where Eugenia had finished talking to James and was getting into her car. Eugenia had planted doubt in Bertie's mind, as she'd meant to. Or maybe she'd just uncovered doubts that were already there. It was true that Bobby was frustrated with Leon for not letting him put a mobile home on the family property. Bobby wasn't at a job the week Leon disappeared. And Bobby wasn't above stealing from family—Bertie didn't keep more than ten dollars in her purse for that reason. Bertie didn't think Bobby had it in him to plan anything against Leon, but she could see him going along. Going along with Cherise LaFaye.

20

Martin

The day before Christmas eve, Martin got up late, as usual. Dennis had left the mail in a pile on the kitchen counter, with the power and gas and phone bills conspicuously displayed. Martin flipped through the stack. Collection notices and two new credit card offers from companies who hadn't researched his payment history. He saved them. The last envelope contained a check from Arnie for $1,028 for his last editing job. There wouldn't be any more checks. He folded the envelope and stuck it in his pocket.

Dennis's key fumbled in the lock. Martin let him in. Dennis mouth-breathed from the climb up the stairs and deposited plastic grocery bags on the kitchen counter. "Those stairs are going to kill me."

Martin poked through the grocery bags and could tell it annoyed Dennis.

"I'm cooking an early Christmas dinner for some friends. I didn't really buy enough for you," Dennis said.

"I'll eat out."

Dennis looked relieved. He pressed the answering machine message button and began deleting messages from creditors, hitting the delete button again and again, with a look of distaste, as if crushing roaches. "I'm fed up, Martin. You're two months behind on the rent. What do you plan to do?"

"Things will pick up in January. Nobody hires this time of year."

"How do you expect to find work when you spend all your time drunk or sleeping it off?"

The doorbell buzzed. Martin walked over and looked through the peephole. Their neighbor from 3B, Mrs. Shapiro, peered up at him. The peephole distorted her already long face. He opened the door. Mrs. Shapiro came up to his chest. She had dyed her hair an unlikely lioness color. Her wrinkled face was peeling from a recent sunburn.

"Martin, the mailman delivered this to my apartment by mistake." She handed him a flat padded manila envelope. The return address was Leon Owenby, the handwriting the big stick letters of someone who rarely wrote anything. Leon had mailed it book rate, the cheapest available. Grease spots dotted the outside. It was postmarked October 1, a week before he disappeared.

"How long have you had this?" he said.

"It came while I was in Florida, visiting my daughter. I'm sorry, the girl getting my mail must not have noticed it was yours. I hope it's nothing important."

"It's fine, Mrs. Shapiro. Thanks for bringing it over."

"Not a problem. Hello, Dennis." She waved at him from the door.

"Hello, Mrs. Shapiro, glad you're back," Dennis said.

Mrs. Shapiro reached up and patted Martin's cheek. "Happy holidays, boys." She turned to leave.

"You, too." Martin closed the door and locked it behind her.

He opened the envelope, and Leon's smell put him right

there in the room. Kerosene and cigar smoke. The shock of it made Martin sit down on the couch. He reached inside the envelope and pulled out what Leon had sent, recognizing it immediately by the worn cardboard cover and his mother's slender handwriting. It was her ledger, the book she used to keep account of her egg money and expenses. His mother was proud that she could read and write and cipher. Martin had assumed his father burned the ledger after she died. He opened it. The binding cracked. A flattened silverfish formed a fossil on the front page, but the book was in good condition. She had recorded her money, not the household's, income neat in one column and expenses in the next, starting in 1942 and going until she died, in 1954. He folded back yellowing paper and found the year he left for college, the ten dollars she sent him to buy a new shirt for his play.

Dennis looked over Martin's shoulder with interest. "Whose was it?" He reached down to touch it, and Martin moved the ledger away from him.

"My mother's."

Dennis withdrew his stubby fingers. "I have at least two clients who would kill for something like that."

Martin gently flipped the pages. He wanted an explanation but knew he would never have one. Leon wasn't a diarist. He wouldn't include even a note. Had he saved the ledger from their father's fire or come across it later? Had it meant something to him? Was their mother dear to Leon after all, this Esau brother of the fields?

In the back, another envelope. Martin took it out. The rusty clasp broke in his hand when he undid it. He gently shook the contents into his lap. Photographs. Small, square black-and-whites with white borders, stuck to each other in spots, all with the same June 1958 development date. He separated them carefully. They were mostly of one young woman. He didn't recognize her. Leon was a poor photographer, with no concept of lighting. The woman's face was in shadow in every picture. Only her teeth gleamed white in a smile. A button-down blouse with the tails tied above her navel showed her midriff. In some shots she stretched her pretty legs out like a pinup girl. There were a few photos of Leon, tall and smiling, as though he were getting away with something. The girl had been a better photographer than Leon. Martin gathered up the photographs to put back in their envelope. He wondered if Leon had meant to send them, or if he had forgotten they were tucked in the back of the ledger.

"I'll pay you a hundred dollars for the book," Dennis said.

Martin held the ledger to his chest.

"You know you need the cash."

"Fuck off, Dennis," he said.

Dennis waved his hands, giving up.

When Dennis's first guest arrived around two o'clock, Martin put on his coat and left the building. He got a cheap meal at a Cuban dive between Fourteenth and Fifteenth streets, then ambled down Eighth Avenue. He had nothing to do. It was cold, but not impossibly so. He passed restaurants, shops, Korean vegetable stands. Vendors yelled, "Whaddelse, Whaddelse!" When he was new to New York he had felt battered by the rudeness, missing the soft southern "What-mayIhepyouwith?"

He turned left onto Christopher Street, gauging how much walking he needed to do before he showed back up at the apartment. In his years in the city he had seen Christopher Street go from sleazy to campy to almost-but-not-quite chic. Just after Sheridan Square he passed the Stonewall Inn.

Stonewall. Whenever two or more gay men of a certain age gathered together in New York City, there would be a discussion of Stonewall. Where were you the night of the riot? Martin always kept his mouth shut because he had run.

He and Dennis were out with a friend of Dennis's that Martin didn't care for, a mouthy guy named Kyle, who favored bell-bottoms and tank tops and wore his hair too long. They weren't at the Stonewall Inn that night. Martin and Dennis were in their thirties. The Stonewall clientele made them feel old. Plus the Stonewall watered the Scotch. They spent the evening at another dive down the street, where the booze was less diluted. Martin drank while Kyle big-talked. Kyle had just been fired from a job for telling off the boss. He yammered on about how his First Amendment right to free speech had been violated. Martin stopped drinking long enough to tell him that the First Amendment only protected him from government action, not a private employer. Kyle might have punched him if a man hadn't rushed through the front door of the bar just then and announced, "They're raiding the Stone-wall."

Martin's first thought was, *Let's get out of here in case we're next.* The cops were known to raid several bars in one night, to convince the public they were doing something about the homosexual problem. You'd be in a bar and the lights would go on, warning you to stop touching your friend. Then the cops would come in. Martin had never been detained, but he dreaded it.

"Come on, man, let's go watch the fun," Kyle said. Dennis got up to follow him.

"Let's just go home, Dennis," Martin said.

"Oh, come on. They can't do anything to us."

Martin tagged along behind Dennis and Kyle. The hot June air carried city smells, diesel exhaust and garbage waiting to be picked up, here and there a waft of food frying.

When they got to the Stonewall, cops were leading the first arrests out. A tall, blond transvestite cursed and screamed at the policeman twisting her arm. A crowd had gathered. Kyle led them up to the front. Men farther back called the cops names from a safe distance. Then people starting tossing pocket change, harmlessly at first, the pennies jingling as they landed at the cops' feet.

"Bullshit," Kyle said. The crowd was too limp-wristed for him. He reached in his pocket and started hurling change, hard, at the cops' heads. He caught one officer in the forehead and drew blood. The cop looked around to see where the projectile had come from. Kyle was out of change. He bent down and picked up a piece of cement that had crumbled from the curb and lobbed it at the police, hitting another officer on the shoulder. Guys around them started doing the same thing, picking up whatever they could find on the ground to throw.

Martin was ready to leave. He turned to Dennis, who was usually as risk averse as he was, but Dennis wore a look of absolute exhilaration. Other faces around them were the same. Something had let loose. Glass shattered as someone broke one of the Stonewall's upstairs windows. The cops who had been inside poured outside to attempt crowd control. A cop lifted his nightstick and caught the first bystander he came to in the side of the head. The man went down. The people near him surged forward.

Martin touched Dennis's elbow. "I'm going home." He ducked through the crowd until he was free of bodies. The sounds of yelling and batons on bone receded. As he walked, fast, he met people heading toward the noise. "What's going on?" He didn't answer.

Back at the apartment, he waited. He thought Dennis would come to his senses and follow him home, but hours went by before he heard the locks rattle. He let in Dennis and Kyle and two other men he didn't know. Kyle's head was split open, but it hadn't shut him up. He was already rehashing his performance. "Did you see the look on that cop's face? I *pounded* him, man." Dennis wet a dishcloth and put it on Kyle's wound, then he and the other guys hopped around the little kitchen, acting out what had happened. Finally, they ran out of stories. Dennis turned to Martin, so satisfied. "Martin, you should have stayed."

Martin always ran.

He ran away from Willoby County at eighteen when his mother needed him. Ran away from Liza and never explained why. Wasn't around for Shane. Ran again when he turned down Hodge's offer and boarded a plane back to New York instead of staying until they found his brother's body. If just once he could stand his ground and do the right thing instead of scuttling away.

Ivy. The first person he let down. The sheriff deputy's arm hard in Martin's puny grip as Martin rode his back. Raw wood splintering along a bedroom doorframe. Ivy sitting in the dirt, her animal cries. His guilt again years later when Shane killed himself and he didn't feel the loss the way he had the first time. When did he lose his outrage? During what drunken blackout did he misplace it? Ivy's matron face was smooth now, scars, if she had them, on the inside.

The cold was getting to him. He pulled his collar up around his throat and headed home, stopping at a liquor store. Dennis's friends were still there when he got back. Dennis tensed up, afraid Martin would crash his party.

"I just need a glass." Martin opened the cabinet.

Dennis's friend Byron sat at their small kitchen table with pillows propped behind his back, so emaciated from AIDS that it hurt him to lean his spine against the wooden chair. "How are you, Martin?" Byron's brown eyes were liquid, like a dog's. This would be his last Christmas.

"I'm good." Martin didn't know what else to say. He carried his booze into his room and closed the door. He could hear them laughing and talking, and fought back childish thoughts that they were laughing at him.

His room was just big enough for a single bed, dresser, and a small desk for his computer. Leon's padded envelope, with the egg book, was on the desk where he'd left it earlier. He tossed it gently onto the bed. He poured a glass of Scotch, took his shoes off, and sat on the bed to take another look at the ledger. He lifted it to his nose, hoping for some scent of his mother, but smelled only mustiness. He looked through the book, carefully examining each page. When he didn't find anything, he did the old Bible trick, closing the ledger and then letting it fall open where it would, to reveal its secrets. It opened to a page filled with ordinary things, sugar purchased and jelly sold at the county fair.

His mother had used a book like this to teach him how to add and subtract, before he started school. She sat at the table, and he stood at her elbow. She pointed to numbers, seventy cents for eggs sold to a neighbor one week, eighty cents the next. "What does it add up to?"

The figures seemed huge to him.

"Now look." She put her thumb over the zeroes in seventy and eighty. "If I cover up the aughts, what's seven and eight together?"

"Fifteen," he said.

She took her thumb away. "Now put back the aught."

He saw what she meant. "One hundred fifty."

"That's it." She turned to a clean page in her ledger and

wrote out $7,000 and $8,000, then handed him her pencil. "Now cross out the aughts."

He took the pencil and marked through the zeroes. "Fifteen. Fifteen thousand."

"You've got it." She reached an arm around him and pulled him in close for a hug.

"Mama."

"What, son?"

"You're never going to sell that many eggs."

Laughter trilled from her throat, tickling his ear.

It had to mean something that Leon had sent the ledger. Paper rustled in Martin's pocket. He took out the envelope containing his last check and fingered it. He remembered the cheap food at the Whelan Bojangles'. His remaining money would go a lot further in North Carolina than it would in New York City, especially if he supplemented it with free meals at his relatives' houses. He could mooch off them until they got tired of him, which was inevitable. If he went back, his brother and sisters couldn't say he was running away from his obligations, though his creditors might have other views. Dennis would be pissed about losing help with the rent, but Martin's help was sporadic at best. And he would no longer have to listen to the constant whispered body counts, who was infected and which Byron or Joe or Tom had died that week.

He left his room and maneuvered around Dennis's company to unplug the kitchen phone. Dennis gave him a look but didn't say anything. Martin took the phone back to his room, plugged it in, and called Hodge. "Is that job at the community college still open?" he said when Hodge answered.

"As far as I know. You gonna take it?" Martin could hear the delight in his friend's voice. Hodge actually wanted him around.

"I think so. Yes."

"That's great, Martin. And you'll stay at our place, right?"

"Can't beat the rent."

"We'll get it cleaned up for you this week. When will you be down?"

"After New Year's." Holidays inflamed emotions. Christmas alone in New York would be better than suffocating around his family. "That'll give me time to tie up things here. Can I ship some stuff to your place?"

"Of course."

"I'll let you know the exact day." Martin paused. "Is Liza ticked at me?"

"A little. You'll have to butter her up once you get back."

"It might take more than butter."

"Flowers, then," Hodge said. "You know she can never stay mad at you long."

"Any more news about Leon?" Martin didn't really want to know but felt he had to ask.

"No answers yet. I'll catch you up when you get here. I'm calling the dean right now. Merry Christmas, buddy!" Hodge hung up.

Martin's room was stuffy. He opened the little window, looking out into the growing darkness at the drab wall of the building next door. It would take no time to wrap up the details of his life here. No employer to give notice to. No bank accounts to close. No friends to say a weepy good-bye. Nothing to pack that he minded losing, except his mother's ledger and his computer, the tool of his trade. He breathed in the cold air coming through the window, trying to separate each city smell, savory and foul, each noise. It should have dismayed him to be leaving such a small ripple in the city he had lived in for so long, but he felt nothing.

A little bird reports that Mr. Martin Owenby,
recently of New York City, will soon be
returning to Willoby County on account of the
tragic disappearance of his brother, Leon
Owenby, age 65. Older readers may recall the
performance of Mr. Martin Owenby's play,
"Second Coming," at the Playmakers Theatre in
Chapel Hill in 1958, for which a substantial
contingent of our local citizenry were in
attendance. Archives of this paper indicate that
upon returning, the mayor, Elijah Ledford, now
deceased, stated that he didn't know quite what
to make of the performance. Other members of the
Willoby party, however, reported that it had
indeed been a cultural experience.

—WILLOBY NEWS & RECORD,
Society Page, January 7, 1987

21

Liza

The phone rang in Liza's kitchen as she and her younger daughter, Alissa, were unloading groceries from her truck. Alissa bolted into the house to answer it. Liza threaded the handles of four plastic grocery bags over her arm and nudged the truck door closed with her shoulder before going inside.

"It's for you." Alissa handed her the phone, sounding disappointed.

Liza dumped the bags on the counter by the refrigerator and took the phone, waving Alissa out of the kitchen. "Hello?"

"I'm back." Martin's voice, so familiar.

"So I heard."

"Still speaking to me?"

She opened the freezer and pushed things aside to make room for the frozen foods she'd bought. "I haven't decided yet." She transferred the phone to her other ear and lined perishables up along the counter so she could put them away with one opening of the refrigerator door.

"I'm sorry for leaving without telling you," Martin said.

"Are you sorry for not calling for two months?"

"Sorry for that, too."

"Your manners leave a bit to be desired." She shoved the crisper drawer shut with more force than necessary.

"They always did."

She closed the refrigerator door. "I hear you've found work."

"It's not official yet, but yes. Any pointers?"

"Yes. Pee before class starts, and don't let your students smell your fear."

"Don't let my students smell my pee. Got it."

"You'll do fine."

"I really am sorry, Liza."

"Yeah, yeah."

"I'll make it up to you."

She held the phone between neck and shoulder and used both hands to ball up the grocery bags. "Good. I think you should."

"What do you want me to do?"

"I'll think of something."

"Let me take you to lunch."

"It'll take more than a lunch."

"I know. I just want to show you something."

"What?"

"I got a package from Leon when I was in New York. It went to my neighbor's apartment by mistake. A ledger my mother used to keep and in the back some photographs Leon took."

Nausea swept over her. "Photos of what?"

"Leon and some woman I didn't recognize. Nothing pornographic. I just wish I knew why he sent them to me."

She let out a slow breath.

"Don't mention the photos to Hodge or my family, please. I haven't shared them yet."

"All right."

"You okay?"

"I'm fine."

"You're still mad."

"Yes, I am. And I can't do lunch this week or next. My daughters have horse shows. I'll call you when I think of a suitable way for you to make up for being a jerk."

"Fair enough."

They hung up. Liza leaned against her kitchen counter. She remembered Leon Owenby's camera very well. Apertures, cold chrome dials, the way he gazed down into it to find the picture, never lifting his head to look up at the people he was hurting when he clicked the shutter.

There were five in the Solace Fork School graduating class of 1954—Liza, Martin, Hodge, and the two Gaddy sisters. Liza's aunt Fran helped Mr. Samuels set up chairs in the schoolyard, where the shiny dark leaves of rhododendron bushes provided a backdrop. Aunt Fran covered a long table with her best lace tablecloth and borrowed a punch bowl and glass cups from the Episcopal church. She and Mrs. Gaddy made cookies. The week before, as Aunt Fran measured Liza for alterations to her white graduation dress, her aunt worried, "Should I ask Nell Owenby to bring anything?" Liza didn't have an answer. Given Mr. Owenby's reaction to Martin's college announcement, none of them was sure the Owenbys would come to the ceremony.

Graduation day was hot and humid, the sky cloudless. Yellow jackets buzzed around Aunt Fran's punch. The Gaddy twins' faces were pink and sweaty, their hair frizzed. Liza handed Nancy Gaddy her silver compact so Nancy could powder the shine from her nose. "You both look beautiful," she told the twins, watching the road for Martin. A few dozen people milled about, family members and students from the grades behind them. Her father passed out fans he'd begged from Ferris Funeral Home. Hodge struggled to stabilize a rickety podium on the uneven ground, finally leaning a chair against it to keep it from falling over. The middle button of his new suit strained over his pudgy middle. Five minutes before it was time to begin, as Aunt Fran and Mr. Samuels were beginning to whisper nervously, the Owenbys' farm truck drove up to the schoolhouse, with Leon at the wheel. Martin and his brother James jumped out of the back. James brushed the dust off Martin's wool suit. It was some brother's hand-me-down, but it fit him well. James's girlfriend, Bertie, helped Martin's mother out of the passenger side. Liza assumed Bertie was responsible for getting James here. It was anyone's guess why Leon had come along. He sat in the truck, his left leg dangling out the open door, fiddling with something in his lap. The other Owenbys walked across the schoolyard. Liza's father went to greet them.

Mrs. Owenby looked frail. She wore a stiff navy blue dress and thick stockings. The bun in her salt-and-pepper hair was so tight it pulled her ears out from her head.

"Nell, we've saved a special seat just for you." Liza's father took Mrs. Owenby's arm and led her to a seat next to Hodge's parents. Aunt Fran walked over and patted Mrs. Owenby on the shoulder, whispering something in her ear to make her smile, putting her at ease. Liza walked over to where Martin stood with James and Bertie.

Leon finally got out of the truck, slamming the door, and joined them. A camera hung around his neck, in a square case of brown leather, with circles cut in the leather for knobs and handles to stick through. Liza's father had a Brownie camera that was broken at the moment, but she had never seen a camera like this. It swung against Leon's chest, its sophisticated gadgetry incongruous against Leon's plain white shirt.

Her father returned from seating Mrs. Owenby and whistled when he saw the camera. "Where'd you get it?"

"Bought it cheap off a German who works at the plant. He needed the money. It's the kind professionals use." Leon held the camera out for her father to examine, but didn't take it from around his neck.

Liza's father fingered the knobs, intrigued, careful not to touch the lens. "Where do you develop the film?"

"The German fellow says he'll do it for me in his darkroom."

"Isn't that something," her father said.

Leon took the camera strap from around his neck and slipped it over Bertie's head. The weight of it bent her forward. Leon grabbed Martin roughly around the neck and pulled him close. "Take a picture of us, Bertie."

Bertie looked flustered. "Oh, I couldn't. I wouldn't know what to do with all these knobs and things. I might break it."

"It ain't hard. I'll show you." Leon let Martin go. Martin rubbed his neck.

"This here's the focus." Leon and Bertie stared down into the top of the camera. Leon's dark hair was perfectly parted, comb marks preserved in Brylcreem. "See how it gets fuzzy, then sharp?"

James looked at Martin and Liza. "I believe I've heard all I care to about that camera."

"Knock it off, Leon," Martin said. "I'm here to graduate."

Mr. Samuels approached them, clearing his throat. "We should get started."

Bertie took the camera strap from around her neck and handed the camera back to Leon. Martin and Liza went with Mr. Samuels to the part of the schoolyard designated as a stage, where the Gaddy sisters and Hodge had already taken seats. Aunt Fran's deep, genteel voice echoed around the yard as she herded people to their places.

When everyone was still, Mr. Samuels went to the lectern, careful not to lean on it. "Ladies and gentlemen, thank you for joining us for this momentous occasion. Hodge Goforth will now deliver the invocation, after which we will hear a recitation from each of our other graduates. I have some awards to give out, and then we will adjourn and celebrate with refreshments."

Hodge gave the invocation, his eyes scrunched tight. Nancy Gaddy read an excerpt from Henry Wadsworth Longfellow's *The Song of Hiawatha*, while her sister, Betty, too shy to speak in public, beat a soft rhythm on the bottom of a bucket. When they sat down, Liza approached the podium to read from Elizabeth Barrett Browning's *Sonnets from the Portuguese*. Her father winked at her from the front row. Behind him, Bertie sat between James and Leon. James picked at a callus on his hand. Leon reached a finger and thumb and gently lifted a fallen hair from Bertie's shoulder. She looked up at him to smile her thanks, then turned back to listen to Liza. When Liza finished, Martin went to the podium and recited Thomas Moore's *The Meeting of the Waters* from memory.

"Show-off," Liza whispered when he sat back down next to her. He grinned.

Mr. Samuels took the podium again. "Ladies and gentlemen, it has been my privilege to teach these young people this year. They have all worked hard. You know we don't designate valedictorians or salutatorians here at Solace Fork School, but I have awards to present to each graduate." He looked back at the graduates, a stack of calligraphied certificates of achievement in his hand, and called them up one by one. The Gaddy sisters got perfect attendance awards. Hodge got most improved student. Liza was best all-round. When Martin came forward to accept his certificate for most likely to succeed, Mr. Samuels reached behind the podium for a small package. He rested a hand on Martin's back, hardly able to contain his pride. "This young man has shown a talent for writing unsurpassed by any student I have ever taught. I expect great things from him. In recognition, I am presenting him with a book award." He held out the package. "Martin, it's Eugene O'Neill. I hope it will inspire you and that one day we will see your own work in print."

Martin accepted the book with reverence. Liza felt her eyes tear up for this boy she loved, for everything he had overcome and the man she was sure he would be.

"Would the other graduates please come up."

They joined Martin next to the podium, and Mr. Samuels presented them with their diplomas. "Ladies and gentlemen, parents, friends, I present to you, the graduating class of 1954."

Their families clapped loudly. People streamed forward to congratulate them. At the refreshment table, Mrs. Gaddy began ladling out punch, and younger children shoved cookies into pockets.

Martin positioned himself behind Liza. She could feel his breath on her hair. Body heat rose from his wool suit, which was too warm for the weather. She wished all these people would disappear and leave the two of them alone. She would take his hand, lead him through cool woods to the clearing where the creek forked, get him out of that suit, push him down on his back on the rocks, feed him early blueberries and sour grass, dots of nectar from shepherd's whistles. She reached back and squeezed his hand.

Leon muscled his way toward them, head bent over his camera's viewfinder. He waved his long arms, directing them without looking up. "Martin, Liza, move closer together." Liza didn't need urging. She put her arm around Martin's waist. He put his hand over hers, interlacing their fingers.

Leon fumbled with buttons and blew invisible lint off the lens. Liza's father and aunt and Mrs. Owenby waited behind him, afraid to come forward and spoil the photograph. Liza could feel Martin growing impatient beside her. She looked at his profile, smooth-shaven, precious. Leon snapped the picture just as she leaned in and kissed Martin's cheek.

After graduation, Martin was stuck in the fields, his father determined to get as much work out of him as possible before he left for college. Liza wanted time with him before the fall separated them, but the one evening he made it to her house for dinner, he fell asleep at the table, head lolling forward, fingers still clutching his fork, until Liza's father cleared his throat loud enough to wake him. Liza's own summer job as a counselor at a YMCA day camp wouldn't start until July. With nothing to do one morning, she drove up to the school to see if Mr. Samuels needed help closing up his classroom now that the younger students were out for the summer.

The school was built two feet off the ground. When she walked up to the small porch, she earned a growl from a dog that had crawled underneath the building to sleep.

"Be quiet. I belong here, not you." The front door was propped open to let in the breeze. She stepped into the dark center hallway, breathing chalk dust and old paper, the smells that made her want to be a teacher.

From the classroom down the hall she heard Mr. Samuels talking to someone, his voice rising and cracking. "Why are you doing this?"

She stopped at the doorway, where she could see but a book rack hid her. Mr. Samuels stood behind his desk, leaning on it with both hands flat. His starched white shirt sleeves were rolled up to his elbows and veins stood out on his tanned arms. In front of him was Leon Owenby with his camera around his neck.

"I saw you," Leon said. "Coming out of the men's room at the Lenoir bus station. I know what you boys do in there that time of night."

"You don't have any proof."

Leon brandished the camera at Mr. Samuels, swinging it by the straps like a lantern. "You can deny it, but the camera don't lie."

Liza knew just enough to understand what Leon was talking about, from pulpit stories of Sodom and Gomorrah and jokes overheard from men on the porch at the general store. They didn't have a word for gay in Willoby County then. Until you can put a name to a thing, you can pretend it doesn't exist. Mr. Samuels's face paled. Sweat circles darkened his underarms, outlining his undershirt.

Leon tapped his camera. "You be gone by tomorrow, or I'll show these to anybody who'll look." He turned and headed toward Liza, sweeping papers off Mr. Samuels's desk with the side of his hand as he came.

Before Leon could see her Liza snuck back down the hall and outside and waited for him on the porch. When he came out, she grabbed the camera strap with one hand and twisted off the lens cap with the other. She had some idea of ripping the film out, if she could figure out which catch to press to expose it, but Leon grabbed her wrist, wrenching it, until her breath caught with pain.

"*It ain't your business.*" He thrust her away, then whistled. The dog under the school scrabbled out to meet him, arthritic hip bones grinding, a pencil-size erection obscenely pink.

"Not you, too," Leon said to the dog with disgust. "Nothing but perverts around here." He and the mutt headed down the deer path, into the woods. Without looking back at Liza he called, "I'll send you that graduation picture when I get the roll developed."

Liza shoved Leon's lens cap into her skirt pocket and kneaded her bruised wrist. It made her sick to think of her image trapped in Leon's camera on the same roll of film as the photographs he was using to blackmail Mr. Samuels. She ran back into the school.

Mr. Samuels squatted on the classroom floor, trying to gather up the papers Leon had scattered. She knelt beside him. "Mr. Samuels, don't let Leon Owenby bully you. I'll tell Daddy. He'll talk to the school board."

Mr. Samuels's face was red now, with embarrassment and fear. She reached her hand out, to let him know she didn't think less of him, but he moved away. "There's nothing anyone can do." He stood up, knees cracking, and looked around the room. He grabbed a wooden apple crate that held supplies, dumped it out on the floor, opened his desk drawers, and began throwing personal items into the crate. His framed college diploma, an ivory-handled magnifying glass, the arrowhead he'd found the day of the first class hike, all tossed now like ballast.

"You can't just give in," she said.

He stopped. "Oh, Liza. You don't understand." He reached into the crate and handed her the arrowhead. Sun from the classroom window struck it, defining every facet. He drew in a long, tight breath. "You're going to be a fine teacher. Remember my teaching, not my skulking away." He turned back to his packing.

She stared at him for a moment, then headed for her car and roared down the mountain until she had to brake, hard, behind a slow-moving chicken truck. She passed it on a curve, scaring the driver. The truck swerved toward the ditch, feathers flying. She slowed down in town, mindful that if she didn't, the neighbors would report her to Aunt Fran. When she got home she left the car door hanging open and ran around the side of the house to her father's infirmary, bursting in just as he was walking a woman and her sobbing little boy out to the waiting room.

"That hurt!" the child shouted through his tears.

"I know, son, but the shot hurts less than smallpox." Her father reached into the candy bowl he kept on a windowsill and handed the little boy a sucker.

Liza opened the door for the woman to get them to leave faster. "Do you have any other patients, Daddy?" she asked once they were gone.

"No, I'm closing up for lunch."

Liza locked the door.

"What's the matter, honey?"

She told him. If she expected shock, she didn't get it. A look of knowing, of pieces fitting together, settled on her father's face. "Ah. I see."

"You have to do something, Daddy."

"What can I do?"

"Talk to the school superintendent. Mr. Samuels is the best teacher this county has ever had. Or the police. Isn't blackmail illegal?"

"Honey, talking to anybody would ruin him. Men like Mr. Samuels, they have to be careful."

"Men like Mr. Samuels. Why does it matter, Daddy?"

He rubbed his face. "I don't know, but it does."

"You're going to let Leon Owenby get away with this?"

"All I can do is offer Mr. Samuels a good reference and tell everybody he left for personal reasons."

It was the first and only time her father let her down. She unlocked the infirmary door and stormed out.

"I'll phone him right now, Liza," he called. The door slammed behind her, cutting him off.

She walked back to her car, parked crooked in the yard, its open driver's-side door hanging like the broken wing of a big blue bird. She got in and drove. Stupid town. Stupid mountain, stupid road, stupid people on the road. Something skidded across the front seat. Leon's lens cap had fallen out of her pocket. She grabbed it with her right hand and squeezed until it dug into her skin. At Balsam Gap, a railroad trestle ran parallel to the road, the ground under it dropping away to bottomless gully. She parked on the shoulder and got out. The train tracks cast a short shadow on the steep rocks descending below. Behind the railroad bridge, the Blue Ridge Mountains rolled on top of one another. She fingered the lens cap. As the one o'clock Norfolk Southern blew its first warning whistle miles away, she hurled the lens cap as hard as she could into the ravine.

She never told Martin. The Martin she knew then was a fighter and would have gone berserk. She wondered sometimes whether Martin had had an inkling back then about Mr. Samuels's sexual orientation—if he might have sensed something in the teacher before he recognized it in himself—but there was no point in dredging up Mr. Samuels now.

She never saw the photograph Leon took of her and Martin and didn't know if Leon had ever developed it. In the days following Leon's disappearance, Liza had tried to support the Owenby family, bringing casseroles and standing with the Owenby women, Eugenia always moving, Bertie so different now from the girl she had been at their graduation, when Leon dazzled her with the camera. As Eugenia and Bertie worried out loud about what had happened to Leon, Liza kept a studied, sympathetic look on her face, fighting the shrieks of the wild girl inside. "Leon Owenby, it serves you right!"

22

Martin

Martin scheduled the interview with the dean for eleven o'clock in the morning, late enough to get over any hangover he happened to have and early enough that he wouldn't yet be craving his next drink. He got ready in Hodge's basement apartment, putting on his one wrinkled suit, which he had never taken out of his suitcase after the last trip to North Carolina. When Hodge and his wife, Claudie, showed him the apartment after picking him up from the airport, they apologized for its small size, but Martin liked it. It was one long room, with a screen separating the bedroom area from the kitchen and bathroom. The bathroom was near the entrance.

Claudie, a sweet, plump little woman with her gray hair cut in a pageboy, had opened the bathroom door to show it to him. "Hodge did it himself. It used to be a closet."

Martin peeked past her. The toilet had handicap bars. Good to know that if he got really drunk, he could still hoist himself off the can. "Great." He walked into the room to see the rest of the space. The apartment smelled like a basement, but they had brightened it up by painting the dark paneling white and putting in rose-colored carpeting. The bed was a hospital bed.

"Sorry about the bed," Hodge said.

Martin lay down on it and tried the controls. Head up, feet down. Head down, feet up. It entertained him for a few minutes, then made him uncomfortable. "I feel like I should be wearing an adult diaper." He returned the bed to its flat position.

"We'll see if we can't find a regular bed somewhere for you," Hodge said.

"No, no need. This will do nicely." Martin sat up. Really, it would do. The room was almost as big as his entire apartment in New York, bigger when you considered it wasn't crowded with Dennis's antiques. He stood and kissed Claudie on the cheek. "You two are the best. Thank you."

Hodge and Claudie couldn't take him to his interview because they had to work, but James had the day off and volunteered to drive him. James picked him up a little before eleven and drove him to the community college, silently handing him an extra coffee from the Bojangles' drive-through. James was quiet, his profile tired. Looking at the hearing aid in his brother's ear, Martin got the bizarre idea that James was listening for something. Martin sipped the scalding coffee, careful not to spill it down his front.

The buildings on the community college campus formed a long, low brick quad, with interstate highway on one side and the county's only four-lane commercial strip on the other. People crawled out of the coves to shop at the Kmart and eat at the chain restaurants. James parked in a visitor's space in front of the administration building. "I'll wait," he said. Martin set his coffee cup in a drink holder and got out.

The building had an underfunded institutional feel. A few surly students smoked around the entranceway, grinding their ashes into the cigarette urns. They were not the fair young people one saw on brochures for four-year colleges. Inside, in the lobby, the original architectural drawing of the college leaned on an easel. Something seemed amiss. Martin realized it was the plants, nicely water-colored onto the drawing. Any plants put in when the building was erected had died long ago. The courtyards where they were supposed to bloom were hard dirt.

He followed yellow cinder-block walls down the hall to the English department offices. The dean, Jay Daniels, came out to greet him. Jay was even more rumpled than Martin. He wouldn't look Martin in the eye, not out of shiftiness, but out of extreme shyness, or perhaps embarrassment at how much he expected Martin to do for so little money. He periodically blew air out through his cheeks, like a horse, his version of clearing his throat. The first thing Jay told Martin as he led him to his office was that he was only the acting dean, had been for two years, and that he would be relieved when they got funding to pay someone else to be a real dean.

To Martin's embarrassment, Jay was actually a bit star-struck. After they sat down in Jay's small, book-filled office, Jay rattled off the short list of Martin's published plays.

"You remember them better than I do." Martin wasn't joking.

"I'm sorry the only classes open are freshman English," Jay said. "It would be wonderful to have you teach our creative writing class, but unfortunately that position belongs to an older member of our faculty, who has had some pieces published in *Guideposts*. I'm afraid I can't see her surrendering it."

"Just as well." Martin hadn't written a creative word in years.

"You might consider teaching a creative writing class as part of our adult education program in the summer." Jay blew air out in a whinny. "Though that pays even less than adjunct pay, depending on how many people sign up for the class."

"We'll see," Martin said. Who knew if he would still be here by summer.

Jay made clear that the job was Martin's if he wanted it, based on good words from Hodge and Liza and the fact that no one else had applied. He was especially impressed that Liza thought well of Martin. She sent Jay good students from the high school. Martin thought it was brave of her to put her reputation on the line for him. He would be teaching two classes, during the day, for a ridiculously small amount of money. Jay grew even more apologetic when he told Martin the sum, and made vague references to eventually changing Martin's status from adjunct to permanent. Martin couldn't think that far ahead. At least his students wouldn't be the worst ones. They would all have placed out of remedial English and actually be able to read. The textbook was already selected. He flipped through the anthology Jay handed him, interested in spite of himself. He scanned the contents page, famous short stories standard in every high school and college text in America, but which he still appreciated. "The Lottery," "Hills Like White Elephants," "An Occurrence at Owl Creek Bridge." Stories that had been precious to him as a young person. Martin wasn't jaded enough to make fun just because they had become cliché. There was a unit on American poetry. He told himself it wouldn't be too horrible.

Jay handed Martin a much-photocopied sheet of paper called "Instructions for Adjuncts," which told him he had to do a syllabus and post his office hours.

"Do I have an office?" Martin said.

"Erm, no, adjuncts don't get an office, but you can hold your office hours in the faculty lounge." Jay gave him tax-withholding forms to fill out and took his driver's license down the hall to copy.

Martin had asked for this job. He would make the best

of it. He filled out the forms. When Jay came back with his driver's license, Martin shook the dean's hand and walked out of the building. James was sitting in his truck, with the engine on for heat. As Martin climbed in the passenger side, Jay ran out of the building, waving something red. "It's your faculty parking sticker," he said, handing it to Martin. Martin thanked him and Jay went back in the building, bending over to recover his breath.

"Parking sticker," said James. "You're going to need a vehicle."

Martin honestly hadn't thought about it, but James was right. He couldn't rely on his family or Hodge to chauffeur him to class and back three times a week.

"I can't afford a car," he said.

"Leon's truck still runs okay. We can go up there and get it now if you want."

By "up there," James meant the home place. Martin had managed to avoid it on his last visit and didn't want to go now, but James was going out of his way to help and Martin couldn't say no. "All right."

James drove along familiar back roads, while Martin tried to suppress the trepidation he felt. James turned off onto the road that went up to their father's place. When Martin was a kid it was just dirt, but Leon had covered it with gravel. James stopped the truck in the yard, and they got out. It had been years since Martin was here. The house was falling in. Wood had shifted. One shoulder of the house shrugged higher than the other. He swallowed despair at being back. Why in the world had he returned? He hated this place. Trees pressed in on all sides, January bare, complaining in their nakedness.

"You want to go inside?" James said.

"No."

Leon's boxy 1968 Chevy pickup truck sat forlornly under an old cherry tree. James walked over and checked the tires. Martin followed him. The truck had been parked under the tree since Leon's disappearance. A length of heavy chain rusted away in its bed, almost covered by decayed leaves and bird droppings. James felt around in the left rear tire well and pulled out a little magnetic box. He opened it and handed Martin a truck key. "Climb on in. You have to get in the passenger side. The driver's-side door don't latch."

Martin looked and saw that the driver's door was secured with a coat hanger, to keep it from swinging open. He went around to climb in the passenger side as James directed.

"Watch out for mousetraps," James said.

Martin stopped. "You're kidding, right?"

James shook his head. "They crawl up in the seat cushions to get out of the cold. Last time I was here I found one drowned in a Dr Pepper bottle. I threw the whole thing in the woods, but you can still smell it."

Martin got in and pulled the heavy door shut behind him. The dead mouse smell hit him, but he had smelled worse. He scooted along the wide seat, upholstered in green leather stamped with a saloon pattern. The sun had baked cracks, then crested waves, in the green plastic dashboard. Martin hadn't driven much of anything for the past thirty years. He tried to adjust the rearview mirror, but it hung broken-necked, unable to hold its head up. He took the steering wheel and gazed out on the hood, stretching for miles in front of him.

James stood at the driver's-side window and motioned for Martin to roll the window down. Martin wrestled with the handle and managed to get the window down halfway before it stuck. "Start her up," James said. The key in Martin's hand seemed too thin and flimsy to start such a beast. He put it in the ignition and turned. Music blared from the AM radio, some contemporary Christian crap, not what he would have expected from Leon. He fumbled for the volume button, but the knob had fallen off.

For some reason known only to Leon, when he bought the truck in 1968 he had had a race car motor installed. The noise was appalling. The truck strained, begging to go. Martin was glad to see that Leon had left a half tank of gas to feed it.

"Mash on the brake." James went behind the truck to check the brake lights. "Well, the left one works, anyway." He patted the truck like a horse flank and called out, "You're good to go." He walked back to his own truck, leaving Martin with eight horses throbbing under him.

He took off the parking brake and put a tentative foot down on the gas. The truck surged forward, throwing him back against the seat. He imagined his ears and face flapping like a test pilot's at fifty g's. More bad music blared from the cassette deck, but he was afraid to loosen a hand from the wheel to try to turn it off. The truck surged down the mountain, throwing gravel, with Martin hanging on tight. On impulse, he yelled out the window a long "Yee-hah!" He now had a vehicle, or maybe it had him.

He drove back to the apartment. Hodge's wife, Claudie, had left a plate of sandwiches in the minifridge. He ate them all, then unpacked his suitcase. Leon's padded envelope, with their mother's ledger and the photographs in it, lay flat between two pairs of pants. Martin took it out and put it in the zippered carry-on he used as briefcase and mobile office. He had the rest of the afternoon free. He could take the ledger to show Wally Metcalf and stop by the liquor store on the way home.

He got back in Leon's truck and drove carefully to the

Sheriff's Department, glad for the wide spaces in the parking lot. He could hear Wally on the phone in his office as he approached. Wally's voice slid into that good old boy joking-around drawl that Martin supposed was crucial to his success as sheriff. Wally hung up as Martin reached his office door, still chuckling about something. Martin knocked on the doorframe, and Wally motioned him in.

"Hey, Martin, I heard you were back." Wally rose and offered his hand. His handshake was strong and practiced, with a hard squeeze at the end to let you know who was boss. He sat back down. "What can I do you for?" Wally was a busy man, but he had a way of making people feel he had time for them.

Martin reached in his briefcase and took out Leon's padded mailer, with the ledger and photos inside. "I don't think this is anything, but Leon mailed it to me about a week before he disappeared. I thought I'd better show it to you."

"Let's see what you got there." Wally reached for it, and Martin handed it over. Wally gently pulled the ledger out of the envelope.

"It was our mother's," Martin said. "And there are some photos in the back. He didn't include a note."

"Of course not." Wally carefully flipped through the egg book. "I'm sure you've been through it. Did you find anything that might be significant?" He looked up. "To the case, I mean. I know the book is significant to you."

Martin appreciated that. "It's all my mother's handwriting. Leon didn't add anything. I assumed the book had been destroyed long ago. The photos are in that envelope in the back."

Wally opened the manila envelope and carefully shook the photos out onto his desk. "That your brother?"

"Yes. I don't know who the girl is."

"Have you showed them to your family to see if they'd know?"

"Not yet. Should I?" By now, the young woman in the photos had started to look familiar, as if he'd seen her shadowy outline somewhere before. He may have simply looked at the pictures too often, but for some reason he still didn't want to show them to the family. He tried to make a joke out of it. "What if this lady is now the mayor's wife or something?"

"It's your choice whether to share them with your family or not. I don't think pictures from 1958 bear on this case. Just don't tell Hodge unless you want everybody to know." Wally handed the photos back to Martin.

Martin smiled. "Hodge isn't a secret keeper, is he?" He dropped the photos into his briefcase.

"That's what I like most about him." Wally pushed the ledger toward Martin but kept the mailer. "I'll hang onto this until we find your brother. The outside's contaminated, but once we know what we're looking for, I might want to send it to the SBI lab in Raleigh." He didn't sound very optimistic. It was all right with Martin. He didn't have a stake in being the one to break the case.

"If he mailed me things all the time, I wouldn't have brought it in, but I don't think I ever got a piece of mail from him before in my life."

"Seems he was in a giving-away mood there at the last." Wally opened a drawer and pulled out a tagged plastic bag. It held Leon's ugly knuckle knife. The sight of it shocked Martin, even though Hodge had told him about the sheriff confiscating it from Steven. Martin had never seen the knife without his brother attached to it.

Wally pushed it over to him. "We had it tested. All kinds of interesting things on it, but no human blood. Give it back to Steven for me when you see him."

23

Bertie

Bertie couldn't believe her eyes when she saw Martin at church on Sunday morning. She and James got there right as the service was starting and saw him, two pews from the front, sandwiched between Hodge and Claudie Goforth on his left and Eugenia looking proud as punch on his right. He gave them a little wave. Solace Fork Baptist Church had an organ it got when the county lost its minor league baseball team. It could sound like any instrument. The organist made it sound like a bell and hit the same key eleven times to chime the hour and get things started.

After the service half the congregation went up to the front to say hello to Martin. Bertie and James went up there to stand with Eugenia and Zeb, to act like family was supposed to. Bertie knew church bored Martin, but he did a good job not showing it. He was charming to all the older people who remembered him from when he was a boy. She was willing to bet he wouldn't be back next week, but he made the best of this week.

When most everybody had shuffled away, leaving just the Owenby family and Hodge and Claudie, Martin said, "Stay here a minute. I left something in Hodge's truck I want to show all of you." He went out the church's side entrance and came back a few minutes later holding something flat wrapped in a plastic bag. "Look at this."

"What is it?" Eugenia nudged Bertie out of the way to look.

Martin unwrapped it carefully. "Mama's egg book." He opened it. Nell Owenby's neat, old-fashioned handwriting filled the pages.

"Oh." Eugenia looked disappointed.

"Leon mailed it to me in New York before he disappeared. It got delivered to a neighbor's by mistake."

James stepped forward and touched the book. "Why in the world would Leon send you that?"

Martin shrugged.

"Was there a note with it?" Eugenia said.

"No."

"Maybe he was trying to send you a message." Eugenia took the book and held it up to the light that streamed in from the church's one stained-glass window. Martin winced as she bent the binding back, peeking down into the spine, looking for a clue. He gently took it away from her.

"No secret messages, Eugenia. I don't know why he sent it."

"Can I look at it?" Bertie said.

"Sure." He handed it to her. Bertie turned the pages. The simple entries made her want to cry.

"I can make photocopies for all of you if you want," Martin said.

James looked puzzled. Eugenia said, "It's just an old book."

Bertie felt for Martin. The Owenbys were not a sentimental bunch. "I'd like a copy, Martin, to keep with my clippings and other family things. I can copy it at the library tomorrow if you want."

Martin looked grateful. "That would be great, Bertie."

Eugenia couldn't stand it. She reached for the book. "Give it here. It was our mama's. I'll copy it."

Before she could grab it Martin put his arm out to block her. "Bertie already offered, Eugenia. I know she'll take care of it." He handed Bertie the plastic bag to protect it.

Bertie gave Eugenia a big smile. Martin standing up to Eugenia gave her heart a bigger lift than the whole church service had. "Martin, why don't you come home and eat with us. James can drive you back to Hodge's later," she said.

"I'd love to."

Eugenia's lips pursed. Bertie allowed herself a moment of un-Christian pleasure at having beat Eugenia to the dinner invitation.

When they got home, Bobby's truck was in their drive-way. He and Cherise came for Sunday dinner after church every week, whether Bertie and James invited them or not. When Bertie and James walked in with Martin, Bobby and Cherise were on the couch, watching a car race on television. James and Martin went to wash their hands. Bertie set Martin's ledger on top of the microwave and put an apron on over her good clothes. The roast she'd put in the oven before they went to church was just right. She took it out and put it on a plate with the carrots and potatoes she'd cooked with it. She set the table and took four little plates out of the refrigerator, each with half a pear sitting on lettuce, with a maraschino cherry in the middle. She lifted the plastic wrap off. Martin could have the one she'd fixed for herself. "Dinner's ready."

Bobby and Cherise came into the kitchen. Bobby was in a good mood. He kissed Bertie on the cheek, something he almost never did anymore, and when Martin walked in Bobby let Martin choose a seat first, before he and Cherise plopped down and started filling their plates.

"Look at this, Bobby." Bertie took the egg book out of its bag and showed it to him. "It belonged to your grandmother Nell. Leon sent it to Martin right before he disappeared, but he just got it recently."

"Leon mailed it before he went missing?" Cherise's eyes seemed to glitter. Bertie didn't like that girl. Cherise was always conniving about something.

Bobby turned a few pages of the ledger. "Why'd it take so long to get there?"

"The mailman took it to the wrong apartment," Martin said.

Bertie wrapped the book back up and put it in a cabinet to keep it safe.

James came in and they started eating. While Martin told them about his job at the community college, Bobby and Cherise ate without saying anything. Cherise chewed with her mouth open, picking her maraschino cherry up with her fingers to pop it in her mouth. James's plate got low, and Bertie cut him another piece of beef without him asking. When everybody was done Bobby leaned back and burped real loud.

"Bobby, show some manners," James said.

"That's how the Eskimos say they liked a meal," Bobby said.

"You're no Eskimo," James said.

Bobby reached over and put his arm around Cherise's fleshy shoulder. "You ready to tell them, Cherise?"

"Fine with me."

Bobby leaned back in his chair. "We've got an announcement."

Bertie could see he enjoyed saying it like that. Bobby hadn't had many things to announce in his life. A feeling of tired knowing seeped through her body. She looked at Cherise's face, puffier lately than it used to be. Bertie knew what Bobby was going to say, and she didn't want to hear it.

"Cherise is pregnant. We're going to have a baby."

Bobby had a big grin on his face, proud to have proved his manhood by knocking Cherise up. Bertie could feel James's stillness beside her. A clock ticked in the living room.

"Congratulations," Martin said.

"When are you due?" Bertie asked Cherise.

"End of March." She was further along than Bertie had thought, carrying the baby high so her regular fat hid it.

"Are y'all going to do the right thing?" Bertie could hardly ask the question. Bobby ought to marry the girl, but the thought of him stuck with Cherise made Bertie sick.

"Not right now," Bobby said. "There's no hurry. We'll get around to it."

Cherise picked potato skin out of her teeth. Martin folded his napkin into a square, studying it.

"You don't have a job, Bobby," Bertie said.

The smile faded from Bobby's face. "That's just like you. You ought to be happy for me, and instead you shoot me down."

Bertie looked to James for help.

"Son, she's just saying you need a steady job to raise a child," James said.

"Your daddy could keep a job," Bertie couldn't help saying.

"I will have a job by the time Cherise has to stop working." Bobby pushed his chair back from the table. "Come on, Cherise." They left without thanking Bertie for the meal or even taking their dirty plates to the sink. Bertie felt her eyes tear up.

James laid a hand on hers. "Bertie, I know it's disappointing."

Outside, Bobby's truck tires squealed as he pulled out into the road. Disappointing. That's what it was.

Martin cleared his throat, changing the subject. "Have you heard anything from the sheriff about Leon's medical bill?"

"Not yet," James said.

"Whatever he had done at that place, it was expensive, so it must have been serious," Bertie said.

"Maybe that's why he sent me Mama's ledger. So I'd have it if he died," Martin said.

At the word "died" James's face got all pink. Martin touched James's arm. "Forget I said that."

James just shook his head. "I'm going to go lie down for a minute." He got up and left.

Martin helped Bertie clear the dishes and wipe the table. He found Bertie's cigarettes on the counter and took one, passing the pack to her. She reached up in the cabinet for his mama's book, and they sat back down at the table to smoke.

Bertie opened the ledger, turning pages to find the date of the last entry. "Your mama kept on writing in here, up until just a few days before she died, weak as she was."

Martin looked at the page she'd found. "How bad was it for her?" He asked the question like he wanted to know but was afraid to at the same time.

"You mean there at the end?"

"Yes."

Bertie stubbed her cigarette out. It seemed disrespectful to smoke while talking about Nell Owenby. "She was in a lot of pain, I can't lie to you. She'd got to where she couldn't eat or drink. That's how it is, you know." She checked Martin's face, to make sure that what she was telling him wasn't hurting him. "Your daddy finally got Dr. Vance to come and give her something for the pain. That last day, me and Eugenia were both with her in the bedroom. I had one of Nell's hands and

Eugenia was holding the other." That was back when Bertie and Eugenia were close, before Bertie left James and Eugenia wrote her off as a sinner. Bertie rubbed the back of her own hand, remembering the sharp, still bones beneath Nell Owenby's dry skin. "Her breathing got slower and slower, until it was just a few times a minute. We sat there listening for it in that quiet room. And then she finally expired. It was a peaceful passing, Martin, really it was."

Martin nodded. "Thank you." He tapped his mama's ledger with two fingers, drumming out a rhythm.

"You're welcome," she said. His hair had fallen over his eyes. Bertie reached over and pushed it aside with one finger, as if he were still the boy he'd been when she first joined the Owenby family.

24

I v y

I love my little house. Nobody else's dirt fills the cracks, a nice change after my life of cleaning motel rooms. An eat-in kitchen with a bay window out to the backyard, so I can watch my bird feeders. Sun jumping in everywhere. I keep it perfect. It still smells of fresh paint and carpet glue. When Steven or Trina comes they smoke outside to help me preserve the smell. And the aloneness of it, not having to share it with some man, nor most of the time with the ghosts, who don't care for its newness, its cleanness, the shortage of upsetting memories. Except that sometimes in the middle of enjoying the house an if-only thought catches me. If only I could have provided such a house for my children, and my sadness calls up Shane. There he is now, in his windbreaker and favorite tennis shoes. Ducks into my clean bathroom and flushes the toilet, runs the water. I hurry my step but can't catch him.

When Shane lived at home with me and my boyfriend Ricky Ball, he slept fully dressed, with quarters in his shoes, in case he had to run down to the Piggly Wiggly on the corner and call 911. I should have put an end to it but didn't. Ricky took such a load off me. The money, for one thing, and also when we fooled around, I could be in just one place, ghost voices not intruding, it was such a grand relief. I needed Ricky to help me sort out what was real and what wasn't. Ricky's explosions could clear a room of spirits.

My children tiptoed around Ricky the way I tiptoed around the ghosts. His mood could change in a minute, like the weather up on Spivey's Bald, clouds rolling in without warning, flash floods suddenly crashing down on what had been a sunny day. Sometimes I'd feel it building up, the way pressure builds inside a house right before a big storm, and it was a relief when it finally blew. Sometimes I provoked him on purpose, when the kids weren't home, to have it over with. Shane took it hardest. He took everything hardest. He pulled out all his eyebrow hairs, until the skin was two pale, raw strips. The kids didn't bring friends home, because they couldn't tell when Ricky would be at work or when he'd be stretched out on the sofa with a six-pack of Pabst Blue Ribbon, yelling orders until he got mad enough to get up and go after whoever had made him ill. It was his trailer. The lease was in his name. The alternative was for me and the children to live in my car.

Shane has left the toilet lid up. I spray cleaner on a sponge and wipe the rim out of habit before I put the seat down. I think about the time Ricky put me in the hospital with a cracked vertebra after he knocked me down and then jumped on me. While I was still in the emergency room, Social Services came and loaded up my children. They let me have supervised visits at McDonald's every other week. Sometimes the social worker didn't bring them and said the mix-up was my fault for not having a phone. When they did come, Trina clung to me the whole visit. Steven cried, asked me when he could come home. At first, Shane tried to be a man and said everything was fine. As time pressed on he began to disrespect me or didn't even bother to show up.

This time I couldn't get my children back. Social Services

gave me a long list of things I was supposed to do. Take parenting classes twice a week, go to counseling twice a week, but still somehow get and keep a job. And stay away from Ricky Ball, which I did, which kept me from meeting one more requirement, keeping a stable home. I cleaned toilets at different motels in exchange for a room. In court every three months, the social worker stood up and told how the visits upset the children, how I had missed this or that appointment, and recommended that my kids stay in foster care. Social Services is a locomotive. Once it gets rolling it doesn't stop, and it carried my children clear away.

The floor of the courthouse where they heard my case was always crowded, the hall outside full of screaming children and grandparents trying to wrest custody away from Social Services on behalf of some no-good child or other. To pretend like there was privacy, they pulled a partition across to separate the courtroom from the room full of people waiting for their cases to be called, but from the outside you could hear what they said behind the partition. Whenever it was my time to go inside, the seats in the back would be full of lawyers and social workers, all gossiping and rolling their eyes, and interpreters for the Mexicans and once even for some deaf people who couldn't hear their baby crying so didn't feed it. That wasn't much privacy to my way of thinking. Not that I ever had privacy, because the ghosts were there, too, wayward girls in old-fashioned clothes who passed through the partition, clutching still bundles in their arms and looking lost.

The judge gave me one court-appointed attorney after another, always some child fresh out of law school, who put their name on the list out of fear of not being able to earn a living otherwise. My case always came up in front of the same judge. I asked one of my lawyers, couldn't we get a new judge, and he hemmed and hawed about continuity. By then the court's file on me was a good three inches thick. I think the state only appointed the lawyers to make it look like it was being fair. There wasn't anything the lawyers could really do. Every time we lost, they filled out their fee sheets to give to the judge before we left the courtroom, set on getting paid above all else. One after another they wrote me letters saying they weren't doing that type of work anymore. One of them, a young man I really liked, was honest enough to use the words "burn out." I was burned out, too, but nobody would let me off the list. I was on it for good.

My brooding has issued an invitation. Alma and Missouri have come to call. Before me in my living room they play out a scene. For once Missouri abandons her youthful beauty, and Alma lets go of her age. Missouri appears as fifty, causing mischief in her daughter's ordered household. In middle age, Missouri's hair has gone from red to a striking gray, as thick as before. She wears black, not to be proper but because she knows she looks good in it—it offsets her hair. The skin on her face has thinned and dried, too much sun for her coloring. Her figure is still fine under sober clothes.

The younger Alma's face is pretty, her teeth are white. She has married early to get away from her mother. Her husband is a shiftless man named Zeno, a grandfather I never met because he fell drunk off of Rendezvous Falls before I was born. It is hog-killing time. I hear the death squeals outside. Zeno's brother has come to help and Missouri is sowing trouble.

Missouri winks at me and sidles up to Zeno where he stands bloody in front of Alma's stove, shoving biscuits in his mouth. Alma and the brother are in the smokehouse, making sausage.

"A pity you get biscuits when Alma has slipped the sweetbreads to your handsome brother." Missouri's own hands are clean, no bloody work for her.

"What?" Zeno speaks with his mouth full, spitting crumbs on the floor he has soiled.

"Keep an eye on your wife if you're wise," Missouri says. Zeno wipes his hands on his front and starts fast for the door.

Missouri is pleased with her joke.

"You ought not to lie on her like that," I chide.

"I'm only having a bit of fun. Nobody could suspect Alma of being unfaithful, not even one as slow as him."

Alma steps through the door. Zeno has busted her eye. Pigs' blood from his fist outlines the bruise. Missouri didn't plan this part. She reaches for Alma's face in spite of herself. Alma grabs her wrist before she can touch her. Alma's jaw is set, her face now more like the Alma I know. "I'll take being hit for a domain of my own. You will leave here tomorrow."

I have never before seen Missouri contrite. She raises her hands and it is night. We all three stand over Zeno's bed. He stinks of moonshine, his snores pull air. In one hand Missouri holds up a pig's privates. In the other the iron forceps used to snip them off. She jabs the forceps into Zeno's crotch, hard enough for him to wake up yelling. He sees her holding the hog's manhood in her fist and thinks the jewels are his. He screams and stumbles from the bed, a hand on what he thinks is missing. Off he goes, a howl into the night.

Alma, her proper old age again, tries out the denim love seat in my living room, puts her thin legs up on my ottoman and eyes her mother. "You did that?"

Missouri lowers her arms. "Daughter, I would do it again."

For the first and only time, it is a smile and not a sneer that reveals Alma's teeth, three of them the blue of cloudy opals.

Outside on my porch I hear Shane's step. After he died, my other two children raised so much hell and ran away so many times, the social workers finally gave in and let them come back to me. We did all right. With children, I got government help with my rent. Steven and Trina shared a paper route for pocket money. At least I had them for those years, though the three of us were pitiful, holding hands in a circle game around the hole Shane left, trying to keep each other from falling in.

I open my front door. Bird feeders swing, set in motion by an idle boy's touch.

Steven's truck pulls up to the front of the house. He gets out and walks toward me, a big grin on his face. Leon's knuckle knife dangles loose from his fingers.

25

Martin

Martin woke up in his clothes, teeth furry, the outside door to the apartment unlocked. When he got up to pee his head still buzzed. He looked out the basement window, set just a few inches above the frosted ground. February was depressing no matter where you were. It was late morning on a Saturday. After two whole days of white-knuckled self-deprivation, he had fallen headfirst off the wagon, landing mangled on the pavement like roadkill. No memory of how he got home from the bar last night. Leon's green truck sat in the driveway, parked more or less straight. He went outside to check it. No new scratches or dents. A Styrofoam box, his leftover supper, sat in the passenger seat, so no one drove home with him.

Another lost trip home.

Back inside, the house was quiet. Hodge and Claudie were in Georgia for a bridge tournament. Martin couldn't relate to their passion for the card game, but there was something sweet about this thing they had found to do together in their middle years. And it gave Martin the house to himself most weekends.

He straightened the apartment, emptying his wastebasket into the garbage bag Claudie left in the downstairs hall, but bagging his liquor bottles separately, to drop in a Dumpster the next time he was out. Hodge and Claudie liked him. He didn't want them counting the bottles. During the week, when abstinence failed, he did his drinking late at night so he'd be sober if they invited him upstairs for dinner or to watch television.

His briefcase was spilling over with the irrelevant memos that clogged his faculty mailbox every day. The college didn't pay him enough to read them. He threw them away and pulled out the first stack of papers his students had turned in. He had made the assignment glibly, forgetting how much work it was going to be to grade the papers. He put them on top of his minifridge. In the side pocket of his briefcase were the photos Leon had sent. He took them out for another look. Still no word on Leon's medical problem. Martin had thought at first that Leon sent the photos by accident, forgetting they were tucked in the back of the ledger, but if Leon were seriously ill, he may have wanted the photos out of his house, afraid of who would find them if he died. If so, Martin was an unlikely trustee.

He put the photos back in his briefcase, trying to identify the tight feeling in his rib cage, the tinny taste in his mouth. He thought it might be hunger and went upstairs to the family kitchen to forage. Claudie had cleaned up before she left. The Formica tabletop gleamed. Packages of cookies sat on the counter, but nothing tempted him. The harvest yellow refrigerator hummed in the quiet, displaying family photos, birthday cards, scribbled notes. Martin realized he was lonely.

He was not one to take time for loneliness. He had spent the past decades surrounded by men. One-time men in bars where he went equipped with his bar name and not enough money. The loud, fluid group of men he and Dennis called friends, the ones AIDS hadn't culled, men he realized now were more Dennis's friends than his, if they were anyone's.

Always someone around to shout down any introspection. Until now.

He opened a package of vanilla wafers, just for something to do. One other time he had felt like this, during the mosquito-ridden summer of 1955, when Deke Armstrong got a part in the *Lost Colony* outdoor drama in Manteo, on Roanoke Island on North Carolina's outer banks, and Martin followed him there.

It was Deke's second summer in Manteo, a waterfront town of a few hundred people if you didn't count tourists. A friend of Deke's got Martin a job as desk boy at the newly opened Queen Elizabeth Inn, its fake English half-timbering a tribute to the queen's failed colonization efforts. The hotel took money out of employee paychecks for room and board and the cost of laundering their logoed shirts, but the job still paid better than picking cucumbers or tobacco. Even if Deke hadn't invited Martin to follow him, Martin would have found a job somewhere other than Willoby County.

Deke didn't suggest Martin live with him, and Martin didn't ask. Deke and three other men in the cast rented a dilapidated house on the beach south of Nags Head, over the Washington Baum Bridge from Manteo. Sand drifted against the east side of the house, threatening to bury it. Weather had warped the wooden shingles on the outside walls and knocked some out like teeth. Green mold streaked the window frames, and storms had ripped away the screens on the sleeping porch, but the house's crooked wooden stairs led right to the beach. Deke and his friends partied there every night until three or four in the morning. The actors didn't have to be back at the theater until the next afternoon. Martin's own shift started at eight in the morning, but he was young. He bought a used bicycle to make the five-mile trip from the inn to the beach house, pedaling over the long, flat bridge. On the Nags Head side, old hurricane floods had caved in the sides of the road. Sand blew over pavement. Scrub grew along the road, keeping its head low, knowing the wind would strip bald any branch that reached too high. In the early mornings Martin could ride the entire flat route without meeting a single car.

For four weeks, it was paradise. The houses on either side were unoccupied that summer, and at night the beach was pitch-black—except for the bonfire they built, the stars, and the faraway light from the Bodie Island lighthouse. Martin and Deke could be ten yards away from the others, screwing right there in the sand, and no one could see. They knew but they couldn't see. He and Deke came back to the fire with sand burns on their bodies, their eyes feverish. Deke moved away from Martin around the circle, molding the conversation, putting upstarts in their places, standing at ease in his perfect skin. Martin tossed driftwood and debris onto the fire, watching sparks cascade, then die on the sand. When Deke looked at him, the heat that shimmered over the fire softened his hard face. Martin rode back to the inn at sunrise and suffered through his shift until he could return for more.

Liza wrote him long letters that summer, witty and full of questions. When the first one arrived, Martin realized that in his infatuation with Deke, he hadn't thought of her once. Feeling guilty, he stole a postcard from a room the maids had left open, with a picture of the hotel on the front, and wrote her a few words on the back. He would have to tell her his plans had changed but not yet.

The fourth week, an Englishman named Clive Davies moved into the beach house after his landlady in Manteo evicted him. Clive played Sir Walter Raleigh in the play and coached the other actors on the proper British accent for their lost colonists. He was a prick. He pronounced his last name "Davis." The extra *e* only reinforced Martin's contempt. He was loud, had lived in London, and was far more interesting than Martin or anyone else there, except Deke. Deke made fun of Clive, using Martin to test out his cutting jokes about English pansies.

Monday was Martin's day off, and there was no performance of *The Lost Colony* that day. Deke usually slept until one. Early in the afternoon, when he thought Deke would be awake, Martin got on his bike and pedaled out to the beach house.

When he walked in the door, a stray cast member lay face-down on a tattered sofa, snoring. One of Deke's housemates stared bleary-eyed into the refrigerator, as if waiting for something palatable to appear. He didn't acknowledge Martin, who was as much a fixture at the house as he was. In the bathroom off the kitchen, a toilet flushed and someone in the shower screamed at being scalded. Martin walked down the hall to the back of the house and opened the door to Deke's room. He didn't knock because he thought he belonged there.

Deke's single bed was built into the wall. Deke's fabulous back and thigh muscles strained as he held himself above Clive Davies. That image elbowed space in the front of Martin's brain for years. Deke's perfect body, no longer his.

He stood there for a second before Clive noticed him and said, "Shit."

Deke turned his head. And with Martin standing there in the doorway, he finished what he was doing, then pushed himself off Clive. Clive got up, patting Martin on the shoulder as he passed on his way out. "Sorry, old boy."

Martin stared at Deke, unable to speak. The window above the bed was open. Seagulls complained and the ocean twisted and roared as it always did.

Deke picked up his shorts from the floor and put them on. "Don't be a baby about it."

"You don't even like him!" Martin shouted stupidly.

"What does that have to do with it? Look, Martin. What

did you think? That we'd live happily ever after together? Grow up, sport." He turned his back and went over to the closet, rifling through it for a shirt.

Martin left. Out past the groggy housemates to his bike. The ride back seemed interminable. Sweltering sun had softened asphalt. It sucked at his bike tires, slowing him down. His breath ripped around the lump in his throat. He turned his handlebars and rode over sea oats and sand to the beach, where he left his bike on its side and started walking. Hot wind whipped sand against his right side, stinging his face and filling his ear with grit. When the wind let up, horseflies descended. He stepped into the water to escape the flies and felt the surf plotting, wrapping itself around his ankles and shins, trying to pull him in. The beach ran for miles, the cottages nicer and more numerous as he looked north. Staring up the beach, he was struck by the flatness of it and wanted his mountains. But he couldn't go home.

He walked down the beach until the right side of his face was numb, then turned around and went back. The hotel manager took one look at his drooping cheek and mouth and sent him to a local doctor. The doctor diagnosed Bell's palsy, brought on by the wind. He told Martin he would have feeling back in his face in a few days or a few weeks. The hotel manager took him off the front desk because his face scared the guests and put him in the laundry room. Martin was glad not to have to deal with the public. The feeling gradually returned to the right side of his face. It took longer to get other feeling back. When he could drink without drooling, he went back to the front desk. Tourists, honeymooners trooped out nightly to *The Lost Colony* and came back mosquito-bitten, talking about the performance. He listened for them to mention Deke by name. Once, a couple dropped their autographed playbill in the lobby. Martin saw them lose it, and when they went upstairs, he took it. Later, in his room, he rubbed his thumb over Deke's strong black scrawl before tucking the playbill away in a drawer.

At the beginning of the summer, Martin had shunned the other hotel workers in favor of Deke's theater crowd. By the time Deke dumped him, the hotel social group had solidified without him. He made a feeble attempt to join in, but couldn't fake enough enthusiasm for the heterosexual intrigue that went on among the young people who staffed the hotel. He worked extra shifts at night to have an excuse not to go out and slept his days away in a fog of depression.

The inn housed hotel staff in a row of closet-size rooms in the basement. The first week in August, he lay on the bed in his room with the door open to keep cool. The communal phone at the end of the hall rang. Staff were allowed incoming calls on the phone, which was connected to the hotel switchboard, but couldn't call out long distance. It suited Martin. He had no desire to call his family. They would have been bewildered if he had.

When the hall phone rang, he ignored it because it was never for him. One of the girls, who camped by the phone to take calls from a boyfriend in Raleigh, knocked on the door. "For you, Martin."

He thought it was Deke. He got up off the narrow bed and arranged his voice, ready to sound reluctant, disinterested, when Deke asked to meet him. He took the receiver. "Hello."

"Martin?"

It was Liza but not as he had ever heard her.

"Liza?"

"It's Daddy, Martin. He had a stroke. He's dead."

She was crying. This was the one loss that could break Liza's cool. Martin held the receiver away from his ear, knowing that grief was coming his way, crackling through the telephone line.

"Can you come home?" she pleaded. "Please, please come home." In the background, he could hear a female voice, soothing her.

"Who's there with you?"

"Aunt Fran. Will you please come?"

"Yes."

"He was out seeing a patient and he collapsed. He was dead by the time they got him to the hospital." Her voice gulped in hysterical waves. "I didn't even get to say good-bye."

He told her he would catch the ferry to Manns Harbor in the morning and get a bus from there. He got her to put her aunt on the line, to assure him that she wouldn't leave Liza alone. As he walked back to his room, he wondered how he would pay for school now without the doctor's money, and then felt ashamed for thinking of himself instead of mourning this kind man who had believed in him. He packed his things. In his bottom dresser drawer he found the playbill he had stolen, with Deke's autograph. He had seen Deke practice his signature when he thought no one was looking. Martin tossed it in the trash can, with a pain like the tearing off of a scab.

The phone rang in Hodge's kitchen. Martin let the machine pick up, thinking the call was for Hodge or Claudie, but it was Steven. "Hey, Martin. They're putting Shane's monument in at noon on March second. It would mean a lot if you'd come. Holler back at me."

On Claudie's pristine counter a single black ant darted among the vanilla wafer crumbs Martin had dropped. He crushed it with his thumb. The doctor. His mother. Shane. Leon. When he looked back on it, it was always death that brought him home.

26

Liza

Bright sunlight streamed through the windshield of Liza's pickup, trying to fool her into thinking it was warm outside. She knew better. They'd had three days of highs in the twenties, and wind gusts rocked her truck.

She had finally called Martin to accept his lunch offer. On the passenger seat, in a long manila folder, was the task she had come up with if he was serious about redeeming himself for his rudeness. He was going to hate it. She grinned as she drove the last mile to the restaurant he'd named, Bailey's Olde Time Tavern, a chain near the community college that specialized in burgers and cold draft beer. She slowed for cars trying to exit Kmart and pulled into Bailey's parking lot. They were eating early so Liza could make her daughter Sandra's horse show, and only a few other cars dotted the lot. Martin had parked his green truck as close to the entrance as he could without taking a handicap space. The truck's narrow tires seemed too flimsy to support its heavy body. Martin wasn't in the truck. She gave him points for getting here early.

She left the folder in her truck and went into the restaurant. Martin was waiting for her in front of the hostess stand, holding his briefcase, his coat draped over his arm. His eyes were bloodshot but he looked well. He'd put on some weight, no doubt from Claudie Goforth's cooking, and it became him. He kissed her on the cheek. The hostess led them to a wide booth in the nonsmoking section. Bailey's tried to look like an English pub. The booths and other woodwork were stained a dark walnut. The lighting was dim. Their booth gave them a view of no fewer than three television sets, all with the sound down, showing different Saturday sports events.

She took off her coat and held her menu close to the table's red mosaic candle holder, which sat on doilies left over from Valentine's Day, with candy hearts scattered over them.

Martin made his selection and put down his menu. He poked through the candy hearts and handed her a yellow one. "They don't have one that says 'I'm sorry.' Will this do?"

She took it and read the message. "'Hubba-hubba'?"

"And I mean that sincerely."

"Then I accept your apology."

Their waitress came and introduced herself. "Can I interest you in one of our draft beers today, or perhaps one of our featured cocktails?"

Liza watched Martin closely, sure that he was tempted, but he declined. "Sweet tea."

"Tea for me also," she said. They gave the rest of their order.

When the waitress left, Martin lifted his briefcase onto the table. "Here's what I wanted to show you." He pulled out a ledger and a stack of photographs. He spread the pictures out on the table between them.

"This is what Leon sent you?"

"Yes."

Liza picked up the ledger. "I know you're happy to have this." She turned the brittle pages.

Martin pointed to the photos. "Any idea who she is?"

Liza looked, not wanting to touch any photograph taken by Leon Owenby. "No. Too bad they're so unclear."

"My brother was no Ansel Adams. Oh, well." He gathered the photos. Liza handed him the ledger, and he put everything back in his briefcase.

The waitress returned with two frosted beer mugs of iced tea. She tossed down cardboard coasters and straws and disappeared again.

Liza lifted her tea to her lips. Sweet but not too sweet. "Are you ready to hear what you'll be doing in order to restore yourself fully to my good graces?"

Martin looked wary. "I was hoping you'd forget about that."

"No such luck."

"All right. Lay it on me."

She put her tea down. "In my truck are the semifinalists from our high school short story contest. The winner gets twenty-five dollars and publication in the school newspaper, for which yours truly is the faculty adviser. You, my dear, are my final judge." She smiled at him, daring him to say no.

He cleared his throat. "How many stories?"

"That's the good news. Only fifteen, none longer than twelve pages. Enough to torture you but not kill you."

He nodded his head slowly. "I can do that." He seemed to be trying to convince himself.

"Thank you. All you have to do is pick the winner and two runners-up. And maybe write an encouraging comment or two on each one. You don't have to do a detailed critique."

"When do you need them?"

"A month from today." She gave a deadline six weeks before the paper actually went to press, so she could find another judge if Martin didn't come through.

He raised his mug in a toast. "It shall be done."

The waitress brought their sandwiches. Martin slid out of the booth. "I need to use the restroom. Back in a minute."

Liza bit into her club sandwich and turned to watch the overhead television set that was closest. The noon news was on, text running across the bottom of the screen for the hearing impaired. The word "body" jumped out at her. She swallowed her food and got up, standing on tiptoe to turn up the volume. A local reporter described the spot where a hiker had found the body of a male, on state land where the lower Jefferson River fed into the creek that flowed through Solace Fork and the Owenby farm. The site was less than five miles from Martin's family home place.

Liza glanced toward the restrooms. Martin hadn't come out. There was a pay phone between the men's and women's bathrooms. She headed for it, fishing in her pocketbook for change and her address book. She tried Hodge at home first, but no one answered. She called his office, and a dispatcher put her through.

Hodge picked up on the first ring. "Hodge Goforth."

"Hodge, it's Liza. The body on the news. Is it Leon?"

"No, it isn't. This fellow was younger, looks about forty, a homeless guy. I've been here all morning, trying to reach the Owenbys before the story hit. I've tracked down everybody but Martin."

"He's with me. He hasn't seen it yet."

"Thank you, Jesus. Tell him it's not his brother. It's a good thing we don't get too many unidentified bodies turning up in this county. I don't think I could take the stress."

Liza hung up and returned to the booth. Martin came out of the bathroom and walked toward her. He looked up at the television, where the reporter was still talking about the body. Before Martin could register what he was hearing, she said, "It's not Leon, Martin. I just called Hodge. It's not him."

Martin watched for a few more seconds, until the reporter signed off and the weatherman came on, then sat down. "That could have ruined a perfectly good lunch." His words were flippant but his voice shook. She let him eat his sandwich so he wouldn't have to talk.

The hostess seated another couple at the booth behind them. The man got up and changed the channel to a NASCAR race. Liza and Martin finished eating. When the waitress brought the check, Martin handed her cash, waving off Liza's offer to pay the tip. They put on their coats and waited for the waitress to return with change.

"Did I tell you Ivy bought a monument for Shane's grave?" he said.

"Hodge mentioned it."

"They're having a ceremony next week to install it." He looked at Liza and sighed. "I hate going to things like that."

"I know you do, sweetie." She searched through the candy hearts at the base of the candle holder and nudged a pink one across the table to him.

He picked it up and read it. " 'Awesome.' "

"Go to the installation," she said. "Be awesome."

"Hubba-hubba," he said.

When the waitress came back, Martin left the tip, and he and Liza walked outside. She got the folder of short stories from her truck and handed it to him.

"I suppose the punishment fits the crime," he said.

"Don't think of it as punishment. Think of it as an opportunity." She pulled her coat tighter around her. "Don't let them down, Martin. My budding authors are very sensitive."

"I won't." He squinted against the glaring sun. "Hey, Liza. Thanks for calling Hodge like that."

"You're welcome."

He raised the folder of stories to his forehead in a salute and got in his truck. Liza climbed into her own truck and drove behind him to the parking lot entrance. Cars streamed past on the four-lane road in front of them. No one would let them out. She could hear the throb of Martin's engine even with her windows closed. Black smoke from his tailpipe puffed around his one good brake light. When there was finally a gap, his truck leaped left into traffic, its wheels almost lifting off the ground, leaving her behind.

27

I v y

Today is the day Shane died. Every year on this day we put his picture in the paper. As my other two children's faces age, Shane's face in the photograph looks younger and younger. This year we're adding a nice poem Trina wrote about him. I wish I could write my own poem that would tell more of his story. How sweet he was as a baby and as a big brother to the other two, teaching Steven to ride a bike and Trina to tie her shoes. How he loved me even when he was giving me lip. Then the drugs that he must have thought would make the pain go away, but all they did was weaken whatever it is that makes us fight to stay here.

It would be hard to make all that rhyme.

There's another thing we're doing this year. Thanks to money Leon gave me, Shane's monument is finally paid for, and we can put it over his grave, instead of the little flat marker that's been there up until now.

Shane isn't buried in the family plot, high on a hill back of the home place, where my brothers and sister sometimes picnic for Decoration Day. When he died Eugenia called to say she considered it a sin for Shane to have killed himself and I ought to bury him somewhere else. Of all the meanness Eugenia has flung at me with her skinny little arms over the years, that one stings the most. I don't reckon she told the others she said that to me. I guess I could have told them and called for a vote, but Shane's dying had pressed all the argument out of me. So I buried him in the funeral home graveyard, which is between the funeral home and a Methodist church. The church doesn't have anything to do with the graveyard, but people driving by on the road don't know that. It looks like a place that God thinks is all right, not just dirt full of sinners who don't deserve a real resting place.

We are installing the monument at noon, but I drive to the cemetery early. I pass through the gate and park along the road. When I slam my car door it echoes. It's always quiet here. This graveyard has been here awhile, and the sidewalks that run in straight lines between the graves are cracked, some pushed up uneven where tree roots grow. I have never seen a ghost in this cemetery. Maybe they have too much else to do to stick around, or maybe the wind that blows through the shade trees, hot or cold depending on the time of year, wafts them away. Today the March wind is fierce and makes my nose run, even though the forsythia blooming yellow around the edges of the graveyard says it's spring, and robins are fighting worms out of the ground. I walk to Shane's grave. The monument people haven't delivered his stone yet.

Social Services had custody of Shane all those years, but when he died they said I could afford to bury him and handed him back to me. I rounded up pallbearers. Steven, Hodge Goforth, Leon, a teacher of Shane's, Martin came home for it, and then there was a man the funeral home lent for a fee. The coffin was a pretty cherry stain and heavy. I set a framed photograph of Shane on the lid. When he died I didn't have a recent picture of him. The principal at the high school gave me his eleventh-grade school picture, the one stapled to his permanent record, for me to enlarge and frame. It's the same photo we run in the paper every year.

I thought I'd never get the funeral paid for, much less be able to buy a monument. With everything, including the little flat plaque to mark Shane's place until we could get something better, the funeral cost me four thousand dollars. Four thousand dollars is hard to pay off at twenty dollars a week, with interest. Every Friday I went by the funeral home and made a payment, which meant that every Friday I had to remember Shane dying. It about wore me down. And that flat marker got me down, too. I wanted a real tombstone, so people wouldn't forget where Shane was buried. Then, when I finally got the funeral paid for and went to see about a monument, the monument people told me I had to pay for the whole thing in full before they'd start on it. I wasn't able to start paying on it at all until I got my disability money. Then I was back to paying a little bit every month.

One evening last August I was leaving the monument company after making my payment, and Hodge rolled up beside me in his truck, with Leon in the passenger seat. It was hot, but Leon wore a flannel shirt under his overalls. The arm that stuck out his open window was buttoned at the wrist. He wouldn't even roll his sleeves up.

"Who died?" Hodge called through Leon's window.

I waved hello. "Nobody."

Hodge pulled over to the curb to talk. He was never in a hurry. I bent down on Leon's side so I could see Hodge. Leon was quiet between us. It took a lot to make Leon talk.

"Picking out your tombstone ahead of time?" Hodge said.

"No. I'm paying on one for Shane."

Leon spoke. "He ain't got a stone?" Leon hadn't been out to see Shane's grave since we put Shane in the ground.

The leaning was hurting my back. I straightened up. "Just

a flat marker. I have a nice monument picked out, but they won't cut the letters until I pay for it."

Hodge said, "I reckon it's like a birthday cake. Once one person's name is on it, you can't sell it to anybody else."

Leon's mouth worked. He looked mad, but that was pretty normal. "How much you owe on the monument?"

"Eight hundred ninety-five dollars," I said. "I'll get it paid off one day."

Hodge shifted his truck gears. "Well, I'm glad nobody died today. You worried me, Ivy, walking out of there. I thought somebody had passed without me knowing about it."

Leon didn't say anything else. I told them good-bye and walked to my car. The next time I went to Leon's to get his laundry, he handed me twelve hundred-dollar bills, some crisp and some that looked like they'd been wadded somewhere for a while.

The day after Leon gave me the money, I went back to the monument company. The monument company is next to a hair cutting place. It's small. Sample headstones sit in a little yard outside, behind bars and barbed wire, leaning different ways in shallow dirt and crabgrass. To the side of the building is a big pile of mistakes, leftover granite scraps with one side smooth and the other rough, some with one letter carved in them. It makes you wonder whose name they'd been trying to spell when the chisel slipped.

I went inside. They had paneled off a little front office, but the thin wall didn't keep out the noise of saws and sanders, or the granite dust. There were no ghosts here. If there had been, the dust would have made them visible even to other people. I breathed shallow so I wouldn't choke.

The owner's wife, who ran the front office, knew me well by now. I knew exactly what I wanted. Granite that was so deep a gray it was almost black, with these words:

SHANE ABSHER OWENBY
JUNE 20, 1949–MARCH 2, 1966
We will always remember,
We will always be true.

I plopped down my cash, proud to finally be able to place my order.

"He'd a liked this stone," the lady said, counting my money.

"He was a good boy," I said.

"He had a good mama," she said.

And here the headstone is. Three men from the monument company drive their truck through the cemetery gate. The older man driving sticks his head out and says to me, "Owenby?" I tell him yes and point to Shane's plot. They park and unload the monument off the back of their truck onto a big dolly. It's wrapped in a brown quilt.

I've seen the stone, in the dusty dimness of the monument company's workshop, but I can't wait to see what it looks like in the sunshine. "Can you unwrap it?"

The two younger men take the quilt off and work to position the stone on Shane's grave. The monument is beautiful, more so because the grass around Shane's grave has had so long to grow. The stone is wide and as high as my waist. Its polish throws the sun back to heaven.

The driver hands me papers. I sign where he points and hand them back. Trina and Steven drive through the gate in Trina's Corvette. Hodge and Martin are right behind them in Hodge's pickup. They all get out and walk over to where I stand. The monument men step back so we can do our thing.

"It's nice." Trina touches the stone, tracing the words I took from her poem.

Martin stands back at first, like he doesn't want to get too close, but then steps forward and rests a hand on the monument's smooth top.

Steven shifts from foot to foot. We give it a moment of silence. I breathe on my hands to warm them. The tips of Hodge's ears turn pink. I look at Steven. He was supposed to say a little something, but I see now he won't be able. He lays his palms on the tombstone, and the words he can't say sink into the granite. I hope Shane can hear them.

Hodge clears his throat, and I look over at him. "Hodge, could you say us a prayer?" I like Hodge's praying because he knows better than to go on too long.

"Surely." He thinks a minute, then prays in one long string. "Lord, we know you have your arms wrapped around this family's son, and, Lord, we pray that you will bless this family and heal the pain that they still feel, and, Lord, bless this hallowed spot and let this fine marker be a monument to your love and grace, in Jesus's name we pray."

As Hodge finishes up I throw my own thank-you out to Leon, wherever he is, for the monument. I know the stone doesn't really change anything, but it makes me feel better.

"Amen," Hodge says.

Martin mutters another "Amen" as an echo.

Trina and Steven move in front of the stone with their shoulders touching. Hodge goes and puts a hand on each of their backs. The smooth granite reflects their legs and the long blades of grass that blow at their feet.

Martin comes over to me. His face shows more pain than Shane can account for. "What are you thinking about?" I ask him.

"About all of them," he says. "Shane, Leon. Mama."

He turns and searches my face, the way some people do when they know about me. They're mostly sure I'm crazy, but there's just the tiniest bit of wondering about the things I say I can see.

"What happens to them, Ivy? Where do they go?"

"Some don't go anywhere," I say.

"What about Mama?"

I take his arm and squeeze it hard, so he will believe what I say and never have to wonder again. "Mama is at rest, Martin. She's in a better place."

The monument men move in closer. "You ready for us to install it, ma'am?" I tell them yes. Trina and Steven each take one of my arms, and we all walk back to our cars. We leave the men to sink Shane's monument in cement, to make it permanent and real, a spot to mow around and take notice of, instead of mowing over.

28

Bertie

Bertie took advantage of the first warm day in March to get out in the yard and coaxed James into getting out there with her. They'd about cleared all the rotten leaves from the front flower beds when Bobby and Cherise drove up. It wasn't Sunday, and Bertie hadn't made enough supper to feed them. James straightened up and leaned his rake against a bush. He'd lost weight since fall. His dungarees were too loose in the seat, and bony wrists showed between his shirt cuff and the top of his worn leather work gloves. It made Bertie think she needed to feed him better.

Bobby got out of his truck and headed toward them. Cherise eased herself out of the passenger side, breathing hard. She had ballooned in the last month. Bertie remembered what it was like to be that pregnant and almost felt sorry for the girl.

Bobby was carrying a paper. "We got something to show you."

James took off his gloves and took the paper Bobby handed him.

"It's a deed," Bobby said. "We got it in the mail yesterday, from Leon. It must have got lost, just like that package Leon sent to Martin in New York."

Cherise waddled over to stand beside Bobby. Bobby had this big surprised smile pasted on his face. Bertie wondered if he'd practiced it in the mirror.

"Where's the envelope?" James handed the deed to Bertie to look at.

"Cherise didn't keep it," Bobby said.

"I threw it away when I opened it, before I realized what it was." Cherise looked James straight in the eye when she said it. She'd had long years of practice at lying, but her eyes dropped when they got to Bertie.

"Why would he mail it to you, instead of just handing it to you?" Bertie said.

Bobby shrugged. "Maybe he knew he was going somewhere."

James tried to talk them out of the lie. "Bobby, if that deed is a fake and you try to claim it's real, the sheriff is going to assume you had something to do with Leon's disappearing."

"Who says it's a fake?" Bobby got hot. "I can't believe my own parents don't believe me. I'm telling the God's honest truth!"

"Leon did all kinds of things like that right before he went missing. That money for Ivy and giving his knuckle knife to Steven," Cherise said.

"He liked me and Cherise way more than them, so why don't you believe he gave us the deed to his property?" Bobby said.

Bertie had never looked closely at a deed, but she didn't trust Cherise LaFaye one bit. The document in her hand was dirty and creased, which it would have been if it came from Leon's house. It described the boundaries of the Owenby property. It was notarized, but the name on the seal hadn't come through and the notary's signature was smudged.

"Can you at least hold off telling anybody about it?" James said.

"We're taking it to a lawyer today." Cherise reached for the deed. Bertie held it away from her, like they were playing keep-away.

"Give me that," Cherise snapped. She reached up for it, then bent over in pain and gasped. "Shit!"

Bobby said, "What'd you do, pull something?" But Bertie had seen the wet patch spreading over the crotch of the girl's sweatpants.

"She's having the baby," Bertie said.

Whatever Bertie might think of Cherise LaFaye, Cherise was carrying her grandchild. "James, get your truck." Bertie ran inside, dropped the deed on the kitchen table and grabbed a stack of towels for Cherise to sit on so she wouldn't mess up James's truck seat. When she ran back outside, Bobby was standing there with a dumb look on his face. He had no idea what to do. Cherise was bent over, swearing with pain. Good. A little pain served her right.

James pulled the truck around. Bertie helped Cherise, all two hundred pounds of her, into the front seat, spreading out the towels before she sat.

"Bobby, we're taking Cherise to the hospital. You follow along behind." Bertie and James would do Cherise a lot more good than Bobby would. Bertie made the girl scoot over so she could get in and then slammed the door. Bobby was just now starting to move. At this rate, he might get to the hospital sometime after the baby had already come. Bertie rolled the window down. "Hurry up!"

Cherise leaned across her. "Bobby! Get the deed!" As in pain as she was, she could still connive. Bobby disappeared into the trailer. James, perfectly calm, drove to the hospital.

Of course Cherise didn't let Bertie be with her for the

birthing. Bertie would have understood it better if Cherise had had her own mother there, but Cherise probably didn't even know where her mama was. Cherise had to have a cesarean section. Bertie started to follow along behind her and Bobby when they wheeled her to surgery. Cherise pointed at her, real mean, and said, "Not her!"

Bertie sat with James in the waiting room until Bobby came out, looking shaky. "It's a girl. They're both okay. They took Cherise's liver out and laid it to the side to get the baby out, I swear to God."

Bertie didn't know enough about anatomy to know if he'd seen right or not, but he got green telling it.

"I liked the old days when the daddy got to wait in the lobby and pass out cigars," James said.

Bertie was so doped up when she had her children, she didn't remember a lot. That was how they did it then. "Where's the baby?" she said.

Bobby motioned down the hall. "They're cleaning her up, then you can look through the window and see her."

Bertie didn't need to be told twice. She took off down the hall. The nurse was writing "Owenby" on a sign on the front of a little crib, and there the baby was. When Bertie saw the baby she didn't care that Cherise and Bobby hadn't included her in the birth. The baby was just precious. Perfect little hands and feet, not too fat or thin, those big, knowing eyes peeking out from under the beanie they'd put on her head to keep her warm. Bertie couldn't get enough of her.

Bobby and James came up behind her. The nurse saw Bobby and mouthed, "Do you want to come in?" Bertie nodded yes for him, and the nurse motioned them around to the door.

The nurse asked Bobby, "Do you want to hold her?"

His eyes got real big, like he wasn't sure.

"Yes, he does," Bertie said.

The nurse lifted the baby out of the crib, wrapped in her blanket, and laid the baby in Bobby's arms. Bertie tucked the blanket in and made sure Bobby supported the baby's head. The baby started to fuss, smacking her lips and arching her back. Bobby looked scared to death.

"Give her here," Bertie said. He handed the baby over, and she settled right into Bertie's arms. Bertie tickled the baby's palm with two fingers, and the baby grabbed hold. In the clutch of the little fist, Bertie felt like she'd been handed another chance, a feeling she hadn't had in forever. She needed another chance.

29

L i z a

The horses snorted a greeting when Liza entered the barn. She could hear Sandra's horse, Jaybird, moving around in the far stall. Alissa's Baby Doll stuck her long brown face over the door of her stall to say hello. Liza loved the smell of a barn, sweet hay, leather, even the manure.

"How you feeling today?" She rubbed Baby Doll's nose. The vet had been out the day before to drain an abscess in the horse's left hind foot. Liza picked up the antibiotic ointment and gauze he'd left and entered Baby Doll's stall, gently lifting the horse's hoof and unwrapping yesterday's bandages. The wound was clean. Baby Doll didn't seem to be in any pain. "Good girl." Liza applied the smelly ointment to the hoof and rebandaged it. Baby Doll's skin twitched and her tail stung Liza's face, but she let Liza finish. Liza had just set the horse's foot down and was wiping ointment off her hands with a rag when the barn door opened. Blinding sunshine flooded the dim barn. Raby and Martin stood in silhouette against the light.

"Look what the cat dragged in," Raby said.

Martin stepped into the barn, wrinkling his nose. "Pungent."

"Don't act like you never smelled manure before. You're forgetting your roots," Liza said.

"Trying my hardest." He held up a folder. The short stories. "I did it. They are judged. I want you to know my own students' papers are still sitting in my apartment ungraded, but I have done what you asked of me."

She accepted the folder over the stall door. "I'm thrilled. Thank you."

"You didn't think I'd do it, did you."

"I had all the faith in the world," she said.

"I bet."

Raby peered into the stall. "How's Baby Doll?"

"She looks good. We need to tell Alissa to be more careful when she rides on gravel." Liza gave Baby Doll a last pat and stepped out of the stall, closing the door behind her.

Raby opened the barn's double doors all the way and propped them with bricks. "The weather's so nice today we can air things out."

"Feels like May, not March," Martin said.

"Good day for sitting on the porch," Raby said. "Y'all come on up to the house. I'll get us something to drink."

"Can you carry these inside?" Liza handed Raby the folder of stories. He took them and left.

She washed her hands in the double sink by the door and walked outside with Martin. The day was truly gorgeous, the temperature in the low seventies. She lifted her face to enjoy the feel of warm sun after the long, gray winter. Beside her, Martin walked without speaking. He looked tired, bluish smudges under his eyes, his mouth tugging downward.

"How's your family?" she said.

"All right, considering. Bobby and Cherise had a baby girl."

"Really? What did they name her?"

"You would ask that. Something with a crazy spelling. Kylee. Raylee. Something with a *lee* in it."

"It'll be good for Bertie."

"True. She needs a hobby."

They walked around to the front of the house, a one-story gray ranch with a railed porch. The wind chimes Liza had hung murmured softly above their heads. It would soon be warm enough to put her hanging plants back outside. Raby came out onto the porch with two bottles of beer and a glass of iced tea for Liza. He passed out the drinks and pulled three rocking chairs into line so they could sit. Liza took the middle chair. Martin sat on her left, closest to the steps. On her right, Raby stretched out his long legs and put his feet up on the porch rail, letting out a long, satisfied "Ahh."

"Where are your daughters today?" Martin said. Liza wondered if he remembered her daughters' names.

"Alissa had a soccer game, and we made Sandra drive her," Raby said.

"I'm sure she loved that."

"If I'm paying the car insurance for a teenage driver, I'm going to get some benefit out of it." Raby drank his beer and belched. "Look at us. Me, my wife, and my wife's old boyfriend. Who'd have ever thought we'd be sitting on the porch together at this point in our lives, having a beer?"

"Raby," Liza warned.

"I'm serious. It's a beautiful thing."

Liza looked over at Martin, not sure how he would take Raby's teasing. An amused twitch played at the corner of his mouth. Liza was the only one uncomfortable. Raby and Martin were enjoying themselves at her expense.

"Did Liza ever tell you how we got together?" Raby said.

Martin smiled at her. "I don't think she ever did."

Liza reached over and took Raby's beer bottle away from him. "Give me a swig of that. I think I'm going to need it."

"Liza was rooming with my sister, Sally. Your junior year, was it?"

"Sophomore," she said. The fall after her father died.

"I'd met Liza, but my sister said she wasn't available. Some fellow named Martin had just broke her heart."

Liza's face burned. "Raby, honestly."

Martin tipped the neck of his beer bottle toward Raby. "The best man definitely won."

"My sister was student teaching. I got a call from her saying Liza was deathly ill and could I come check on her while Sally went on some overnight field trip with the Future Homemakers of America."

"Flu," Liza said. "Sally didn't want to leave me, but I told her I was going to die anyway, there was nothing she could do. I've never been so ill." The whole awful time had dissolved her immune system, leaving her wide open to the bugs Sally brought home from school. It started on a Friday afternoon. Liza felt "peaked," as Raby would say, and restless. By her two o'clock class, she couldn't hold her head up without propping her chin with her hand. The professor sent her to the infirmary, where a nurse took her temperature and called Sally to come get her.

"Vomiting, diarrhea. Spewing at both ends," Raby said.

"Raby, you are destroying Martin's image of me as the perfect woman," she said, giving up any hope that her dignity would survive this story. The flu sapped her of every bit of energy and motivation she could ever remember having. On Saturday morning after Sally left the house, Liza crawled on her hands and knees down the hall to the bathroom. She couldn't stand up without fainting. She made it to the toilet to throw up water, the only thing she'd been able to swallow. On her crawl back to the bedroom she passed out.

"I found her unconscious in the hall. Got her back in bed. Found some chicken soup in the cabinet and spoon-fed her," Raby said.

"I threw up all over the poor man," she said.

"It was worth it. That flu was my excuse. I knew Liza was too sick to put me off. I left my daddy's farm during haying season to go over there to Greensboro. My daddy about killed me for that, but when he met Liza he understood why I did it. Liza Vance was going to be mine. Good thing you'd left the picture, Martin, or I would have had to kill you."

"Good thing," Martin said.

Liza handed Raby's beer back to him. "Sally claimed afterward that she was matchmaking all along, but I think she saw how green I was and didn't want me to die and stink up the apartment while she was gone."

"Liza was talking out of her head that weekend from the fever. She said all kinds of interesting things," Raby teased.

"Stop right there." Raby would never tell her what she said in her delirium those two days. With all she had on her mind, God knows what came out about her and Martin. Over the years, to kid her, Raby had threatened to tell all if she ever left him. She wasn't going to leave him.

"I got to pee. Another beer, Martin?" Raby offered.

"No, I'm due at Eugenia's for supper." Martin sounded regretful.

"Call ahead next time and we'll feed you," Liza said.

Raby went inside.

Martin picked at a piece of the paint flaking off the arm of his rocking chair. "Shane has a headstone now."

"How was that?" she said.

"Sad."

"Who was there?"

"Ivy, Trina, Steven, me, and Hodge."

"Not Eugenia and the rest?"

"No." He brushed the chipped paint to the ground with his hand. "I kept wishing my mother could have been there. She loved Shane. She'd cradle him on her lap." He showed her with his arms. "Even after he got so big his arms and legs hung over the sides."

Liza looked sideways at him. "She held you like that, too, you know."

"I suppose."

Raby came back out. "Martin, Liza's got tickets to the symphony next week. You'd be doing me a favor if you'd go with her so I don't have to," Raby said.

Martin raised his eyebrows at her.

Liza sighed. "You really would be doing us a favor. If Raby goes he'll just squirm the whole time."

"I can't stand that scratchy violin music. Makes me crazy," Raby said.

"I'd love to go." Martin stood up and set his beer bottle on the porch rail.

"That your truck?" Raby pointed to the green monstrosity parked crooked in the yard.

"It was Leon's."

"Let me take a look at that thing." Raby walked Martin out to the yard, asking him questions about the truck that Martin couldn't answer. Martin climbed in the passenger side and slid over to the driver's seat. The truck started with a roar. Martin gave Liza a last quick wave as he drove away.

Raby joined her on the porch, "You cold?" The sun was still keeping winter hours, and the air was starting to chill.

"A little, but I don't want to go inside yet."

Raby went in the house and brought out a sweater, draping

it over her shoulders. His thumb touched her cheek. "Don't stay out too long."

"I won't."

He walked toward the barn to settle the horses for the evening. A flock of starlings returning from their winter to the south flew overhead, some landing to rest on the telephone wires that ran along the road, others scolding them to keep up. Liza pulled her sweater closer around her neck and put her feet up on the porch rail.

After Raby finally talked her into getting married, she taught until Sandra was born, then stayed home. Alissa came a couple of years later. By the early 1970s, she and Raby were in trouble. They weren't bored like some couples, but they were out of sync, constantly hurting each other's feelings without knowing why, cats with fur rubbed the wrong way. Liza was tired, so tired, of the constant negotiation that was marriage, and found herself thinking about divorce at least three times a day. Divorce. She had no one to confide in, and she missed her father more than at any other time since his death. She volunteered at a women's center in Winston-Salem then, but couldn't talk to those women about Raby because they would tell her to leave him. It was a time of bra burning and women needing men like fish needed bicycles. She straddled two sides of an abyss, one leg on each bank, the sides moving away from her, forcing her further and further into a split. Too late to jump to one side, she was going to fall.

The women's center had a storefront on the edge of the nice part of downtown, in a strip that included a convenience store, a launderette, and a substance abuse counselor. Money from an anonymous donor paid the first few months' rent. The women were supposed to raise funds for the rest. Liza got involved through a woman named Cassie, whose daughter went to gymnastics with Sandra once a week—Liza's excuse to get off the farm. Cassie's husband was a junior professor at Wake Forest University. Cassie was younger than Liza, as were most of the mothers of Sandra's friends, because it had taken Liza and Raby a while to conceive. Cassie was thin and wore her dark hair loose down her back. She would have been pretty but for the intense, defensive look on her face. She didn't shave her underarm hair, something that startled Liza every time she saw her.

To celebrate the center's opening and to brainstorm about how to raise money to keep it going, one of the women hosted a potluck dinner. Liza stood in front of the mirror in the bedroom, trying to decide what to wear, finally choosing a white peasant blouse and a skirt of dark orange India cotton. She pulled her hair back and curled tendrils in front of each ear with a curling iron. She started to put on her normal makeup, thought of the pale faces of the other women, and almost stopped, then scolded herself for caring what anyone thought. Raby came in as she was applying lipstick. "Getting ready for your hen party?"

She knew he meant it in fun, but it still annoyed her. "It's an important cause, Raby."

He leaned against the doorframe, arms crossed. "Learn to take a joke, Liza. What time do you think you'll be back?"

"I'm not sure."

"Sandra wanted to know if you'd be home in time to read her a story."

"You'd better plan to do it."

"She won't be happy."

"She needs to learn I'm not the only parent who can do things for her. If I had a dollar for every time I've heard the word 'mama' this week, I'd be a rich woman." She blotted her lipstick.

Raby's eyes narrowed. "Something eating you, Liza? A little girl ought to be able to call for her mama without getting on your last nerve."

"Nothing's eating me," she said, ashamed.

Raby stood there a moment, looking at her in the mirror, then turned away. "You girls have fun."

All she could think was that she was glad to have an evening away from him.

Marietta, the woman hosting the potluck, lived in a three-story apartment building in an older part of Winston-Salem. Cassie was getting out of her car as Liza drove into the parking lot. She waited for Liza, holding a pottery bowl. "What'd you bring?"

"Deviled eggs." Liza showed Cassie the eggs, nestled securely on Aunt Fran's deviled egg plate. "What about you?"

"Hummus." Cassie must have seen Liza's blank look. "Chickpea paste with tahini. I'm going to make it here. You eat it on pita bread."

"Interesting."

They walked up the two flights to Marietta's apartment. Voices and laughter spilled out onto the landing. Marietta's door was propped open. Cassie knocked on the doorframe, and they stepped into the foyer. The apartment had its original 1920s hardwood floors, in good shape except for water stains around a radiator. Liza caught a glimpse of built-in bookcases through the bead fringe that served as a living room door. There were so many layers of old paint on the walls that the corners and angles in the apartment had lost their definition and were rounded instead of sharp.

They followed party noise into a big, old-fashioned kitchen, where all the guests had gravitated. Several women and two men leaned against walls and counters, sipping wine or preparing food. Liza knew most of the women by face, if not by name. Cassie introduced her to the men. Vic was the only guest who looked older than Liza. His gray hair was cut short, and he had a small, neat beard. A few dandruff flakes spotted his dark green turtleneck. Chad was plump, with bright yellow hair and sideburns. He wore a nylon Hawaiian-print shirt. Plastic inserts kept the pointy collar stiff.

"We're honorary women," Vic said, shaking Liza's hand.

"What is *that*?" Chad took Aunt Fran's deviled egg plate out of Liza's hands. "Oh my God, a deviled egg plate. Only in the South."

"Chad loves specialized cookware," Vic said.

"And mayonnaise." Chad slipped an egg out from under the plastic wrap and popped it in his mouth.

Their hostess, Marietta, waved from the sink, where she was chopping vegetables for a salad. Her sleeveless cotton dress was tied too high in the back to be flattering. "Liza, I'm so glad you made it."

"Can I help?"

"Sure. You can wash these alfalfa sprouts." She handed Liza a container of little sprouts.

Liza tasted one. "I didn't realize humans could eat these. We grow alfalfa to feed our horses." She ran the sprouts under the faucet.

"They're really good for you. Totally organic, no pesticides or herbicides," Marietta said.

Cassie set her things on the kitchen counter to Liza's right and started crushing chickpeas with a pestle. "What else do you grow?"

"Soybeans, mostly, to supplement my husband's job selling farm equipment. And some fruit trees and vegetables just for us," Liza said.

"Are you organic?"

"Raby sprays the fruit trees. If he didn't, the bugs would get everything."

Cassie gave her a look. Liza could tell Cassie saw her as misguided, someone to rehabilitate. "You've got to read *Silent Spring*, Liza. You'll never spray again."

"Maybe not." Liza didn't mention that they also sprayed their tobacco. If Cassie didn't like pesticide on her apples, Liza could imagine how she would feel about tobacco.

Vic unscrewed the top of a big jug of Gallo wine and poured glasses for Liza and Cassie. He and Chad watched Cassie mix tahini into the chickpea paste.

"Cassie, we saw your hubby at the mall the other day. What a hot body," Chad said.

"Hands off. He's straight," Cassie said, unperturbed.

"Oh, for God's sake, I said he was cute. I didn't say I wanted to jump him," Chad said. He and Vic laughed.

Liza realized then that Chad and Vic were a couple. She had never been around any openly homosexual men before. She stole a look at Cassie and Marietta. Neither of them seemed at all uncomfortable. Liza shook water off the sprouts and spread them on Marietta's salad.

Marietta wiped her hands on her dress. "I think we're ready. Come get a plate, everybody. We'll eat in the other room."

They got their food and took it to the living room. Other than the built-ins, the only furniture was a low couch and a coffee table made from packing crates. Marietta had served in the Peace Corps in Ghana. African masks and statues, some of them blatantly phallic, decorated the walls and every available surface.

"I like your couch," Liza told Marietta.

"Futon," Cassie corrected her.

"Thank you," Marietta said.

They settled cross-legged on the floor. Chad ran his hand over a well-endowed fertility statue on the coffee table. "Almost as big as Vic."

"You flatter me," said Vic.

Liza averted her eyes from the statue, then felt disappointed in herself for being so provincial.

After they ate, Marietta introduced the evening's business. "The plan is to be open from ten until two, four days a week. That's school hours for those of you who have children. I'll be there most of that time, but I'd like at least one other person there with me, to man the desk and phone."

"To *woman* the desk and phone," Cassie said.

"Sorry, you're right," said Marietta. "Here's the sign-up sheet." She passed it to her left. "Now let's talk about money. We have a three-month grace period before we have to come up with our own rent, but we're on the hook immediately for the power, phone bills, and printing costs for the pamphlets we're putting out. Ideas?"

"I can try to get us some corporate sponsors," a woman said, sounding doubtful.

"It's worth a try," Marietta said.

"We could do a bake sale," Liza suggested.

Cassie snorted. "We're a feminist organization. Our fundraiser shouldn't endorse the traditional happy homemaker role."

Liza looked around. "But most of us here are homemakers."

"Speak for yourself. I'm an activist," Cassie said.

"Given the amount we need to raise, I think grants may be the way to go." Marietta hefted a large paperback book to her lap. "This lists a bunch of foundations and their grant guidelines. Liza, you're the English teacher. You know how to write. Would you be willing to do some applications?"

Liza reached for the book. "Of course."

"Great. Any other thoughts?"

No one said anything.

"Okay, people. Business meeting adjourned." Marietta twisted around and reached for a drawstring bag on the bookcase behind her. She opened it and pulled out a plastic baggie of crushed dried leaves and little squares of thin paper. She rolled a cigarette and lit up. A sweet smell that was not regular tobacco wafted toward Liza. Marietta passed the cigarette to the woman beside her, and Liza realized just how square she was. Before the joint could make it to her, she left the circle and went into the kitchen to pour herself another glass of wine. When she got back, Cassie, Vic, and Chad were sitting on the floor with their backs against the futon, discussing which members of the Wake Forest University faculty were homosexual.

"Practically the whole foreign language department. I've never seen so many repressed souls," Vic said.

"It is a Baptist college, after all," Cassie said.

"That Anton Zaltow. He claims he has a girlfriend out of state, but I know he's gay," Chad said.

"You think everybody's gay," Cassie said.

"Not everybody. Just every single person over the age of thirty," Chad said.

"And a lot of the married ones," Vic said.

"Not every middle-aged single person is gay," Liza said, trying out the new word. "I have a friend in New York City who lives with a male roommate. He isn't gay."

Cassie raised an eyebrow at her. "Does he date women?"

"He doesn't share that with me. We used to be boyfriend and girlfriend, and he may not want to hurt my feelings."

Cassie and Chad looked at each other and burst out laughing.

"Doesn't date women. Lives in the city. Has male room-mate. Sweetie, your friend is gay," Chad said.

"I don't believe that," Liza said.

"Marietta, roll another joint," Chad called.

Liza took a sip of wine. Martin came back to Solace Fork from time to time, and when he did, she enjoyed the attention of both her husband and her first love. That made her twice as attractive, didn't it? But now memories were lining up in her mind like pictures on a slot machine. The contempt in the voice of Martin's roommate when she called. The polite but indifferent reaction from one of Martin's male friends at Chapel Hill—Liza was used to getting more of a response from men. The countless times Martin put her off when they were teenagers and she wanted sex. That last time, at Rendez-vous Falls, when he unwound her arms from around his neck and she knew there would never be another time.

She looked around Marietta's apartment. The African stat-ues with their uncovered male genitalia seemed to lean toward her. Across the room, two women held hands. Marietta was taking a hit off the joint. Liza picked up her wine glass and the grant-writing book and went over to Marietta. "I need to get home. It's a bit of a drive. Thanks for hosting."

Marietta exhaled. "Oh, no problem. Thanks for doing the grant applications. Let me know if you need any help."

Liza got Aunt Fran's empty egg plate from the kitchen and left the apartment. Chad's loud laughter echoed after her down the stairs.

She still drove the Ford Sunliner that had carried her and Martin through high school. Raby maintained it with the same care Liza's father had, polishing it monthly and wiping child spills off the leather before they could set. She got in the car, tossed Marietta's book on the floor, stuck the key in the ignition, and gunned the motor. She was a good driver, had never so much as nicked another car in a parking lot, but upset and not looking, she backed into something with a crunch. She got out. The cement base of the lamppost she'd hit was unscathed, but the taillight on the right fin of the Sunliner hung by its wires like an eye from a socket.

Three stories up, someone looked out of Marietta's apartment window. Liza got back in the car and drove out of the parking lot, the taillight banging against the bumper.

At home she parked the car in front of the house and went inside. She could hear Alissa babbling to herself in her crib and bathwater running. She went to the bathroom door. Sandra was in the tub, playing with a plastic measuring cup. Raby turned the water off and wiped his hands on a towel, then saw Liza. "Back already?"

"I wrecked the car."

He was immediately protective, touching her to make sure she wasn't broken. She pulled away. "Just the taillight."

He relaxed. "Lord, honey, you scared me. Let me go take a look." He went to inspect the car.

Liza knelt on the bath mat next to Sandra. "Are you ready to wash your own hair tonight?"

"You wash it." Sandra said it "wass." She couldn't say the "sh." She poured water from the measuring cup over her tummy.

Liza reached for the shampoo. "You're a big girl now. You need to learn how to wash your own hair."

"But you love washing my hair, Mommy."

How they knew these things. Liza squeezed shampoo on her hands and lathered Sandra's dark hair. She checked for the day's crud behind Sandra's ears and rubbed the extra suds down her back and arms. "Lie back."

Sandra wiggled down into the water, and Liza rinsed her hair. "I love you," Liza said.

"What?" Sandra yelled, her ears under water. Liza couldn't tell if she really couldn't hear or was just pretending.

"Never mind."

Sandra sang a wordless song, to hear how it sounded through water. Her hair floated around her face.

Raby came back in. "It should be easy enough to fix. I can take it in tomorrow."

"I don't want it anymore."

He gave her a quizzical look but let her be. "It's your car."

Down the hall, Alissa started to fuss. Raby left to check on her.

Sandra sat up, water beading over her shoulders. "Why you crying, Mommy?"

Liza reached for a towel. "I got something in my eye."

Raby got the car fixed and found a buyer on their local radio call-in show. The morning of the day the man was supposed to pick it up, Liza watched from their front living room window as Raby polished the already spotless car. Their neighbor Mrs. Cooper walked across the street and spoke to him, and they both came toward the house.

Liza opened the front door. "Good morning, Mrs. Cooper. What can we do for you?"

Mrs. Cooper looked at Raby, confused. "I'm here to babysit."

"She's going to watch the girls for the day, while you and me take the Sunliner to Howling Rock. One last cruise." Raby rocked on his heels, his hands in the back pockets of his jeans. Liza could tell he was pleased with himself but also afraid she would turn him down. She wondered when she had become someone who most often said no.

"Let me get my pocketbook," she said.

Raby drove the winding back roads to Howling Rock instead of taking the highway, to feel the power of the convertible on the curves and hills. His hands slid expertly along the steering wheel as he maneuvered the turns. "They don't make 'em like this anymore."

"If you don't think I should sell it, I won't."

"I'm fine with you selling it." They crested a low mountain, and the town of Howling Rock appeared below, first the Swiss-cheese rock formation that had given Howling Rock its name, then the little tourist town itself, its shops and galleries pressed in a curve against the mountain like crowded teeth.

"But first we need to take some pictures, for posterity." He pulled into the paved area in front of the famous outcrop, ignored the No Parking signs and parked the Sunliner right in front. The rock rose forty feet above them, ravaged with a dozen holes, the smallest the size of a basketball, the largest as big as Liza. A hundred thousand years of nature and curious hands had worn the surfaces smooth. Wind piped through the holes, the deep tones loud even with the car windows rolled up.

Raby opened the glove compartment and took out their Kodak Instamatic. They got out of the car. Liza's light coat flapped around her.

Raby backed away with the camera. "Lean against the car, Liza."

She leaned against the hood and smiled.

Raby took a picture and cocked the camera for the next one. "Act like you're in a showroom trying to sell that thing."

She tilted her hip and batted her eyes at him.

He took another picture. "Climb on top of the hood there."

"I might dent it. The buyer wouldn't be happy."

"You couldn't dent that thing if you tried. They knew how to make cars back then."

She climbed gingerly onto the hood. Raby was right. The

metal was solid under her. She lay back on her elbows. "How's this?"

Raby took the picture. "I guess that's enough." He turned his back to her to check the camera. She lay a hand on the Sunliner's warm hood. "Good-bye, car," she said softly. She slid off onto the ground.

Raby turned around and grinned at her, slipping the camera into his pocket. "Let's get something to eat."

They drove into Howling Rock and found a parking place right in front of a diner called Babe's Café.

"This okay with you?" Raby said.

"It's fine." It was the type of primitive establishment Raby favored. They stepped through a screen door. The diner was packed, a good sign, the only seats two high stools at the lunch counter. They climbed up. Babe's had no menu. Customers were supposed to know what to order. The drink choices were lined up in their cans and bottles on a high shelf. Paper towel rolls served as napkins. Three beautiful cakes sat incongruously on the counter, a reward if they had room afterward.

A waitress, in her fifties with a beehive hairdo and red lacquered nails, slapped her palms down on the counter in front of them. "What can I get you folks?"

"Are you Babe?" Raby said.

She gave him an appreciating look. "For you I am." It was nothing new for women to admire Raby.

"Hot dog plate and sweet tea, then, Babe," Raby said.

The woman raised a mercilessly plucked eyebrow at Liza.

"BLT?" Liza hazarded.

"We're out of L and T."

"Grilled cheese, then."

"That we got."

"And a Sundrop, please."

The waitress whipped behind her to grab a cold Sundrop out of the cooler case and poured Raby a big iced tea in a Styrofoam cup, yelling their order into the kitchen. Liza looked around for restrooms and saw none. When the waitress swung around with their drinks Liza asked her where the ladies' room was.

"Outside. Down the stairs. In the basement."

Raby winked at her. "If you aren't back in five minutes I'll come hunting for you."

"I'll look after him for you, hon," the waitress said.

Liza draped her coat over her bar stool, went outside and down the narrow brick staircase between the diner and the next building. A tiny hand-lettered sign with an arrow said Toilet. She stepped up two cinder block stairs into the building's basement. The toilet door didn't close all the way, and when she hooked it there was an inch gap. She pulled her pants down and peed with record speed. The low ceiling squeaked as people walked around in the diner above. She heard the low rumble of Raby's laughter and the waitress's muffled cackle.

When she got back upstairs Raby slid off his stool. "My turn. How was it?"

"You might as well pee in the yard. I don't think they'll mind."

He left and Liza situated herself on the stool. The waitress came out from the kitchen and set food down in front of her. Cheese dripped beautifully out of Liza's sandwich. Onion rings and fries spilled off Raby's plate. The waitress picked up the spilled ones with her scarlet talons and piled them lovingly back on. "We gave him extra. The girls in the kitchen just can't get over him. Your man is a prize, hon."

"Thank you," Liza said.

Raby came back and they ate their lunch, then split a piece of chocolate cake. Raby left a big tip for the waitress, who blew him a kiss from across the room as they left. They walked down the town's main street, window-shopping, going into a store here and there when they felt like it. In a gallery where oil paintings shared space with jewelry and other accessories, Raby bought her a scarf.

"It's blue, like your car. Something to remember it by." He hung it around her neck. The silk was so soft she could hardly feel it on her skin.

Back at home late that afternoon, she watched from the living room window again as Raby handled the sale of the Sunliner. He stood relaxed, patient while the excited buyer checked out the car.

"Mommy!" Sandra called from her room down the hall. "Alissa isn't sharing!"

"Just a minute," Liza said.

There was a passage in *Little Women* when Laurie, the young man whose love for Jo has gone unrequited for so long, goes away after Jo turns down his marriage proposal and then falls in love with Jo's sister Amy. He comes back and tells Jo he'll never stop loving her, but that the love is altered. "Amy and you changed places in my heart, that's all." Those words always bothered Liza. She didn't see how it could be true, that you could love someone so passionately and then trade them out, like an interchangeable part. That afternoon, with late spring sun touching Raby's hair and glinting off the convertible, she understood. In that moment she made the decision that she would turn her mind, would assign to Raby all the romance with which she had endowed Martin for so long, would from that day on look at Raby with the eyes of the town women whose gazes followed him whenever he and Liza were out together.

"A prize. Your man is a prize."

Liza was over Martin Owenby. Almost.

30

Bertie

Another meeting. Bertie almost begged off and told James to go without her, but she couldn't do that to him. The sheriff needed to tell them what he'd found in Leon's medical records. This time Hodge offered his house, since he and Martin would already be there. Bertie was glad they weren't meeting at Eugenia's again, but she still didn't want to go. There was no way around it. She and James were going to have to tell the family about Bobby and Cherise's deed. Cherise was still on bed rest, recovering from her cesarean, but soon she'd be up and around and lying again. Bertie dreaded the righteous look on Eugenia's face.

James drove without speaking, clenching and unclenching his jaw. It started to sprinkle. Raindrops beaded on the windshield, their shadows growing huge on Bertie's lap when other cars passed with their brights on. James turned on the wipers and the spots disappeared. Bertie wished she could just as easily wipe away her fears about what Bobby might have done to Leon. "James?" Her voice quavered. "Do you think Bobby had anything to do with it?" All her doubts were in the question. She had to ask it.

"No." He sounded so sure Bertie felt better right away. "But you know he's lying about that deed, and he ain't smart enough to get away with it." He ran his fingers through his thinning hair. "Stupid," he said. "Just stupid."

At Hodge's house, Hodge opened the door before they could knock. Martin and Eugenia stood in the living room behind him. The sheriff wasn't there yet. Eugenia hadn't brought Zeb.

"Is Ivy coming?" James said.

The others all looked at each other. "It didn't cross my mind to call her," Hodge said.

"She doesn't really understand things anyway," Eugenia said.

"You know they just put up a nice headstone for Shane. Martin and I went. It was real nice," Hodge said.

Martin looked uncomfortable.

Hodge was used to dealing with Owenby family awkwardness. He changed the subject. "Bertie, you look awfully young to be a grandmother." He clapped James on the back. "Can we start calling y'all Papaw and Mamaw?"

"Not unless your name is Haylee," James said.

Bertie got out the picture of Haylee they'd taken at the hospital right after she was born. Her hair stuck out, and her face was all squinched up because of the big light the photographer shone in her eyes, but she still looked beautiful. Bertie passed it around. Everybody said Haylee was cute, even Eugenia. "She's got the red hair, from Daddy's side of the family." Eugenia handed the photo back to Bertie. "None of us had it, but they say Missouri was a redhead, our great-grandmother."

"Granny Alma's mother," James said.

Martin pretended to shudder. "Granny Alma. That was a scary woman."

"Do you remember her? You weren't but about four when she died," Eugenia said.

"I remember a dark presence in the corner and her bellowing and pointing a long bony finger at me." Martin pointed his own finger at Eugenia, crooking it like an old lady's.

Eugenia batted his hand away. "She'd had a stroke by then and couldn't talk."

"Just as well," James said. "She never had anything nice to say. She told Mama I had shifty eyes and couldn't be trusted. I wasn't but six at the time. What six-year-old can't you trust?"

Feet stomped on the mat outside. Sheriff Metcalf let himself in, knocking as he entered. He looked tired. Bertie appreciated the special attention he was giving the Owenbys, out of friendship to Hodge. The sheriff shook hands all around and settled in the middle of the couch, where he could open up his briefcase and spread papers on Hodge's coffee table. Hodge was the only one willing to sit down next to him on the couch. The rest took seats farther away. James touched his hearing aid, adjusting it so he wouldn't miss anything.

"We've got Leon's medical records, one set from the hospital and another from the neurologist he saw after that." The sheriff slipped a pair of little reading glasses out of his front pocket and put them on. "He admitted himself to the emergency room back in July, saying his face was tingling and it felt like his tongue wouldn't move. They did a CT scan and found what they called 'ministrokes.' It says here, 'transient ischemic attack.'" Even the sheriff tripped up over the medical words. "He saw the neurologist three times after that. He told the doctor he was having spells more and more often."

"Does it really say 'spells'?" said Martin.

"I think the doctor was quoting Leon. They sent him for an MRI in August. He refused to take any medicine." The sheriff flipped through the rest of the papers in his hand. "That's about it."

"Why in the world didn't he tell us?" Eugenia said.

The sheriff shrugged. "He may not have wanted to worry you."

Hodge cleared his throat. "If he was sick, that would explain something." They all stared at him. He looked guilty.

"I guess I should have mentioned it before, but it didn't seem connected, and I know Leon wouldn't have wanted me to talk about it. Lately he would come hunt me down when he was in town, to ask me questions. About repentance, good works, setting things right. I think he was making a turn toward the Lord."

Eugenia's hands flew up to her mouth. "Oh, Hodge, thank goodness. I've been so worried that he wasn't saved."

"Leon? Interested in church?" Martin said.

"I can't say I'd got him to church yet, but maybe he thought God was trying to tell him something with those strokes, rapping him on the wrist to get his attention, so to speak," Hodge said.

"The strokes explain why he didn't want to drive anymore," the sheriff said.

"Do you think he could have had one of those transient attack things and wandered off somewhere, gotten disoriented?" Hodge said.

"It's possible. We just don't know," the sheriff said.

"Well, that has to be it, doesn't it?" Bertie said. She wanted that to be it. Leon's medical records gave an explanation for Leon's disappearance that didn't involve her son.

"What puzzles me is why we haven't found him yet," the sheriff said. "If he was sick, he couldn't have wandered far. We've searched that entire property." He knocked the papers on the coffee table to straighten them and put them back in his briefcase. "Anyway, we'll hold on to these. They might be important."

"Do you have any other new information, sheriff?" Eugenia said.

"No. I was going to ask y'all the same thing."

James cleared his throat. He looked at Bertie and she nodded. "There's something me and Bertie thought we better tell you about. We don't think it has to do with Leon's disappearance, but we might as well get it out in the open."

Everybody stared at him, waiting.

"Last week, before Cherise had the baby, she and Bobby came over to the house with what they said was a deed from Leon to them." James looked down at his hands, then back up. "I can't say for sure it was a fake. I don't think I saw Leon's signature more than a time or two in my life, so I can't compare. But I think it was a fake. We're telling all of you in case Bobby tries to take it any further. I hope he won't." He shook his head. "He's a liar, but I don't think he hurt Leon."

Bertie could feel James's shame. She moved closer to him and touched his slumped shoulders.

Eugenia said, "Well!" The look of satisfaction on her face made Bertie feel just sick.

"So Bobby could have killed Leon in order to get his property," Eugenia said. It was the first time anybody had said the word "kill." James stiffened.

"Now, Eugenia," Hodge said.

"Actually, it wasn't Leon's farm," the sheriff said. "I had a deputy check the property records. The title is recorded in the names of Rory and Nell Owenby. Nobody ever probated your daddy's estate."

"We didn't know he had an estate." Eugenia was wide-eyed. "Pop didn't own anything to parse out."

"He had that land. Did he have a will?" the sheriff said.

"Of course not."

"We all assumed it went to Leon as the oldest son," James

said. "I never really thought about it, to tell you the truth. Nobody but Leon wanted to live up there."

"Primogenitive inheritance. They never should have abolished it," Martin said.

Eugenia turned on him. "Martin, you're the educated one, why didn't you ever ask about it?" She hit him on the arm.

Martin didn't answer, but Bertie could have answered for him. Martin didn't care who owned that property. He had never planned to come back here and probably even now didn't consider himself here for long.

"How does it work?" Eugenia asked the sheriff.

"Well, I think all you siblings get an equal share," the sheriff said, sounding not particularly interested in that part of it.

"What have we got to do to make it official, that we all own it together?" Eugenia was certainly interested.

Hodge said, "One of you will need to go down to the probate office at the courthouse and get sworn in as the administrator of your daddy's estate."

"What does an administrator have to do?" Eugenia said.

"I think inventory his personal property," Hodge said.

"Zero," said Eugenia.

"Put a notice in the paper and pay off his debts if he had any, though it's been so long you're probably off the hook."

"Pop was never beholden to anybody," Eugenia said.

"I guess once you do the paperwork, you get a new deed in all of y'all's names. Which one of you wants to do it? James?"

James looked startled. "Not me."

"Martin?"

"Me? I don't even live here."

"You do now," Hodge said.

"You're the one's been to college, Martin," Eugenia said.

"You would be the best choice," Hodge said.

James looked upset. "Shouldn't we wait until we know something on Leon? It doesn't seem right to carve it up without him."

"It's just to get all your names on the deed, to get the ownership straightened out," Hodge said. "It doesn't mean you have to do anything with the property."

James still looked disturbed. "Is that property even worth anything?"

"The timber on it is worth a little something," the sheriff said.

"Why can't you do it for us, Hodge? You know how it all works," Martin said.

"It needs to be a family member."

"Oh, just go down and do it for us," Eugenia said to Martin.

Martin sighed. "I guess I can go down there and report back."

"I have all your mama's and daddy's papers, their death certificates and such," Bertie said. "I'll get them to you."

"Great." Martin didn't sound very enthusiastic.

The sheriff turned to Bertie and James. "I'm going to need to talk to Bobby and his girlfriend about that deed."

Bertie's heart started to speed up. She could feel the pulse flicking in her neck.

"You want to give me their phone number?" the sheriff said.

"They don't have a phone," James said. "You can call our house, we'll give them the message. And one of us will come with Bobby, Sheriff."

"That's fine." The sheriff snapped the locks closed on his briefcase and stood up. "I'll let you folks know if anything develops."

"Thank you, Sheriff." Eugenia followed him to the door. Bertie could hear Eugenia whispering to him, about Bobby, about Bertie. Eugenia cut her eyes back at Bertie, and Bertie heard her tell him as clear as day, "The apple doesn't fall far from the tree."

That was enough. Bertie started toward Eugenia. "You got no right to be saying that."

James put his hand on Bertie's arm to hold her back and shook his head at her. "We need to be going."

"Martin will let you know about the probate thing, won't you, Martin?" Hodge said.

Bertie followed James out the door. Eugenia was still gossiping with the sheriff out on the stoop, though it eased Bertie's mind a bit that Eugenia was the one doing all the talking. Bertie would have felt worse if Sheriff Metcalf was joining in. James said a short "Good night" as they passed. Bertie kept her mouth shut for James and opened her eyes real wide so the tears couldn't pool up. She and James climbed in the truck. James started the engine and pulled out of Hodge's driveway. Bertie leaned her head against the window. Her sad face stared at her from the truck's side mirror. Eugenia's sharp words festered in her brain. *The apple doesn't fall far from the tree.* Eugenia had to know Bertie would go back and change things if she could, that she'd regretted leaving James almost as soon as she'd done it, but she couldn't go back.

It was the dancing that did it, a thing as simple as a country two-step. Whiskers touching her cheek not quite by accident, warm skin beneath them.

She had gone to Lenoir to see a doctor. Not the local man who replaced Dr. Vance, but a gynecologist, one not in her town, who wouldn't be tempted to gossip. She went because James wanted a son. They had the two girls, and they hadn't been able to conceive a third child. Two weeks before, when her monthly showed up, James, thinking he was being kind, remarked that after all, she was getting older. She got the doctor's name out of the phone book. She didn't tell James. She left the girls at her mama's and took the bus to Lenoir. The doctor had his nurse in the room during the examination, but still it was humiliating to have a man prod her like that, even if he was a doctor. When she had dressed again and the nurse had left, Bertie asked the doctor if she could have more children. He said he thought so, he didn't see anything wrong. Then she asked him whether there was a way to make sure it was a boy. She didn't know. What did they know up there in the coves? It seemed like there ought to be a way people could choose. The doctor laughed at her. He told her if she figured out how to fix the sex of a child, to come back and see him and they would patent the process together. She felt so stupid and ashamed.

She left the doctor's office and walked down Main Street toward the bus station. People who passed, headed home for their suppers, didn't notice her. She was invisible, a middle-aged mother, too ignorant to know you couldn't pick having a boy or a girl. The walk took her west, and even in her misery the twilight demanded her attention. The dying sun made lightbulbs of new buds on spring trees and stained the long boarded porch that ran along the front of the town's stores and eateries. She stepped up on the porch, hearing the deep boom of her footsteps, and wished she could just keep walking along it forever, instead of going home.

And then she heard the music, old time, the same that played when she and her girlfriends used to go out dancing. Change came slow to this part of the world. Even Elvis hadn't made inroads here before he left for the army. Bertie saw him once on *The Ed Sullivan Show*, and his noise hurt her ears.

She was just going to peek in, not let anybody see her. The place wasn't even a real dance hall, just a barbecue restaurant that put the chairs on the tables in the evening to open up its floor and had local people play. The band had a banjo, a fiddle, a guitar, and a mandolin. Bertie loved a mandolin. As she stepped up to the door she heard them start "Are You Lonesome Tonight?" a song the Carter family sang that always called up in her a false memory, sad but sweet, of somebody she had lost. But when she stopped to think who it might have been, she realized there never was anybody and she was looking back at nothing.

As she leaned against the doorframe, watching the few people who were dancing, she felt a touch on her shoulder. She turned and he was standing there. The light of early evening gleamed on black hair that was still wet from a bath. His face was tanned from outdoor work, and he looked a little tired, like he had worked all day but then just had to come out. He smelled of soap and aftershave.

"Well, hey." She tried to think of an explanation for why she was there, but he didn't seem to require one.

"You're looking pretty, Bertie."

She looked down at her dress, a faded shirtwaist of dotted swiss mostly hidden under her long sweater. She didn't feel pretty, hadn't in a while, but she appreciated the compliment.

He peered inside the restaurant. "James here?"

"No. I had some errands to do. I'm about to go home."

He looked at her, really looked at her. He was standing close. "Why not stay a while." His blue eyes, tired as they were, flashed mischief. James's eyes never flashed mischief.

She turned toward the music again. "I didn't know you were back."

"Haven't told the family. Sometimes it's nice to slip in

without anybody knowing." Then he took her hand, looking at it, not up at her face. It was so strange. Leon had never been any more to her than James's brother. Now they stood together in the bewitching light. His hand was soft and hard at the same time, so pleasing. She wanted to move closer.

"Come dance one with me, Bertie."

She followed him inside. He helped her take off her sweater, folded it, and set it with her pocketbook on a chair. She didn't see anybody she knew, so she relaxed. She did love to dance. The musicians finished their song. The half dozen people who had been dancing sat down in the restaurant's straight back chairs, fanning themselves and looking around for iced tea. Leon went up and spoke to the fiddle player. The man nodded, and as Leon came grinning back toward her, the band struck up "Tennessee Waltz," a song that tapped out a rhythm in the heart of even the clumsiest dancer.

Leon took her hand, and they stepped out on the wood floor. Looking down, she could see their movements reflected in his polished shoes. He wore trousers then, not the overalls that became his uniform later. His strong hands slid down her sides to her hips, no apology, he just wanted them there. And Bertie wanted something, too, even if she didn't know what. She rested her head in the crook of his neck. Leon was tall, able to kiss the top of her forehead. She didn't know if other couples joined them on the dance floor or not.

The band slowed the song to a stop. Bertie's hand slid to Leon's chest. She felt the ridge of a scar through his shirt. He brushed her hair back, touching her right cheek. "Do you want me to take you home?"

She told him no.

He had a camera, a fancy one. At the motor court in Asheville he showed her how to load the film. She didn't care about that, but she liked the way his fingers looked when

269

they pressed the film in, matching up the little holes along the edges of the film with the line of bumps that held it in place. She liked it, too, when he looked down into the top of the camera to see her through the lens, then cut his eyes up to look at her for real. He liked what he saw, both places. She posed for him, there on the bed, in a white button down shirt that belonged to him and shorts he'd bought her at Efird's Department Store. She tied the tails of the shirt in a knot over her navel and arched her back to make her rib cage show, like the girls in *McCall's*. She stuck her legs up and pointed her toes, pretending she was a pinup girl. The two of them went a little crazy with the camera, using up the whole roll of film.

That last morning, when they knew it was over, they moved around each other in the motel room, packing up their meager things, and she heard Leon toss the film canister into the trash can. She imagined the finished roll of film curled up inside the canister, never to be developed, and wondered what she would have looked like in those photographs. Would they have shown her to be as beautiful as she felt those few days, or would they just have been one more disappointment?

Nine months later Bobby was born. Even with the shame of everybody whispering, Bertie felt again the shadow of the hope she'd felt when she ran off. She could place hope in a boy that she couldn't in a girl, just because of the way the world was. She clung to that hope when she bounced Bobby on her knee and when he accepted Jesus Christ as his Lord and Savior at Solace Fork Baptist Church. She held onto it when his teachers told her he was causing problems, when he quit school. She kept hold of it when he started running with that tramp, Cherise, even though Bertie knew it was only a matter of time before he got her pregnant. Bertie still clutched it now, despite Eugenia saying out loud the word "kill," but she could feel it slipping through her fingers. Her son, conceived in hope and a last deep breath of freedom, had done nothing but let her down. She couldn't retrieve in him even a taste of what once felt good about her life.

She never told anyone who it was she'd run off with, and over the years she came to feel like it couldn't have been Leon. The laughing man who had led her away from the dance by two fingers was just too different from the one who'd sat up in that old house all those years, letting his life shrink in.

Beside her in the driver's seat, James stared ahead, the way he had for so long, like if he didn't look at her, at what she'd done, maybe it wouldn't be true. The brake pedal was within reach of Bertie's left foot. She had the crazy thought of stomping on it, as hard as she could. She imagined their seat belts jerking them up short, her pocketbook sliding off the seat and spilling on the floor, James turning to her to ask what in the world she was doing. The two of them stopped there, in the middle of the road, until they finally talked about that time and got it out of the way.

James felt her staring at him and turned his head. "What, Bertie?"

"Nothing," she said.

31

Martin

Martin was unaccountably nervous about going to the probate office. He threw a pair of crumpled khaki pants and a white dress shirt in Claudie's dryer to get the wrinkles out. He was glad she and Hodge weren't home. Claudie would want to get out the real iron. The probate office was in the county courthouse building. He was due there by eleven. When he'd called, the clerk told him not to come any later than that or he'd make the girls who worked there late for lunch and they wouldn't be happy.

He took his warm clothes out of the dryer and got dressed. Bertie had given him a folder of papers, including his parents' yellowing death certificates. He put it in his briefcase. His family seemed to have such faith in him. He wasn't sure what he was supposed to accomplish.

Bertie hadn't found his parents' original deed among her other papers, and no one else knew where it was, either. If Bobbie and Cherise had seen it, they weren't saying. At Hodge's suggestion, Martin stopped first at the Register of Deeds office on the ground floor of the courthouse to confirm what the sheriff had said about who owned the home place. A nice lady in the records room showed him how to search the title.

"Owenby. Isn't that the name of that missing man?"

"My brother," he said.

"Bless your heart."

Martin followed her instructions and couldn't find any transfers of property after the one to his parents. He went to the sole computer and typed in Leon's name and his parents' names, in all their variations. Nothing. He called the clerk over.

"I need to make sure I'm doing this correctly." He gave her his most charming smile and told her what he had already done.

"That's right," she said.

"So if it doesn't show a transfer to my brother, there was never one recorded?"

"If there was a conveyance recorded, it would show here on the computer." Her faith in the machine was absolute.

The clerk helped him print out his title search and made him an official copy of his parents' deed. He thanked her and then walked up wide, curving stairs to the mezzanine to see the probate clerk.

A woman with shellacked black hair sat at the front desk, taking dainty bites from a sandwich. She smiled when she saw him and swallowed the bite in her mouth.

Martin held out his hand and introduced himself.

"You're the one I talked to on the phone yesterday," she said. "Did you bring all your paperwork?"

"I think so." He spread his documents out on her desk. "Here's the last deed to the property." He didn't mention Bobby's fabricated deed. "My mother died in 1954. My father died in 1965. His estate was never probated. My family wants me to find out who owns his property."

"Your mother's interest went automatically to your father when she died. Do you have brothers and sisters?"

"There are five of us." He almost said four.

"Then if you probate your father's estate now, you'll take the property in equal shares."

"I'm embarrassed the family never did anything about this before," he said.

"Don't be. You'd be amazed at how many folks never bother with the paperwork, until they get word a highway's coming through or Kmart wants to build on it. Mountain people don't care for paperwork."

"What if one of us died before the property was divided up. What would happen to his share?"

"If he had any children, they would get it. If not, the other four of you would divide up his share."

"So, what do I need to do to probate it?"

The woman plucked his father's death certificate from the pile. "Let me get you under oath." She swore him in as his father's administrator, two decades late. She handed him an inventory sheet to list all of his father's personal property, and he entered zeros on every line except the real property line. She didn't look surprised. There were probably a lot of farmers in Willoby County who didn't own anything but their land.

Martin read the mimeographed sheet she gave him, listing things to do and the address of the local newspaper to run an ad for his father's nonexistent creditors. He felt a depression coming on at the thought of suddenly owning property here, as if something heavy had grabbed at his leg. "What does a person do if he doesn't want his share?" he said.

"You can renounce."

The word appealed to him. "Renounce," he repeated.

"It has to be in writing and filed with the probate court. If you do that, it will be like you never got a share." She collected his forms. "Come back when the newspaper ads have run."

Martin put all the documents and forms in his briefcase,

then walked back down the mezzanine stairs. The marble steps dipped in the middle, worn down by a hundred years of trudging feet. Voices from the ground floor lobby echoed up, a man pissed off about his traffic fine, the calming answer of the deputy who manned the front door. Martin reached the bottom step and passed them, pushing through heavy doors out into the sunlight in front of the building. A bench faced the parking lot and the iron box where people could deposit their water bills. He sat down and put his briefcase on the bench beside him. On the other side of the parking lot, an old man got out of a dirty white Cadillac. He looked enough like Leon that Martin froze for a moment, then felt embarrassed at how fast his heart was beating. The man came toward him and dropped his water bill into the depository, nodding to Martin. "Good morning."

"Good morning." Up close the man looked nothing like Leon. Martin watched him shuffle back to his car. The man opened his door and scraped the car next to him before folding himself into the seat and pulling the door closed. He wasn't Leon. Leon wasn't coming back.

Martin walked down the block to where he had parked Leon's truck and drove to the community college for his afternoon class. The last of his students' oral presentations were due today, a thorough and well-considered report on the twentieth-century poet of their choosing. He wished he had a flask to see him through it. He hadn't had a drink in five days, not out of self-discipline but because he had no money. Adjunct pay stretched only so far.

When he opened the classroom door, his students were waiting for him. They were slack-jawed and uniformly white—there were no ethnic minorities to speak of in this part of the state. Their oral presentations were worth a big chunk of their grade, and a third of them hadn't bothered to do it or even to show up. Martin actually preferred the ones who weren't interested at all to the ones who thought they were poets. The rhymers. Girls who wrote their poems on torn-out notebook paper with big circles or hearts dotting their *i*'s and brought them to him after class, the paper bits from their spiral notebooks dropping all over his desk like confetti. Encouraged by publication in their church bulletins. Christians weren't allowed to tell each other they stank. No one could laugh at you in church.

"So. Whose turn is it?" Martin sat down behind the teacher's desk. Silence. He checked his grade book to see who hadn't gone yet. "Eldon, go for it. Who's your poet?"

Eldon Mayhew was one of the few males who came with any regularity, and Willoby County's only punk rocker. He wore a black leather jacket and leather bracelets with studs, and had dyed his dirt brown hair green and spiked it up in a Mohawk. Martin had to respect him for trying to reach beyond the county's boundaries for someone to be, though he didn't think Eldon would ever physically leave this place. Martin could tell by the scabs Eldon picked on his head and the back of his neck, the mange sores of a dog who would chase his own tail here forever.

Eldon slouched at his desk. "Allen Ginsberg."

"I met Allen Ginsberg once," Martin said. All but Eldon stared at him blankly. They had no idea who Allen Ginsberg was. Martin felt a secret satisfaction. The one time he'd met Ginsberg, in a smoky coffeehouse in New York City in the late 1960s, Ginsberg told him his work reeked of Faulkner-esque putrefaction, of the conventions of a decaying southern aristocracy, that the time for Martin's style of writing had passed and he ought to try LSD to loosen up. Ginsberg's friend Bill Burroughs was with him and tried to soften the criticism by talking to Martin about their mutual hero, Thomas

Wolfe, but as much as it stung, Ginsberg's criticism was right. Martin's success was fleeting. It went the way of crew cuts and Buddy Holly eyewear. By the late sixties it had danced away from him, disappearing in a swirl of psychedelia, and he couldn't sell a thing.

Eldon swaggered to the front of the room and stumbled through his report on Ginsberg, drawing a titter from the class when he detailed Ginsberg's drug use and homosexuality. Behind Martin, an oversize institutional clock ticked on the wall of the classroom. A headache wedged itself between his eyes and began to spread outward to both ears. He needed a drink to make it go away. Eldon finished and sat down, his long body sprawling, pleased with himself.

"Thank you, Eldon." Martin marked an A in his grade book. Why not. Just one more report to go. Mary Lacy Morgan was the worst of the rhymer girls, her love poems like fingernails on a chalk board, her ambition in life to start her own greeting card line. "Mary Lacy, you're next."

She stood up. She was overweight, her not-quite-blond hair held back with a thin wire hair band that had to hurt. She smelled of gardenia perfume. "My report is on Helen Steiner Rice, the poet laureate of inspirational verse," she said.

This was what Martin got for not assigning them particular poets. He rubbed his temples, trying to press the pain back toward the center of his head. "Ah, Helen Steiner Rice-A-Roni, the San Francisco treat." Mary Lacy blinked her dull eyes. The other students were silent. Nobody around here got Martin's jokes. He really, really needed a drink. "Go ahead, Mary Lacy."

"Mrs. Helen Steiner Rice was an independent woman," she began. Martin couldn't take it. He didn't care how pioneering Mrs. Steiner Rice, queen of the rhymers, had been. He wrote an A beside Mary Lacy's name because he knew she would come find him if he gave her anything less, and tuned her out.

He owned a share of the family farm. Part of him wondered how much it was worth, and part of him just wanted to divest. He could certainly use some money, if Eugenia, James, and Ivy were willing to sell. Then he remembered Leon, who also owned a share. They might not be able to sell it without proof of what had happened to him. Martin had watched enough *All My Children* episodes to know they'd have to wait seven years before they could have him declared dead.

Mary Lacy walked around the room, handing out photocopied portraits of Helen Steiner Rice. She placed one on Martin's desk. Mrs. Steiner Rice glared up at him, proud and perfectly coiffed, as if to chastise him for thinking about property values instead of his missing brother. He turned her facedown. His thoughts always settled on self. It had been the same at the installation of Shane's monument. To avoid remembering Shane, he had focused on the piles of dried bird poop that topped the headstones, how the cold of the graveyard permeated his coat, where he might go and drink when it was all over.

The department secretary tiptoed in the classroom door and laid an envelope in front of him. His paycheck. Thank God. He smiled at her, and she tiptoed out again. Mary Lacy was finishing up her presentation by reading one of Mrs. Steiner Rice's more famous poems, from a yellow sympathy card with flowery gold lettering and glitter outlining a bouquet of calla lilies. Martin felt like he needed a sympathy card himself. Deep-felt regrets for the demise of your early promise and the subsequent ruination of your life. Our warmest thoughts are with you as you endeavor to locate a source of booze to ease your pain.

Mary Lacy was done. So was Martin, even though class

wasn't supposed to end for another thirty minutes. "Thank you, Mary Lacy. Class dismissed. Don't forget the exam is tomorrow morning at nine o'clock."

Mary Lacy waited until the others slid their books into backpacks and sauntered out. "Mr. Owenby, could you look over some poems for me? I'm going to enter them in a contest." She held out three pages of typed poems bound with a paper clip. The words of the first poem curved around the page in the shape of a fish.

"Fancy typing, Mary Lacy," he said.

She beamed beneath her hair band. "That took me a while."

"I'll look at them tonight." He tucked them into the breast pocket of his blazer.

"Mr. Owenby, are you going to review before the exam tomorrow?"

"We can take about a half hour for questions."

"I want to do good on your test. This is my favorite class."

"You'll do fine, Mary Lacy. I gave you an A for your report today." He hoped that would satisfy her and allow him to escape. He picked up his things and started for the door.

"Thanks for everything, Mr. Owenby." As he left she was walking around the room, retrieving the photocopies of Helen Steiner Rice that her classmates had discarded.

He went by the English department on his way out. Flora, the department secretary, was about ten years older than him, her short hair permed on top in painfully tight curls. She called everyone "hon" but was adept at deflecting students who came in with stories of dead grandparents, begging for a higher grade. Martin stopped at her desk. The dean had given him a copy of last year's multiple-choice exam to use as a model. He got it out and handed it to Flora with a wink.

"Can you type this up for me and just put the questions in a different order? I need sixteen copies by tomorrow morning."

Adjuncts were supposed to do their own typing, but Flora liked him. "I'll put them in your box, hon."

"You're the best, Flora." He blew her a kiss and left. Her giggles followed him down the hall.

He was meeting Liza at the symphony later, but he had a few hours to kill. He ought to be a good boy and go straight home, but one drink wouldn't hurt. He went by the college business office to cash his paycheck and called Steven—they said one shouldn't drink alone. It was almost quitting time. It didn't take much to talk Steven and Trina into meeting him at Cappy's, a bar downtown where he'd become a regular despite his best intentions.

Cappy's wasn't fancy. The bar gave out free peanuts. Martin's feet crunched empty shells as he walked across the concrete floor. The place smelled of stale beer and the melted Cheez Wiz the bartender kept on a hot plate behind the bar to dribble on nachos for the braver customers. Dim lighting kept the patrons from looking too bad.

Martin pulled a stool up to the bar. "Scotch. Neat." He chatted with the bartender for the first hour, enjoying the smooth taste of the liquor after days of deprivation. Steven and Trina walked in as he was ordering his fourth drink. Steven smelled of cologne. He had put on a nice shirt. Trina had come as she was, in a jean jacket and tight white pants. Cappy's sold canned beer for a dollar. If you wanted a glass you had to ask. The Scotch wasn't so cheap. Steven and Trina ordered two cans of Budweiser apiece and followed Martin to a booth in the back. They sat on one side and Martin sat on the other, facing the door.

Steven leaned back and stretched. "I'm glad you called, Martin. It feels good to get out."

Trina looked around. "I haven't been here in a while."

The bar's only waitress passed by and gave them a bowl of peanuts, still in the shells. Martin took one, popping the warm shell with his fingers and dropping the nut in his mouth. It was hot as buckshot. He spit it out.

Over the bar's music system, the Oak Ridge Boys belted out "Elvira." "I love this song." Trina drummed her fingers on the edge of the table. "Ba dump bump."

"I used to date a girl named Elvira," Steven said.

"You did not," Trina said.

"I don't tell you everything, sis. Hey, Martin, we had a lady from up your way in the shop today."

"A New Yawker," Trina said, imitating the unfortunate woman.

"Her car got dinged in the hotel parking lot. She brought it in this morning and asked me where she could get some breakfast. I pointed her to the lunch counter at the drug-store across the street for some eggs and grits. She asked me what grits was. When I told her, she said maybe she'd try one grit."

"She wasn't the dumbest one we had this week, though," Trina said. She and Steven told one tale after another about their customers. Steven was a natural storyteller, and Trina chimed in when he left out a good part. It was pleasant there in the bar, cool and dark. Country music played not too loud. Pool balls from a corner pool table knocked softly against each other. Once in a while a siren passed by outside.

Martin's glass was empty. He motioned to the waitress, and she headed for the bar to get him another. "Steven, tell Ivy I need to talk to her. I went down to the Register of Deeds today. It turns out all of us siblings own equal shares of the farm."

Steven whistled. "That's great. Maybe Mama will get some money out of it. Lord knows she could use it."

"She'll finally get something for being an Owenby. The family sure hasn't done much for her up to now," Trina said.

"I don't know how much it would bring. And with Leon missing, it might be a while before we could sell it," Martin said.

"Mama's waited this long. She can wait a little longer," Steven said.

The waitress brought Martin's drink. The room was starting to swim, so he went ahead and paid her while he was still sober enough to count his money.

"Whose idea was it to go check out the property title?" Steven said.

"Bertie and James told us Bobby claimed to have a deed from Leon. The sheriff said Leon didn't own the property, so he couldn't convey it. It seemed wise to check it out."

"You've got to be kidding me. That Bobby is about useless," Steven said.

As he spoke, the door to the bar opened, and Bobby came in with a girl Martin assumed was Cherise. Cherise looked puffy. It was less than two weeks since she'd had the baby.

"Speak of the devil," Martin said. Willoby County was too small for comfort sometimes.

Steven turned around to look. "Speak of the dumbass."

Martin sipped his Scotch. It seemed like there was something he was supposed to be doing, but he couldn't remember what it was. Up at the bar, Bobby and Cherise ordered beers. The bartender put the cans down in front of them. Bobby popped his open and turned his back to the bar. He spotted them at the booth and headed their way. Cherise followed him.

"Is this a family reunion?" Bobby held out his hand for Martin to shake, snubbing Steven and Trina.

"Hi, Bobby." Martin reached for his hand and missed completely.

"You're shit-faced, man," Bobby said.

"I guess so," Martin said.

"I hear Leon deeded you his property," Steven said, straight-faced.

Bobby looked wary. "That's right. He did. His share of it, anyway. Enough to put a trailer on."

"That was awfully nice of him," Trina said.

"Awfully nice," Steven said.

"We were the only ones cared about him. That's why he gave it to us," Cherise said. The V-neck of her light blue body suit came down way too far. Her breasts, swollen from recent childbirth, fought with each other to see which one could escape first. The sight made Martin queasy.

"You say you're the only ones cared about him?" Steven squeezed his beer can. It dented with a loud pop.

Martin could feel the conversation going bad, but he didn't know how to stop it.

"That's what Leon thought, anyway," Cherise said. "Plus he knew we were planning a family."

"Planning? That's a good one," Trina said.

A cackle escaped Martin's lips. He put a hand up to cut it off.

Cherise glared at Trina. "Yes, planning. Just because we aren't married yet doesn't mean we didn't plan it. Y'all ought to know that. Your mama never bothered marrying any of your daddies."

"Leave our mama out of it," Steven said.

"It's the truth," Cherise said.

Trina smiled sweetly at Cherise. "Slut."

"What did you say?" Cherise puffed out her chest. Her

breasts loomed so close Martin could see the acne in her cleavage. He reached for his Scotch to fight off nausea.

"I said you were a slut," Trina said, speaking loudly and clearly enough for a slow hearer to understand.

Cherise set her beer can down on the table. "Come over here and say that."

Trina clambered over Steven to get out of the booth. The two women faced each other, a foot apart. Trina came up to Cherise's shoulder and weighed half as much.

"You were a little bitch in high school, and you're a worse one now," Cherise said, looking down at Trina.

Trina didn't bother to answer. She reached up and grabbed a fistful of Cherise's starched bangs and yanked. Martin winced. Cherise screamed. Trina opened her hand and hairs floated down onto the table. Cherise grabbed her forehead with one hand and flailed at Trina with the other, spilling beer all over the table. Trina kicked Cherise in the shins. Steven was up now, going for Bobby. The bartender headed their way. Martin shrank back into the corner of the booth and held his drink up out of the way to protect it. Steven drew back to punch Bobby in the face, but the bartender had arrived. He grabbed Steven's arm. "Cut it out! One more move and I'm calling the cops. Get the hell out of my bar." He pointed to Bobby and Cherise. "You two first. You get a thirty-second head start."

Bobby and Cherise headed for the door, fast.

"You *better* run," Steven called.

"Now you two," the bartender said to Steven and Trina. He looked over at Martin, cowering in the corner of the booth. "You can stay, Martin. You weren't hurting anybody."

Steven reached for his wallet and threw a couple of singles on the wet table for the waitress. He grinned. "Most fun I've had in a while, Martin. We'll let you know how it turns out."

He and Trina took off. Outside Bobby's truck tires screeched as he and Cherise pulled away from the curb.

The bartender went back to his place behind the bar. The table was covered with beer. Martin tried mopping it up with the thin cocktail napkin that came with his drink. It disintegrated into soggy shreds. He reached in his breast pocket for a handkerchief and started to sop up the mess, then realized he was wiping the table with Mary Lacy Morgan's poems. Round Courier letters bled off the page. Her carefully typed fish swam in a pool of Budweiser.

He left the poems where they lay and made his careful, balanced way to a drier booth.

32

Liza

Liza kept her sweater on the back of the chair next to her to save Martin's place during the orchestra warm-up and through the first twenty minutes of the performance, then put it in her lap. She would not allow herself to be hurt by something so predictable.

When the performance was over she was first out of the auditorium so she could escape the parking lot before the crowd. She drove to downtown Whelan, knowing Martin would be at Cappy's, one of the few bars in Willoby County that sold both liquor and beer. She had seen his green truck there a few times since he'd come back, once at two o'clock in the afternoon. The truck was there now, sitting comfortably in the loading zone in front of Cappy's. She parked across the street and went into the bar.

By this time of night a cigarette haze hung over the room, making her eyes water. The bartender, Jason, was a former student of hers. He looked surprised to see her, but gave a wave from behind the bar. She walked toward the back.

Martin was drunk. He listed to the right in a booth, arm outstretched, clinging to his Scotch glass to anchor himself. When he sensed her standing there, it took great effort for him to raise his eyes enough to see who it was. "Liza," he managed. "Liza, Liza." She could see his brain slowly working, trying to remember. "Was I s'posed to . . ." He put his head down in the crook of his elbow.

"The symphony," she said.

"Ah, shit," he slurred. "Sympomy. Shit." He lifted his head and tried to sit up straight. "I forgot. I'm sorry. I'm sorry." The words were an echo. She wondered how many times he had uttered them drunk to how many people. And how many, like her, couldn't help but forgive him.

"I'll give you a ride home," she said.

"I can drive." He patted his blazer randomly, couldn't find a pocket, much less his keys.

"Better let me." She looked around to see who could help her get him outside. Jason was watching them from behind the bar. She motioned him over. "My truck is across the street. You take one arm, I'll take the other."

"I can walk," Martin insisted. He slid out of the booth, missing the six-inch step down. His reaction time was too slow to get a foot out to catch himself, and he sprawled on the cement floor, facedown. He rolled over, peanut shells sticking to his hair and clothes. "I renounce," he said.

Jason looked at her. She could imagine the word getting around town—Miz Barnard in a bar late at night, lugging a crazy drunk man to her truck. "On second thought, I think I'll call my husband. Can you keep an eye on him, Jason?"

"Yes, ma'am." Jason didn't bother trying to get Martin off the floor. Liza walked to the entrance to call Raby on the pay phone. Behind her, Martin's mantra grew louder. "I renounce. I renounce."

Raby answered on the first ring.

"It's me," she said.

"You all right?"

"Yes, I'm downtown. I'm fine. Is Sandra still up?"

"She's right here. What do you need?"

"Martin's down here at Cappy's, too drunk to drive. If you bring Sandra with you, we can get him and his truck back to Hodge's."

"Better just to bring him here," Raby said. Her fine husband. He didn't ask why she and Martin were at a bar instead of at the symphony.

"Be there in fifteen minutes." Raby hung up. She went back to where Martin lay on the floor. Jason was glad to be relieved. The few other customers in the bar were staring, though some of them looked as impaired as Martin.

"We've had a time with the Owenbys here tonight, Miz Barnard," Jason said. "You should've seen them earlier. Steven and his sister on one side, and Bobby and Cherise on the other. I guess we'll learn tomorrow who got the best of who."

"Whom," Liza said automatically.

"Whom. Glad they took it somewhere else. We don't need the trouble." He went back to the bar.

Martin had gone to sleep on the floor. Liza stepped over him and sat down at the booth to wait. She found a spot on the table that wasn't sticky and set her purse down.

"Liza."

She looked down. Martin's eyes were still closed, but he was conscious.

"What, sweetie?"

"Why do you put up with me?"

"I'm not sure."

He didn't say anything else.

When Raby and Sandra walked in the door, Liza's daughter had a big grin on her face. It wasn't often she got to come pick up her mother and her mother's old boyfriend at a bar at midnight. Raby had a protective hand on Sandra's back. He was already sizing up the situation.

"So this is your old beau, Mom?" Sandra said.

"Don't start," Liza warned.

Raby bent down over Martin and put his hand on his shoulder. "You awake, Martin?"

"No," Martin said, eyes still closed.

"Help me out," Raby told him, hefting him up by the arm. Martin groaned, but managed to stand up flat-footed. Raby put one of Martin's arms over his shoulder, and Liza took the other one.

"Sucker's heavy for a skinny boy," Raby said. They walked Martin toward the door. Sandra picked up Liza's pocketbook and followed behind. Jason got the door for them, then left them on their own.

"My truck's across the street," Liza said.

"He's riding with me," Raby said. "Sandra, you drive my truck. Me and Mr. Owenby here will follow y'all in that green thing." Raby had parked behind Martin in the loading zone. They leaned Martin against his truck, and Raby fished in Martin's pockets until he found Martin's keys. They wrestled him into the truck, tucking in loose arms and legs, then Raby went around to the driver's side and found it wired shut with a coat hanger.

"Piece of crap." Raby came back around and somehow managed to get his big body around Martin's prone one and fall into the driver's seat. "We're going to laugh about this one day." He put Martin's key in the ignition. "Let me see y'all get in your trucks."

Liza closed the passenger side door and went across the street to her truck. Sandra got in Raby's truck. They let Sandra pull out first, then Liza, then Raby followed with a roar. Liza kept an eye on him in her rearview mirror, in case Martin's Chevy gave up and died on the way. They drove in a convoy until they pulled into the front yard of Liza's house.

The green truck throbbed to a stop beside hers. They turned off three sets of headlights. Liza got out and opened the passenger door of Martin's truck. Raby crawled around Martin and got Martin up the front porch steps and into the house without her help.

Sandra handed Liza the keys to Raby's truck. "I'm going to bed."

"Thanks for the help." Liza followed Sandra inside. Sandra went down the hall to her room. Liza could hear Raby tucking Martin into bed in the front guest room, shoes hitting the floor. Raby came out and closed the door behind him.

"So," he said.

She looked at him, waiting for any smart remark he might care to make. He was within his rights, but he passed.

"What are you going to do with the boy?" He didn't mean just tonight.

"I have no idea."

Raby stepped close. He reached a hand up, pushing his fingers gently into her hair, his palm warm against the side of her face, then dropped his hand and led her by her fingertips down the hall to bed.

Her husband was the sexiest man in the county.

33

Martin

Martin woke up in an unfamiliar room, wearing a pair of large men's Christmas pajamas, the red flannel still bearing the creases of store packaging. One of the more surreal awakenings he'd experienced but not the only strange one. He sat up in bed and put his feet on the floor, rating his hangover an eight on a ten-point scale. He walked over to the window and looked through the blinds. Liza's front yard. At least now he knew where he was. Scattered memories from the night before pasted themselves together in a familiar collage of remorse.

The house was silent. An alarm clock by the bed said eleven o'clock. Liza and her daughters would be at school. He had missed his exam at the community college. So much for his job. He opened the bedroom door and walked out the front door to the porch, closing the door softly behind him. The sun was bright enough to stab. He held onto the porch rail and closed his eyes.

The screen door flapped open, and Raby stepped out on the porch. The door banged behind him, hurting Martin's head. Raby handed him a mug of black coffee, keeping another for himself.

Martin wrapped his fingers around the mug, too dispirited to thank him, and looked out at the yard. "I'll be out of here shortly." He was sure Raby would want him gone, and probably Liza would too.

"Don't go avoiding her. You owe her that much, at least."

"I doubt she'll want to talk to me after last night."

"She ain't wrote you off yet."

"Why hasn't she," Martin said under his breath, not for Raby to hear.

"Boy, you know how it is with certain people in your life. People you knew when you were young, when the cracks to your heart were still open. She'll take all kinds of crap from you. If I thought it hurt her I'd put a stop to it, one way or another, but it doesn't. She's not stupid about you. She just loves your sorry ass, as much as you'll let her."

"I love her, too," Martin said.

"I know you do, as best you can." Raby clapped him on the back, rippling Martin's coffee.

"I was never jealous of you." Raby was completely matter-of-fact, not threatening or insulting. "When I first started going with Liza, everybody told me I could never compete with you, but I never worried. I've known some other men like you. I say, so what. Liza knows, too. You aren't fooling her either."

"I figured that," Martin said.

Raby set his coffee mug down on the rail. "You want anything to eat?"

Martin shook his head, wincing as his brain sloshed from side to side.

"Anyway, you need to tell Liza you're sorry the next time you see her. Right now, go ahead and get cleaned up."

Martin looked down at the pajamas he was wearing. The felt Santa stitched to the front leered up at him.

"You can keep those," Raby said. A laugh tried to crack his straight face.

"Let me guess. From your girls."

"I hadn't had a chance to open them yet."

"I bet."

Raby picked up his mug and poured the rest of his coffee over the porch rail. "Come on. I'll lend you a razor. Liza washed and pressed your clothes."

Thanks to Raby's hot shower and shaving supplies, Martin didn't look or smell too bad when he left Liza's. He got in his truck. Raby had pushed the seat back, to accommodate his longer legs. Martin readjusted it and drove toward his apartment, thinking about Liza.

When her father died, Martin made his way by ferry and bus across the state, arriving in Whelan the evening before the funeral. He hitched a ride to Liza's house. A full moon lit up the yard, its white light overpowering the artificial lights that blazed in the house and on the porch. The visitation was winding up. People walked back to the cars they had parked all along the street and on to the next block. Couples passed him, shaking their heads, still murmuring their regrets. Dr. Vance was much loved.

Dirty and rumpled from traveling, Martin stood in the front yard for a moment before going in. The door opened. Liza's aunt Fran told a visitor a gracious good-bye, her deep voice following the man down the wide porch steps and out to the walk. Martin started up onto the porch, and Aunt Fran saw him. "Martin." She grabbed his arm, almost pinching it as she pulled him inside. "Honey, I'm glad you're here. I'm so worried about Liza."

He stepped into the foyer of Liza's house. A slight clinical odor from Dr. Vance's infirmary underlay the house's other smells: funeral cooking, aging books, the housekeeper's furniture polish, the light scent of wildflowers that was Liza's own.

He left his duffel bag in a corner and followed Aunt Fran to the formal dining room, where covered dishes weighed down a large antique table and matching sideboard. A dozen people huddled in small groups, eating and talking quietly. Liza stood on the far side of the room, her hair pulled back in a tight ponytail. She was as pale as he had ever seen her. She clutched a white china cup, as if for warmth. A woman beside her talked at her, her fingers touching Liza's arm. Martin could tell Liza wasn't taking in anything the lady said.

Aunt Fran said, "Liza, Martin's here." He walked across the room. Liza saw him and reached out helplessly. He took the cup out of her hand and set it on the table and wrapped his arms around her. Her sobs were hoarse. He felt them rattle against his chest. Aunt Fran waved the other mourners away from them. Liza drew in a deep breath to try to calm herself. She lifted her head. "Can you take me away from here? I don't want to see any more people."

"Go change clothes. I'll get your car keys," he said.

Liza left the room, wiping her eyes. Aunt Fran sent him a questioning look from over by the door. He tried to reassure her with a nod and went into the kitchen, where the keys to Liza's Sunliner hung on a hook above the sink. Aunt Fran entered the kitchen.

"I'm going to take her for a drive," he said.

"Do what you can for her, Martin. She's about to fall apart. I don't know how she's going to get through the funeral tomorrow." Aunt Fran blinked back tears. Her striking gray hair, normally perfect, was falling out of its bun. She could have used Martin's comfort, too, but Martin just stood there, awkward.

Liza came into the kitchen wearing jeans and a sweater. The night air was cooling off. She slipped a cold hand into his and tugged him toward the door without speaking.

"We won't be out too late," he told Aunt Fran.

Liza let him drive. In high school she always drove. She was better at it than he was and didn't adhere to the southern female tradition of ceding the wheel to a male. But that night she was in no shape to drive. Her whole body shook. Long shudders ran through muscles that had held tight for too long. He grasped her hand to try to calm the shaking.

He took the winding road up to Rendezvous Falls, where there would be no traffic and they could just drive. Moonlight flooded farmland on both sides, then spiked plant shadow into the road when they entered woods. The Sunliner climbed without effort. Liza cried in a whisper in the passenger seat.

The car glided around a last curve, and Rendezvous Falls rose up out of the darkness, wide bands of white water dropping forty feet to the rocky base below. Martin parked and got out to open Liza's door. The waterfall sprayed them with a greenhouse mist. She shivered, but before he could tell her to get back in the car, where it was warm, she had brushed past him and started up the worn trail to the top of the falls. He grabbed a flashlight from the car and stumbled after her. Plants on either side of the trail reached for his clothing, rhododendron and holly branches, a tangle of galax and sedge, dog hobble and others his mother had taught him the names of. Where overhanging branches obscured the moonlight, Martin shone the flashlight just in front of Liza's feet so she could see where to step.

They came out on the bald rock face above the falls. Martin called out to Liza to be careful, but the noise of the waterfall covered his voice. He stepped closer and touched her arm. "Let's go back."

She pointed to the long crevice that ran like a gutter down behind the waterfall itself. "Come with me."

"No, Liza."

"Please," Liza said. In the moonlight, Martin could see the tracks tears had made on her cheeks. When he didn't move, she took the flashlight from him and sat down in the fold of rock, letting herself slide a few steep inches at a time until she disappeared behind the wall of water.

Droplets thickened the night air. Over the pounding of the water Martin thought he heard Liza call his name. He knew how little he had to offer her, but he couldn't leave her on her own. He followed her down.

At the bottom, Liza stood on a relatively dry shelf of rock about five feet deep. The stone wall behind her angled forward, leaving just enough headroom for them to stand. He reached out to touch the sheet of water that coursed past them. It stung his hand. He turned back to Liza. She had set the flashlight down and was taking off her sweater, then her blouse, moving toward him as she undid the buttons. She wasn't wearing a bra. The light from the flashlight carved a deep shadow between her bare breasts. She dropped her clothes and stepped toward him, pressing against him, slipping her hands under his shirt. He traced her breasts with his thumbs. She pulled his head down and kissed him, vulnerable, needy, her tongue pushing into his mouth, her teeth clicking against his. She tilted her hips upward, grinding against him, fumbling with the zipper on his pants.

He and Liza had made out many times, before he met Deke Armstrong. Martin remembered heat between them but felt none of it now, only the coolness of the rock behind him sweeping a stripe across his back. He pulled away from her and held her wrists when she tried to reach down to touch him. She was frantic. "I want you inside me. Why are you stopping?"

He couldn't answer. She searched his face and then let out a wail that echoed past the tons of water that rushed in front of them. He let go of her arms. She turned and picked up her clothes from where she had dropped them, pushing Martin away when he tried to help her put them on. He retrieved the flashlight and helped her climb back up the crevice to the rock face. She wept all the way back to the car, her mouth and arms open but empty of him.

It was one of the great blessings of Martin's life that Liza had become his friend again after enough time had passed, and now he'd blown it.

He drove the rest of the way to Hodge's house and let himself into the apartment. The garbage bag he used to hold his empty bottles bulged from under the kitchen sink. He pulled the bag out. He could sneak and dump it before Hodge and Claudie got home. His last bottle of Scotch sat on top of the minifridge, an inch of amber liquid in the bottom. Not enough. He pulled out his wallet and counted the bills remaining from his paycheck. When he took out the money for his rent, there was just enough left for the booze he needed. He would worry about food later. He stuffed bills, mostly singles, back into his wallet. The money made the billfold too fat, and he started taking things out that he no longer needed—his New York library card, his expired Authors Guild membership, the stub from his last plane ticket. Behind a dead credit card he found the photograph of him and Liza that Leon had taken at their graduation. The image had flaked, leaving a white gash like a wound across Liza's cheek.

34

Bertie

Bertie ended up being the one that had to go with Bobby to see the sheriff.

"I can't get off work for it, Bertie. I already used up all my leave," James said.

"Can't it wait until your day off?"

"I don't think it'd look good if we tried to put it off."

"James, please don't make me. Can't he go by himself?"

"Somebody has to keep him from talking too much or getting his temper up. I'm sorry." He looked as upset as Bertie felt, so she let him alone.

Bobby picked her up a little before eleven and told her Cherise would drive her own car and meet them at the Sheriff's Department. When they got there, Cherise was walking Haylee in the lobby, trying to get her to stop screaming. Bertie started toward Cherise with arms stretched out to take the baby, but Cherise pulled Haylee away. Bertie dropped her arms.

Sheriff Metcalf must have been watching for them. He came right out.

"Hey there, Bertie, Bobby, Cherise. I appreciate y'all coming. If you don't mind, I'm going to meet with Cherise by herself first."

Haylee was still squalling.

"Bobby, how about taking the baby so Cherise and me can talk," the sheriff said.

Bobby didn't look happy. "Can't we go in together?"

"I'd rather talk to each of you separately." The sheriff waited. He was calm, but he expected to be obeyed.

Cherise shrugged a diaper bag off her shoulder and dropped it on the floor, then rolled the screaming baby into Bobby's arms. The way he held her was all wrong. As soon as the sheriff and Cherise had disappeared down the hall, Bertie took the baby from Bobby, and Haylee stopped crying. Bertie reached down with her right hand and felt around in the diaper bag until she found a bottle of formula. Cherise didn't want to mess with breast-feeding, which was too bad because a mother's milk does make a baby stronger. Bertie breast-fed all hers. Eugenia tried with her daughter, but her milk didn't have any strength to it. The doctor made her go out and get Karo syrup to mix with condensed milk. That was the only thing Bertie ever did better than Eugenia. Of course Eugenia's daughter lived off somewhere now and made a lot of money, and Bertie's breast-fed Bobby was still here, causing aggravation.

"Get that bag," she said to Bobby. "I'm going to go sit over here." She sat down in the lobby's softest chair and gave Haylee the bottle. The poor little thing sucked on it like she was starving. Bertie bent down to kiss her head. Cherise wore some perfume that had rubbed off on Haylee, but Haylee's natural baby smells came through it, so sweet.

Bobby sat in the chair next to Bertie. He leaned forward, fidgeting. "What's he asking her in there?"

Bertie looked around. Deputies and secretaries ignored them. "Don't talk so loud."

He lowered his voice. "That deed is genuine, Mama."

"Bobby."

"It is!"

Haylee took her mouth off the bottle to breathe. "Hand me a cloth," Bertie said. Bobby dug in the diaper bag and handed her a burping cloth. Bertie draped it over her shoulder and lifted Haylee up. The baby's head wobbled against her cheek. "You're better off not saying anything than saying something that's a flat lie," she whispered. "I mean that, Bobby."

Bobby swore and got up. He went outside to pace. That was all right. She and Haylee were fine without him. Bertie burped the baby, then laid her on her lap and played with her fingers until Haylee fell asleep.

Cherise was in with the sheriff for about twenty minutes. Bertie couldn't read her face when she came out. Cherise was used to hiding things from people.

"The sheriff says go on back. Give me the baby."

Bertie handed Haylee over without waking her up and went outside to fetch Bobby, and she and Bobby walked down the short hall to Sheriff Metcalf's office.

Men didn't decorate. The only thing hanging on the sheriff's wall was a map of Willoby County. His desk and the bookshelf behind him were dark brown laminate. On the shelf were a dozen or so trophies the Sheriff's Department's sports teams had won, going back to the two sheriffs before Wally Metcalf. Things were dusted, though. The sheriff was not messy, Bertie had to admit. There were papers and files here and there, but they were patted into neat piles. He had one file open in front of him. She tried to see if it was Leon's, but the sheriff had laid a piece of paper over it.

"Y'all have a seat. Thanks again for coming in." There were two chairs facing his desk. He came around and pulled one out for Bertie, then closed his office door. Bobby waited until the sheriff had sat back down before taking the second chair.

Bobby looked surly, there was no other word for it. Bertie wished James was here instead of her.

Sheriff Metcalf didn't waste time. He leaned forward, lacing the fingers of his hands together, and locked eyes with Bobby. "Tell me about this deed."

Bobby squirmed. "Didn't Cherise tell you?"

"I'd like to hear it from you."

Bobby gave a big sigh, like he was put out. "Leon must have mailed it before he went missing, and it got delayed. It had Cherise's trailer park address on the envelope but not the lot number."

This was a twist to the story Bertie hadn't heard before.

"So you saw the envelope?"

"Yeah, I saw it before Cherise threw it away."

"Why in the world did she throw it away?"

"I don't know. It got in with some other stuff she threw out."

"That's quite a coincidence, Leon sending a package to your uncle in New York and getting the address wrong, then doing the same thing with y'all."

Bobby rubbed his finger under his nose, the way he always did when he was guilty or about to tell a lie, either one. "I guess he didn't know much about mailing stuff."

"Which raises another question. Why would he mail you something? Why not just hand it to you the next time he saw you?"

"How should I know?" Bobby's voice went high. "How should I know why the man did what he did? Why'd he mail that book to Martin?"

Bertie reached over to lay a warning hand on Bobby's knee. He moved away from her, but he stopped talking.

Sheriff Metcalf leaned back in his chair. "See, Bobby, I just don't buy it." He looked over at her. "And Bertie, I know you and James had nothing to do with this nonsense."

Bertie couldn't show that she agreed with him, but she was glad he understood.

"Here's the thing, Bobby," the sheriff said. "Even if that deed was the real thing, signed by Leon and notarized by the pope himself, it wouldn't help you out, because Leon didn't own that piece of property. I know your mama and daddy told you that after our meeting the other night."

"Well, he could still deed his share over to me, couldn't he?" Bobby said.

"Here's what I got to say about that, and Bertie, forgive me for giving this boy a talking-to." The sheriff pointed a finger at Bobby. "That deed is a lie. You know it and I know it. If I thought your lying about the deed meant you were lying to me about anything else connected to Leon, I'd haul you to jail so quick you wouldn't have time to blink. But I don't think that. The reason I don't think it is I don't think you're smart enough to have planned killing Leon in order to get that land."

"Now, hold on," Bobby said.

"You hold on, son. There's a reason I didn't ask you to bring the deed in here with you. The reason is, if you gave the deed to me, acting like it was real, I'd have to do something about it. As it is, you haven't shown it to me, and you haven't tried to record it. Let's keep it that way. Keep it at home in your bureau drawer. Consider it a souvenir of a big mistake you almost made. Don't ever try to tell anybody else it's for real. I'm giving you this chance because you got a new baby and nobody's been hurt yet by your lie. It's the only chance I'm giving you. Do you understand?"

Bobby was almost doing a dance in his chair, stamping his feet to show how offended he was, swinging his head to look anywhere but at the sheriff.

"I want to hear you say you understand me."

"Fine!" Bobby looked down at his feet. "I understand."

"Good."

That was the end of it. The sheriff stood up. He walked around and held the door open for them to leave. "Thanks again for coming in."

Bobby jammed his hands in his jeans pockets and stalked out of the office. Bobby might not be too happy, but Bertie felt better than she had in a while. If Wally Metcalf didn't think Bobby had anything to do with Leon disappearing, then he must not have. She felt an easing of the anxiousness that had come from not being sure about her son.

Cherise was waiting for them in the lobby. She and Bobby exchanged a look, and Bertie knew they would compare notes later, when she wasn't around.

They pushed through the double glass doors of the Sheriff's Department, out into bright sunlight. Cherise knew enough to pull a corner of Haylee's blanket over her head for protection.

"Y'all come back to the house for some lunch," Bertie said. "Leave Cherise's car here, and we'll all ride together. I'll watch the baby for you this afternoon so you can get out." She made the offer carefully, afraid Cherise would say no just for spite, but Cherise was ready for a break. "All right," she said. They walked to Bobby's truck.

Bertie rode in the middle, with Cherise on her right holding the sleeping baby. Bobby and Cherise wouldn't use a car seat, even though James got them a perfectly good one at a yard sale. Cherise said a baby belonged in its mother's lap. Haylee's little lips moved in a dream, like a dog's legs do when it imagines chasing rabbits. Bertie felt like all the cars on the road were aiming at them, ready to hit them and make that sweet child go flying through the windshield. Bobby got right up on the tail of other drivers and gave the finger to two people he said cut him off. Bertie was relieved when he finally pulled into her driveway and stopped.

Cherise climbed out first and carried the baby toward the trailer. Bertie slid across the seat. She'd been forced to leave her house too many times of late and was looking forward to holing up inside. Bobby got out and slammed his door. When he did, his glove compartment opened and a man's wallet fell out in Bertie's lap. She picked it up to give to Bobby, thinking it was his, then saw the vulgar condom ring worn in thirty-year-old black leather. It was Leon's wallet.

She ran into the trailer, where Cherise and Bobby were settling the baby in the bassinet Bertie had bought to have at their house. She waved the wallet at them. "What did you do?"

Bobby's eyes got big. He raised a hand to rub under his nose, then dropped it again.

Bertie opened the wallet and turned it inside out over the floor. It was empty. "Where's his money? Leon always kept cash. Where is it?"

Bobby looked over at Cherise for an answer. She wasn't going to help him. "I don't know, Mama," he said.

"You took it!" The wallet felt cold and dead in Bertie's hand.

"What if I did?" Bobby said, defying her. "So what if I took money out of his billfold? He owed it to me. I drove the man around whenever he needed, ran errands for him. He could have said thank you by letting me put a trailer up, but no, that was too much to ask."

Cherise's eyes beaded out of her fat face. Bertie pointed at her. "Was she with you?"

"What?" Bobby said.

Bertie stepped up to him and slapped him with the wallet as hard as she could. "Was she there with you at Leon's?" she screamed, shocking him. Haylee woke up and started to howl.

"Jesus, Mama, get out of my face! She was there. It ain't no big deal." He clutched his cheek where Bertie had hit him. The skin reddened under old pockmarks.

Bertie turned on Cherise LaFaye. She drove her fingernail into Cherise's chest, backed her up until Cherise had to sit down on the couch. "You put him up to this. I know you're the one got him to do it. What did the two of you do to Leon?" Bertie was screaming her throat raw. Cherise looked genuinely scared, and Bertie wanted to keep her that way.

"We didn't hurt him," Cherise said. "All we did was take the wallet, honest! It was laying there. Leon wasn't around."

"You lying hussy," Bertie yelled at her.

Outside in the yard, Leon's dogs heard her and set to barking. Their noise disturbed Bertie's mama. Bertie heard her mama's screen door knock against the house and imagined her starting to walk across the road.

"Get rid of it!" Bertie grabbed Cherise by her arm and tried to haul her off the couch. Cherise lurched to her feet. Bertie shoved the wallet into Bobby's hand. "Get rid of it!" She pushed them both toward the door. Cherise dug in her heels and slipped behind Bertie, heading back into the living room toward Haylee's bassinet.

"You leave that baby here!" Bertie shrieked.

"No!" Cherise grabbed Haylee and shoved past Bertie, holding the baby away so Bertie couldn't get her. Bertie followed them out and stood in the yard while Bobby started up the truck and they pulled away. Then she kept on standing there, crying.

"Bertie?" Bertie's mama stood on her porch in her house-dress.

"It's nothing, Mama." Leon's dogs howled, as miserable as Bertie. "Go on back inside."

35

Martin

The Dumpster Martin frequented was behind a gas station on the way to downtown Whelan. Hand-lettered signs taped to it said No Public Dumping, but no one had ever bothered to come outside to tell Martin to take his empties elsewhere. He pulled into the parking lot and drove around to the back, planning to toss his bag of bottles and head downtown to the liquor store, but he braked when the Dumpster came into view. His nephew Bobby stood next to the Dumpster, his pickup truck idling beside him. As Martin watched, Bobby's right arm arced and he threw something small and black into the Dumpster.

Martin thought of turning around and leaving, but he couldn't drive around Whelan with a bag of liquor bottles in the bed of his truck. Word might get back to Eugenia or Bertie. He parked behind Bobby's truck and got out, holding his breath against the smell of rotting garbage. Bobby turned around. When he saw Martin he froze for a second, glancing back at the Dumpster.

"How's it going?" Martin said.

The passenger door of Bobby's truck opened, and Cherise LaFaye heaved herself out, holding the new baby. She came around to where Bobby and Martin were standing. James would have said her stretch pants made her rear end look like ten pounds of potatoes stuffed into a five-pound sack. The baby slept, her strawberry hair curling in a spiral around the top of her head.

Bobby eyed Martin. "What are you doing here?"

"Just dumping my trash." Martin reached into the bed of Leon's green truck for the bag of bottles. He lifted it out as gently as he could and held the bag against his leg, to minimize the telltale noise of glass on glass.

Bobby stuck his hands in his jeans pockets. He looked tired, the skin under his eyes puffy. The baby was probably keeping them up all hours. Things hadn't gone Bobby's way lately, and Martin almost felt sorry for him.

"Hey, Bobby, about last night with Steven and Trina, I hope it all worked out," Martin offered. He didn't want to make an enemy of Bobby.

"Whatever. They didn't catch up to us," Bobby said.

"You heard what we found out about who owns the property?" Martin said.

"Yeah. I don't get shit." Bobby kicked a tin can that lay at his feet, sending it clanging against the Dumpster.

Cherise shifted the sleeping baby in her arms. "It's not right. After all we put up with from that stupid old man. Jumping every time he needed to go somewhere, taking care of him up in that filthy house." She looked at Martin, narrowing her eyes. "Hey, what about your share?"

"What?"

"We could put a trailer up on your part. Everybody knows you don't want it."

Bobby took his hands out of his pockets. "That's an idea, Martin. Why not?"

Martin thought of Leon. Whatever his brother had been when they were younger, he was nothing but an old man when he disappeared and Martin felt protective. He wasn't going to let Bobby live on the property. He could do that much for Leon. "It's not going to happen. I'm sorry."

"I should have figured," Bobby said, disgusted.

The bag of empties was getting heavy. Martin switched it to his other hand. Glass shifted, giving him away.

"Your family's useless, Bobby," Cherise said.

Martin swung the bag up over the side of the Dumpster, listening to the bottles break as it landed inside.

On Main Street he found a parking space just down from the liquor store and slid across the seat of Leon's truck to get out on the passenger side. In front of the antiques shop next to the liquor store he stopped to get out his billfold, to calculate exactly how many bottles of Scotch he could afford. The antiques store was open. A woman inside was dusting a display of vintage picture frames in the front window. She smiled at Martin through the glass. The picture frames were lovely, some gilded, some silver. A small one in the corner caught Martin's eye, ornate sterling silver with a bead border where the picture would fit, a picture the size of the photograph of Liza he kept in his wallet.

He couldn't read the tiny price tag from outside so he stepped into the shop and asked. The shopkeeper told him the cost, almost as much as he had on him. She lifted the frame out of the window and set it on the counter in front of Martin.

"It's more than I expected," he said.

"Would it be a gift?" she said.

"Yes."

"For your wife?"

"A friend," he said.

"It'd be money well spent," the woman said.

He should have been able to buy it for Liza without a thought, but he could feel the liquor store to his right, like a human being standing next to him, close enough to warm his skin with body heat. This was the last of his money. He could taste the Scotch it would buy, that first swallow especially, soothing on the back of his tongue.

"I can gift wrap it for you," the woman said.

Martin's fingers knotted around his billfold. He felt ridiculous. It was a simple matter of motor control, his brain instructing his hands to count out the money and his hands obeying, but he couldn't do it. He was pathetic. He tried to laugh at himself but couldn't force air past the tightness in his chest. Instead his eyes teared up.

The shop owner smiled at him. "Sometimes I get nostalgic about these old things, too." She rested her hands on the counter, perfectly patient, waiting for him to make up his mind.

That night with Liza at Rendezvous Falls, she snatched the car keys out of his hand and drove the two of them back down the mountain, gunning it around sharp turns until Martin felt sick to his stomach. At the bottom, when the road straightened out, she finally spoke. "Where are you staying?"

He had planned to stay with her. That was impossible now. "I don't know." He would rather sleep in the road than go to his father's, and it would frighten Eugenia if he showed up at her place this time of night.

Liza drove toward her house. Moonlight striped her face, illuminating her mouth and cheekbones but leaving her eyes in shadow. "You can sleep in Daddy's infirmary tonight. I'd appreciate it if you'd leave in the morning."

"I will."

They reached her street. The cars that had lined it earlier were gone. Clouds rolled over the face of the moon, obscuring it. Aunt Fran had left lights on, on the porch and inside. They could see her though the dining room window, putting china away. The infirmary was dark.

Liza turned off the engine. "The infirmary's not locked. I'll put your bag outside on the porch."

Martin couldn't think of anything to say. He had come home to comfort her and had only caused her more pain. He opened his door to get out.

"In case you wondered," she said.

He stopped.

"He left you the money to finish school. We read his will today." She was crying again. Her hands slid from the steering wheel to her lap.

"I don't have to accept it," Martin said. The doctor had based his gift on the expectation that Martin and Liza would marry.

"He'd still want you to have it. I'll have Aunt Fran handle it." She pulled the keys out of the ignition and got out of the car, closing the driver's-side door quietly. She walked up the porch steps into the house, and a moment later put his bag out on the porch and turned the light off, leaving him in darkness.

The next day Martin went to the doctor's funeral. He declined Aunt Fran's invitation to sit up front with the family, instead taking a seat in the back, where women's wide hats blocked his view and he didn't have to watch Liza suffer. No members of his own family came to pay their respects. When the service was over he skipped the receiving line and headed for Whelan to start the long, lonely bus ride back to Chapel Hill. Every month for the next three years, Aunt Fran mailed him a check, each envelope bringing with it a mix of guilt and resignation that he hadn't had a choice.

* * *

The antiques shop owner was still waiting politely. Martin flexed his fingers and found he could move. He counted out bills one by one. He extracted Liza's picture from its place in his wallet, holding it by its frayed edges, and had the shop-keeper put it into the frame before she wrapped it.

Outside, he walked toward his truck, head down, deliberately not looking back at the liquor store. He put the wrapped gift in his glove compartment for safety and drove home. At Hodge's house he pulled into the driveway. Hodge and Liza were in the yard. They walked toward him, Liza raising a hand against the sun that glared behind Martin, concern carving a deep crease between her brows. Hodge looked flustered, his thinning hair mussed. Martin turned off the truck's monster engine and got out.

"They found him, Martin. They found Leon's body," Hodge said.

Martin would not have predicted the sick, falling feeling that coursed through him, the vacuum created in the space vacated by a brother he hadn't known he cared about. Liza reached for him, her familiar scent of wildflowers touching his nostrils, allowing him to breathe.

36

Bertie

When Bertie answered the phone in the kitchen and Hodge said, "Bertie?" she knew why he was calling. She could hear it in the careful way he said her name. They had all been expecting such a call.

"Where was he?" she said.

"At the home place. Down by the sawmill. A hunter found him."

"How did he die?"

"Can't say yet. There's a hairline fracture on the left side of his skull. Wally thinks it could have been caused by being hit, but also by falling. Animals and bugs had got to him, so there wasn't a lot left to tell how he got the crack on his head. I'm sorry, Bertie."

She fought back moving pictures in her head of Bobby and Cherise hitting Leon with something and said, too quick, "He must have had one of those strokes and fell, don't you think?"

"Could be. We'll know more after the autopsy."

"James is at work, Hodge."

"I already called him. He's on his way to the morgue."

"Why didn't he call and tell me himself?"

"He's taking it hard, Bertie."

"How in the world did they not find the body before, when everybody was looking?"

"He was under a bush, with leaves over him. Still, it's hard to understand. We must've passed by him a dozen times." Hodge sighed. "Do you want to call Eugenia, or do you want me to?"

"I'd appreciate it if you would." Bertie didn't want to deal with Eugenia. "Tell James to call me." They hung up, and Bertie sat down at the table and lit a cigarette.

After she and Leon came to their senses and she rode the bus back home to James, there was just one other time that Leon came around. It was during a winter storm, when Bobby was about two. Pine trees loaded with ice eyed the trailer. Branches popped off with a sound like rifle fire, making Bertie jump. It was just her and the kids at home. The storm had come up fast, the temperature dropping thirty degrees in an hour. James, patrolling the plant floor at work, hadn't noticed until it was too late to get home. He called and said he was going to work the next shift, to make some overtime. The electricity went out, and the trailer got colder. Smoke puffed from the chimney of her mama's house. Bertie could have bundled up the kids and taken them across the road, where there was a fireplace, except that her daddy tended to drink when he was stuck inside. Dacey thought it was funny when Papaw stumbled and lunged around the house, but Bertie didn't. It was too cold to smoke outside, but she did anyway. The cold stillness calmed her some, numbing nerves that were raw and bleeding from listening to children fight, smelling baby pee, feeling the trailer shake when three children chased up and down the hall in an animal stampede. Bertie usually didn't allow running in the house, but she was too tired to fight.

She felt trapped in the trailer and trapped in her marriage.

James ducked his head whenever he talked to her. She just wished he would yell at her, hit her even, treat her like she'd treated him so they'd finally be even and could put things behind them, but he was too gentle a man to act like that.

She stared out on her ice-covered yard. Pines hurled widow makers. Grass frosted gray. Ice wrapped the bird feeder so that when songbirds tried to land they skidded, indignant, back into the air. And then came a man's figure tramping up the road. It was Leon, his good shoes sinking in crusted snow. He slipped now and again as he walked and put his arms out to catch his balance.

Bertie thought, *Lord, what is he doing here.* She was not in the mood for company. He made it to their porch and grabbed the post for support. His eyebrows and nose hairs had frozen silver, turning him old. He could hardly move his mouth. "Can I come in for a spell?"

"What in the world." She put out her cigarette and opened the door so he could get out of the cold. "The heat's off," she warned.

"S'all right." He kicked snow off his shoes and stepped inside, shedding his coat and leaving a puddle on the floor. He flexed his fingers. "I think I'm frostbit. My hands are burning."

She took his hands and examined them. His breath near her face smelled of cigars. His fingers were red, not white, and she let them go. "You're okay. Blow on them. I'll get you some warm water to soak them in." She got a plastic bucket from under the kitchen sink and filled it with the last of the warm water in the pipes. "What were you doing out in this mess anyway?"

He sat down at the table. "I don't know."

Another man would have had an excuse ready.

The kids came chasing into the kitchen, Bobby in just a

low-riding diaper and pajama shirt, jogging along after his sisters. They didn't pay any attention to Leon.

"Out," she said, but they were already chasing back down the hall. "You want a biscuit, Leon? They're left over from breakfast, before the electricity went off. I can't offer you any-thing hot."

"All right." He dipped his hands in the water.

She got him a biscuit and a paper towel and set it down on the table in front of him.

Leon took his hands out of the water and used the paper towel to dry them off. Biscuit crumbs spilled on the table. "I got a letter." He reached his frozen hands in his coat pocket and fumbled it out. "A fellow I knew down east when I worked there, wants me to come to Kinston and run his sawmill."

"That's something." She brushed the crumbs off the table into her hand and put them in the garbage, then pulled up a chair and sat down across from him. "You going to go?"

"Depends." He kind of bowed his head, creasing and re-creasing the letter, then he looked up and held the envelope out to her. His Adam's apple rose and fell in a long swallow. "We could go together." His mouth drew up and held still. Outside, the sky turned from white to gray with late after-noon. Leon's blue eyes squinted in the dimness of the kitchen, waiting for her answer.

What she mainly felt was mad. Mad at the loneliness that had made her run off with him in the first place. Mad that their time together hadn't been real. Mad that she'd ruined things with James. Mad at the smell of diaper bucket that surrounded her. Mad at Leon for pretending that they could start over, when it was so clear they never could. Anger rolled up out of her. Her hands started to shake, and it was hard to breathe. "Are you crazy?"

Leon reached for her hand, grabbing it hard, pleading.

"Come with me, Bertie. Please, girl. I think about you all the time." He had tears in his eyes.

"No, Leon. No. Absolutely no." She pulled her hand away. Down the hall something crashed—the kids had broke something. Pain stabbed behind her eyes. She pressed the sides of her head. Leon's shoulders sagged. She saw that half of him had expected her refusal.

"Go home, Leon," she said.

He got up and went, picking up his coat as he left, not putting it on until he got outside. She sat at her table for a long time after he left, staring at his uneaten biscuit.

Leon didn't go to Kinston. As far as she knew he never went anywhere again. He never said another word to Bertie about the two of them. When they talked after that, she watched for some hint in his eyes, any suggestion that he held on to a memory of her. There was nothing and that was fine by her.

She pondered it at her kitchen table now. How one man could be many. First young and spirited, worth sampling at any cost. Then old, swaddled in sameness. Then finally a bundle of bones lying quiet under a bush.

*Leon Owenby of Solace Fork died on an
undetermined date in October, at age 65.
Mr. Owenby was an army veteran of the
Second World War, during which he fought
in the European theater. He worked many
years for Oakley Mills and also farmed. He
is survived by his sister Eugenia Nash and
husband, Zebulon; sister Ivy Owenby;
brother James Owenby and wife, Bertie;
brother Martin Owenby; and numerous
nieces and nephews. Arrangements are by
Ferris Funeral Home.*

—WILLOBY NEWS & RECORD,
April 9, 1987

37

I v y

We are first out of the church after the funeral because we sat in the back, feeling unwelcome. I stand in the churchyard with Trina and Steven. Pine knots swirl under the church's thin white paint. Steven's suit is too small. He has split a seam where sleeve meets coat. I paw around in my purse for a safety pin and fix it for him. I watch my relatives file out of the sanctuary. They use different doors, don't even talk to each other. Martin stands with Liza Barnard under a tree. Hodge makes the rounds, says the right thing to whoever. Eugenia bosses the undertaker, orchestrates the drive to the family plot. James stands under a tree, fiddling with his hearing aid. Bertie holds her new grandbaby. The little girl's red hair curls all over her head, and Bertie can't keep her hands off her.

Steven is about to explode. He can't take another second with these people. "You want me to go with you to the burial, Mama?"

"No, I'll be ready to go home in a minute." We have driven separate cars. Ghosts mill about, the women stern, the men sniffing for a free meal. Leon is not among them.

The funeral director escapes from Eugenia and comes up with a clipboard to assign us a place in the car line. He is relieved when we tell him we aren't going. He shoos other people to their cars, tells them to put their headlights on. Steps out into the street in front of the church and starts to direct traffic.

"You ready to go, Trina?" Steven says.

"Yeah. Hey, Mama, I'll call you later on." Trina kisses my cheek. They walk to Steven's truck as the line of cars pulls out of the parking lot.

I go to my car and leave by a back way. I have never been one for burials. Other people see them as an ending, but I know better. I drive up the developer's road that runs along the back of my family's property, up to my special place. I park near enough that my knees won't have far to go. I walk down to the creek and knock pine needles and a curled dead spider out of my jelly jar, get me a drink, and walk up to my spot.

It's been six months since I was here.

The last time, I brought a towel to sit on. I heard somebody walking around the old sawmill down below and got up to see Leon down there, sorting through a pile of lumber scraps, stacking what he wanted under a juniper bush. I sat back down. He couldn't see my car from where he was, and I didn't have any particular need to tell him hello that day. I listened to the pleasant sound of wood tossed on wood, hollow and springy, like a baseball bat thrown down as a man heads to first base. Each toss sent an echo knocking between hill and creek.

Somebody hollered for Leon. I recognized James's voice. I could hear all that they said, the fall air was that clear.

"Whatcha looking for?" James said.

"Wormy chestnut." Wood slid down the pile as Leon picked through it.

"Ain't much of that around. Remember that big tree Pop

had over by the barn that died? You could make some money off that if you had it today."

"I'm hoping they's some pieces of it under here, to finish a cradle I'm making for Bobby and Cherise." Leon's breath came fast from his efforts.

There was a silence. I stretched up on my knees so I could see. James stood a few feet from Leon while Leon worked. He held a pair of tin snips in his right hand, and he looked a little puzzled. "Cradle? You know something I don't?"

Leon straightened up and faced James. From above I could see the top of Leon's balding head, count the strands of the hair he had combed over. He looked like he was thinking hard on something. "Look here, I got something to say." He dropped a last board on the stack he had salvaged and ground the toe of his shoe into the dirt. "I got to make it right. When Bertie left you that time—"

"We don't talk about that," James said.

"It was me."

James adjusted his hearing aid, like he wanted to be sure what he'd heard. "What was you, Leon?"

"I'm the one ran off with her. If Bobby ain't yours, he's mine."

Leon was always the bigger, meaner brother, but James got in a lucky hit. The arm with the tin snips came up fast, crashed into the side of Leon's head, sent him down into wood chips and sawdust. A single cry tore from James's throat, the length of half a breath. He turned and stalked away toward the house.

I saw Leon get up. I think I did. Saw him rise from where he fell, his legs bending too far at first when he tried to walk, then steadying up. Saw him stop and wipe his shoes one at a time on the back of his pants legs. Heard the soles crack dry leaves as he walked into the brush away from me. Smelled the drift of a cigar he'd lit. But that's not all I saw, and it's the also-sawed I'm never sure of. Did I see him keep lying there, still as a sleeping child while James raged up the hill? Did I see October wind flick back wisps of his hair, like a mother tickling him to wake up? Did deep leaves really gossip in a whisper, quilting him a cover, burying him with his wood scraps? I told myself I would tell the sheriff if he came to me and asked, tell him both tales and let him sort out which was real.

But nobody ever asked me anything.

38

Bertie

They buried Leon in the family graveyard, lowering the casket into a rectangular hole in the hard red clay. Woods and kudzu surrounded the graveyard on three sides. Bertie and James stood up front with the rest of the family and close friends, Eugenia and Zeb, Hodge and Claudie, Bobby and Cherise with the baby, Martin standing with Liza Barnard. The other thirty or so people who had come had to find a place as best they could. The graveyard was old enough that the family couldn't remember the names of everybody buried there. Round rocks marked the graves of babies who'd died too fast to claim a name. The older markers were split by time and weather, the carved names long worn off. Bertie looked at the other grave markers and imagined future years, when the words would be worn off Leon's stone and whatever family came up here would have to remember him by story.

Eugenia stood to Bertie's right, tearful. "I know it's the Lord's will, but I just wish we had an answer."

Hodge put his arm around her. "It's a shame the autopsy came back inconclusive."

Bertie looked over at Bobby and Cherise, standing to her left with the baby. For Bertie the autopsy was a prayer answered. She would have to live the rest of her life knowing what Bobby and Cherise had done to Leon, but at least her son wasn't going to prison and Haylee would have a father. The baby started to fuss. Cherise shifted her from one arm to the other. Bertie reached for Haylee, and for once Cherise handed the baby to her without arguing. Bertie put Haylee over her shoulder, patting her back, enjoying the feel of the little head against her cheek.

They finished lowering the coffin and that was that. People started to move, coming up to the family to say one more time that they were sorry before picking their way down the dirt road to where they'd parked.

Bertie touched Martin's arm. "I'd like to get those family papers back from you, if you're done with them."

"I am. Your folder's in my briefcase, in the truck." Martin started to go get it.

"We'll get it. We're going now anyway," James said.

Bertie gave Haylee back to Cherise and followed James out of the graveyard to where Martin's green truck was parked, taking up half the road. James reached in the open passenger side window and fished Bertie's folder out of Martin's briefcase, and they went to their own truck. James was quiet, had been since they'd found the body. Bertie wondered when he would start to talk to her again.

At the house she went in the bedroom to change into comfortable clothes, pants and a sweater and shoes that didn't pinch. "Do you want me to make you a sandwich?" she called. James didn't answer. She finished getting dressed and went into the kitchen.

James was standing by the kitchen table with his head bowed. His face was stricken. She thought the day had just caught up with him, but then she looked down. The folder of family papers lay open on the table. A stack of little square black-and-white photos were spread out in a crooked fan on top of the other papers. She reached to straighten them, then saw what they were. Her. Her and Leon.

She looked up. James turned without saying a word and pushed through the door, out to his truck. His engine started up. She ran out of the trailer after him.

It was too bright outside. She banged on the truck hood as James drove past her, but he didn't stop. She ran back in the house and dragged her fingers through the kitchen drawer looking for the extra keys to her parents' car, a rusting brown Buick that sat under the sweet gum tree across the road. She found the key and ran outside. She drove only when she had to. The Buick's pedals felt strange under her feet. She prayed the car into starting and it did. She backed out of her parents' driveway, then put the car in drive and sped off after James, honking her horn. He ignored her. He headed out into the country, in the direction of the home place. She followed him up the winding road, the car bouncing hard in the ruts. James parked in the yard of the home place and got out.

She stumbled out after him. "James!"

He swung around. "Go home, Bertie."

"Let me explain."

"You don't have to explain."

"I didn't love him, James. I never did. I had gone invisible, is all."

His head hung down. His voice was a whisper. "I should have done better by you."

James the martyr. Suddenly she was so angry at him she could have killed him.

"Jesus Christ, James, will you just go ahead and get mad at me for it? I slept with your brother. Don't you care enough about me to get mad?"

James turned away and looked at the sky, then turned toward her again and let out a breath that he seemed to have been holding forever. "How could you go and do it?" he hollered. "Leave me with those sweet little girls and just walk off! With *him*!" He turned around and kicked at the porch's rotting post, making the whole house shake. He kicked it again and again, then turned back around to Bertie. "I had to tuck the girls in those nights and explain away why their mama didn't love them enough to stay, didn't love me enough to stay. Dacey cried the whole time. You put us through hell, woman." He commenced kicking again. Hornets whose nests held the post together came out to see what the commotion was about. "I was a good husband to you, Bertie Owenby," he yelled, kicking slower now and breathing harder. "I am a good husband to you, and you are just a woman who will never be happy with what you've got." The porch post gave way, and James backed into her as part of the porch roof fell down in a splintering of wood and a buzz of surprised insects. She caught him in her arms, and they both sat back hard on the ground. The house stood stunned by James's assault.

The air seemed clear, cleansed by James's fire. Bertie breathed it in, laid her cheek on the top of James's head and breathed him in. "I am happy with what I've got."

They watched hornets circle the house in confusion. Finally, James moved. He got up and walked over to the end of the porch and picked something up, a baby cradle, partly finished. He held it up, running his hands over the unsanded parts, examining the dovetails that held the sides together. "I need to do the rest."

Bertie got to her feet and came to look. "I'll help. A little mattress and coverlet and something around the sides so she won't bump her head." She fingered the smooth curve of one of the rockers, imagining Haylee in the cradle she and James had made together, the baby's little hands exploring what was hard and what was soft. James set it down, and it started to rock, just a little, even though there was no wind.

39

Liza

Liza sat with Martin at the table in Hodge's kitchen, where he'd invited them after the funeral. Hodge poured coffee from a battered aluminum coffeepot. The veined white Formica of the tabletop had separated from its base. Martin flicked it with his thumb, making rubber band music. Liza gave him her schoolteacher look, indulgent but suggesting that perhaps he should quit damaging property. He stopped. The kitchen was painted 1960s avocado green, the walls marked by the scuffs and accidents of Hodge's children. Stove burners had branded oven mitts. Papers and photos rippled down the yellow refrigerator. Liza could feel Martin wishing the kitchen were his. Claudie had told them good night and gone to bed.

Hodge set the coffeepot on the counter and sat down. They all looked at each other.

"The three musketeers," Martin said.

"The three stooges," Hodge said.

"The three wise men," Liza offered. "Wise people."

"I like that one," said Martin.

"We're not that wise," Hodge said. "Or you aren't, anyway. I'm pretty wise."

Martin snorted.

"Reverend Davis did a nice job with Leon's eulogy," Hodge said.

"Considering he never met him," Martin said.

"Got his name right, anyway," Hodge said. "I went to one last month where the preacher got the poor man's name wrong the whole service." He grinned at Martin. "That's what happens when you don't attend church regular."

"I don't want anybody yapping at my funeral. Especially not you, Hodge," Martin said.

"Too late. I've already got my sermon written. The wages of sin is death and all that." Hodge blew across his coffee to cool it. "By the way, Martin, the developer that owns that property back of yours called me yesterday, to see which one of y'all he needed to talk to about buying your place. He's going to give you a call."

"Did he mention a price?" Martin said.

"He floated two hundred thousand."

"You're kidding me," Martin said.

"You can probably get more than that," Liza said. The bigger cities nearby were expanding, rising like a slow tide, their waves beginning to lap at properties in surrounding rural counties.

"That would be nice," Martin said.

"Of course, you could buy out your brother and sisters and live up there yourself," Hodge said.

"Like I said, the money would be nice, seeing as I'm currently out of a job. I may be moving on soon," Martin said.

"Now, don't go and say that," Hodge said. "We'll find you another job. The community college wasn't a good fit for you anyway. The headmaster at Wakefield Academy told me they're looking for an English teacher. I told him about you. Private schools don't pay much, but you'd make more than at the community college, and I bet the students are better."

Wakefield was where wealthier Willoby County families sent their daughters to high school.

Martin pushed hair out of his eyes and flashed a wicked grin. "Is Willoby County ready for a flaming homo from the city to teach its impressionable young ladies?"

It was the first time Liza had ever heard him put words to his homosexuality. She giggled. "This county could only benefit from a little flamboyance."

"It really could," Hodge said.

"Then maybe I will stay," Martin said.

Liza got up, rinsed out her coffee cup in the sink, and set it upside down on the drain board. She put a hand on Hodge's back. "I'm heading home. You two stay out of trouble."

Martin walked her outside. At her truck, he pulled something out of his pocket. "This is for you." He handed it to her, a palm-size package, store-wrapped by expert female fingers.

She raised her eyebrows. "Shall I open it now?"

He nodded.

She slipped a fingernail under the tape and unwrapped it. In an antique silver frame, her younger self leaned in to kiss Martin Owenby's cheek. It wasn't her own image that made her throat catch, but Martin's, the happy, confident look on his smooth face. She wanted to weep for him. "Where did you get this? Did you find it at Leon's?"

"I've had it," he said. "I've always had it."

The photo was worn, the pigment faded from handling. He had loved it. He had thought of her.

"I may need to borrow it back from time to time," he said. "The girl in that picture has seen me through a lot."

She ran her thumb over the frame's patterned surface. "I'll share it. You know where to find it."

Martin hugged her. For once he felt solid in her arms. Liza realized that she was ready to go. That she was freed from the what-ifs that had tugged at her for thirty years. She knew that even though there would be other nights at Hodge's table or her own, the hemorrhage of feeling, of regret for things unfinished, was stanched. She wanted to laugh and cry with relief.

She touched Martin's face and said out loud what she had always counted on him to read in her mind. "I love you, sweetie. I hope you stay here. You know you're welcome at our place anytime."

He put his hand over hers. "I love you, too, Liza." He squeezed her fingers and then let go. She climbed in her truck. Martin walked back to the house and stood in the doorway, keeping the porch light on until she pulled out, then turning it off and disappearing back into the house. Liza headed home.

For years after Martin broke it off with her, they hadn't seen each other or spoken. Then, on the evening after another funeral, Shane's, something made her get in the Sunliner and drive over to Eugenia's, where she had heard Martin was staying. When she got there he was sitting on the porch by himself, smoking a cigarette. His sideburns were long, but otherwise he looked the same. When he saw the car he crushed out his cigarette and stood up. She got out and leaned against the car, crossing her arms.

"Nice wheels," he said. "An old friend of mine had a car like that."

"She still does," she said.

He took a few steps toward her and stopped, then held his arms open. She stepped into his hug, finding a place in it that was hers. Their skin was warm against the moist chill of the night air. Their fit was perfect.

They separated and Martin helped her put down the convertible's white top. Curtains fluttered as his sister Eugenia peered through the front window at them. They got in the car and went for a drive, as if nothing had ever interrupted their friendship.

When she got home from having coffee with Martin and Hodge after Leon's funeral, she saw Raby through the window, his reading glasses down on his nose. Raby of the strong face and sly wit, who had coaxed her into marrying him, who checked the oil every time his wife or daughters started out on a trip. Raby, as solid as the mountain that rose beyond the fields on their farm. She pushed through the screen door, and he looked up at her with a little grin. "I was about to send out a posse."

"Hodge had us over after the funeral."

"How's your Martin?"

"Fine. What are you doing?"

He held up the bridle Sandra used for horse shows. "I am sewing tiny pink ribbons on our daughter's bridle so that she will not die of embarrassment at her horse show Saturday. I feel like a sissy."

Liza unwrapped the photograph Martin had given her and set it on the mantel, then walked over to Raby and put her arms around his neck, rubbing her smooth cheek against his rough one. He put down the bridle and slid his hands along her arms, then nodded at the photograph. "I remember her," he said.

40

Martin

After Liza left, Hodge rooted around in his kitchen cabinets and pulled out a skillet. "I'm in the mood for eggs and bacon. How about you?"

"Is it included in my rent?" Martin said.

"I'll put it on your bill."

"Two eggs, sunny-side up."

Hodge opened the refrigerator and got out eggs and bacon wrapped in white waxed paper. He peeled strips into the skillet. Grease began to pop.

"Is there any species on earth that doesn't like bacon?" Martin said.

"Bacon is a gift from God. This is the real thing. I get it every year from a fellow up the road who keeps hogs."

"It smells like my mother's." Martin breathed deeply. He remembered waking up to that smell on cold mornings, trying to get downstairs early to claim his share before his brothers did.

"She could cook some bacon." Hodge poked around the skillet with a fork. "Your mama would be proud of you, Martin."

Martin shook his head. "I did not do well by my mother." Hodge was facing the stove, and Martin couldn't see his face.

It was easier to talk to him with his back turned. "What kind of son was I, not to be there with her when she died?" Bacon smoke filled Martin's eyes.

"She kept it from you."

"What?"

"She kept it from you, how sick she was, because she didn't want you coming home."

"How do you know that?"

"I went and saw her about every weekend. I could see she was failing. She forbade me to tell you. I respected that." Hodge turned around, a pudgy middle-aged man holding a fork. "I'll never forget what she said, the last time I saw her. Your mama was a person of words just like you, even if she didn't know as many big ones. We were out on her porch. She pointed to how red clay had crept up the sides of the house and outbuildings. She said she had seen it creep up the legs of people who stood still too long, and I wasn't to call you back, lest it stain you, too."

Martin stared at him.

"She was glad you got away, Martin. But that doesn't mean you can't come home again." Hodge turned back to the stove, pushing the bacon to one side of the skillet and cracking eggs into the grease. "Did I ever tell you about the time I heard the voice of God?"

Martin groaned.

"Don't worry, I'm not going to witness to you, I'm just telling you about it." Hodge touched the edges of the eggs with his fork, testing to see if they were cooked. "It was the end of my first year at the farm school. First time I'd been off on my own, and I had not behaved myself. I had lost my way. Too much drinking and wildness, and then there was a girl who thought I might have got her into trouble, she didn't know for sure yet. I was out by the fountain at the school. I thought my life was over. It was five in the morning. I remember there was a little wren bathing in the fountain. I was watching it, and all at once I heard a voice say, clear as day, 'None of that old mess matters.'" Hodge slid the eggs and bacon onto two plates. "People always want God to repeat Himself when He says something. I listened for it again. I went around the fountain to see if somebody was playing a joke on me, but no. I didn't hear anything else. God just said it the one time, but I decided that was enough. I've never forgotten it. Every time my own mistakes pile up on me like manure, I remember it and the burden is lifted." He brought Martin his plate and put a hand on Martin's shoulder. "None of that old mess matters, Martin."

Martin felt the sureness of his friend's touch, the love it contained. Hodge gave his shoulder a squeeze. "Eat your breakfast," he said.

They finished their food. Hodge got up and took their dishes to the sink. "I think I'm ready for bed. You going to turn in?"

"No." Martin stood up. "I've been thinking I'd like to go to the clearing. I haven't been there since I came home."

"Do you want company?"

"Not this time."

Hodge nodded. "It's different now," he warned. "Don't be sad at how things have fallen in."

"I won't."

"All right, then." Hodge stood in front of Martin, his arms at his sides. On impulse Martin reached out and hugged him, the way men were supposed to hug other men, quick and hard, as if they could imprint all their love in one squeeze. To his surprise, Hodge turned it into a real hug, holding him long enough to make it matter. When they stepped back, Hodge wasn't embarrassed at all. "You go on, friend," he said.

"I won't worry about you till morning." He walked down the hall toward his bedroom.

Martin went down the narrow basement stairs to his apartment, to change out of his funeral clothes and get a coat and the truck key. Next to the key on top of his refrigerator was the almost empty bottle of Scotch that had been there since before they found Leon's body. He hadn't touched it. He could look at it and not want it. He didn't know if it was finding Leon that had dampened his desire for alcohol, or if he had finally just had enough. He knew the not wanting wasn't likely to last, but for now he didn't have to drink.

He went out the ground-floor entrance, turning on the porch light for his return and closing the door quietly behind him. The night was damp and hazy. The almost-full moon shone bright but out of focus. There were no stars out. A few frog voices rose from the grass around Hodge's house, but he didn't yet hear the excited cacophony of peepers that would come with full spring. Leon's truck sat in the yard. In the moonlight its shadow loomed against the grassy bank behind it.

The morning Martin left for college his mother had made him a special breakfast, a double serving of bacon and fried eggs cooked as he liked them, runny, instead of fried hard the way his father insisted. The simple task of standing up to cook seemed to cost her breath, and she stopped every few minutes to lean against the stove. When she carried the skillet to the table and slid the food onto his plate her wrist strained to hold the weight.

Leon came into the kitchen, buttoning his shirt. Martin wolfed his bacon down before Leon could steal it. Leon ignored him, speaking only to their mother. "I'm going to town. You need anything?"

"I don't believe so."

A car horn honked in the yard. "That's Liza." Martin jumped to his feet. He reached around his mother's waist, hugging her hard, making her wince. "Bye, Mama."

"God bless you, Martin."

His packed duffel bag sat by the door. He grabbed it and stepped out onto the porch. As he paused to lift its strap to his shoulder he looked back inside the house. His mother was at the stove again, her back to him, cooking Leon's breakfast. Leon stood beside her, his hair combed into a perfect duck tail at the nape of his neck. As Martin watched, Leon put a hand on his mother's upper arm, his fingers encircling it, squeezing it gently, then letting go. She turned her head to look up at him. Her profile was sharp. The smile she gave, just for Leon, crinkled the thin skin around her eyes.

Liza honked her horn again, and Martin walked out into the yard. He didn't see his mother again.

He opened the heavy passenger door of Leon's truck and slid over to the driver's seat. A spark of static electricity shocked him when he turned the key in the ignition. The truck rumbled horribly, the noise bouncing between cornfields and houses all along Hodge's road, but no lights came on. The people here ignored loud truck motors at midnight the way New Yorkers ignored car alarms.

He drove to the dirt parking lot of what used to be the Solace Fork school grounds and pulled in. Orange plastic netting blocked off the construction site. The concrete foundation of the new book depository was half-poured. Two portable toilets loomed in the darkness. He dug a flashlight out of Leon's glove box and climbed out of the truck. The old deer path was still there. Animals didn't change the way people did.

At one time Martin could have walked this path blindfolded. He started along it, holding the flashlight low. Small pink and white flowers had stuck their heads up along the trail, groundhog style, to test the weather. He imagined them shouting the all-clear back to their brethren in the ground. The air held the not-quite-warm wetness of spring. Then he heard the sound of the creek. He left the path and walked toward it. The water was so cold, ice had formed tubes around small saplings that leaned too far over into the stream. If Martin stuck his hand in, his fingers would ache with cold. He made his way through a canopy of winter branches, noting here and there the light green of new growth on the forest floor. May apples formed droopy green umbrellas under the trees. He saw wild orchids, jack-in-the-pulpits, trillium. He arrived at the clearing. The trees were still there, though they leaned or lay at different angles.

Liza had called them church ladies. She should have been the writer instead of him. Looking at the trees, he wished for her metaphoric eye. Or, more, for his sister Ivy's glimpses of people who had passed. He turned off his flashlight and invited the moonlight to trick his sight, imagining bowed trunks as backs, bark as sun-roughened skin, hanging vines as sundries bought for trimming at Riddle's general store. And then he saw them, sitting in a circle. He searched the crowd, and there was his mother among them. She smiled at him. He put his cheek down on the nearest tree, which grew sideways in front of him like a gate, and watched her. She was quilting. She chatted around the straight pins she held in the corner of her mouth. Her face was rested.

"Where was I when you needed me?" he asked her out loud as she talked to her friends.

She looked over at him, surprised. "Law, Martin, you were right where I wanted you to be."

He thought of the sheets he lay on the night she died and felt a laugh hopping up his throat. "I don't think so, Mama."

"You were. You were at school. I wanted you at school, away from here." She put down her sewing and gestured him over. "Come here, boy. Stop your aching." He walked over, and she pulled his head down to her ear. She smelled of rose hips and clean laundry hung on a line. He sat down beside her on the ground and put his head in her lap. The other women, polite, averted their eyes while he cried.

41

I v y

At the home place the morning after Leon's funeral, the porch has caved in on itself. The porch roof hangs almost to the ground. The rotten corner post that supported it lies in the yard, light morning rain dampening the splintered wood. The house has given up, has crumpled to its knees like a cowboy dying slow in an Old West movie.

I am back again to clean it, this time to clean it out, to get the rest of Leon's things before the whole house falls in. Eugenia is supposed to help me, but I don't see her yet. Rain mists my face. I lift a cardboard box of garbage bags and cleaners from my car. The fingers of my yellow rubber gloves wave over its edge. I go around to the side door so the porch roof won't collapse on my head. I enter the kitchen and leave the door open behind me for light, set my box on the kitchen table. I am glad this is the last cleaning, that I won't have to come back here anymore. The house, usually so crowded with spirits, is empty and dark, and still no Leon. I wonder if he will ever come.

I carry plastic garbage bags to the room where Leon slept. On the way I catch sight of Shane's back and legs disappearing around a corner. I call out, "Shane!" He ignores me.

In Leon's room I find a closet full of brand-new dress shirts, still pinned and wrapped in store plastic.

Missouri, my redheaded great-grandmother, appears at the foot of Leon's bed, her favorite age of twenty-one. She wears her pink dress.

"Save them shirts for Eugenia," she says, a mean twinkle in her eye. She knows Eugenia gave Leon a new shirt every Christmas, hoping he would wear them to church.

"No, I'm not going to hurt her feelings." I put them in a bag to carry to Goodwill.

Missouri lies back on the bed, her dress pleasingly tight around her slender rib cage. "You bore me to death."

"That's all right," I say.

Shane never owned a dress shirt, except for the one I bought for his funeral. The shirt was white. The funeral home people buttoned the collar high on his neck to hide the long rope burn and bruises. Somehow they fixed his swollen face. Still, most people who came by to view his body were afraid to look down and stared instead at the photograph I'd laid on the coffin lid.

I didn't see my son die, but I smelled it. I wasn't supposed to know where the foster home was, but Hodge told me, and I drove there before I went to the morgue. A police car was still outside the house, blue lights circling in the darkness. I parked behind it and got out. The foster mother stood in the front porch doorway, talking to the cop, fear of blame on her thin face. I couldn't hear her words, but her hands rolled over one another, listing all the reasons why it wasn't her fault. As I got closer I could hear the cop murmuring, "Yes, ma'am," over and over. I went up the steps and pushed right between them, and was inside before they could do anything. I broke yellow tape and walked up carpeted stairs to the second floor.

The smell of death is terrible, even when there is no blood. The stench of Shane's last fear coated faded wallpaper. The rug stunk of all the things that are loosed when a body lets go. The policeman came up behind me and forced my arms behind my back, kicked my legs out from under me while the foster mother screamed. With my face pressed to carpet that was wet with my son's waste, I wondered if Shane had known how a body betrays itself, would he have tied that last knot, stepped up on that chair, kicked it away with the white rubber toe of his beloved tennis shoes?

"What are you moping about?" Missouri asks me.

"Nothing." I tie shut the plastic bag that holds Leon's shirts, as Shane passes by the bedroom door once again and doesn't come in.

"Oh, for Pete's sake." Missouri hops off the bed and stamps a small, booted foot, blowing impatience from her nostrils. Red hair flames down her back, then turns to cinders, and she appears as her oldest self, the age she left the world, an age she hates.

"You!" she calls to Shane. I hear his footsteps pause out in the hall, but he doesn't answer her.

In two strides Missouri rounds the doorframe and chases down the hall after him. I hear a struggle.

"Let loose of me!" Shane yells.

"I'll learn you to ignore me."

They come back into the room, Missouri dragging Shane by his ear. She shoves him toward me. "I'm tired of you pining for him and him slinking off."

I hold my arms out, but Shane ducks and runs for the door. Missouri starts after him, but someone else blocks his way.

Leon stands in the doorway, Leon as he was when he was young, when there was still some fun in his face along with the meanness. His hair is dark with Brylcreem, no strand out of place, and his black dress shoes are buffed to a high polish. Shane's head barely comes up to his chest. Leon grabs Shane's windbreaker at the back of the neck, almost lifting Shane up. He spins him around toward me, still holding on. And I get to see my son face-to-face for the first time since he died.

"Talk to your mama," Leon says.

Shane squirms out of Leon's clutch but doesn't run.

Missouri, her work done, becomes young again. With a smile for Leon she prances out of the room, petticoat showing at the hem of her dress. If she had a hat she would toss it. Leon follows her, his step heavy down the short hall and out onto the porch.

I reach for Shane. I have had years to form the question in my mouth. "Was it me, son?" I quaver. "Was I the reason? Did I make you do it?" I hold onto his arm, feel nylon over hard bone, weep with the realness of it. I can't get ahold of myself.

Shane looks at me. He is so close I can count the shaving nicks on his face that never had time to heal. He reaches up and touches my hair, tracing the gray among the brown, letting his fingers rest cool against my cheek. "It wasn't you, Ma," he says.

"Ivy!" Eugenia comes running. She finds me blubbering and speechless, holding onto air. My son has laid out his answer in a circle, a funeral wreath for me to treasure.

Outside, sun leans over the mountain, sucking rain back into the sky. On the porch, Leon whistles. Eugenia lifts her head. She takes my hand, and we listen as dog noises tear at the air. Excited whines, the scratch of toenails, the tickling sniff of warm noses searching for palm.

Acknowledgments

So many people encouraged me while I was writing this novel. I am profoundly grateful to the Flatiron Writers of Asheville, past and present, especially Genève Bacon, Toby Heaton, Diana Stoll, Maggie Marshall, and Jennifer Fawkes. My deep thanks to Jill McCorkle for her thoughtful feedback at Sewanee and to the other members of the 2008 McCorkle-Earley workshop, especially Sarah Crow and David McGlynn, who gave me a second read on their own time; to my other readers, Suzanne Newton, Lynda Gralla Mottershead, April Spencer, Bill and Julie Latham, Joanne Ryan, Craig and Cari Newton, Mark Mennone, David Snyder, and all the rest of you who read all or part of it and told me what you thought. My appreciation to Walter Cox for his memories of four-room school houses and phone service in rural North Carolina; Jay Latham for his descriptions of cars and college life in the 1950s; Margaret Errington and my other lawyer pals for their expertise on probate law; Deborah Steely for Helen Steiner Rice-A-Roni; the Outer Banks History Center; Jenny Cox and the Castelloe family for entertaining my child while I wrote; Tommy Hays for helping me get on with my next project; and UNC Asheville's Greatest Smokies Writing Program for its valuable support of me and other western North Carolina writers. I am indebted to my agent, Liv Blumer, and my editor, Gabe Robinson, for going to bat for the novel. In developing the character of Martin Owenby I found two books to be particularly helpful: *Stonewall* by Martin Duberman and *Boys Like Us: Gay Writers Tell Their Coming Out Stories* edited by Patrick Merla. Finally, and by no means least, I thank my parents: Carl Newton, who always assumed I could do anything, and Suzanne Newton, who showed me the discipline and joy of the writer's life.